PR/

D0776181

"It's hard to say if   s a wicked
sense of humor to round off the horror, should be eligible
for an Edgar Award or a Bram Stoker or both."
Booklist

"Both horror and mystery readers will be delighted by this
horror-noir adventure."
Publishers Weekly (starred review)

"[*Nekropolis*] is an atmospheric and exciting mystery."
SF Site

"It's a classic. If you're a fan of Simon R Green, who does
a series very much like this one, you'll especially enjoy
Nekropolis. It's a horror spoof done with a sense of wit and
pulp detective done tongue-in-cheek. Sam Spade, watch
out. There's a slow-footed zombie creeping up on you!"
Bewildering Stories

"This is a terrific melding of the horror and private detective
genres. Waggoner's writing is visually led, and the *Blade
Runner/Dark City* atmosphere is well drawn. Richter, with his
seemingly bottomless pockets, makes a good protagonist – a
former cop who can't quite lose all the scruples of his old
profession. A great start to what is hopefully an ongoing
series."
Total Sci Fi

"*Nekropolis* is an engaging read that had plenty to recommend
it to me. There's a mystery to be solved and every question
is answered with another question, just the thing to keep
me reading... Richter is a great character to spend time
with... *Nekropolis* is a solid and enjoyable read... if you're a
fan of detectives or zombies then you'll get something out
of it too."
Graham's Fantasy Book Reviews

BY THE SAME AUTHOR

Tim Waggoner

NIGHT TERRORS
A Shadow Watch Novel

**ANGRY
ROBOT**

ANGRY ROBOT
An imprint of Watkins Media Ltd

Unit 11, Shepperton House
89 Shepperton Road
London N1 3DF
UK

angryrobotbooks.com
twitter.com/angryrobotbooks
To dream the impossible dream

An Angry Robot paperback original, 2009

Copyright © Tim Wagoner 2020

Cover by Kieryn Tyler
Set in Meridien

All rights reserved. Tim Wagoner asserts the moral right to be identified as the author of this work. A catalogue record for this book is available from the British Library.

This novel is entirely a work of fiction. Names, characters, places, and incidents are the products of the author's imagination or are used fictitiously. Any resemblance to actual events, loales, organizations or persons, living or dead, is entirely coincidental.

Sales of this book without a front cover may be unauthorized. If this book is coverless, it may have been reported to the publisher as "unsold and destroyed" and neither the author nor the publisher may have received payment for it.

Angry Robot and the Angry Robot icon are registered trademarks of Watkins Media Ltd.

ISBN 978 0 85766 900 1
Ebook ISBN 978 0 85766 370 2

Printed and bound in the United Kingdom by TJ International.

9 8 7 6 5 4 3 2 1

This one's for all the coulrophobics out there.
Mr Jinx hopes to visit each and every one of you real soon.

ONE

Jinx lifted his nose and scented the air. He reminded me of a wild animal whenever he did this, and even after all our years together, it still creeped me out. Of course, it didn't help that his skin was chalk-white, his lips dark red, and his eyes covered by large blue crescents resembling sinister eyebrows.

He turned to me and smiled, red lips stretching wider than humanly possible.

"He's close."

His voice was a mellow tenor, pleasant on its own, but disconcerting when emerging from that face. The combination created a real lunatic/serial-killer vibe, which I knew amused him. His voice was one of the things about Jinx that I hadn't gotten used to yet. I wondered if I ever would.

Without waiting for me to comment, he stepped out of the alley and started heading north. I didn't like it when he got bossy, but we were on the trail of a rogue Incubus named Quietus, and that meant he was in charge – for the time being. So I slipped out of the alley behind Jinx and hurried to catch up. He's over six feet, and with those long legs of his, he can cover a lot of ground when he wants to. At five and a half feet, I sometimes have to work to keep up with him. Good thing I always make sure to wear comfortable shoes.

Speaking of shoes, Jinx's oversized red-and-whites slapped the sidewalk like bloated swim fins. They looked awkward, but he could move easily – and silently – in them when he wanted. He probably made so much noise only because he knew it annoyed me. I ignored it, because I knew *that* annoyed *him*.

"Is it Quietus?" I asked.

"Ask me no questions, and I'll tell you no lies." He let out one of his hyena giggles – loud, high-pitched, and not altogether human.

It was after ten, but it was a warm night in April and the sidewalks were far from deserted. Jinx's appearance always attracts attention – who wouldn't look at a six-foot bald clown wearing a gray business suit, a blue tie with orange polka dots, a large yellow flower pinned to his lapel, a WWJD bracelet (which stands for What Would Joker Do?) and, of course, those gigantic shoes? But that eerie giggle of his sets off all kinds of *What the hell was that?* alarms in anyone who hears it, and everyone within earshot turned to look at us.

I sighed. "Do you have to sound so psychotic when you laugh?"

"It's not my fault. *You* dreamed me this way." He paused, then added, "Mommy."

As usual, he was baiting me, but this time I was irritated enough to respond. "I'm not your parent. I'm your *Ideator*."

Jinx twisted his features into a grotesque parody of a sad face. "What's wrong, Audra? Don't you wuv me anymore?"

I was trying to decide whether to punch him in the shoulder or stomp on one of his banana boats, when someone said, "Dude! The circus is in town!"

"Ignore it, Jinx. We've got work to do." I doubted there

was a chance in hell that he would let this go, but I felt I had to at least make the effort.

Jinx stopped walking. A trio of young men in their early twenties blocked our way. They were only a few years younger than me – physically, at least. Mentally was another story.

I stepped between Jinx and the boys. I pegged them for kids who'd driven in from the suburbs to hit some of the downtown bars. They wore light jackets, T-shirts, jeans, and running shoes. One had a Cubs cap and sported a scraggly soul patch, another had an anarchy symbol emblazoned on his shirt – *How retro*, I thought – and the third's shirt said *Down Here, Ladies!* with an arrow pointing to his crotch. *Charming.*

All three of them were smirking, and I *really* wanted to slap the smug little bastards – hard and repeatedly. But Jinx and I couldn't afford to waste the time. With every passing second, Quietus' trail grew fainter, and the longer we lingered here, the greater the chances that Jinx wouldn't be able to pick it up again. And if that happened, there was an excellent chance someone would die tonight. Quietus was already responsible for three murders in the city – three that we knew of, anyway – and I was determined there wouldn't be a fourth.

"Look, guys, my friend and I are kind of busy right now. I know he's dressed like a clown" – I glanced at Jinx – "and a freaky one, at that. And out in the 'burbs, I'm sure he would be quite the spectacle. But this is downtown. Here, *he's* the normal one, and the more you make fun of him, the more you just look like hicks from the sticks."

I knew I was overstating my case by referring to Jinx as *normal*, but I was hoping to knock these guys off balance verbally – the best defense, etc. – so they'd let us go without pissing off Jinx any further. But I could smell the beer fumes wafting off them, and if they weren't falling-down drunk, they were well on their way, which meant their judgment was – as the don't-drink-and-drive ads say – impaired.

And it didn't help that I don't present the most imposing presence. As I said, I'm only medium height, and I was wearing a white pullover shirt under a gray suit jacket, gray slacks, and the aforementioned comfortable shoes (my job requires a fair amount of running). My auburn hair – I like describing it that way; much nicer than saying *brown* – falls past my shoulders, and while I like to think that I'm pretty enough, there's nothing remarkable about my features. I've been told that I'd look better if I wore makeup, but I've never liked the stuff. Besides, Jinx is made-up enough for both of us.

They, of course, ignored me and focused on Jinx.

"So who are you supposed to be?" Cubs-Cap said. "The Joker?"

"Naw," Anarchy-Symbol said. "He's Bozo!"

"Bozo has red hair, dumbass," Down-Arrow said. "He looks like a cross between a Cirque du Soleil clown and a lawyer."

Jinx and I exchanged a look.

"Five points for originality," Jinx said.

I thought about it for a second. "Four. The lawyer part was a bit too easy."

Jinx nodded. "Yeah, you're right. Four."

Cubs-Cap scowled. "You makin' fun of us?"

Jinx turned to him and gave him one of his famous too-wide smiles.

"*Us?* Make fun of *you?*" Jinx touched ivory fingers to his chest in a display of mock alarm. "Heaven forefend!"

Down-Arrow frowned. "Heaven what?"

Anarchy-Symbol didn't speak. Instead, he stared at

Jinx's overlarge smile. He was starting to get it. There was something *wrong* about Jinx. *Twilight Zone* wrong.

I took Jinx by the elbow. "Time to jet. Places to go, nightmares to catch, remember?"

I tried to get him moving again, but he wouldn't budge. Incubi are stronger than humans, and when they don't want to be moved, nothing short of a dynamite blast will do the trick.

"But our new friends are just getting warmed up. I'm sure they're going to get to their A material soon." He turned to face the three boys. "How about it? You fine gentlemen have anything else to say about my..." He paused as he searched for the right words. "Lifestyle choice?"

He smiled again, and this time he showed teeth so white and straight, they almost didn't seem real.

Anarchy-Symbol was starting to look nervous. Some humans are more sensitive to the presence of Incubi than others, and it looked like he was one of them.

"Uh, guys, maybe we should get going," he said. "I– I got to get up early for work tomorrow."

"Shut up, Dale," Cubs-Cap said, not bothering to look at him. Instead, he kept his gaze firmly fixed on Jinx. "You think you're funny, huh?"

I couldn't let that one go, even though I knew better. "Seriously? You *do* know you're talking to a clown, right?"

"Are you a happy clown or a sad clown?" Down-Arrow said.

"Is there a third choice?" Jinx said. His teeth were slightly pointed now.

Down-Arrow went on. "Should we sing 'Laugh, Clown, Laugh' or 'The Tears of a Clown'?"

I groaned. "Don't tell me: you were in the drama club in high school, weren't you?"

"I've always been partial to Smokey Robinson," Jinx said.

Down-Arrow leaned in closer. "How about musical theater?" he asked. His smile was a human smile, but it was no less cold than Jinx's. Despite his moronic shirt, it looked like Down-Arrow was no dummy, and he was determined to make sure we knew it.

But his mention of musical theater sent a chill rippling down my spine.

Jinx leaned in toward the boy. "Love it."

For a moment, Down-Arrow just stared at Jinx. He was close enough now to realize there was something not quite right about Jinx's makeup. Namely, that it didn't look like make-up at all, but rather an elaborate tattoo job. Or maybe it wasn't Jinx's bizarre pigmentation that had caught his attention. Maybe it was the clown's ice-blue eyes. They glittered like diamonds, and his gaze was just as hard and cold.

"Randy, forget about it," Anarchy-Symbol said, tugging at his friend's sleeve. "Let's go!"

The fear in the kid's voice was palpable, and I prayed Randy/Down-Arrow would hear it and heed it. But he didn't.

"I especially love Sondheim," he said.

"Me, too."

"Then you won't mind if I sing a little?" Randy asked.

"Go right ahead."

Randy grinned. Then he began singing. "Isn't it rich? Aren't we–"

Jinx's ivory fist pistoned forward and smashed into Randy's face. Blood spurted from his nose, and I heard the sickening sound of cartilage crunching. The fact that the kid didn't go flying backward a dozen feet – not to mention that his head remained attached to his body – told me that Jinx had pulled his punch.

Randy clapped his hands to his face and took a stagger-step backward. Blood ran through his fingers and splattered onto the sidewalk. "Fuck!" he shouted, although it sounded like *Fwuk!* "Fuck, fuck, fuck!"

"Jinx *really* hates that song," I explained, although I doubted Randy heard me.

Anarchy-Symbol's face went about as white as Jinx's, and Anarchy-Symbol took a step backward. I expected him to turn and run, but he remained where he was. Maybe Anarchy-Symbol couldn't bring himself to abandon his friends, but more likely he was too terrified to do more than stand and stare open-mouthed at Jinx.

Despite the fact that these three morons had interrupted our investigation, I could sympathize with Anarchy-Symbol. I'd seen this reaction many times before. Lots of people are freaked out by clowns, but Jinx isn't just a scary clown: he's something out of a nightmare. My nightmares, to be exact.

Jinx's attack on Randy had taken Cubs-Cap by surprise, but he recovered quickly. Anger clouded his face and his hands curled into fists.

"What the *hell* is wrong with you, man?" Cubs-Cap demanded. "Are you crazy or something?"

"Or something. Definitely."

"You clown-faced bastard!"

Cubs-Cap started forward, obviously intending to make Jinx pay for hitting his friend. Jinx didn't make a move to defend himself. He didn't brace his gigantic feet, didn't raise his fists. He simply stood there, smiling. But before Cubs-Cap could take more than two steps, a stream of liquid jetted forth from the flower on Jinx's lapel. It arced through the air and splashed Cubs-Cap in the eyes.

The kid screamed and broke off his attack. He rubbed at his eyes with both hands, shouting, "It burns! God, it *burns!*"

"You promised me you wouldn't use acid anymore!"
I accused.

"I didn't," Jinx said. "It's juice from the Moruga Scorpion, one of the hottest peppers in the world." He paused, then added, "With added ingredients of my own."

Then Jinx started in with his unearthly hyena impression, his laughter growing in volume and intensity until it sounded as if it issued from the air around us. His laughter continued growing louder until it echoed up and down the street.

Randy forgot about his broken nose, which was still gushing blood onto the front of his shirt, and stared in horror at Jinx. Cubs-Cap's eyes were red and swollen, but he no longer rubbed at them, either because he'd adjusted to the pain or, more likely, he was too terrified by Jinx to care how much he hurt. Anarchy-Symbol looked on the verge of tears, and if I could've heard anything over the din of Jinx's maniacal laughter, I was confident I would've heard Anarchy-Symbol keening softly, as if he were on the verge of losing his sanity.

Pedestrians on both sides of the street stopped and stared at Jinx, and while most were too creeped out to do more than look, their eyes wide and jaws slack, a few still possessed enough presence of mind to pull out their phones and start taking pictures. Traffic had ground to a halt, and drivers and passengers were reacting the same way as those on foot, goggling at Jinx and holding out their phones as if they were some manner of technological talismans to ward off evil.

I could imagine the headline in tomorrow's *Tribune: Psychotic Clown Terrorizes Loop!*

Sanderson would *not* be pleased.

I punched Jinx in the shoulder as hard as I could. The flesh beneath his suit was rubbery, but the bone it covered was hard as marble, and pain flared in my hand. I ignored it.

"Cut it the hell out!" I shouted.

Jinx gave no sign that he heard me – or for that matter, felt my punch. He continued laughing, his eyes now the size of golf balls, his teeth sharp as a shark's.

I pulled my trancer from its holster and jammed the silver muzzle of the weapon – which looks too much like a toy ray gun – against Jinx's temple.

"I'll fire if I have to. You know I will."

I didn't shout this time, didn't raise my voice above my normal speaking tone. But Jinx's laughter cut off as if a switch had been thrown somewhere inside him. The sudden silence was startling – which I knew was precisely the effect he wanted.

I still had my trancer pressed to Jinx's head, and now he turned until the muzzle rested at a spot just above his eyebrows. His gaze locked on mine.

"Go ahead," he said in a low, dangerous voice. "Make your day."

Ice water flooded my gut. Jinx had never tried to harm me – as his Ideator, I wasn't sure he could – but that didn't reassure me much. As you might've guessed by now, I had a thing about clowns. Big-time. I didn't trust them, and that included the one I created.

Especially him.

I lowered my weapon, and when I spoke, I tried to sound tougher than I felt right then. "We don't have time for this crap. We need to–"

That's as far as I got before Randy – owner of the oh-so-amusing *Down Here, Ladies!* T-shirt – let out a choked gurgle. I turned to look at him, figuring that he had probably swallowed some blood from his broken nose and it was making him gag. But when I saw the hilt of a

knife protruding from his throat, I knew that Randy had
a more serious problem than a busted beak. The hilt was
black, as was the blade itself, but it wasn't an ordinary
black. Instead of reflecting light, it absorbed it, giving the
impression that if you tried to touch the blade, your fingers
would pass through its nonexistent surface and keep going
into a realm of nothingness, deeper and deeper... I'd seen
shadow daggers like this before, and I knew where it had
come from. I also knew what would happen if I didn't get
it out of Randy fast.

"Shield me!" I ordered Jinx, and without looking to see
if he was going to do it – with Jinx, you never know – I
ran toward Randy.

As bad as his broken nose was bleeding, it was nothing
compared to his throat wound. Blood sprayed from it
like a fountain, and while I knew there was a very real
chance he would bleed out within moments, it wasn't
the bleeding I was most concerned about. I managed to
reach him just as his knees buckled, and I was able to catch
Randy and lower him to the blood-slick sidewalk. I knelt
next to him, and I felt the knees of my slacks soak through
with his blood, but I ignored it. His eyes were wide with
confusion and disbelief, and I couldn't blame him. First
he got punched in the nose by a clown, and now he had
a dagger sticking out of his throat. It definitely was not
his night.

His eyes shifted to look at me, and he opened his mouth
to speak, but all that came out was a dribble of blood.

"Shhh," I said. I wanted to tell him that it was OK, that
he was going to be all right. But I couldn't lie to him, even
if it would've given him a few moments of hope before
he died.

The dark blade had already started its work. Thin lines
of black spiderwebbed out from the wound, running

beneath the surface of Randy's skin like a rapidly spreading infection, which I suppose in a way was what they were. He grimaced in pain, teeth gritted, neck muscles tensed, and I had to resist the urge to grab the dagger's hilt and pull it out of him. If I so much as brushed my fingers against the blade, its taint would spread to me.

I still had my trancer, and I switched the gun to its highest setting. Trancer fire concentrated Maelstrom energy, and since that's what the dark blade had been made from, I hoped that a short burst would destroy the dagger, and – if Randy was lucky – nullify the effect of its poison. And once *that* miracle was accomplished, then I could see what I could do to stop Randy's bleeding.

It had only been a few seconds since Randy had been wounded, and his companions hadn't had time to do more than stand and stare in shock. Now Cubs-Cap said, "No, he didn't! No, he didn't!" He kept repeating that phrase, but I wasn't sure exactly what he was trying to say. Maybe he wasn't trying to communicate anything in particular, just speaking nonsense out of sheer terror. Anarchy-Symbol was doing something similar, only instead of talking, he was shaking his head rapidly, as if by doing so he could alter reality and negate what had happened to his friend.

I glanced at Jinx. He stood facing the street, gigantic shoes planted far apart, arms stretched wide. I couldn't see his face, but I had no doubt he was grinning.

"Come at me, bro!" he shouted.

Relatively reassured that a shadow dagger wasn't going to slam between my shoulder blades in the next several seconds, I turned my attention back to Randy. I could see the black threads covered his entire neck and were now moving down onto his chest and up onto his chin and cheeks. His breathing had become shallow and rapid, and I knew he didn't have much time left.

I placed the muzzle of my trancer a fraction of an inch away from the dagger's ebon hilt and squeezed the trigger.

There was a flash of multicolored light, and I felt a wave of vertigo wash over me as Maelstrom energy was released. The sensation passed quickly, leaving me feeling mildly nauseated – as it always does – but I was thrilled to see that the burst from my trancer had cancelled out the shadow dagger's energy, just as I'd hoped it would. The blade was gone. Randy still had a seriously nasty hole in his throat, of course, but at least he no longer had a mystic dagger poisoning his system.

But then I saw the black threads of dark energy were still spreading through his skin, and I knew that I'd been too late.

I switched my trancer to its lowest setting and aimed it at Randy's head.

"I'm so sorry," I said, and pulled the trigger.

Randy's eyes widened in surprise, but then a short burst of Maelstrom energy washed over him, and his eyes closed and he fell still.

"What the fuck did you do?" Cubs-Cap demanded, an edge of hysteria in his voice.

"He's just sleeping. If you want him to wake up again, you better call an ambulance."

I knew there was nothing medical science could do for him now, but at least he'd be spared the agony of the dark energy negating his life force, in a very real sense eating him alive. Still, I pressed my free hand to Randy's throat in an attempt to stop – or at least slow – the bleeding.

I hollered over my shoulder at Jinx. "Do you see him?"

"No, but he's close."

"Can you smell him?" I asked.

"Don't need to." He turned around and grinned as he displayed the half-dozen shadow daggers embedded in his chest. Although he was bleeding from the wounds, no black threads of infection spiderwebbed across his bone-white skin. Like Quietus, Jinx was formed from pure Maelstrom energy, so aside from making him look like a human pincushion, the shadow daggers had no more effect on him than a bee's sting.

His body jerked several times, and when Jinx turned around to face the street, I saw he had three new daggers in his back.

Not for the first time, I wondered what sort of nightmare had birthed Quietus into existence. I mean, who dreams about a shadow assassin that can create throwing knives from shards of his own dark substance? I bet a psychologist would have a field day with that one.

The situation was rapidly getting out of control. Some of the onlookers were beginning to panic – and who could blame them? They'd witnessed a lunatic clown break a guy's nose, then saw one of the guy's companions catch a knife in the throat. And now the clown was standing guard and being struck with one dark blade after another, seemingly with no ill effects, grinning all the while. It was only a matter of time before another bystander was hit by one Quietus' dark shards. Or he might decide to take a hostage in order to force us to allow him to escape.

And how long would it be before one or more of Chicago's Finest got wind of what was going on and showed up, guns drawn, ready to kick ass first and ask questions later? I wasn't worried about what the cops might do to us. I was afraid of what Jinx might do to them.

"Do you have a fix on him?" I called over my shoulder.

"He's in one of the buildings across the street," Jinx said. "I can't tell which one or how high up he is, though. You know how he blends in with the shadows."

"Keep looking," I said. Then I turned toward Randy's

friend. "Hey, Anarchy-Symbol!"

At first, the kid didn't know who I was talking to, but then he glanced down at his shirt, and it clicked.

"Uh, my name's Dale."

"I don't give a damn what your name is," I snapped. "Get your ass over here!"

He hesitated, and I thought this time he really would break and run. But he came over and I put my trancer on the ground, reached up, grabbed his hand, and pulled him down to a crouching position. Then I removed my bloody hand from Randy's throat wound and replaced it with Dale's.

"Keep the pressure on until help arrives," I told him. "It probably won't do any good, but it's the only hope he's got."

Dale was pale and shaking, but he kept his hand pressed tight to his friend's neck.

"What the hell is going on?" He spoke in a near whisper, almost as if he wasn't certain he wanted an answer.

I decided he'd sleep easier in the future if I kept my mouth shut. I mentally apologized to Randy as I wiped my blood-slick hand on his pants leg, then I picked up my trancer and stood. Keeping my head low to avoid catching a dark shard in one or both of my eyes, I made my way over to Jinx, making sure to keep his body between me and the street.

I checked on Cubs-Cap. He was standing and gaping like an idiot, his gaze moving from his wounded friend to Jinx and back again.

"You moron! You're lucky you haven't been hit yet! Get your ass down!"

Cubs-Cap looked startled, as if the possibility he might be struck by a blade hadn't occurred to him. He flung himself belly-first to the sidewalk, hitting so hard that his face smacked the concrete. Ouch.

Constructs formed from the substance of an Incubus' body don't last long, and the dark shards embedded in Jinx's back were already starting to fade. Jinx jerked his head to the side as a shard came flying at him. It flew past him, missing my head only by inches. It struck the building behind us, shattering the window of a pawnbroker's shop.

"How about a little warning next time?" I scolded him.

"My bad," Jinx said, and then gave a soft giggle. "Emphasis on *bad*."

By this time, most of the pedestrians had cleared the street, although a few idiots remained, unable to stop watching the action. I wanted to shout, *This isn't a TV show, dumbasses!* But I knew it wouldn't do any good.

Still using Jinx as a shield, I said, "I don't get it. Since when does Quietus start attacking random people on the street?"

Quietus was an assassin for hire, and he had a reputation for working quick, neat, and – you guessed it – quiet. It wasn't like him to be wasteful with his weapons, either. One shard, one strike, one kill. That had been his MO up to this point. Something had happened to change that, but what?

"Maybe he decided he needed a change of pace," Jinx said. "Every Incubus needs to cut loose now and then."

"Emphasis on *cut*," I said as another shard streaked past. This one hit the side of the building, bounced, and clattered to the sidewalk.

Jinx started to chuckle, but then he stopped. "There he is."

I looked past Jinx and saw a slash of darkness in one of the third-floor windows across the street. The window was open, and a shadow emerged and fell silently through the air – to land just as silently on the sidewalk below.

Quietus looked like a tall, thin man garbed from head to toe in midnight-black spandex. He had no visible facial features – for all I knew, he didn't have any – but his head was pointed at us, and I had the impression that whatever sense he might've possessed in place of sight, he was using it to "look" straight at us.

And then he turned and began sprinting eastward down the sidewalk.

Why was he fleeing? It wasn't as if Jinx and I had had a bead on him. Was there a limit to how many dark shards Quietus could create from his body in a short amount of time? If so, that could mean – for the moment, at least – that he was weaponless. But I didn't have time to strategize. Jinx and I needed to haul ass if we didn't want to lose him.

The dark shards in Jinx's back were gone now, as were those that had struck him in the front. His clothes were blood-stained and had vertical cuts in the fabric where the shards had hit, but his wounds were already in the process of healing. I have to admit that there are certain advantages to being a nightmare made flesh.

"Let's go," I said.

Jinx started running east down the sidewalk, his huge shoes beating a rapid *slap-slap-slap* cadence as he went. I cast a quick look back at the unlucky trio. Randy lay on the sidewalk, his skin ashen. If he was still alive – and that was a big if – I knew he wouldn't be for much longer. Dale knelt next to his friend, both hands pressed to Randy's throat wound now, not that it would do much good. Cubs-Cap – whose name I still didn't know – lay flat on his belly, unaware that he didn't have to worry about being hit by flying daggers anymore.

I wanted to say something, apologize for not capturing Quietus before he'd lodged one of his dark shards in Randy's neck. But I knew nothing I could say would help, so I turned and ran after Jinx, once more grateful that I value function over fashion when it comes to footwear. Flats may not be stylish, but you try chasing down a homicidal nightmare in heels.

Quietus headed eastward toward the lake, moving as swiftly as the shadows he resembled. He wove between pedestrians without knocking them down – which is more than I can say for Jinx. If someone didn't get out of his way fast enough, he'd shove them to the side, or jam an elbow in their ribs. Sometimes he'd leap over them, as if his legs were made of coiled springs. There was no way I could keep up with Jinx at his full speed, so I ran as hard as I could and tried to make sure I at least kept the two Incubi in my sight.

As I ran, I shouted, "Out of the way! Official Shadow Watch business!" in the hope that my warning might spare a few pedestrians bruises or cracked ribs. I've found that in the midst of chaos, people look for whatever guidance and reassurance they can get. So even if they've never heard of the Shadow Watch – and since we're *way* beyond a secret organization, no one has – shouting in an authoritative voice and using the word *official* was enough to get most people's attention and ensure their cooperation.

As we ran, my mind raced as fast as my feet. I still couldn't figure out what was happening. Why would Quietus – up to now a thoroughly professional and, more importantly, *restrained* assassin – suddenly go batshit crazy and start throwing dark shards around like they were confetti? It didn't make sense. Sure, we'd been on his trail, but we hadn't been *that* close. As an Incubus, he was as capable of sensing others of his kind as Jinx was, and there was a good chance he would've caught wind of us in time to make a run for it. So why attack us? Quietus had to know his dark shards would have no lasting effect on Jinx.

All he'd managed to do was alert us to his presence and kill an innocent bystander in the bargain.

Then it hit me. Not only was Quietus highly skilled at what he did, he was an Incubus, which meant he was *inhumanly* skilled. I'd assumed that Quietus had been trying to hit me or Jinx with his first dark shard but accidently hit Randy instead. But Quietus never missed, which meant that he had *wanted* to hit Randy. Randy had been his intended target all along. Jinx and I had stumbled across him by accident, forcing Quietus to act.

Anger and frustration welled inside me. Without knowing it, we'd located Quietus' target, and instead of protecting him, we'd gotten into a fight with him and his friends, and ended up standing around like morons as Quietus took him out. Sanderson wouldn't just be displeased. He'd be *furious*. But I didn't care. There was no way our boss could be madder at me than I was at myself.

My calf muscles started to cramp. The pain was mild at first, and I was able to keep running without losing much speed. But the pain soon intensified and spread to my thighs. I gritted my teeth and tried to fight past the pain, but I began to slow down despite my efforts. Ideators like me don't need to sleep, but our bodies still require rest, just like anyone else.

I wasn't about to let a little thing like weary muscles keep me from doing my job, though. I reached into my jacket pocket and pulled out an object that resembled an asthma inhaler. I jammed it in my mouth and sucked in a deep lungful of chemicals A wave of warmth rushed through my body and washed away the weariness. Not only did my legs no longer hurt, they felt ready to run a marathon.

Strong and refreshed, I started picking up speed again, and I tucked the inhaler back into my pocket. Thank the

First Dreamer for rev. Sometimes I think I couldn't survive my job without it.

I was more determined than ever to catch Quietus and bring him to justice. And if he happened to get killed while trying to evade capture... well, I wouldn't shed any tears over his loss, and I doubted anyone at the Rookery would either, Sanderson included.

I figured Quietus' main objective at this point would be to find a Door. Their number and location change every night, which makes locating them a real pain in the ass. Shadow Watch officers get a little help in this department, though. Our wispers – communication devices that resemble wide silver bracelets – can locate Doors, provided we're close enough to them. Only Incubi can open Doors, however, so if I don't have Jinx with me, it doesn't matter how many Doors I find; I'm not going through. Incubi can sense Doors without any technological help, but it's hard for them to do on the fly. As long as we kept Quietus running, he wouldn't have the opportunity to stop and search for a Door, which was exactly what we wanted. Catching him would be a hell of lot easier if he remained on this side. If he found a Door and passed through to Nod, tracking him down would be a lot harder.

After leading us down various streets and alleys, Quietus brought us to Millennium Park. Specifically, to the AT&T Plaza, where the sculpture called *Cloud Gate* is located – although because of its shape, locals refer to it simply as the Bean. If you've never been to Chicago, you've probably seen pictures of it or watched a movie in which it was featured. As numerous Internet sites will tell you, it's made from almost two hundred stainless steel plates welded together and highly polished so there are no visible seams. It's thirty-three by sixty-six by forty-two feet, and weighs one hundred tons. Its surface reflects and distorts the city's skyline, kind of like a gigantic three-dimensional funhouse mirror, and it's a favorite stop for tourists.

I wasn't sure what Quietus was thinking, leading us to so much open space. At this time of night, the plaza was empty, and the lack of bystanders – coupled with the scarcity of cover – meant that I could get off any number of clean shots at Quietus. Of course, that would work both ways, and with Jinx having outdistanced me by a dozen yards or more, I no longer had my psychotic clown partner to intercept Quietus' dark shards for me.

The instant the thought occurred to me, I dodged to the side, just as Quietus spun around, flicked out a hand, and sent a dark shard hurtling toward me. If I hadn't changed course, the shard would've pierced my heart, but as it was, it flew past, missing me by less than a foot. A bit too close for comfort, but a miss was a miss, and I'd take it.

Quietus had barely paused to throw his dark shard, but in the split second it had taken him to complete the maneuver Jinx found the chance he needed. He gave another of his great leaps and closed the distance between himself and Quietus. The assassin had already spun back around and resumed running, and so he didn't see Jinx coming.

Jinx landed on Quietus' back like a ton of bricks covered in clown-white makeup, and the two of them went down in a rolling heap of living nightmare. They were both on their feet in an instant. A pair of dark shards appeared in Quietus' hands – actually, it looked as if they *were* his hands – while Jinx reached into his inner jacket pocket and withdrew an impossibly long sledgehammer.

Jinx had an advantage over the assassin. While Quietus created weapons out of his own substance, Jinx used his Incubus abilities to store weapons on his person. Jinx swung his hammer, struck Quietus a blow on his left shoulder, and the shadowy assassin went flying.

"Fore!" Jinx yelled.

Quietus flew toward the Bean and slammed into its side hard enough to leave a good-sized dent before bouncing off and falling to the ground. *Crap*, I thought. Now Sanderson would have to send M-gineers to fix the Bean. I sighed. There went my holiday bonus.

Quietus lay on the ground, stunned. Jinx had hit him hard enough to kill a human, but Incubi are made of tougher stuff. Quietus wouldn't lie there long, so we had to work fast.

Jinx ran toward Quietus, sledgehammer lifted high over his head. Subtlety isn't one of my partner's prime attributes.

"Stay clear!" I told him. I stopped running, aimed my trancer, and flicked the selector switch to the highest setting. Since Incubi are made of Maelstrom energy, they tend to be immune to it – at low levels. But higher levels create an energy overload within their system, wounding and in some cases killing them.

Using my trancer at the highest setting would quickly deplete the remaining charge, but I knew it was the best chance we had at taking Quietus down, so I fired. A blazing beam of swirling multicolored light shot toward Quietus, so bright that Jinx averted his eyes. I squinted mine and kept my gaze trained on Quietus as best I could.

In the time it had taken me to stop and fire, the assassin had started to rise, and he was already halfway to his feet when the trancer's beam streaked toward him. His reflexes were inhumanly fast, though, and he managed to leap out of the beam's path. The beam struck the Bean – making an even larger dent this time, damn it! – and ricocheted, this time angling upward toward the sky. The beam dissipated as it should have, but then a small sphere of Maelstrom energy appeared in midair above the Bean. Golf ball-sized at first, it rapidly increased until it was as large as a car.

I ran over to Jinx, who had lowered the sledgehammer to his side and was gazing up at the expanding sphere of multicolored energy.

"What the hell is happening?" I asked. "Is that... an Incursion?"

He shrugged. "I don't know. You want me to throw the sledge at it?"

To show how desperate I was, I actually considered it. But before I could say anything, the sphere shuddered and then exploded in a burst of light so intense that I had to shield my eyes. Afterimages danced on my retinas, and I knew that Jinx's vision was similarly obscured, which meant we were vulnerable to attack.

"Back to back!" I told Jinx, and given our proximity – not to mention how long we'd worked together – we had no trouble sensing where the other was and pressing our backs together. This position wouldn't keep me safe from a hurled dark shard, but it was better than nothing. I had no idea if the burst of light had temporarily blinded Quietus – remember, he had no visible eyes – but I hoped it would momentarily distract him if nothing else.

And that's when I heard the sound.

A strained groaning, loud and deep. It made me think of a sleeping giant starting to come awake and stretch his gargantuan limbs. My vision hadn't cleared yet, and at first I didn't believe what I was seeing. Steel legs – thin and jointed like an insect's – emerged from each side of the Bean, six in all. They braced against the ground, pushed, and one hundred tons of tourist attraction slowly rose into the air.

Jinx started laughing. The worse things get, the more he likes it, and when six stainless steel tentacles protruded from the top of the Bean and began writhing in the air like giant serpents, his laughter grew until I thought he might literally bust a gut. I hate it when that happens. He's useless for hours afterward, and the mess is *horrendous*, not to mention the smell.

As Beanzilla lumbered forward, steel tentacles lashing the air, I could only stand and stare. If we'd been in Nod, I'd have had no trouble accepting Beanzilla's existence. The rules are different over there – *very* different. But as far as I knew, this sort of reality distortion wasn't possible on Earth, but there it was, big as life and twice as ugly.

At first I thought Quietus had done something to animate the sculpture, although I had no idea how he might've accomplished such a feat. But he appeared as surprised as we were. For a moment, he stood and watched as the monstrous living artwork advanced, but then he began hurling dark shards at it with both hands, throwing them so fast that it was almost as if he were firing an automatic weapon at the creature. The shards struck Beanzilla only to bounce off, without doing more than leaving behind dings and scratches.

More work for the M-gineers, I thought. Of course, the M-gineers wouldn't be able to do squat unless we could figure out A) what had brought Beanzilla to life and B) reverse the process.

Quietus' barrage of blades had one other effect: it drew Beanzilla's attention. The creature swung toward Quietus and although – just like the assassin – it had no identifiable facial features, I could feel it scrutinizing him with a primitive intelligence. Quietus, perhaps out of desperation, continued firing dark shards at Beanzilla as if they were fléchettes, but to no better effect than before. One of the creature's tentacles whipped toward Quietus and wrapped around him, pinning his arms to his side. Then it lifted the assassin into the air and waved him around as if eager to show the world its new toy.

Jinx stopped laughing. "No fair! He's ours!"

He let forth a battle cry that sounded like a cross between a dyspeptic Viking heading into battle and a deranged lion that had overdosed on PCP. He ran toward Beanzilla, sledgehammer gripped in both hands.

Beanzilla turned to meet his advance, and as Jinx leaped into the air, ready to do his best John Henry impression on the monster, two of its tentacles streaked toward him. One caught him in midair and coiled around his midsection, while the other tore the sledgehammer from his grip. The tentacle squeezed, and the sledge's wooden handle splintered. The tentacle then relaxed its hold, and the pieces of Jinx's hammer tumbled to the ground.

Jinx let out a wail of grief. "Cuthbert! Nooooo!"

Did I mention that Jinx likes to name his weapons?

Without thinking, I aimed my trancer at Beanzilla and fired, but as I'd anticipated, the last blast had depleted the weapon, and nothing happened. I holstered my trancer, and desperately tried to think of a way that I could – alone and without any weapons – single-handedly bring down a one-hundred-ton monster that had taken out a pair of Incubi without so much as batting one of its nonexistent eyes.

I thought Beanzilla would attack me next, but evidently it didn't view me as much of a threat, for it turned and started crab-walking westward. I couldn't help feeling a trifle insulted by that. So far, with the exception of Jinx's beloved sledgehammer, Beanzilla hadn't done any damage, but once it got outside of Millennium Park, it would become a real threat. New York might be known as the city that never sleeps, but Chicago has its fair share of night owls, and those in the vicinity would be easy pickings for Beanzilla.

I couldn't let that happen. I started running.

Beanzilla moved quickly for its size, its legs thudding into the ground one after the other, leaving patches of broken concrete in its wake. My hit of rev was starting to wear off, and my legs felt like they were filled with wet sand. But I ignored the burning in my lungs and cramping leg muscles as I ran to catch up with Beanzilla.

I had started chasing the ambulatory sculpture before I had even the inkling of a plan, but I guess my subconscious had come up with something, for my hand reached into my jacket pocket and felt three coiled chains. Each was made of a silvery metal and measured eighteen inches when stretched out end to end.

Of course!

As I ran, I withdrew one of the chains and touched the two ends together. They fused with an audible *snick* and the chain snapped into the shape of a solid metal ring.

Bound as he was in Beanzilla's coils, Quietus could do nothing but go along for the ride as his monstrous captor hurried to begin its rampage of terror. Jinx's arms were still free, though, and he used one of his hands to aim his lapel flower. A stream of liquid arced from the flower's center to strike the surface of the stainless steel tentacle that held him fast. I was too far away to smell anything, but I could hear the faint sizzling sound of acid eating away at the metal. The bastard had switched the pepper juice back to acid! But I told myself I could be mad at him later. Right now, I had a work of art to stop.

"Jinx!" I shouted. "Catch!"

I said a quick prayer to the First Dreamer and hurled the silver ring toward Jinx. It spun through the air in an arcing trajectory, and I feared it was going to fall short. But Jinx snatched it out of the air.

He looked at the ring. "I'm flattered, but I'm not sure I'm ready for this kind of commitment."

I ignored his joke. "Maelstrom energy brought this damn thing to life, right? So let's see if we can turn off its power!" I said.

Jinx gave me one of his disturbingly too-wide grins. He pulled the ring apart, and it immediately fell slack. Then he wrapped it around Beanzilla's tentacle, the metal stretching to encompass the tentacle's girth. He then touched the ends together, and the ring stiffened and fastened itself tight to the tentacle's polished steel surface. For an instant, the ring glimmered with a sheen of multicolored light, which quickly faded.

I wasn't sure, but it looked as if the tentacle drooped a bit, and the coils around Jinx loosened a touch. And did Beanzilla slow down a little? I thought it did.

I caught up with the walking sculpture and as one of its legs came down, I jumped and wrapped my arms around it. Then I held on as the leg rose into the air again, this time carrying me with it. I caught a disorienting glimpse of myself reflected in the mirrored surface of Beanzilla's body, and a wave of vertigo hit me.

I looked away from the image and reached into my pocket and removed a second chain. I wrapped it around the leg, doing my best to ignore the nauseating sensation in my stomach as the leg carried me downward, and tried to touch the ends together. But even though the chain stretched, the leg was too wide. I pulled out the second chain, attached it to the first, and that did the trick. The ends met, *snicked* closed, drew tight to the leg's surface, and then shone with a glimmer of multicolored light that lasted only a second or two.

Nothing happened right away, and I feared my hastily improvised plan had failed, but then Beanzilla began to slow down. I felt its leg begin to shudder, and I knew the negators were working.

Negators prevent Incubi from accessing Maelstrom energy, thereby nullifying their abilities and rendering them, if not exactly powerless, no more of a threat than an average human being.

I heard Jinx yell, "Geronimo!" and an instant later, I saw him land on the ground in a crouching position. He immediately rolled out of the way of a severed tentacle that slammed into the spot where he'd landed. It looked like his acid had finally done its work.

He came up on his absurdly large feet and jogged over to where I still clutched Beanzilla's leg. The creature had stopped walking, but the leg I held onto had frozen at its highest position, stranding me almost thirty feet in the air. From where I was, I couldn't see Quietus, and I had no idea if he was still caught in the tentacle that had grabbed him or if, like Jinx, he had managed to get free. If Quietus was still trapped, I knew he wouldn't be for long.

Jinx stood beneath me, arms out.

"Jump!" he said. "I'll catch you!" He paused a beat. "And this time, I mean it!"

"Like you meant it when you promised you'd give up using acid?"

Still, I didn't see that I had any other choice. So I closed my eyes, let go, and dropped. When I opened my eyes again, I found myself looking up at Jinx's face. I expected him to make some sort of smartass comment, or maybe make one of his scary faces – bulging eyes, too-wide smile, sharp teeth. But his normally ice-blue eyes were warm, and the expression on his face might almost have been one of tenderness.

But then he grinned and dropped me on my ass. I said a word that I'd learned from my mother – Lord, can that woman swear! – and then Jinx offered me his hand to help me up.

"Joy buzzer," I said as I rose to my feet.

He grinned wider and showed me the metal device concealed in his palm.

The Bean was no longer alive – if indeed it ever truly had been – but it still had its legs and tentacles. Well, almost all its tentacles. The M-gineers were going to have their hands full with this cleanup job.

I looked at Jinx. "Quietus?"

He pointed skyward and took a step back just as the assassin landed in front of me, a pair of dark shards in his hands. The assassin lunged toward me, but before he could plunge the blades into my flesh, there was a blur of motion behind him, followed by a sickening thud. Quietus' head snapped to the side, he staggered, and then collapsed to the ground. Behind him stood Jinx, holding a new sledgehammer and grinning.

"Say hello to Cuthbert Junior."

TWO

Jinx found a Door in the middle of an alley. It didn't look like a passageway between dimensions: featureless wood surface, peeling white paint, tarnished metal knob... If I – or any human – tried to open it, I'd find it locked, and if I returned tomorrow night, I'd discover the Door gone, only brick in its place.

Hell, without Jinx along, there was a good chance I wouldn't be able to even *see* the Door. Doors aren't invisible to human eyes exactly, but there's an intrinsic wrongness to them, one that humans sense on a subconscious level. I was a trained officer of the Shadow Watch, and I'd been through Doors dozens of times, and I still felt a compulsion to turn and walk away whenever I looked at one.

We had Quietus in custody, a negator around his neck to nullify his Incubus powers, and another wrapped tight around his wrists to keep him from attacking us by more mundane means. Negators might prevent Incubi from using their special abilities, but they don't remove their training and experience. Superpowered or not, Quietus was still a master assassin, and we weren't taking any chances.

Well, *I* wasn't. Given Jinx's penchant for random acts of chaos and mayhem, I had to watch him almost as closely as I did Quietus. I knew my partner would love for Quietus to make a break for it, just so he could fight some more. I wouldn't put it past Jinx to "accidentally" allow Quietus to escape, so he could have a little more fun.

I'd searched Quietus while he'd been unconscious to see if he carried any other weapons on him. I'd never touched Quietus before, and I was surprised to find his substance – I can't bring myself to refer to it as flesh – was cool and spongy to the touch. As near as I could tell, he wasn't wearing any kind of outfit. I could find no zippers, buttons, or seams.

Quietus appeared to be a creature molded entirely from living shadow. He had no pockets, but then, why would he? He didn't need to carry anything because he could create weapons from his own darkness. He had no wisper on him, which was too bad. The M-gineers could've hacked into its system to search for the identity of his employers. Which was, of course, why Quietus didn't have one.

We walked toward the Door, Quietus between us, each of us holding onto one of his arms. Since my trancer needed recharging – something I couldn't do on this side of a Door – I held a blade to the assassin's ribs. M-blades are made from concentrated Maelstrom energy, and while they can kill Incubi if used right, stabbing an Incubi with one interferes with the Maelstrom energy that forms their bodies, causing a kind of short circuit. This results in agony so intense that all an Incubus can do is fall to the ground, drooling and twitching. It's a wonderful sight to behold, and I was almost sorry that Quietus hadn't given us any trouble. *Audra*, I thought to myself, *you're starting to get as bad as Jinx.*

Jinx had been in merry mood when we'd captured Quietus, but as time passed without the advent of additional ultraviolence, he'd turned grumpy and taciturn. Normally, anything that got Jinx to shut his nonstop mouth for a while was a good thing in my book, but the grumpier he became – or First Dreamer help me, the more *bored* he became – the more likely he was to do something impulsive and potentially fatal to anyone in the vicinity, including me. The sooner we opened the Door and stepped through and into Nod, the better.

But just as we reached the Door and Jinx stretched his ivory-colored fingers toward the knob, the Door opened from the other side.

Jinx and I assumed battle-ready positions without releasing our hold on Quietus. We are professionals, after all. I pulled the M-blade away from Quietus' ribs and pointed it toward the opening Door. Lone Incubi in Nod aren't supposed to have free access to Doors, but their location on the other side shifts randomly, just as it does on Earth.

In Nod, the Shadow Watch does its best to locate and guard Doors as soon as they appear, but we can never find them all. There are literally thousands of them. So if a rogue Incubus had managed to find an unguarded Door and was using it to sneak into Earth's dimension, I figured the sight of my M-blade should give it pause. And if the blade didn't intimidate the living nightmare, then Jinx's joy buzzer – which he held palm out and was throwing off sparks of high-voltage electricity – should do the trick.

But the being that stepped through the open doorway wasn't an Incubus. He was human. And what's more, I recognized him. I lowered my blade and repositioned it against Quietus' side. Jinx continued to hold his joy buzzer at the ready for several more seconds – before he finally powered it down and lowered his hand to his side.

"Hey, Neil," I said.

The man stopped, startled. He glanced back and forth between Jinx and me, then he fixed his gaze on Quietus – noting the negators around his neck and wrists – before finally turning his attention back to me. I gave him my brightest smile, but he only scowled in return.

"I should've known you and your clown" – he shot a dark glance at Jinx – "would try to sneak out of the city before we arrived."

Jinx gave Neil a smile too, only his was the sort a shark would give, all teeth and no humor. Neil swallowed and focused his gaze on me once more.

Neil Gonnick was a thin man in his early fifties with a receding hairline and a neatly trimmed mustache. He wore the standard M-gineer uniform: a slightly rumpled gray jumpsuit with a black belt and boots, the dream catcher symbol of the Shadow Watch emblazoned on the right breast. The jumpsuit was covered with pockets, all of which bulged with various tools and tech.

The M-gineers are proud of their uniforms almost to the point of arrogance, but I've always thought they were ugly things that looked as if they'd been inspired by bad 1960s' science fiction films. Neil carried a trancer holstered at his side, along with a nine-inch crystalline rod slid through a loop on his belt. The M-rod was the prime tool of his trade, allowing whoever had the knowledge and skill to wield it to use Maelstrom energy to affect solid matter. And I had a pretty good idea why he was here and less than pleased to see us. He'd come to clean up our mess.

Still smiling his shark smile, Jinx said, "I thought you pocket-jockeys used your own dimensional portals when you traveled. What happened? Rod go limp?"

Neil clenched his jaw. He hated it when Jinx used the word *pocket-jockeys*, which meant Jinx used it around the M-gineer whenever he could.

"You two caused a truly impressive amount of damage tonight. In fact, I'd say you achieved a personal worst."

"It's not our fault," I said. "At least, not entirely. There was an Incursion. I called in a full report–"

Neil cut me off. "I'm well aware of that. But I'm also aware of you and your..." – he paused to give Jinx a dubious look – "partner's record when it comes to collateral damage. You might not be the best officers employed by the Shadow Watch, but I have to admit, when it comes to wanton destruction, you're unequalled."

Jinx looked at me. "You hear that, Mommy? We're number one!"

A noisemaker appeared in his mouth and he blew on it, making a loud blat that sounded like an elephant breaking wind. He tossed a handful of confetti into the air at the same time. I cringed, waiting for the confetti to explode, but it drifted to the ground without igniting, and I was as grateful for Jinx's restraint as I was surprised.

Neil ignored Jinx and continued. "Because of the severity of the damage, we couldn't afford to expend any energy on creating personal portals. We already had to waste energy locating Doors that led to Chicago. We're going to need every bit of M-power we have left to fix this mess before dawn."

And since the M-gineers couldn't be certain precisely where in Chicago those Doors led, each member of Neil's team had chosen a different one, hoping at least some of them would let them out close to the Bean.

"So you're forced to travel by Door like the rest of us ordinary schlubs," Jinx said. "That must really put your little gray undies in a twist."

Neil scowled but otherwise didn't rise to the bait. "Now thanks to you two, I have to jog to AT&T Plaza – unless I can get a cab this time of night." He nodded to Quietus. "I assume *he* had something to do with your monumental screw-up."

I was used to how crotchety Neil could get when he had to do a rush repair job – especially a big one, and I had to admit that Jinx and I had caused an impressive amount of damage, even by our standards. But that didn't bother me as much as the fact that we'd failed to prevent Quietus from claiming another victim tonight, and I was in no mood to put up with Neil's crap.

"Better get moving," I said. "The clock's ticking, and you've got work to do."

Jinx grinned. "A *lot* of work."

Neil's scowl deepened, and for a moment I thought he was going to start yelling at us, but instead he sighed.

"Which direction?" he asked.

"North," I said, and pointed.

Neil gave us a last dark look before turning and jogging off in the direction I'd indicated.

Quietus had, naturally enough, said nothing during our conversation with Neil, nor had he displayed any physical reaction. He'd remained statue-still the entire time, which I found way creepier than his silence.

"Let's go," I said to Jinx. "The sooner we get this sonofabitch to the Rookery, the better."

"You think Sanderson will let me interrogate him?" Jinx asked, practically salivating at the thought. "I've got some new toys I've been dying to try out."

I shrugged. "You can ask, but after what you did to Scuttleback, I think Sanderson will say no."

Jinx made an exaggerated pouty face. "That wasn't my fault! I didn't think his shell would break that easy!"

If Quietus thought anything about our exchange – or for that matter, even heard it – he gave no sign.

Neil had left the Door open when he departed, but only dark was visible inside – thick, impenetrable shadow that was blacker than the blackest night, blacker than the inside of the deepest subterranean cavern. Which, considering it led to a city inhabited by living nightmares, was only appropriate.

Maintaining our mutual grip on Quietus, we stepped into the darkness. I reached behind me and pulled the Door shut, sealing us in otherworldly shadow.

The transition from one dimension to another is supposedly instantaneous, but it's never seemed so to me. There's a moment in between when the darkness closes in and clings to you like a second skin – cold, clammy, and claustrophobia-inducing. You're sealed in completely, like an insect caught in amber, trapped, unable to move. There's an instant of panic, a nauseating, soul-chilling fear that this time you're not going to make it through to the other side, that you're going to be stuck here, wrapped in darkness, forever.

The voices are the worst part. I've never told anyone on the Shadow Watch about them because they'd probably think I was crazy, and Sanderson would pull me off active duty. The sound seems to come from inside my ears as much as outside, a chorus of soft, eerie whispers, like distant ocean waves breaking against a cold, barren shore. Sometimes I think I can almost make out words, but just when I'm on the verge of understanding, I emerge from the darkness, and everything is normal again – or at least as normal as it ever gets in my life.

This time was no different. The three of us stepped out of an open doorway not much different from the one we'd entered. Transitioning between dimensions is disorienting for humans, but less so for Incubi, at least when it comes to arriving in Nod. They always know where they are there. So the instant I closed the Door behind us – which was set into a wall of a large brick building – Jinx said, "This is an alley in Soma Street. We're in Newtown, about..." He considered a moment. "Four blocks from Oldtown."

I gave a small sigh of relief and sent a prayer of thanks to the First Dreamer. Nod is *big*, and we might have ended up a lot farther away from the Rookery, so that delivering Quietus into the Shadow Watch's custody would have been more problematic.

"Let's go," I said.

We both still had hold of Quietus' arms, and I kept my M-blade pressed against his side. We moved cautiously out of the alley and onto the sidewalk. The negators were as effective in Nod as on Earth, but I wasn't about to relax my guard around a master assassin.

Incubi don't have to sleep, so Nod is busy all the time. (I was going to say 24/7, but since it's always night there, measuring time isn't one of the Incubi's priorities.) Pedestrians – mostly Incubi with a smattering of humans here and there – thronged the sidewalks.

Some Incubi are human-looking in appearance, but most are creatures straight out of the deepest, darkest, most twisted levels of humanity's collective unconscious. The sort of distorted monstrosities that would make the toughest Earth cop or soldier mess his or her undies. Hell, I've worked for the Shadow Watch for years, and I still get squicked out by the sight of the more hideous Incubi. It's times like those when I'm glad to have a psychotic nightmare clown for a partner. He's enough to give even the scariest-looking Incubus pause.

Most of the Incubi we passed were bare-necked, meaning they weren't wearing negator collars and so were free to use whatever special powers they might possess. But around one in five were collared, and not with the temporary field negators like the ones we'd slapped on Quietus. These were permanent collars, made of thick silvery metal and welded closed. These were criminals, Incubi who'd broken the laws set down long ago by the Nightclad Council, and as punishment had their powers negated for varying lengths of time, depending on their sentence. And if that wasn't punishment enough to prevent them from committing further crimes, they then would be sentenced to Deadlock Prison. I might not always be comfortable with sharing the streets with the more nightmarish Incubi, but I'd gotten used to it, more or less. But I don't think I'll ever become accustomed to seeing criminals walking around free. I'm always on edge when I'm in Nod, senses alert and ready for danger. Which, come to think of it, is probably why I'm still alive.

There are few vehicles in Nod, so the streets tend to be used as pedestrian overflow, especially by those Incubi too large to fit comfortably on the sidewalks. Occasionally, a rider on horseback, a carriage, a car, or some unidentifiable contraption created by the dreams of a mechanically inclined Ideator will go by. But in general, most people get around by what Shakespeare called shank's mare – unless they have special abilities that allow them to travel in more convenient ways.

Most of the Incubi shot us dark looks as we passed. As you might imagine, the Shadow Watch isn't the most popular institution in Nod, and it didn't help that I recognized some of the Incubi as criminals that Jinx and I had captured.

The atmosphere of Nod is breathable, thanks to the unceasing efforts of the Unwakened, but the air has a thick ozone tang that I find unpleasant. Jinx refers to it as *eau de électrique chair*, and I had to admit it's a pretty fair description.

The sky is cloudless, permitting a perpetually clear view of the star-filled sky that Noddians call the Canopy.

The stars are for decoration only – another gift from the Unwakened, although primarily an aesthetic one. Nod is adrift with the turbulent energies of the Maelstrom itself – the raw material of creation – and the simulated night sky hides the seething, multicolored vortex beyond. The energy is so powerful and chaotic that even Incubi can't tolerate looking at it directly for very long.

The most disturbing aspect of Nod, at least as far as I can see, is its moon: a glowing blue-white orb called Espial that resembles a gigantic floating eye, complete with lids and lashes. A silvery iris surrounds a pupil that seems to exert the pull of a black hole, and the moon's phases are created by its torturously slow blinking.

Right now, Espial was past full and its lids just beginning to close. Its cycle is roughly a month long, same as Earth's moon, but unlike our planet's satellite, Espial always seems to be gazing down upon Nod's citizenry with a detached emotionless scrutiny that I find truly disturbing. The Incubi don't seem to think much of it, though, ignoring Espial for the most part. I've tried to emulate them, but no matter what I do, I'm uneasy at the way the damn thing stares down at me, as if I were nothing more than an insect that it's watching idly, hoping she'll eventually do something interesting.

There are any number of explanations for Espial's existence. Some say it's a result of the Incubi themselves, created from the raw material of the Maelstrom through their combined unconscious will. Others say that the Unwakened created it and use it as a way to keep tabs on the city's denizens. Still others – though admittedly not many – claim that Espial is the eye of the First Dreamer, or one of that being's servants, watching over Nod for its own enigmatic reasons. Me, I don't care where the damn thing came from. It gives me the creeps.

Even when wide open, Espial doesn't provide enough light to illuminate the city fully, and there are streetlamps on every corner – chrome poles atop which crouch lightning bugs the size of large dogs. The creatures glow constantly throughout their life cycle and are replaced after they die. Seems like a lousy life to me, but then I've never heard any of the bugs complain.

If you had Espial's view of Nod, the city would look like a series of concentric rings. Oldtown lies in the middle. This is, as the name implies, the oldest section of the city, and it's where the most ancient Incubi live. Some of them are hundreds, even thousands, of years old. The architecture of Oldtown resembles that of an Earth village from the 1700s – small wood and stone buildings, cobblestone streets, or more often, dirt paths. There are some nightmarish touches in Oldtown, but overall, it's more normal than you would expect. The Rookery is located in the center of Oldtown. The Aerie, the most exclusive section – where only the most powerful and distinguished Incubi live – is close by.

The next ring out is, unsurprisingly as well as unimaginatively, called Newtown. The architecture here, as well as the attitude, is more modern. Newtown resembles a small Earth city, steel and glass buildings, some of them quite tall, though not exactly skyscraper-level. There's far more diversity of structure here. Some buildings look perfectly normal – more or less – but others appear to have sprung full-blown from a lunatic's fever dream. Buildings with angles that don't look quite right, and tooth-filled maws that appear and disappear at random in the street. That sort of thing.

After that, the next ring out is the Cesspit, a combination of New Orleans at its most decadent and the Old West at its wildest and deadliest. All your darkest desires can be fulfilled here, often at the same time, provided you survive

long enough. Past that is a ring that's simply referred to as
The Murk. Incubi who are so nightmarish that they even
terrify others of their kind live there, and very few non-
residents go there if they can avoid it. This is where Deadlock
Prison is located. The outer ring is called the Edgelands. It's
a barren, desolate place where only the strongest and most
savage Incubi can survive. Once you enter the Edgelands –
so the stories say – you can never return.

I've been there twice.

Jinx and I escorted our prisoner centerwise, the direction
in which Oldtown lay. Our fellow pedestrians gave us a
wide berth because our reputation, as the saying goes,
preceded us. Jinx grinned maniacally at any Incubus who
was brave enough to meet his wild-eyed gaze, and that
was usually enough to get them to quickly avert their eyes
and pretend we didn't exist. Anyone else would've been
satisfied to have his badassness recognized like that, but I
knew that, at least on one level, Jinx was disappointed. He
grinned like that as much to provoke others into attacking
him as to warn them to keep their distance.

Ah, the joys of working with a psychotic nightmare
clown. They are without number.

But one Incubus didn't step aside as she approached us. I
say *she* only because I knew her. She possessed no outward
signs of gender or, for that matter, humanity – unless
you count the fact that she walked upright. She stood
eight feet tall and her reptilian body was unclothed. Her
shoulders were broad, her limbs thick and well-muscled,
and her scales gleamed as if she'd spent a fair amount of
time polishing them. She had a long, powerful tail which
swayed side to side behind her as she walked, in a kind
of reptilian swagger. Her head was that of a crocodile but
with eyes and a mouth that could, when she wished,
approximate human expression. She had large hands

which were humanlike too, with opposable thumbs, but the wicked-looking claws that jutted from her fingers were longer and – because she filed them every day – sharper than a true crocodile's.

She stopped in front of us and smiled, revealing a mouthful of teeth. Thin lines of electricity coruscated across the yellowed enamel with soft crackling sounds. "Hello, Audra, Jinx."

She gave my partner a nod, her smile widening and her teeth throwing off a few angry sparks.

She spoke in a thick Australian accent, her voice deep and guttural – exactly the way you'd expect a crocodile to sound.

"Shocktooth," I said in acknowledgment, if not in greeting. "I'm surprised to see you bare-necked."

"And *I'm* surprised to see you walking without a limp," Jinx said to her. "I guess I'll have to break both your legs next time."

Shocktooth ground her teeth together, and the electric current that surged between them sizzled and popped.

A few years ago, Jinx and I had caught wind of a jumper operating in the Maul. Jumpers import adrenaline from Earth and sell it on the streets of Nod as jump juice. Since Incubi are nightmares made manifest, adrenaline is a highly pleasurable and addictive drug to them, and one for which they'll pay through the nose.

Shocktooth had been working "security" for the jumper, meaning that she made sure transactions went down smoothly, and if they didn't, she started snapping bones and demonstrating how she'd come by her name. Jinx and I busted the jumper and hauled him and his "associates" in.

The law in Nod is more lax than on Earth. Incubi are expected to behave chaotically. They *are* nightmares, after all. So the jumper was sentenced to Deadlock, but Shocktooth received only a three-year collaring. But she was bare-necked now, and that meant she was dangerous. And of course, she had a grudge to settle.

Quietus didn't show any outward reaction to Shocktooth's arrival, but I felt his arm tense beneath my grip, just the merest amount, but I knew what it meant. Quietus saw a chance to escape, and he was preparing to take it.

I shot Jinx a quick glance to see if he'd picked up on Quietus readying himself for action, but my partner only had eyes for Shocktooth at the moment. If we hadn't been escorting a deadly assassin to the Rookery, I might've simply stepped aside and let Jinx have his fun. But we were, so I couldn't.

A quick look around showed me that, just as I'd feared, we'd begun to draw a crowd. A crowd of Incubi always means trouble of one sort or another. But a crowd of Incubi watching one of their own confronting a pair of Shadow Watch officers – who happen to have yet another Incubus in custody – is reason to go to DEFCON 1.

Raising my voice slightly, I said, "Antwerp." And when Jinx didn't respond, I repeated it louder. "Antwerp!"

Jinx's inhumanly wide grin faltered, and his right eye twitched.

Some couples use safe words to prevent one or both partners from getting injured when their sexual encounters become, shall we say, overenthusiastic. I established a safe word with Jinx to help rein him in for similar reasons. Not because I'm afraid of him hurting me when he goes full-on demonic clown on some bad guy – well, not *too* afraid – but because sometimes I need him to focus, and this was definitely one of those times.

I gave Shocktooth my best "Don't fuck with me" look.

"You're lucky we've got more important things to do," I said, "or I'd let Jinx turn you into a handbag with a matching pair of shoes. Now beat it."

Shocktooth didn't appear intimidated in the least, and I wondered if I was losing my touch. The croc's grin widened and the electric current coursing between her teeth became bright and started throwing off sparks.

"Thanks for the advice," she said in a low growl. "Not gonna take it, though."

I saw movement out of the corner of my eye, and I risked breaking eye contact with Shocktooth to check it out. Two figures were walking toward us from the middle of the street. One human, one more or less canine. The human was male, late twenties or early thirties, and wore a white poet's shirt with poofy sleeves. His pants and boots were black, and he wore a sword in a scabbard at his belt. And if all that hadn't been enough to peg the guy as having a serious pirate fetish, then the purple hooded mask and matching cape cinched the deal.

The canine – and I use the term loosely – padded along at the pirate's side. The creature was the size of a small horse, with coarse black fur and a spiked collar around its neck. The spikes were long and ended in needle-sharp points. The beast's mouth was open, displaying twin rows of wicked-looking teeth and a black forked tongue. The creature's hindquarters were scaled instead of furred, and its long, writhing tail resembled a lizard's more than a dog's. A line of serrated bony ridges ran down the tail's length, ending in a spiked protuberance that resembled a morningstar. Its feet were lizardlike too, with scaled toes terminating in sharply curved talons which clicked softly on the street as it walked. Its eyes were disturbingly intelligent, almost human-seeming, and I knew this Incubus was much more than the nightmarish beast it appeared to be.

They weren't Shadow Watch officers. No way I could ever forget that pair, especially the pirate. Pirates are hot. Besides, there was something almost familiar about him, although I couldn't put my finger on it right then.

I could tell they were bonded, though. Like the saying goes, it takes one to know one. I could *feel* the bond between them, and I knew Jinx could too. I had no reason to think the pirate and his monster-dog were heading for us, other than a tightening in my gut that told me they were. But over the years, I've learned to trust my instincts on this job, and they were telling me that trouble was heading our way.

But before I could even start to think what to do about it, Shocktooth released a bellowing roar and charged.

I jammed my M-blade into Quietus' side. He wasn't human, and I knew a single strike from the weapon wouldn't kill him – as long as I didn't hit any vital organs – but it would seriously hamper him. It wasn't that I had any objection to killing him if necessary. I'm not bloodthirsty, but I am pragmatic. But I wanted him alive for questioning. I wanted to know why he'd been killing people in my town.

Jinx's reflexes are inhumanly fast. As I slipped my blade into Quietus' side, Jinx released his grip on the assassin's arm and rushed forward to meet Shocktooth's attack. The crowd that had gathered to watch let out a cheer – well, more a series of guttural cries and high-pitched shrieks, really – at seeing the promise of violence fulfilled at last.

Without Jinx to support him on the other side, Quietus slumped to his left, his body pulling free of my blade. Instead of blood, tendrils of black mist coiled forth from the wound. Quietus fell to one knee and clapped a hand over the injury, as if the black mist was the equivalent of blood and he intended to prevent his life from escaping. It was possible. There's no telling with Incubi.

Shocktooth opened her maw wide and lunged at Jinx, miniature bolts of blue-white lightning arcing from her teeth. Jinx was ready, though. He raised his right hand in a blur of motion and slapped his palm onto the crocodile's tongue. Bright light burst forth from Shocktooth's mouth, accompanied by a loud *fwoom*! She flew backward a dozen feet, hit the concrete sidewalk, and slid several more feet before finally coming to a stop. Smoke curled upward from her mouth, and the smell of burned flesh filled the air.

Grinning, Jinx turned to show me his hand and the scorched joy buzzer in the burned flesh of his palm. It looked painful as hell, but if it bothered Jinx at all, he gave no sign.

"Go on," he urged. "Say it!"

I smiled. "How shocking."

He let out one of his crazed hyena laughs, but it was interrupted by an ear-splitting growl. I still held the M-blade, and I spun around, already knowing what I'd see. The monster-dog bounded across the street toward me, jaws stretched wide, foam-flecked tongue lolling out the side of its mouth. Its pirate master ran at its side, his sword drawn. The weapon's blade was rapier thin, but its swirling, multicolored hue shocked me as thoroughly as Jinx's joy buzzer. Pirate-Boy carried a sword formed from Maelstrom energy.

As far as I knew, only M-gineers were capable of creating such objects, and every M-gineer in Nod worked for the Shadow Watch. But there he was, carrying a weapon – you'll pardon the seeming double entendre, I hope – much bigger than any I'd seen before. Hell, from what I understood, an M-object that large should've been inherently unstable. I almost wished Neil could've been here to see it. Almost.

At first I thought the gigantic hound was going to attack me, and I braced myself and tried not to think about how much I really could've used a fully charged trancer right then. But before the beast reached me, it leaped into the air, soared over my head, and slammed into Jinx. Jinx is no delicate flower, but the creature's mass combined with the force of its leap knocked my partner backward. Jinx smashed into the building behind us. Breath whooshed from his lungs, accompanied by cracking sounds like multiple gunshots as a number of his bones broke from the impact. He fell face-first to the sidewalk and lay there. The demon dog stepped toward him, growling softly, and I spun around, ready to dash forward and sink my M-blade into the beast's scale-covered haunch. But before I could, Pirate-Boy reached me and swung his sword in a broad, sweeping arc designed to separate my head from my body.

Maelstrom energy doesn't have the same disruptive effect on humans as it does Incubi, but objects formed from it are incredibly strong and can hold a razor-sharp edge. I had no trouble believing my attacker could behead me as easily as slicing through a sheet of paper. So, hoping Jinx would recover before the demon dog could do more than take a couple mouthfuls of clown flesh, I raised my M-blade to block Pirate-Boy's sword, crouching slightly as I did so in order to get my head out of his sword's path.

His blade might've looked thin, but it hit mine with the force of Cuthbert Senior and Junior combined. The impact sent a jolt of pain jangling through my hand, along my arm, and into my shoulder, and I felt my fingers go numb. I managed to keep hold of my weapon, though, and despite the pain, I didn't think anything was broken. And if it was, I didn't have time to worry about it.

Still blocking the sword with my blade, I pivoted left and kicked at Pirate-Boy with my right foot. I was aiming for his knee, but he turned to the side and took the blow on his inner thigh. I'd put a lot of power into that kick, so even if I hadn't shattered his kneecap as I'd hoped, I knew I'd landed a solid blow. I meant to follow up the kick with a blade strike at his midsection, but he moved back several steps to get out of my knife range and give himself some room to get into a better fighting position.

Pirate-Boy was fast, and more importantly, smart. It was exactly what I would've done in his place. I considered hurling the M-blade at him, but my knife-throwing skills are a bit spotty. Despite how massive the sword had felt when it struck my blade, Pirate-Boy swung it as if it weighed nothing. Given the ease with which he could wield his sword, there was a good chance that he'd be able to deflect a hurled M-blade with that weapon of his. So knife throwing was out.

The crowd of violence-hungry onlookers stepped back to make more room for us. They might've wanted to watch the fight, but that didn't mean they wanted to take part.

I risked a fast glance in Jinx's direction and saw that my partner was back on his feet and battling the demon dog with a pair of cast-iron chickens (so much more deadly than the rubber variety). Jinx had a chicken in each hand, and he wielded them like the heavy clubs they were. The metal struck the dog with sickening dull thumps, but although the creature let out a pained whine with each blow, it appeared the impacts weren't causing any serious damage. I wasn't surprised. Some Incubi are so tough, it would take a bazooka strike to make them do more than blink, and it looked like the mutant pooch was as tough as they came.

Jinx didn't seem disturbed by the inefficiency of his blows. Or for that matter, by his shredded clothes or torn skin beneath. He was giggling with mad delight, as if he were having the time of his life. The worse things become, the happier he is. He was bleeding from the wounds the demon dog had given him, but he was already healing. He had to be careful, though. As strong and fast as the beast was, it might be capable of inflicting more damage than Jinx's Incubus physiology could heal – and then he'd be in real trouble.

Thinking of Jinx healing reminded me of Shocktooth. I turned my gaze toward the spot where she'd landed after Jinx short-circuited her, but she was gone. I'd hoped she'd taken advantage of the confusion to leave, but I doubted we'd be that lucky.

Quietus still knelt on one knee, hand pressed to his side. I was surprised that he hadn't tried to escape, even wounded as he was. Maybe I'd hurt him worse than I'd thought. Or maybe there was more going on here than it looked like.

Pirate-Boy had got himself together and now advanced for another attack. He ran toward me, sword held high, and I knew at once that something was wrong. No way would the skilled, confident fighter I'd faced a moment ago make such a clumsy advance. I could kill him half a dozen ways without working up a sweat. It had to be a–

Before I could think the word *distraction*, I heard a loud smacking sound. I turned in time to see Jinx flying toward me. Behind him, the demon dog finished spinning its hindquarters around, and I realized the beast had struck my partner with its powerful tail. Jinx collided with me and we went down in a tangle of arms and legs, and the last thing I saw before I lost consciousness was Shocktooth running forward and scooping up Quietus in her muscular arms.

After that, everything went black.

THREE

"So to sum up, you failed to stop Quietus from taking another life, you damaged a well-known Chicago landmark, and once in Nod, you were attacked by an Incubus you'd previously captured – one who somehow managed to free herself from her negator collar – and during the altercation, you lost Quietus."

Sanderson stopped pacing around the office, turned, and fixed us with an icy stare.

"Would you say that's a fair assessment?" he concluded.

"You forgot the guy in the pirate outfit and his giant dog," Jinx said.

His clothes were still shredded from where the demon dog had clawed him, but the flesh underneath had healed for the most part. Some faint scars remained, testament to how seriously the beast had wounded him. I'm sure Sanderson noticed – no detail, however small, escaped him – but he made no acknowledgment of Jinx's injuries. I was certain he understood their serious implications. Whatever Pirate-Boy and Demon-Dog were, they were hardly ordinary street toughs.

I didn't think it was possible, but Sanderson's gaze grew even colder. "Thank you, Mr Jinx."

Jinx grinned. "Happy to help."

If we'd been alone, I'd have swatted Jinx on the arm for being a smartass. But I didn't want to start squabbling with my partner in front of the boss – especially when he was giving us a dressing-down. It would only make him angrier. I had to content myself with gritting my teeth and shooting Jinx a dark look, which of course he blithely ignored.

"Not to nitpick," I said, "but the Bean came to life because of an Incursion. We had no control over that."

Commander Sanderson was a tall, slender black man in his sixties, with short white hair and a full, neatly trimmed beard that still had a few flecks of pepper amidst the salt. He was dressed, as always, in a sharp, expensive-looking dark blue suit and highly polished black shoes. His tie had an image of the Maelstrom on it, and if you watched long enough, you'd see the multicolored swirls of energy slowly move. Some say he's human, some say he's an Incubus of one kind or another, and some say he's a different sort of being altogether – perhaps even the legendary Sandman himself. To me, he was more like an ill-tempered school principal, and it seemed that Jinx and I spent far too much time in his office being scolded.

His office was Spartan to the point of utter sterility. The walls, ceiling, and floor were white, and the reflected illumination from the fluorescent lights made the entire room seem to glow. I always felt like I needed to wear sunglasses when I was there, and I usually left with a mild headache. There were no pictures or art on the walls, only the dream catcher symbol of the Shadow Watch behind his desk, fashioned from gleaming chrome.

He had no office furniture, save for his desk and chair, and the two chairs that sat in front of it. They were all of modern design: uncomfortable glass, chrome, and plastic monstrosities. His only piece of office equipment was a tablet computer that rested on the desk's glass tabletop. The screen swirled with Maelstrom colors, but I didn't know if the image was simply a screensaver or if the computer was actually linked to the Maelstrom itself. I'd never gotten around to asking and now certainly didn't seem like the time.

Sanderson looked at us for another moment before releasing a weary sigh. He then returned to his desk, sat, and placed his hands on the table, fingers interlaced. I knew from experience that gesture was not a positive sign. Nevertheless, when he spoke again, his tone was calm, his manner relaxed.

"Incursions are rare, but not unheard of. The two of you were simply in the wrong place at the wrong time." He paused, then added, "Which is something you seem to have a particular talent for."

"There've been a dozen Incursions over the last couple months in Chicago," I said. "That doesn't sound so rare to me." Incursions are times when the dimensional barrier between Earth and the Maelstrom grows thin, allowing M-energy to leak through and wreak havoc with reality.

"All of which have been minor for the most part," Sanderson said.

"Until today," Jinx said.

"Until today," he agreed. "But the M-gineering department will be looking into that. As for the other matters at hand, we have all available officers in the city searching for Quietus, and I've relayed your report about the masked man's sword to M-gineering. I've never heard of an M-blade that large – not one that was stable, anyway. Perhaps they'll be able to determine something about the man's identity by investigating from that angle."

Emboldened by Sanderson's calmer manner, I said, "Jinx and I can hit the streets and start asking around about Pirate-Boy... uh, I mean the masked man. A sword like that wouldn't go unnoticed."

"Neither would a big-ass killer dog," Jinx added.

"I don't think that would be a wise move, Ms Hawthorne." Sanderson's voice betrayed no hint of emotion, but I recognized his remark for the rebuke it was.

"I know we could've handled the whole situation better," I began, struggling to keep my emotions on a tight rein. "But there was no way we could've anticipated the Incursion. And as for our encounter with Shocktooth, it had to be a setup of some kind. She was obviously working with the masked man. She took us off guard with her initial confrontation, and then the man and his Incubus attacked, allowing her to scoop up Quietus and carry him away."

Even though I hadn't remained unconscious for long, by the time I'd come to, Quietus, Shocktooth, Pirate-Boy, and the demon dog were gone. Jinx had been stunned by the impact when he struck me, but he hadn't blacked out. Even so, he hadn't seen which direction they'd gone in. After calling in a report to the Rookery on my wisper, Jinx and I had attempted to question witnesses, but – surprise, surprise – they all claimed they hadn't seen anything.

Sanderson looked at Jinx. "Do you concur with your partner's assessment?"

Jinx was slumped in his chair, staring up at the ceiling while he blew spit bubbles. His gaze shifted to Sanderson.

"Sure. Whatever she says."

Sanderson sighed again, more heavily this time.

"So, you're suggesting that despite the fact that there's no way to track officers on Earth from Nod, and no way to predict the precise location of the Door they'll enter through, that somehow Shocktooth and this mystery man knew *exactly* where you would enter Nod, and they arranged to be there waiting for you in order to free Quietus?"

I didn't know what to say to that, but fortunately, Jinx did.

"Why not?" he said, still staring up at the ceiling. "The pirate had a stable M-sword, something no one's ever been able to make before. That's one impossible thing. What's one more?"

Sanderson considered this point for a moment. I smiled at Jinx to let him know I was both impressed and grateful. In response, he stuck his index finger up his nose and began digging around.

A faint expression of disgust crossed Sanderson's face, and he did his best to ignore Jinx's nasal excavation.

"And who do you surmise possesses the capability of obtaining information across dimensions?" Sanderson asked.

I thought for a moment, then gave the only answer that came to me. "The Lords of Misrule."

Sanderson looked at me as if I were crazy, which didn't bother me. But when Jinx did so as well, I knew I better explain myself fast before Sanderson sent me upstairs to Somnocology for a complete psych eval.

"The Lords have been around as long as the Shadow Watch, right? Isn't it possible that they've made some technological advancements that we haven't? What about the masked man's sword? We don't have anything like it, do we?"

Sanderson considered this. "The Lords of Misrule were once our equal in power, it's true, but their organization has fallen into decline over the last century. These days, they're mostly involved with cross-world smuggling and the illegal drug trade. The time when they plotted to rule both Nod *and* Earth is long past." He dismissed the matter with a shake of his head. "I think it far more likely that your encounter with Shocktooth was a random one. At first, she may have simply wished to settle accounts with you, but we've had a bounty out on Quietus for some time. When she recognized that it was him you had in custody, she realized that if the Shadow Watch was willing to pay for him, others would too. And quite handsomely. She saw an opportunity and took it. Simple as that."

"And the masked man?" I asked.

"Same thing. He recognized Quietus and thought he'd cut himself in for a share of the profit by helping Shocktooth. That, or he simply hates officers and thought he'd have some fun fighting with them. Either way, it adds up to a second random encounter, one that further complicated the situation. That's all."

I wasn't so sure, but I'd already stated my case, and since I didn't want to rile Sanderson up again, I decided to let the matter rest. For now.

I changed the subject. "So why don't you want Jinx and I looking for Quietus? Is it some kind of punishment?"

"No, but consider what a mess the two of you have made of things, you *ought* to be punished. I have a different concern." He paused and his eyes narrowed as he regarded me. "Tell me, Ms Hawthorne... Audra. Are you getting enough rest?"

Jinx – finger in his other nostril now – let out a loud guffaw. "He called you by your first name! You're in real trouble now, Mommy!"

"Fuck off," I muttered out of the side of my mouth without taking my gaze off Sanderson.

He went on before I could respond.

"Tonight isn't the first time that you've not performed at optimal level. I'm well aware that in the field, events occur at a rapid pace, and unexpected developments are the norm rather than the exception. All the more reason why officers – *human* officers – need to make sure they're tending to their physiological and psychological needs."

Once humans bring an Incubus to life – in other words, become Ideators – they no longer need to sleep. Ever. In fact, they can't sleep if they try. Sleep aids are ineffective. It takes a massive dose of tranquilizer to put us out, and even then we don't stay unconscious for long.

But not needing sleep isn't the same as not needing rest. Ideators still get tired physically, as well as mentally. And when that happens, we start making mistakes. Not so bad if you're trying to make lunch and accidentally put strawberry jelly on your ham sandwich instead of mustard. A much bigger deal if you're an officer tasked with preventing living nightmares from causing trouble – such as eviscerating people – and fail.

Sanderson was accusing me of not resting enough to the point where it had put me off my game. And the hell of it was, I feared he was right. Not that I was about to admit it.

"I make sure to get the minimum daily requirement–" I said.

Jinx let out an amused snort.

"*At least,*" I continued.

Sanderson looked at me for several moments, face expressionless. A centuries-old statue displays more emotion than he does when he gets like that. I hate it.

I let out a defeated sigh. "Fine. Lately I've been getting only a couple hours rest a day."

"A couple?" Jinx said.

This time, I punched him on the arm as hard as I could. Sanderson didn't chastise me. He probably wished he could've done it himself. Jinx has that effect on people.

"And if you function so well with so little rest," Jinx said, smirking, "then why do you need to take so many hits of rev a day?"

If we hadn't been in Sanderson's office, I'd have slammed

the butt of my trancer against the side of Jinx's head. As it was, all I could do was glare at him – which, of course, only made his smirk wider. Sanderson scowled at me, but he didn't follow up on Jinx's remark, and I thanked the First Dreamer for small mercies.

"An Ideator needs a minimum of five hours of rest per day, Ms Hawthorne. And yes, I realize that your duties as an officer often require you to keep irregular hours. Nevertheless, you do no one any good, least of all yourself, if you don't keep yourself sharp. Am I clear?"

I wanted to argue more, but I knew it would only make things worse. "Yes, sir."

Sanderson narrowed his eyes, as if he were attempting to gauge my sincerity. Finally, he nodded, and then looked at Jinx. "I'm charging you with the responsibility of making certain she gets at least five hours of rest per day. Five *uninterrupted* hours."

Jinx smiled at me. "I could always clonk her over the head with Cuthbert Junior a few times. That should put you down and keep you down for a good long while."

He was kidding. I hoped.

"I promise I'll get some rest as soon as I can, but you need every officer you can get to help track down Quietus. Not only do we need to prevent further murders, we need to find out if he has some link to the Incursion that took place."

"While I'm an admitted aficionado of random acts of chaos, it does seem awfully coincidental that an Incursion would take place as we were trying to capture Quietus," Jinx said.

"Are you suggesting Quietus somehow *caused* the Incursion?" Sanderson said. "Impossible! Incursions are a natural phenomenon." He thought for a moment. "And even if an individual could initiate an Incursion on his or her own, according to your report, Quietus was also attacked by the mutated sculpture."

Jinx shrugged. "Sometimes a prank backfires on you. Not that it's ever happened to me," he hastened to add.

I smirked but didn't reply.

"Rest assured, the Shadow Watch intends to make recapturing Quietus its highest priority."

"Without us," I said.

Sanderson stood and walked from behind his desk. He clasped his hands behind his back and paced around the office once more as he spoke.

"Do you remember when we recruited you, Audra?"

Back to first names. Not a good sign. "Sure. It's not the kind of thing a girl forgets."

"The Nightclad Council wasn't convinced that you and Jinx would make suitable officers. Jinx for obvious reasons..."

Jinx stuck his tongue out at Sanderson. It transformed into a hissing serpent that glared at our boss before slithering back into Jinx's mouth.

"And you, Audra, because you were so young." He stopped pacing and turned to regard me. "And more importantly because you were so afraid. Of everything, but most especially the Incubus you created."

I thought Jinx might make a smartass remark at that, but he said nothing. He just looked at me without expression, his thoughts unreadable.

"That was a long time ago," I said, my tone harsher than I intended. Sanderson let it pass without comment.

"There's a reason all officers work in pairs comprised of an Ideator and his or her Incubus. Since the Shadow Watch is charged with protecting Earth as well as Nod, it only makes sense for our teams to represent both realms. But much more important is the bond that Ideator and

Incubus share. When the bond is strong and healthy, it allows the pair to function as a highly effective team. And if the bond is exceptional, the officers can at times perform as a single individual, with shared thoughts, emotions, and reactions." He sighed. "I don't think I'm delivering any shocking news by telling you that your bond is far from that strong."

He returned to his desk and sat once more.

"It took some doing to convince the Council to grant the two of you full active status as officers, but I did so, for I believed you had the potential to be one of the best teams the Shadow Watch has ever seen. But after tonight…" He trailed off and shook his head.

"So," I said, trying not to sound as bitter as I felt, "who's going to take the lead on the hunt for Quietus?"

Sanderson hesitated before answering. "I'm considering a number of officers…"

He was interrupted by a knock on the door. Before he could answer, it opened, and a handsome man in his early thirties poked his head in. He had chestnut-brown hair, a neatly trimmed beard, and what some women refer to as puppy-dog eyes. He was smiling, but when he laid eyes on Jinx and me, his smile faded.

"I'm sorry to interrupt. When Dispatch said you wanted to see us, we thought…"

Sanderson's features remained composed, but a slight chill crept into his voice, indicating his annoyance. "That's all right. Come in."

The man pushed the door open wider and slipped inside. He was followed by a stunningly beautiful woman who stood a head taller than him. She had long black hair, and her flawless skin was the color of roasted almonds. If you watched her long enough, you'd notice that the ends of her hair waved back and forth, as if stirred by a gentle breeze that only she could feel. Her eyes were completely black – no irises, no whites – but instead of making her look alien or frightening, those eyes somehow accentuated her beauty. She seemed ageless and eternal, like an ancient marble statue brought to life.

They both wore the nondescript gray suit that served as the Shadow Watch's official uniform. But on them the suits looked like *haute couture*. Jinx and I looked as if we shopped at discount clothing stores. Of course, Jinx looked even worse, considering how shredded his clothes had gotten during his battle with the demon dog.

"I should've known," I muttered.

Damon Chambers and Eklips were two of the most highly regarded *senior* officers in the Shadow Watch. They were based in New York, although they went anywhere in the world their duties took them. Chicago's my hometown, and as far as I'm concerned, it's the greatest city on Earth. But one of its nicknames is the Second City. I bet you can guess which city considers itself number one. So, like a lot of Chicagoans, I grew up with a bit of a chip on my shoulder when it comes to the Big Apple.

But that's not why I hated Chambers and Eklips. They were professional, successful, and so good-looking, they could both be models or movie stars. But even all that didn't bug me – at least, not too much. What bothered me about them was how damn *nice* they were. How *modest*. How "Oh no, darling! It's not about *us*; it's about the *team!*" they were. They were stuck-up phonies pretending they didn't care about being the most beloved officers in the Shadow Watch. So beloved, in fact, that even rogue Incubi admired them. I once saw one ask for their autographs as they were hauling him in.

But they didn't fool me or Jinx. We knew who they really were, and what's more, they knew we knew. Which made it all the more galling that they'd been assigned to clean up our mess.

"Audra!" Damon said, smiling. "It's been a while. How are you? Well, I hope." He stepped forward and offered his hand for me to shake.

I stared at his hand as if poisonous thorns protruded from the flesh. He lowered his hand, but his smile didn't falter.

Jinx smiled at him, but instead of teeth his mouth was now filled with rows of rusty nails. Damon's eyes narrowed, but he maintained his smile at full wattage. He nodded. "Jinx," he said, his tone decidedly less warm than when he'd greeted me.

He turned his attention back to me. "By the way, excellent work in taking down that gang of melatonin smugglers last month. Top-notch work!"

Eklips crossed silently to her partner's side, her feet seeming not to touch the floor. She never made a sound when she moved, a quality I had never gotten used to. She reached up and gently placed her hand on Damon's shoulder, and I did my best not to grimace.

Romantic and physical relationships between human and Incubi – assuming the latter possess the proper anatomy – although rare, are accepted by the majority of Nod's citizens and institutions, including the Shadow Watch. But relationships between Ideators and the Incubi they create are, if not forbidden, mostly frowned upon. Ideators and their Incubi aren't linked genetically, of course, so our relationship isn't precisely that of parent and child, but in a metaphysical sense at least, it's close enough. So to most of us, myself included, sex between Ideators and their Incubi comes uncomfortably close to incest.

And many Incubi are reluctant to have sex with humans for another reason. Centuries past, some Ideators considered themselves magicians and viewed the Incubi they created as slaves to do with as they pleased. And some Incubi saw themselves as powerful demons who could whatever they wished to their creators. Rape on both sides was often the result, and the word *incubus* – which originally came from one of the Latin words for nightmare – came to be associated with a demonic sexual predator, primarily a male. Somewhere along the line, someone eventually coined the word *succubus* for the female variety of these "demons", although as far as I know, no one in Nod uses it.

So, because some of their ancestors had been ill-used by humans, and vice versa, most Incubi prefer to stick to their own kind when it comes to carnal pleasure. Obviously, Eklips was of a different mind on the subject. The issue has never come up between Jinx and me, and to be honest, the thought makes me more than a little ill.

"I'm surprised you two were able to get here so fast," I said to Eklips, baring my teeth at her in an insincere smile. "I figured you'd be too busy attending the opening of a new Broadway show, or maybe checking out a quaint new art gallery."

Eklips didn't smile back at me. She never smiled, not in public, anyway. I wondered if she ever smiled at Damon when they were alone.

"Rumor is that you two had Quietus in custody but let him escape? Is that true?" Her voice was like two swaths of black velvet being rubbed together. I'd never heard her raise her voice above a near whisper, even when she was furious. In some ways, that's scarier than anything Jinx does. Classier, too.

Jinx ground his nail-teeth together, and his eyes began to glow red. Not a good sign. Normally, I would've tried to defuse the situation. Having your psychotic clown partner go full-tilt horror movie in your boss's office doesn't make for a positive performance review. But these two always pissed me off – especially Eklips – and so I decided to sit back in my chair and watch the fun.

But before Jinx could do anything interesting, Sanderson laid his right arm atop his desk, palm up, and pulled his jacket and sleeve cuffs back with his left hand. He wore a wisper around his wrist, but just below that was a tattoo of a closed eye. The rest of us in the room with Sanderson stopped talking – for that matter, we stopped breathing – and focused on the eye tattoo. I braced myself for the eye to open, knowing that very bad things would happen if it did. But after several moments passed quietly, Sanderson pulled his sleeve back down. He then looked at Jinx – whose eyes were no longer glowing – and without a hint of emotion spoke a single word.

"Dismissed."

"It wouldn't be so bad if it was anyone else but those two," I said.

Jinx and I were walking down Chimera Street, away from the Rookery. The building is made of black brick and is shaped like a turreted tower. In other words, like the chess piece called the rook – get it? I've heard rumors that the building existed before the Earth game was invented, and the chess piece was modeled after the Noddian counterpart. I don't know if it's true, but it wouldn't surprise me. A high wrought iron fence topped with wickedly sharp spikes surrounds the Rookery, protecting it in ways mundane, technological, and – for lack of a better word – mystical. There are only two entrances, and there are guards posted there at all times, to supplement the Rookery's other defenses.

I was seriously pissed off at how our meeting with Sanderson had gone. I glanced up and saw Espial gazing down upon us from the Canopy above. Irritated, I raised my hand high and gave the enigmatic orb the finger.

"If we're lucky, Quietus will kill Damon and Eklips before they even know he's there," Jinx said.

I should've chastised Jinx for saying something so nasty, but at the moment, I felt the same way.

Jinx pulled three shrunken heads from one of his pockets and began juggling them as we walked.

"What next, Mommy?" he asked.

"What do you mean?"

"I assume you're going to disregard Sanderson's orders. You usually do. So where do you want to go? Who do you want to – as they say in old-fashioned gangster movies – lean on? Or to put it more bluntly, whose skull do you want to bash in first?"

He tossed the heads faster as he spoke, and they began muttering tiny cries of discomfort. Jinx ignored them.

"Actually," I said, "this time, I'm going to do what Sanderson says."

Jinx stopped walking and turned to look at me with an exaggerated expression of surprise. The shrunken heads froze in the air and remained motionless, staring at me with similar expressions.

I stopped and turned to face Jinx. "Maybe Sanderson's right. Maybe Quietus got away because I was off my game. Maybe some rest will do me good."

Jinx frowned. He plucked the heads out of the air one by one and slipped them back into his pocket. Then he turned to face me once more.

"You know I'm not good at interpreting human emotions in my Night Aspect." He paused. "Any emotions, really. So correct me if I'm wrong, but you seem kind of… down."

Night Jinx rarely shows any awareness, let alone interest, in how I'm feeling, but when he does, it makes me uncomfortable.

"You think?" I said, a bit harder-edged than I intended. I faced forward and started walking again. "C'mon. I need you to find us a goddamned Door home."

Jinx didn't follow me at first, and I wondered if I'd hurt his feelings. But then I remembered he didn't have any feelings to hurt.

A few seconds later, I heard the soft *slap-slap* of his overlarge shoes on the pavement as he followed after me.

We reentered Chicago through a Door in the outer wall of a bank close to Union Station, right next to an ATM. The instant I closed the Door, it began to fade, and I knew we'd made it back to Earth just before sunrise. I was glad. The last thing I wanted to do right then was be stuck in Nod until nightfall.

Already the streets were filled with cars, although not so many that traffic was congested. Handfuls of pedestrians made their way along the sidewalks, bleary-eyed and moving slowly, most of them carrying cups of takeout coffee.

I looked at Jinx. Although the sky was still tinged by night, it didn't need to be full daylight for Incubi to change. All that mattered was that enough sleepers had awakened, weakening the connection between Earth's dimension and the Maelstrom.

Unlike Doors, Incubi don't vanish during the day. Instead, they become denatured, changing from their Night Aspect to their Day. It happens quickly, so fast, in fact, that the transformation is almost impossible to detect. One instant, Jinx was his regular sinister clown self, and the next, he looked like a normal human. Well, almost normal. His clothing remained shredded, thanks to the demon dog, but his gigantic clown shoes had shrunk to normal sneakers, and while his tie was still orange with blue dots, it was no longer as large, and the colors were more muted and less garish.

Most noticeable was his skin. The clown-white was gone, replaced by Caucasian-white, and while he remained bald, the skin around his eyes and mouth was flesh-colored, too. He even had a pair of eyebrows now, although they were thin and almost undetectable.

He looked down at his shredded clothes with disgust. "I wish my other Aspect took greater care of our wardrobe." He looked to me, and his gaze filled with concern. "Are you all right, Audra? That meeting was less than pleasant, to put it mildly. Bad enough that Sanderson was dressing us down, but then to have Damon and Eklips walk in like that... I don't for a moment believe their arrival was an accident. More likely they wanted to rub our noses in the fact they were assigned to be lead officers on the case."

Day Jinx is, as you've doubtless gathered by now, somewhat different mentally and emotionally than Night Jinx. He can, however, be equally irritating in his own way.

"I'm fine," I told him, hoping he would leave it at that.

He gave me a skeptical look that said he wasn't buying my bullshit, but he didn't call me on it.

"Sanderson was right about one thing," he said. "You *have* been pushing yourself too hard lately. A bit of rest will do you a world of good. Let's start heading home. We'll grab the first taxi we see. Sound good?"

Without waiting for me to reply, Jinx set off down the sidewalk at a brisk pace.

"Too bad you have to rest today," he called back over his shoulder. "There's a new Titian exhibit at the Art Institute I've been dying to see. I was planning on asking you to come with, but I suppose I'll have to go by myself."

Both Jinx and Sanderson were wrong, I thought. I didn't need a rest. I needed a full-fledged vacation.

While Jinx's back was turned, I drew my rev inhaler from my pocket, took a quick hit, and then tucked it away. Then I followed after my partner.

One of the perks of being a Shadow Watch officer is that the agency supplies you living quarters. Unfortunately, the agency's cheap. Noddian currency, called M-units – or yoonies – isn't worth anything on Earth, and the Shadow Watch doesn't have access to much Earthly currency. We officers are lucky we get any housing at all.

Our apartment building is located in McKinley Park, on the city's southwest side. It's a working-class area and safe enough – at least as safe as any city gets. The complex is called Lakeside Apartments, which – despite the name – isn't anywhere near Lake Michigan. It's a decent-enough place, even if its best days are behind it. Our building is three stories tall, there's no elevator, and of course we live on the top floor. At least we get in a little cardio every day.

As we trudged up the stairs – well, *I* trudged; Jinx never seems to get tired, regardless of his Aspect – I inhaled the faint sour-cabbage odor that permeated the building, a smell I put down to decades of human beings cooking in a cramped, confined space. I hate that smell, but I'd be lying if I didn't admit that it was part of what makes the place feel like home.

Our apartment is 3F, about midway down the hall. The fluorescent lights in the hallway hum too loud and have a tendency to flicker, the walls are painted a stomach-turning olive green, and the gray carpet is stained and fraying at the edges. Be it ever so crumbled...

I unlocked our door and went inside. Jinx followed and closed it behind us, throwing the deadbolt and sliding the chain into place. Our apartment is a small two-bedroom with a tiny living area, an even tinier kitchen, and a single bathroom. Jinx may not be entirely human in his Day Aspect, but he's close enough, which – unfortunately for me – meant he needed to use the bathroom, too. I grew up as a single child, and I'm not big on sharing.

Jinx headed for his room to change, and I went into the kitchen and got a bottled water from the fridge. I opened it, tossed the cap into the trash container beneath the sink, then returned to the living room. When we first moved in, Jinx and I made a deal. I told him I didn't care what he did with the rest of the apartment, as long as he left my room alone. Jinx – his Day Aspect, that is – readily agreed.

So, while we might not be in the biggest or fanciest apartment in the city, inside, our place looks like it deserves a spread in *Better Urban Living* magazine. Our furniture is modern, sleek, and surprisingly comfortable, if a trifle sterile-looking.

The rooms are painted in warm colors with curtains in complementing hues, and the carpet – which Jinx also picked out – is so soft and cozy, it feels positively sinful to walk on in bare feet. The decorations are all his doing as well. Framed paintings – all originals bought from promising newcomers from various downtown galleries – and *objets d'art* displayed on wall-mounted shelves.

The only part of the living room that I had anything to do with is the large wall-mounted flat-screen TV. At first, Jinx resisted the idea of having a TV, but when I told him I'd be even crankier than I usually am if I didn't get to watch my Bears and my Cubs, he relented. He still complained about it for the first two weeks, until he discovered the various arts and food channels on cable. Now I think he watches the damn thing more than I do.

Normally, I like what Jinx has done with the place, not that I'd ever tell him that. But today, it depressed me. There was little of *me* in here, in my own home. It was like I didn't live here at all. Almost as if I didn't even exist. I told myself to knock it off, that I was just feeling down after bungling Quietus' capture and getting thrown off the case. But it didn't help. I still felt like crap.

I flopped onto the couch and took a long sip of water. I considered turning on the TV to catch the early-morning news. I knew today's top story would *not* be the destruction of the Bean. I had faith that Neil and his fellow M-gineers had repaired the damage to it by now, but making sure would give me something to do. But a manila folder lying on the coffee table caught my eye. I left the TV off, put my water down, and picked up the folder. Inside were background reports on Quietus' victims – not counting last night's. The Shadow Watch has many operatives on Earth, but most of them serve in less obvious ways than Jinx and myself. They work as police officers, federal investigators, doctors, lawyers, elected officials – any position where they might be of use in the struggle to keep the world of dreamers and the realm of nightmares separate. The Shadow Watch has operatives working for news organizations as well, and it wouldn't be long before they delivered a report on the latest victim to the Rookery. Not that Jinx and I would see it, though. That report – along with fresh copies of those that I held in my hand – would go to Damon and Eklips.

Even though Jinx and I were officially off the case, I couldn't help looking over the reports again. I told myself that maybe I'd missed something, that some new tidbit of information, some connection, would jump out at me this time. But in reality, I knew that I wanted to review the reports because I didn't want to let go of the case, despite Sanderson's orders.

I picked up my water, tucked the folder under my arm, and started toward my room, which is across the small hallway from Jinx's.

Jinx came out of his room, dressed in a satin robe and comfortable but stylish slippers. He stopped when he saw me. "Aren't you going to have breakfast? I'm planning on making eggs Benedict. You know what they say–"

"Breakfast is the most important meal of the day," I finished. "I know. You tell me that every morning. I'm not really hungry. I figure the sooner I get some rest, the sooner I can get back to work."

Jinx continued looking at me, his thin eyebrows furrowing into a frown. He noted the folder under my arm, and his frown deepened into a scowl. "You're not going to do anything foolish, such as continuing to work on Quietus' case after Sanderson removed us from it, are you?"

"I told you – Night You, that is – that I wasn't going to do that. I'll admit that's exactly the kind of thing I'd normally do, but not today. Today, I'm just tired of all the bullshit, and I want to get some rest before I burn out completely."

He frowned at me a moment longer, as if trying to gauge my sincerity. Night Jinx is more apt to take what I say at face value. His Day Aspect, not so much. Finally, he said, "Very well. I'll put your breakfast in the refrigerator, and you can heat it up later, if you wish. And if you do, use the actual oven, not the microwave."

He started to walk away, but then paused. "Have a good rest."

Then he continued down the hall.

"Thanks," I half whispered, then I opened the door to my room and walked inside, glad that Jinx had bought my lie.

FOUR

My bedroom looks more like a hotel room – or maybe a prison cell – than a place where someone lives. My bed sits longways against one wall to give me more room; a desk with my laptop on it rests beneath the single window, which is covered with the plastic blinds that came with the place. No curtains, and the room has the same bland white paint it had when I moved in.

Opposite the bed is a set of shelves crammed with books and DVDs. Since I don't sleep, I have to occupy myself somehow when I "rest". Meditation is the preferred method for officers to "refresh and renew", as the Shadow Watch's somnocologists put it. But since I suck at meditation, it's books, movies, and the Internet for me.

I tossed the folder onto my bed, then put my water on the nightstand, along with my fully charged trancer. Once loaded with M-energy, trancers can function on Earth day or night, but they can only be recharged at one of the M-stations in the Rookery – which I had done before leaving. I took off my suit jacket, shirt, and pants, slipped them onto hangers, then hung them up on the back of my closet door. I took off my bra for good measure. I then slipped into a Leon Redbone T-shirt and a pair of comfy shorts.

I sat cross-legged on the bed and began rereading the files. I don't know how long I read. A half hour, maybe. But no new insights came to me. Aside from living in the Chicago area, the victims had no connection that I could see. Two were male, one female. A newspaper reporter, a lawyer, and a physician.

There was more information, of course. Places of residence, names of family members and coworkers, medical histories, organizations they'd belonged to, hobbies they'd had... Hell, even their pets' names. But none of it was any use. Maybe the report on last night's victim would shed some light, but not for Jinx and me. Not unless I could scam a copy of the report. There had to be someone at the Rookery who owed me a favor.

I decided to worry about it later. I got up, put the folder on my desk, and then went over to my bookshelf. Sitting next to my collection of Jane Austen novels (don't judge) were a half dozen leather-bound journals. I selected the one on the end, then returned to my bed. On the way, I grabbed a pen from my desk, and after sitting cross-legged on the middle of my bed, I opened the journal to the first blank page – about two-thirds of the way through – and began to write.

I started keeping a journal when I was ten, at the suggestion of Dr Kauffman, the psychiatrist my parents took me to see when my constant nightmares became too much for them to deal with. I've continued the habit ever since. When I was in high school, I'd considered becoming a journalist. I even worked on the school newspaper for a couple years. But then Jinx – who'd been becoming increasingly real as the years passed – achieved full Ideation. After that, my life took a different turn. I never became a reporter, but I have kept writing, so I've never fully lost touch with that part of myself.

I spent an hour or so writing before closing the journal
and returning it to the shelf. Sometimes, I think I should
hide them, maybe even keep them in a trunk with a lock
on it or something. Some of the stuff I write – OK, most
of it – is private. But I wasn't concerned about Day Jinx
taking a peek at any of my journals. He's too proper. He'd
never consider violating my privacy like that. Night Jinx,
however, would read them in a heartbeat. But since we
were almost never home at night, I didn't worry about it.

I then selected a movie at random – *Bridesmaids*, one of
my favorites – and put it into my laptop to play. I climbed
back onto the bed, lay down, placed my hands on my
stomach, and stared up at the ceiling. Jinx had said he
planned to go to the Art Institute today. All I had to do
was wait for him to leave. Then I could get back to work
– for real.

As I lay there, I thought back to what Sanderson had
said to us in his office, about how Jinx and I weren't
bonded as strongly as we could – *should* – be, and how it
was affecting our performance as officers. While I had to
admit, if only to myself, that Jinx and I weren't always
the most simpatico of partners, most if not all of that was
due to Jinx's chaotic personality. In his Night Aspect, he
was nuts, even for an Incubus, a barely controllable force
of lunatic energy that caused as much harm as good. It
wasn't my fault he was the way he was… but I knew I was
lying to myself. I *was* his Ideator. Maybe I hadn't brought
him into existence on purpose, but that didn't change the
fact that, in a metaphysical sense at least, I was his parent.

As the saying goes, the acorn doesn't fall far from the
tree. If Jinx could be a psychotic maniac at times, what did
that say about me?

I didn't want to let my thoughts wander down that
road any farther, so I forced myself to close my eyes and

listen to the movie. The longer I listened, the more distant the actors' voices became. It wasn't as if the volume was slowly being turned down, more like someone had picked up my laptop and carried it away from me, one slow step after another. A feeling of distance. I suppose that's why I didn't notice it at first. It happened so slowly.

There was silence for a time after that, but I didn't think anything of it, and I didn't open my eyes. I was still fully aware, of course. As I've said, Ideators can't sleep. But in a way, the state I was in resembled sleeping. Almost as if I were remembering what it was like to sleep. It was wonderful.

I heard sounds then. The rustle of cloth, the soft inhalation and exhalation of someone breathing. Then came a familiar sound – one I dreaded above all others. A low, mocking laugh. It was followed by a whisper.

"Audra? Are you awake?"

Panic filled me, and it took everything I had not to whimper and pull the sheet over my head. But if I moved, he'd know I was awake. If I kept my eyes closed, stayed still and quiet, there was a chance – however slight – that he might go away. But I couldn't do anything to stop my body from trembling. All I could do was hope he wouldn't notice.

But as I feared, it turned out to be a vain hope.

He sniffed the air, loud and deep, like a bloodhound, and when he spoke next, I could hear the wicked smile in his voice.

"I know you're awake. I can smell your fear."

I couldn't take it any longer. I opened my eyes and sat upright in bed. My room was dark – Daddy wouldn't let me leave the light on, and he refused to let me have a night-light. He said I was too old for such foolishness.

At first, all I saw was darkness. But soon I was able to

make out some shapes in the gloom. My dresser, my Barbie playhouse, my shelves full of cutesy stuffed animals... There was another shape, too. A *human* shape, standing at the foot of my bed, hands gripping the footboard, body bent at the waist, head leaning forward. I couldn't make out his face (I knew it was a him, it was *always* a him), but I knew he was looking straight at me, grinning one of his too-wide grins.

"I knew it!" Jinx said, his voice louder. *"Why were you pretending to be asleep? What's wrong? Don't you want to see me?"*

On the word *see*, his eyes lit up with bluish light, illuminating his face and body. He was dressed like a hobo in a tattered jacket with a dead flower fixed to the lapel, a dirty white shirt, and an ugly blue tie with orange dots. I took my lower lip between my teeth and bit down hard to hold back the scream that was building inside me. If I screamed, Jinx would vanish – at least, he always had before – and my mom and dad would come running, just as they always did.

Only they'd gotten tired of my waking up screaming after one of my "nightmares", and by this point, I was almost as afraid of their anger as I was of Jinx. They'd started threatening to take me to "see someone" if I didn't settle down, and even though I was only ten, I knew what that meant. "Someone" was a doctor, and doctors meant shots and pills – and I wanted nothing to do with either. So I fought to hold my scream inside and prayed Jinx would get tired of torturing me and leave soon.

The cold blue-white light from Jinx's eyes illuminated me as well, and his smile widened as he saw the terrified expression on my face.

"You are *awake! And you're scared. That's good. That's very good."*

His ivory-fleshed hands gripped my footboard tighter, and as I watched, his fingernails lengthened into sharp black talons.

"After all, that's what you made me for, isn't it? To scare you."

His smile grew even wider, until the edges of his mouth tore and lines of bright red blood trickled down his white face. I couldn't fight it any longer. The scream came, high and shrill, and all the louder for having been restrained for so long.

Jinx laughed in delight, sounding almost like a happy child before breaking into fog-like wisps and disappearing.

My door swung open, and I prepared to apologize to my parents, to beg them not to send me to a doctor. But they didn't enter my bedroom. Jinx did. Day Jinx, that is.

Even though he looked like a normal human, he was still recognizably Jinx, and the sight of him was enough to make me draw in a gasping breath in preparation for another scream. I'm not sure what stopped me. Maybe it was that the lights were still on in my bedroom – and that it was *my* room. The adult me. But it might have been the look of concern on Jinx's face, an expression so different from anything I'd ever seen on his night face. Whatever the reason, I managed to let out my breath in a shaky exhalation instead of a scream.

Jinx and I looked at each other for a moment, and then he said, "I assume you took a backstep."

Since Ideators don't sleep, we don't dream. But sometimes when we've gone too long without getting enough rest, we experience hallucinatory memories so strong, it's like literally reliving them. The Somnocologists call these episodes backsteps. This wasn't the first one I'd experienced, but it was one of the worst. I'd actually believed I was ten years old, in my bedroom at my parents' house, being terrorized by Jinx in the middle of the night.

I sat up and scooted to the edge of the bed.

"What makes you say that? Maybe I was watching a scary movie and it just got to me."

"You hate scary movies," Jinx said.

He was right. When your job involves dealing with living nightmares, you don't enjoy reading or watching scary stuff in your downtime. At least I don't.

I changed the subject. "Looks like you're ready to go out."

Jinx had changed into a new shirt and gray suit. He wore a conservative blue tie and black dress shoes. His sartorial tastes were vastly different from those of his other Aspect.

"I was just about to head out to the Art Institute when I heard you... well, when I heard you."

His expression of concern – which he'd worn the entire time we spoke – now deepened, and I thought I detected guilt in his gaze. But then he gave me one of what I thought of as his "day smiles". Thin-lipped and barely noticeable.

"Have you changed your mind about coming with me? Aesthetic experiences can refresh the human mind just as well as physical rest in their own way, you know."

"Thanks, but I think I should stay here and rest – really rest – some more." I faked a smile. "I obviously need it."

Jinx's smile fell away and his expression grew serious. "Audra, you didn't... take anything, did you?" he asked.

Anger flashed bright and hot in me, and I had to fight to keep from snapping at him. "Only water," I said, my voice tight.

He regarded me a moment longer before finally nodding. "Very well. I'll be back at least an hour before sunset."

Day Jinx knew better than to allow his night self to roam the city streets alone. Without me to babysit him, there's no telling what sort of mischief he'd get up to.

"Sounds good," I said.

"Promise me you'll stay here until I get back?"

"I promise."

"And try not to get too broody about the meeting with Sanderson. I'm sure he'll come up with another assignment for us soon."

"Sure."

He gave me a last look, one that I couldn't interpret, and then he left, closing the door gently behind him.

I heard the apartment door open and close, followed by the sound of Jinx locking it. I then waited an extra ten minutes just to be sure he was gone. Then I got up and put my suit on.

It was time to get back to work.

I didn't want to waste any time, so I caught a cab to the Near North and got out a couple blocks from my destination. The place I was going to wasn't secret exactly, but when you work for an other-dimensional law enforcement agency, you tend to err on the side of paranoia.

Wet Dreams is a hole-in-the-wall bar that doesn't advertise. No website, no entry in the phone directory, not even a sign out front. No windows, either. Just a plain wooden door, unremarkable except for the ornate brass knob fashioned in the shape of a demon's head. At night, you have to be careful opening the door because if the knob is in a bad mood, it might bite your hand. But it was day now, and the knob was only cold, lifeless brass. I turned it, pushed the door open, and went inside.

As always, the first thing that hit me was the smell. I know what you're thinking, but I'm not talking about the stink of stale beer, dried piss, and old vomit. It was a subtler smell than any of those, a combination of air after a thunderstorm and the acrid tang inside the reptile house at the zoo. It was the smell of Incubi – a lot of them. Over the years, the odor had worked its way into the floor, walls, ceiling, and furniture, and even when the bar was mostly empty – like now – it still smelled as if it were packed full of living nightmares. I've worked with Jinx long enough that I've gotten used to the scent. It helps that Incubi don't smell as strong in their Day Aspects, and there are so many competing smells in Nod that my olfactory sense is usually stunned into submission when I'm there. But here, in the enclosed windowless space, the scent slammed into me like a brick between the eyes. I thought of the backstep I'd just experienced. Jinx had smelled like this when he came to me at night.

My stomach twisted with nausea, and I realized I hadn't eaten anything for breakfast, and it was getting close to lunch. I have a bad habit of forgetting to feed myself. And not resting enough. And disobeying Sanderson's orders whenever I didn't agree with them.

The latter was the reason I'd come here, and I'd come alone because while Night Jinx is a living embodiment of chaos, his day self has a stick up his ass a mile long. He was a stickler for... well, everything. But especially for rules. If he'd known what I was up to, he'd chastise me for going against Sanderson's wishes, nag me to stop, and keep nagging me. At least until sunset. And I simply wasn't up to dealing with that right now. Besides, after the memory I'd relived during my backstep, I didn't want to be around Jinx, regardless of which Aspect he was in.

Wet Dreams' interior is about as no-frills as it was possible for a bar to get. Brick walls, concrete floor (complete with suspicious stains), round wooden tables and uncomfortable chairs, and a bar that looked like, well, a bar. The lighting was dim, which added to the bar's overall miasma of gloom. Incubi, regardless of their Aspect, are more comfortable in dark places. Light doesn't hurt them in any way, but it does make them uncomfortable.

The action at Wet Dreams doesn't really pick up until after dark, but there were a dozen or so regulars present. I was familiar with them all, but some I knew better than others, and none were all that happy to see me. An Incubus named Scattershot got up from his table as soon as I walked in, and headed for the exit. As far as I knew, he wasn't involved in anything shady, but I made a mental note to check up on him later.

Lizzie Longlegs was sitting at a table with Cancer Jack, both of them looking relatively normal in their Day Aspects. Jack eyed me warily as I entered, ever-present cigarette dangling from his lips, but Lizzie gave me a smile and a nod. Lizzie and Jack had been an on-again, off-again couple for years, longer than I'd been an officer. Maybe longer than I'd been alive. Their relationship ran hot and cold. When it was hot, it was very hot, but when it turned cold... well, it was better – and safer – to stay as far away from them as possible.

I tried to get a read on which extreme the pendulum of their relationship was currently at, but their body language gave nothing away. They weren't sitting close, but they weren't sitting far apart, either. They weren't touching, but they weren't shooting venomous looks at each other, so that was a good sign.

Abe Chen sat at the bar, and he glanced over his shoulder at me, face expressionless, and then faced forward once more. Abe's a middle-aged man whose Incubus – some kind of bird creature he called Budgie – left him not long after its Ideation was complete. He had no idea where it might've gone, and he never heard from it again.

There's no law that says an Incubus has to remain near its creator. Once they come into existence, they're separate beings, free to make their own choices and act as they will. Even so, they tend to stay close to their Ideators if they stay on Earth, even if they don't maintain contact with them. There's a bond – or maybe link would be a better word – between Ideators and Incubi. One that goes both ways. It's not uncommon for Ideators to follow their Incubi to Nod, and if for some reason they can't find each other or become separated – or if one dies – they feel as if there's something wrong in their lives, something vital. They often end up lonely and depressed.

Although in Abe's case, no one really believed there ever had been a Budgie. He was commonly thought to be a nightfreak, a human who'd somehow become aware of Incubi and wanted so much to be a part of their world that he posed as an Ideator. Abe was a nice guy and harmless enough, so the customers at Wet Dreams played along with his pretense, myself and Jinx included.

At the opposite end of the bar sat one of the creepiest Incubi I've ever encountered – the Darkness – along with his Ideator, a woman in her sixties named Maggie Martin. In his Day Aspect, the Darkness looked like a young man in his early twenties. In his Night Aspect... well, maybe it's better if I leave that up to your imagination. Maggie was a petite firecracker of a woman who loved life with the gusto of a teenager and who didn't suffer fools. She looked upon the Darkness as the son she never had and made sure to keep the darker side of his nature on a very short leash.

The Darkness ignored me and took a sip of his Coke – Maggie doesn't let him drink alcohol. Maggie, however, lifted a scotch to me in a salute and gave me a grin. I couldn't help but smile back.

I took a seat at the bar between Abe and Maggie and the Darkness. Not because I was being antisocial, but because I hadn't come here to chat.

The man behind the bar was larger than life, even in his Day Aspect. Deacon Booze stands close to seven feet tall, is broad-shouldered and barrel-chested, and his arms are as thick as most people's legs. He has a full head of dense black hair that he wears bound in a ponytail that reaches down to the small of his back. His mustache and beard are just as black as his hair, and the tips of the mustache are curled up in an old-fashioned style. His features are pronounced and sharp, and they look as if they were carved from solid granite. But his eyes are a warm brown, and he always wears a friendly smile. He was dressed in a white work shirt with the sleeves rolled up and jeans. I've never see him dressed in any other way. Some Incubi are so old and strong that they retain a small measure of their power even during the day, and I sometimes wonder if that's the case with Deacon. His shirts aren't just white. They're always spotless, and they practically glow with their own light. He always wears a button pinned to his shirt with the words *In Vino Veritas* on it. Latin for *In wine, there is truth*.

"Hey, Audra," he greeted me as he came over to see me. "Flying solo today?"

"There's an exhibit at the Art Institute that Jinx wanted to see."

"The Titian? That's a good one. He'll really enjoy it."

As far as I know, Deacon never leaves his bar – literally. In fact, that's one of the conditions for his being allowed to stay on Earth. But I didn't ask how he knew about the exhibit.

As a Shadow Watch officer, I'd learned long ago not to ask my friends questions I might not like the answer to.

"What'll it be?" Deacon asked. His voice is a mellow baritone, and every time I hear him speak, I wonder what he'd sound like singing. Pretty damn good, I bet. "A glass of white wine? Or maybe something stronger? I imagine you can use it after what happened last night."

I wasn't surprised that Deacon knew about last night's clusterfuck. When it comes to the Incubi community, he was information central. Which was why I'd come here, of course.

"Neither, thanks. But I was hoping you might be able to offer me a little... insight into what happened."

Deacon's smile widened, revealing teeth so very white they nearly gleamed. "I thought you and Jinx were off the case."

"We are. That means anything you tell me is *off* the record."

He chuckled. "And if I'm able to provide any useful insight?"

"Then Jinx and I will owe you a favor."

"A sizeable one."

"Let's say medium-ish."

He thought for a moment. "All right. I'll tell you what I can. Shoot."

What I can meant what he felt comfortable telling me, but I knew it was the best I'd get out of him. I didn't bother filling him in on the details of our battle with Quietus or the assassin's subsequent escape. I wouldn't dream of insulting him by telling him what he already knew. Instead, I asked, "Any idea who the masked man with the monster dog is?"

"He's an Ideator who calls himself Nocturne. Cute alias, huh? I don't know what his real name is. He calls the dog Bloodshedder."

Nocturne. I wasn't familiar with the name. It struck me as a bit pretentious, but *Bloodshedder*, however, was a perfect name for his beast.

"Who's he work for?" I asked.

"Himself. He's freelance."

"Which is another way of saying *mercenary*."

Deacon shrugged. "From what I understand, he's more of a jack-of-all-trades than hired muscle. Whatever you want done, he can do it. Except killing. He'll do it when he's forced to, mind, but he's not an assassin."

Interesting. A bad guy with a moral code. I've never had a thing for bad boys, but I was beginning to think in his case I could make an exception.

Now for the big question. "He ever come in here?"

Deacon's frown was all the answer I needed. Deacon views himself as a true neutral party when it comes to Incubi affairs, and he insists that Wet Dreams be respected as neutral territory by all his customers. Asking him to reveal whether or not Nocturne was a customer was tantamount to asking him to take sides – and he didn't like it.

Maggie got up from her stool, came over, and sat next to me.

"I couldn't help overhearing, hon," she said.

"Only because you were listening so hard," the Darkness said sullenly.

Maggie ignored him.

"I've seen Nocturne in here a couple times. The first time, he brought that awful dog of his, but the horrid thing took a gigantic dump on the floor, and Deacon told Nocturne that the next time he came back, he had to leave the dog outside. Although where you could possibly leave a beast like that without drawing any attention is beyond me."

As Maggie spoke, Abe got up and came over to join us. "It climbs up the alley wall and hangs there like a lizard or a spider. I saw it once when I was coming in. Damn creepy."

I imagined Bloodshedder clinging to the surface of a brick wall high above me as I walked through the alley. It would make a perfect vantage point to watch prospective prey and then, when the time was right, launch an attack. That was a detail I planned on remembering.

Deacon's frown deepened into a scowl as the conversation continued, but he didn't try to prevent Abe and Maggie from talking with me. As I said, he prefers to remain as neutral as possible, even when it irritates him.

"He came in late both times I saw him," Maggie said. "Three, four o'clock."

"I've seen him several times, too," Abe added. "Always around 3am or so."

Late, but not too late for Incubi or Ideators. There was still an hour or two before dawn. And not every Ideator or Incubus heads back to Nod before sunrise, and since we don't sleep, late and early don't mean much to us. Still, it was another detail to take note of.

"What did he do when he was here?" I asked. "He hang out with anyone in particular?"

"You mean someone like Quietus?" Maggie asked. She has a loud voice, something she seems unaware of, and when she spoke Quietus' name, the few other customers in the bar grew quiet and turned to look at her. I gave them my best "I'm an officer on official duty" look, and they turned away and went back to what they were doing.

"Quietus isn't allowed in here," Deacon said, voice tight with anger. "You know that, Maggie. Too many people hold grudges against him. I can tolerate a fight in here from time to time. After all, it *is* a bar. But I refuse to have people killing each other left and right in here. It's bad for business."

I watched Deacon's face closely as he spoke. He wasn't above lying to protect his bar, and if Quietus did come here from time to time, Deacon wouldn't admit it to me. I decided he was telling the truth, though. He wouldn't want the hassle of allowing Quietus to drink here. Assuming the faceless Incubus *could* drink.

Before I could speak again, Lizzie Longlegs let out a high-pitched laugh that sliced through the air with all the sharpness and force of a finely honed katana. Everyone in the bar turned to look in her direction, suddenly on edge. She smiled and patted Cancer Jack's hand, though, and everyone relaxed.

I turned back to Deacon, Maggie, and Abe. "I'm interested in anyone Nocturne might have associated with," I said. "I'm trying to get a sense of who he is, what his habits are, that kind of thing."

Both Maggie and Abe thought for a while after that.

"He sat at a table by the door when I saw him," Abe said after a time.

Maggie nodded. "Same here. I don't recall anyone sitting with him, though. Do you, Abe?"

He shook his head. "He drank alone. Draft beer."

Damn! I was hoping I could get a lead on any friends or associates of his that I might be able to track down and question. Of course, it couldn't be that easy. On impulse, I asked, "Did he wear his mask?"

Both Maggie and Abe confirmed that he'd worn his mask the entire time he'd been in Wet Dreams.

"Is that important?" Abe asked.

Before I could answer, the Darkness let out a long-suffering sigh.

"Of course it is," he said. "It means Nocturne doesn't want anyone to recognize him, which means he's afraid someone *will*. Someone important."

Deacon had been silent for a while, but now he said, "Could mean he just wants to keep a low profile. When you're not fussy about who you work for, you're bound to piss off a few folks."

The Darkness finished the last of his Coke, put the glass down on the bar a little harder than necessary, and shook his head. "With that Incubus of his? Mask or no mask, there's no hiding who he is with that thing accompanying him. If he's trying to hide his identity, it's so no one knows who he is during the day on Earth."

I was impressed. "That makes a lot of sense."

"Of *course* it does," the Darkness said, his voice rising. "Why do you sound so surprised? Do you think I'm too stupid to come up with good ideas?"

A look of concern came over Maggie's face, and she got up and went back over to the Darkness. She smiled as she put a hand on his shoulder.

"Inside voice, hon."

The Darkness' features twisted into a mask of fury, but then all his anger drained from him, and he smiled sheepishly. "Sorry."

"No worries," Maggie said. "Let's go, sweetie. We'll get some ice cream. That always puts you in a good mood."

I knew what Maggie was doing. The calmer she could keep the Darkness during the day, the easier she'd be able to control him at night.

"I don't want to," the Darkness said, almost pouting.

"You can get extra sprinkles."

The Darkness took that in, considered, then nodded. He rose from his bar stool and headed off with Maggie.

"Good luck, dear!" she called to me as they left. I waved back, and then she and the Darkness stepped outside.

I let out a relieved breath as the door closed behind them, and I wasn't the only one. Even Deacon relaxed a little. The Darkness makes everyone nervous. Everyone except Maggie, that is.

We were all quiet for a time after that. Deacon started talking to Abe about how the Cubs were doing, and I fought the urge to join in. Instead, I contemplated what I'd learned so far. Nocturne and Bloodshedder were known to Chicago's

Incubi community, but not to me or Jinx – which seemed so unlikely as to be almost impossible. Collectively, there are thousands of Incubi on Earth and in Nod, and new ones come into existence every night. There's no way the Shadow Watch – let alone its individual officers – can keep track of them all.

But in my own city, I know all the major players and most of the minor ones. And no way would I have forgotten a masked cutie with a demon dog companion. So Nocturne wasn't only trying to keep a low profile, he'd been avoiding Jinx and me. Until last night, that is. Why? Was he – despite Deacon's assurance that Nocturne himself wasn't an assassin – an accomplice of Quietus? Or perhaps even Quietus' employer? Just because Nocturne didn't like to kill himself didn't mean he minded someone else doing the job for him.

What bothered me more than any of that, though, was the nagging feeling of familiarity I experienced whenever I thought about Nocturne. I *knew* him somehow, I was sure of it. His voice, the way he moved, his presence... But no matter how hard I tried, I couldn't remember.

Cancer Jack picked that moment to slam his fist down on the table he shared with Lizzie Longlegs.

"We should start seeing other people again?" Jack shouted. "Are you *serious?*"

Once more, we all turned to look in the couple's direction, and this time, we were even more tense than before. Jack's face was twisted with anger and Lizzie's gaze was cold and glittering.

Jack noticed us watching, and he gave us a wave, indicating that everything was all right and that we should go back to our business. We did so, but I doubted that would be the last outburst from them, and I decided to keep an eye on the couple.

I then turned to Abe and asked, "Are you holding?"

Abe and Deacon stopped talking baseball and turned to look at me. Deacon arched an eyebrow in surprised interest. Abe went pale.

"I– I don't–"

"Don't worry," I interrupted. "I'm not going to bust you. I just want to know if you got any mem on you."

Abe went even paler. "Seriously, Audra. I don't use–"

"Bullshit," I said mildly.

Not sleeping – and more, not dreaming – is hard on both the human body and mind. When an Ideator psychically taps into the Maelstrom to create an Incubus, something happens to change us mentally and physically so we can survive without sleep. But that doesn't mean it's easy. Ideators who aren't careful can be prone to physical exhaustion, mood swings, and in extreme cases, irrational behavior. Because of this, almost every Ideator needs a little pharmacological help to get by. Myself included, although I'm not proud of it.

It doesn't help that the Shadow Watch has deemed such drugs unsafe and made most of them illegal. But you know what? Sometimes even the police have to say fuck the police. I don't carry drugs on my person, though. Not counting my rev inhaler, which – if not precisely legal – is tolerated by the Shadow Watch. But I'm not above mooching off a friend, acquaintance, or even an enemy if necessary. And although Abe wasn't a true Ideator, he carried Ideator drugs on him as part of his façade.

Abe looked to Deacon and then turned to gaze longingly at the door, as if trying to decide if he could get to it before I tackled him. Evidently he decided his chances of escape weren't good, because he turned back around on his stool and sighed.

"Yeah, I got a couple mem tabs. Holding them for a friend, you know?"

"Isn't everyone?" I said.

Abe reached into his pants pocket and pulled out a piece of rumpled tinfoil. He pried it open to reveal a dozen different pills of various shapes, sizes, and colors. I recognized mems, stunners, and tinglies. There were a couple I was unfamiliar with, and I was tempted to ask Abe what they were and, more importantly, what they did, but I restrained myself. I was working, after all.

There was no jump juice in Abe's stash, though. That's strictly an Incubi drug. If humans take it, there's a better-than-even chance that our hearts will explode. Doesn't stop some morons from taking the chance, though. I was glad to see that Abe wasn't one of them.

Without waiting for Abe to offer, I reached out and took a single mem tab. I considered taking a second in case the first didn't work, but I decided against it. No need to be greedy.

"You want dollars or yoonies?" I asked Abe.

He looked confused.

"For the pill. I want to pay you for it."

"Um, dollars are good, I guess."

I knew why Abe was hesitant. Like a lot of people, he expected me to use my authority as an officer to take what I wanted. But I don't roll that way. I might not be the cleanest officer in the Shadow Watch, but I'm not an asshole, either.

I pulled a couple twenties out of my wallet and handed them to Abe. He took them without comment, folded them, and tucked them into his back pocket. Then he sealed the tinfoil containing his drugs and put that back in his pocket, too.

"What do you need a mem for?" Deacon asked.

I wanted to tell him it was none of his damn business, but he was an information broker. Being nosy was normal for him. And one of the ways you paid for his information was to provide information when he asked.

"I'm convinced I know Nocturne, but I can't figure out from where. I'm hoping my little friend here" – I held up the blue pill – "will jog my memory."

Deacon frowned. "You know they don't work like that. You can't just select a memory like picking a movie to slide into a DVD player."

Mem – short for *memory* – induces backsteps. Some Ideators rely on backsteps to replace the dreams they no longer have. But instead of waiting for backsteps to occur naturally, they use chemistry to make them happen on a regular basis.

"Actually, you can," Abe said. "If you concentrate hard enough. It's not reliable, though."

"So, what's the plan?" Deacon asked. "Go home, crawl into bed, swallow the pill, and hope the right memory pops into your head?"

No way I was going back to my apartment to do this. If Jinx came home and caught me, he'd be extremely unhappy. Backsteps are hard on a person, and experiencing two in one day – hell, within a few *hours* of each other – would be even more of a strain. But if it would help me remember how I knew Nocturne, I figured it would be worth it.

"Keep an eye on me, you two."

I tossed the pill into my mouth, dry swallowed it, and waited for it to start working. It didn't take long.

A great weariness settled over me, and I felt as if my body had been hollowed out and my insides replaced with molten lead. I remained conscious, but I couldn't move, couldn't breathe. I slipped off the barstool and plummeted to the floor. I had a vague impression that Abe tried to catch me and missed.

And then my face hit the floor and darkness descended.

FIVE

I was sitting on a couch in a small room. A large potted plant sat in a corner, and several other plants hung from the ceiling. They were real, not plastic. This surprised me, but I wasn't sure why. On the other side of the couch was a four-foot-high decorative fountain. The water ran down a corrugated bronze-colored metal sheet and into a round bucket-like container. I knew the fountain was here to provide white noise, although I couldn't remember why. The couch faced a door with a nameplate on it that read *Cecelia Kauffman, PhD: Psychiatrist*. I knew that name. Knew it very well. Better than I liked, in fact.

Up to this point, I'd ignored the boy sitting on the couch next to me, but now I turned toward him.

"Hi," I said.

I guessed his age at somewhere around eleven. Our faces were on the same level, and I realized this meant we were the same size. Ergo, I was a child, too. Probably around the same age as him.

The boy had brown hair and eyes to match. He wore jeans and sneakers, along with a black T-shirt with Batman's bat symbol on the chest. After sizing me up for a moment, he must've decided I wasn't going to bite, and he said, "Hi." It was a noncommittal hi, one that didn't encourage further communication, but it didn't discourage it, either. I chose to take this as a good sign.

"My name's Audra."

He considered this, then nodded, as if my name met his approval. "I'm Russell."

I nodded, but only because he'd done so. Russell didn't add anything to that, but he didn't look away, and I decided this was a good sign, too.

"Do you have trouble sleeping?" I asked.

Another nod from him, no hesitation this time.

"Me, too."

We sat looking at each other in silence for several moments. I started tapping my right foot on the carpet, nervously.

"Bad dreams?" he asked.

I nodded. "Scary clown."

Another nod from him. "Scary dog. A big one. I don't sleep much anymore."

"Me neither." I considered asking him what was so scary about a dog, even a big one. I knew about Clifford the Big Red Dog, and he was friendly. But before I could speak, Dr Kauffman's office door slowly swung open. Russell and I turned to look at the open doorway, expecting to see Dr Kauffman standing there, giving us one of her cold smiles.

But instead the doorway was filled with a thick, almost solid darkness. As we watched, it began to drift into the outer room like tendrils of black smoke. The tendrils stretched toward us like shadowy serpents, and I tried to scream, but even though my mouth was open and I could feel the rawness in my throat, no sound emerged. And then two glowing yellow eyes appeared within the darkness, and this time, I did scream. Long and loud.

•••

The first thing I became aware of was a sensation of gentle, repeated pressure on one of my cheeks. *Someone's patting it,* I thought. I considered telling whoever it was to go about their business while I submerged back into the cool, comforting depths of unconsciousness, but I realized then that I was lying down, which – since the last place I remembered being was Wet Dreams – meant that I was most likely lying on the bar's floor. The thought of the dry-cleaning bill that awaited me brought me back to full awareness, and I opened my eyes.

Day Jinx crouched next to me, a look of worry on his face. But when he saw that I was awake, he stopped patting my cheek, and his features became stern and disapproving.

"What were you thinking?" he demanded. "You know it's not a good idea to force another backstep so soon after experiencing one naturally."

I looked around. Deacon was still behind the bar, but he was leaning forward to watch. I realized then that I'd never seen him come out from behind the bar, and I wondered if he could. Abc still sat on his stool, gazing down at me with a mixture of concern, guilt, and more than a little fear. No doubt he was worried that he was going to get in trouble from slipping a mem to an officer, who'd promptly collapsed after taking it.

I sat up. I was weak, and my head pounded like a sonofabitch, but I managed. At first, Jinx reached out as if to help me stand, but then he lowered his hands. He probably figured it would only piss me off if he tried to help me. He was right.

I reached up to feel my forehead and winced. No blood, so I didn't cut myself, but I could feel a knot rising. I was going to have one hell of a bruise there.

"We should get you checked for concussion," Jinx said. "Head injuries are nothing to fool with."

"That's rich coming from you," I said. "I once watched you use your head to smash through a brick wall."

Jinx stiffened. "That was *his* head. Not mine."

I could tell from his tone that he was offended, but right then I really didn't care. I pulled myself to my feet and managed to climb back onto the stool next to Abe. Jinx stood as well, but he didn't take a seat. Wet Dreams isn't one of his Day Aspect's favorite establishments. Too déclassé for him.

"What are you doing here?" I asked him. "I thought you were at the Art Institute checking out the tit exhibit."

I knew damn well the artist's name was Titian, but I couldn't resist.

Jinx let out a long-suffering sigh but otherwise ignored my joke, such as it was.

"Deacon called me the moment you hit the floor, and I got here as soon as I could." He shook his head. "I should've known you wouldn't let this go."

"You left a museum for me? I didn't know you cared."

Jinx looked hurt. "Of course I care. You're my partner."

Despite myself, I was touched, but I didn't want to show it. "Well, as you can see, I'm not dead yet." As bad as my head hurt, though, I was tempted to take a hit of rev, but I knew it would only upset Jinx, and I figured I'd already done enough of that for one afternoon.

"I kept thinking there was something familiar about Nocturne, and I hoped that taking a mem might help me remember him." I smiled, feeling insufferably pleased with myself. "And it did."

"Really?" Jinx said. "Or is that just your head injury talking?"

"His name's Russell. I can't remember his last name, though. I'm not sure I ever knew it. I met him as a child, back when my parents had me seeing a psychiatrist who specialized in sleep disorders. That was after..."

"Me," Jinx said simply.

"Russell's parents took him to the same doctor. Sometimes she saw the two of us together, sometimes individually, sometimes as part of a larger group. She was doing some kind of study, I think. I didn't know much about it, and I didn't care. I just wanted the dreams to stop."

Jinx's gaze became sorrowful, and he looked away. But when he spoke again, his voice sounded normal. "And you know Russell is Nocturne because when he was a child, he told you about his Incubus."

"Yes."

Jinx thought about this for a moment. "It could be a coincidence. And Sanderson *did* tell us we were off the case..."

There are times when I wish Day Jinx was more like his nocturnal counterpart. Night Jinx would've been halfway to the door, ready to investigate before I'd finished my explanation. Day Jinx's reaction might've been lukewarm, but at least he hadn't said no. Better yet, he was no longer chastising me for taking the mem.

Jinx went on. "I was planning on trying out a new seafood place downtown for an early dinner. But I suppose it will have to wait." He sighed, as if he were making a supreme sacrifice. "Our first step should be to determine whether Dr Kauffman is still in practice." He turned to Deacon. "Do you have a phone book we could use?"

Before Deacon could answer, I said, "We can look her up on a wisper, you know."

Wispers can function as phones on Earth and can connect to the Internet. Information is displayed via a holographic screen projected in the air above the user's wrist.

Jinx gave me one of Those Looks. "We're supposed

to avoid using wisper technology on Earth whenever possible. You know this."

"What's the point of having supercool tech if we hardly ever get to use it?" I countered. "Besides, we're in Wet Dreams, not standing out on the street in broad daylight. It's not like anyone in here is going to–"

A loud crash interrupted me, and we all turned to see Cancer Jack lying on the floor, the broken remnants of a wooden chair scattered around him. Lizzie stood over him, half a chair back gripped in her hands, looking down at Jack with an expression of raw anger.

"Looks like the on-again, off-again switch has been flipped to off," I muttered.

"Indeed," Jinx said.

Without thinking about it, I slid off my stool and started walking toward Jack and Lizzie's table. I didn't check to see if Jinx followed me. Day Jinx might prefer pursuing aesthetic pleasures to fighting, but at his core, he was a Shadow Watch officer, and I knew he'd have my back. My legs were a little wobbly on the way over, and I knew I hadn't fully recovered from the mem I'd taken, but I was determined not to let Lizzie and Jack see that I wasn't functioning at full capacity. Incubi, regardless of which Aspect they're in, can be like wild animals. You can never let them think you're weak – especially when you are.

As I approached their table, I made sure to keep my hands down and held away from my body. I didn't want Lizzie to think that I was going to draw a weapon and attack her. I found myself wishing Maggie and the Darkness hadn't left. Jack and Lizzie would've probably continued to behave themselves if they were still around. Even if they hadn't been intimidated by the Darkness' Day Aspect, they wouldn't have wanted to be on the end of one of Maggie's infamous tongue-lashings.

"Hey, Lizzie," I said, keeping my voice casual and pleasant. "What's wrong?"

She looked up at me, eyes wild, face red, chest heaving. At first, there was no recognition in her gaze, and I debated reaching for my trancer. But then her eyes focused more clearly on me, and she relaxed a little. Not much, but enough so that I didn't feel I had to shoot her. Not yet, anyway.

"Nothing's wrong, Audra." She glanced down at Jack, who was moaning and trying to push himself up off the floor. He still had a cigarette in his mouth – I've often wondered if that ever-present cigarette of his is a bit of Incubi magic that follows him even into his day persona – but it was bent at a right angle.

When Lizzie saw her sometime lover start to rise, she placed her foot between his shoulder blades and shoved him back to the floor. "Jack just needed another lesson in how to behave himself."

"What did he do this time?" I asked.

Jinx went over to help Jack up. Lizzie glared at him, but she made no move to stop him.

"I told him I was thinking of getting a new tattoo, and he agreed with me."

"The monster," Jinx muttered.

He'd gotten Jack to his feet, but Jack was far from steady. *Lizzie must've really hit him hard this time,* I thought.

Lizzie wore a tank top, shorts, and flip-flops. A dozen tattoos were visible on her body, and she probably had quite a few that weren't. Some were larger, some small, some realistic, some cartoonish or abstract. But they all had one thing in common: they were all tattoos of insects.

"What's wrong with getting a new tat?" I asked.

"Nothing," she said. She sat back down at the table and crossed her legs. "Except that by agreeing with me, Jack implied that the tattoos I already have aren't enough." She paused. "Besides, you should've heard where he suggested I get it!"

Jinx had given Jack a quick once-over, and he looked at me and nodded. Jack might be the worse for wear, but he'd survive. Incubi can be injured in their Day Aspects, even killed, but once the sun sets and they return to their true selves, all physical damage is repaired, and as long as enough of their body remains intact, they can even return to life. For this reason, no matter how badly hurt, Incubi almost never seek medical attention. It's unnecessary, and if a doctor performed too many tests, he or she might notice that despite appearances, their patient wasn't altogether human.

I turned to Jack. "You all right?" I wasn't just asking about his physical state. I wanted to know if he was planning on attacking Lizzie.

"Hmm?" He looked at me, blinking and squinting, as if his eyes were having trouble focusing. "Oh, yeah. Sure. Better'n ever."

He wore an old black jacket over a black Iron Maiden T-shirt, with jeans and sneakers. He spit out his bent cigarette and reached into the inner pocket of his jacket, presumably to get a fresh one. But instead he pulled out a butterfly knife, flicked it open, and lunged for Lizzie.

I drew my trancer and prepared to fire, but I feared I wouldn't be able to do so before Jack could cut her. Sure, she'd heal the damage by nightfall, but I wanted to spare her the pain if I could. Plus, the more pissed off Lizzie got, the more trouble there would be, if not now, then later tonight when they were both in their Night Aspects. And that, I – and the city of Chicago – could do without.

But Jinx intervened before I could pull my trancer's trigger. He stepped between Jack and Lizzie – and just as Jack swung his knife toward Jinx in a vicious arc that would've laid his throat open, Jinx raised his arm to block the strike. His forearm connected with Jack's, but Jack – still wobbly on his feet – stumbled. His arm slipped, his wrist twisted, and the point of his blade jabbed into Jinx's shoulder.

Jinx let out a bellow that might've been the word *Fuck!* but which just as easily might've been an inarticulate shout of pain. He grabbed Jack by the collar of his jacket and his belt, picked him up as if he weighed nothing, then slammed him down onto the table at which Lizzie still sat. The table collapsed into kindling. Lizzie let out a shriek and tried to push herself back, which only resulted in her falling over backward in her chair and smacking her head against the concrete floor.

Jack lay amidst the remains of the broken table, not moving, and Lizzie lay on the floor several feet away, equally unconscious. Jinx stood there looking at them, the butterfly knife stuck in his shoulder, a bloodstain blossoming on the fabric of his jacket. For an instant, I almost fired on Jinx. If he'd been in his Night Aspect, I might have, if only to distract him from his homicidal rage. But this was Day Jinx. He was much better able to control his emotions than his nocturnal self. At least, that's what I'd always thought. But right then I wasn't so certain.

From behind the bar, Deacon shouted, "Who's going to pay for the table?"

"Put it on my tab," I called back. I holstered my trancer and went over to Jinx.

"Want me to pull it out?" I asked.

"Not yet. I might be tempted to ram it into Jack's chest."

"Wouldn't blame you. Buy you a drink?"

"I wouldn't say no to a soda water."

We headed to back to the bar.

•••

Once we were seated and had our drinks – I ordered a Sam Adams – I called up the Internet on my wisper. Jinx gave me a disapproving look but didn't object. A small holo display appeared above the device, and using vocal commands, I found information about Dr Kauffman. She was no longer in private practice and now worked for a company called Perchance to Dream: Advanced Sleep Solutions. The company specialized in all aspects of sleep therapy: physical, psychological, and pharmaceutical. It was the last that seemed to be their biggest money-maker. They'd produced several popular sleep aids that were currently on the market.

I made a note of the address and then closed the holo display. The bloodstain on Jinx's jacket had spread since we sat down, and I decided that we shouldn't put off taking care of his wound any longer.

Deacon keeps a full medical kit behind the bar. Given the nature of his establishment, he needs to. It gets a lot of use and requires constant restocking. I took Jinx into the women's room, had him strip to his underwear – boxers, if you must know – and did my best not to make too much of a bloody mess as I pulled Jack's knife from his shoulder. I'd stripped down to my bra and panties – no way was I going to pay a dry-cleaning bill if I could avoid it. Besides, bloodstained clothes cause more than a few raised eyebrows at the cleaners.

There was nothing remotely sexual about what we did. Despite Night Jinx's insistence on calling me Mommy, we were more like brother and sister. Besides, I don't get aroused by blood-spurting knife wounds. I guess I'm just an old-fashioned girl that way.

I've had more than my fair share of practice at tending to injuries in the field, both Jinx's and mine, and I managed to get the knife out, then clean and dress Jinx's wound without spilling too much blood on ourselves, the sink, or the floor. Despite the fact that as an Incubus, Jinx probably didn't need it, I put some antibiotic cream on the bandage. His wound would heal completely come nightfall, but a little extra precaution never hurts.

I cleaned up the mess as best I could, and then we got dressed. Jinx's shirt and jacket were bloodstained where Cancer Jack's knife had sliced through fabric and flesh, but as Jinx didn't have a change of clothes with him, he put them back on. He moved stiffly and grimaced as he put on his shirt and jacket, but he needed me to tie his tie for him.

"Want some pain meds?" I asked. "I'm sure Deacon's got some." And if he didn't, Abe probably did.

Jinx tapped his wisper with an index finger and softly glowing numbers appeared above the device. 3.38. After a few seconds, the display vanished.

"Better not," he said. "It's getting late."

Day Jinx was careful about what he put into his body, especially in later afternoon or early evening. No alcohol and definitely no drugs, not even the legal kind. He didn't want anything in his bloodstream when his Night Aspect took over. Not even caffeine. Once he'd forgotten and had a double espresso a half hour before the sun went down. I spent half the night chasing him through the city as he jumped up and down like a demented kangaroo.

"Have it your way, tough guy."

We said goodbye to Deacon, who reminded me one more time that we owed him for the table we destroyed. Abe had left the bar while we were in the restroom – probably because he was afraid I might change my mind about busting him for possession. Jack and Lizzie had regained consciousness and were sitting at a different table. They looked worse for wear, but all they did was glare at us as we walked past. They were both drinking water, which I

knew was a bad sign. It meant they wanted to keep a clear
head for later, when they would undoubtedly try to get
even with us.

I sighed. One more damn thing to worry about.

We stopped before we reached the door, and I used my
wisper to make a quick call. Then Jinx and I stepped outside.

A 1973 baby-shit-brown Pinto came rattling down the
street toward us, a blue-black exhaust cloud billowing in its
wake. The body was dented and rust-nibbled, and a large
horizontal crack ran across the middle of the windshield.
A woman pulled up to the curb outside Wet Dreams, the
Pinto's ancient brakes grinding, tires so badly in need of
air they looked as if they might burst any second. The
windows were down, and the driver – a short, heavily
tattooed woman with a buzz cut – leaned toward the
passenger window.

"Your chariot awaits!" Connie Desposito said cheerfully.

Jinx had taken a deep breath when he first heard
the Deathmobile approaching. He hated the miasma of
exhaust, gasoline, and burning oil that surrounded the
vehicle like a cloud of military-grade defoliant.

He continued holding his breath as he opened the
passenger door – which creaked and sagged as it swung
outward – and climbed into the backseat. Jinx let out a
soft hiss of pain as he settled back, and I knew his shoulder
wound hurt like a bitch.

The car's upholstery had been repaired by duct tape so
many times that the back seat was practically covered by
it. Crumpled fast-food bags covered the back floor, and
Jinx grimaced as he tried to find a relatively clean place
to put his feet. He couldn't hold his breath forever, and
the interior of the Deathmobile smells even worse than
the exterior. It's best just to breathe through your mouth

and try not to think about the millions of exotic bacteria multiplying around you.

I slid into the front seat next to Connie and closed the door behind me. It made a loud *chunk!* sound as it shut, and I wouldn't have been surprised if the damn thing had fallen off. But it didn't. The Deathmobile is always on the verge of total mechanical and structural collapse, but somehow it manages to hold itself together, if only just.

Before Connie could remove her foot from the brake, Jinx and I buckled our fraying seat belts. While safety is an unattainable ideal in the Deathmobile, every little bit helps.

Connie tromped on the gas and pulled into traffic, cutting off a Lexus whose owner honked at her. She raised her middle finger in cheerful salute, then lowered her hand back to the steering wheel. One thing about Connie: she takes her driving seriously.

"Where to?" she asked.

"First to our place since Jinx can get a clean shirt and jacket there. Then to a business called Perchance to Dream," I said. "It's located—"

"I know where it's at," she said, a bit sharply. She takes pride in knowing the Chicago area inside and out, and she hates it when anyone implies otherwise.

"Of course you do," I said. I glanced over my shoulder and saw Jinx's face was red edging toward purple. He can hold his breath longer than a regular human, but not much longer. I knew he'd have to give up soon. Good thing the windows were open.

"How are things, Connie?" I asked.

"Can't complain."

She was dressed in a black tank top and purple short-shorts that were so tight on her they looked as if they would cut off circulation to her legs. Her body is tattooed with a winding racetrack on which various makes and models of cars seem to be zooming across her flesh in a never-ending contest. Connie is, to put it mildly, a car enthusiast. If it's got four wheels and an engine, she's crazy for it.

She went on. "Been a slow day so far. DM and I haven't had many fares. Business will pick up tonight, though." She grinned. "It always does."

Not all Incubi are living creatures – or rather, they *are*, but they don't always look like it. During the day, the Deathmobile is a decades-old car perpetually on the verge of falling apart. At night – well, it's still a vehicle and still just as scary, but in an entirely different way.

Connie's a gypsy cabbie who only services Incubi and Ideators, along with the few humans that know about us. But that wasn't why I called her. The more unusual-looking Incubi ride with her at night, so they don't attract attention going from one place to another. And even though Jinx looks relatively human in his Night Aspect, his behavior is so bizarre that when we need a lift, we usually call Connie. But during the day, we take a cab or ride the El without anyone looking at us twice.

Given the way the Deathmobile smells inside, I'm sure Jinx would've preferred we'd chosen a different mode of transportation today. I wasn't overly fond of the odor either – the car's interior smelled like a mixture of corn chips, sweat, and bubblegum, with a touch of ammonia tossed in for good measure. But Connie, like Deacon Booze, was one of the go-to people in the community when it came to information. So I figured we might as well see what, if anything, she knew about Quietus and Nocturne-slash-Russell while we made our way to our apartment.

As it turned out, she didn't know more than Deacon did, and actually knew a bit less. She'd heard about the Bean coming to life last night, and she asked me a few questions about what had happened. I answered them, feeling as if I was giving more information than I was receiving.

When we got home, Connie and I waited outside while Jinx went inside to change. After a few minutes, he returned with a fresh shirt and jacket, and we started on our way to Perchance to Dream. By now it was close to 4.15. I told Connie we needed to get there before five. I figured a place that conducted sleep therapy would keep odd hours, but why take chances? She said she didn't think it would be a problem, she hit the gas, and the Deathmobile began coughing and rattling down the road once more. Despite the car's appearance, Connie could make good time in it when she wished, and I felt relatively confident we'd reach our destination before the close of business.

As Connie drove, Jinx and I decided that we'd pose as freelance writers who wanted to do a feature story on Perchance to Dream. We'd used similar cover stories in the past, and they'd always worked for us. As we figured out the details, I noticed a shimmering in the air outside the Deathmobile, a rippling and distorting, as if waves of intense heat were rising from the asphalt. I felt a dizzying sense of disorientation accompanied by a twist of nausea, similar to what I experience every time I step through a Door, and the car upholstery beneath my rear shuddered and jerked, as if we were going over a stretch of bumpy road.

At first, I was afraid I was hallucinating, an aftereffect of experiencing two backsteps in so short a time. I turned around in my seat to face Jinx, intending to ask him if he was experiencing the same thing, but my voice froze before I could speak. Despite the fact that it was full daylight out, my partner had assumed his nightmare clown Aspect. His clothing had transformed, too. He still wore his gray suit, but now Jinx had on his overlarge orange tie with blue polka dots, his flower boutonnière, and his absurdly gigantic sneakers.

He grinned at me, but there was a hint of uncertainty in the expression.

"This is different," he said.

I turned forward once more to talk to Connie, but as I did, the Deathmobile changed around us. The upholstery became fine black leather, and the rest of the interior – floor, roof, doors – became black as well. The engine – which up to this point had sounded as if it were perpetually on the verge of shaking itself to pieces – now sounded smooth and powerful, like a large beast growling softly just before it attacks. Like Jinx, the ancient Pinto had transformed into its Night Aspect: a hot-rod hearse. A true Deathmobile.

"Holy shit!" Connie said. "What the fuck's going on?"

"Good question." I turned back to Jinx, but he just held up his hands.

"Don't look at me. I don't have a clue."

I looked out my window again. We'd left downtown a while ago and were driving through a lower-middle-class business district – fast-food restaurants, liquor stores, short-term loan joints. People on the street looked confused and terrified. There was a scattering of Incubi among them, humanlike for the most part, but there was one that resembled a cross between a velociraptor and an armadillo that was making folks decidedly nervous.

Worse was what was happing to the surroundings. Buildings canted at strange angles, their windows distorting into all manner of geometric shapes, and the sidewalk undulated beneath pedestrians' feet as if they were standing on the back of a giant writhing serpent.

"It's another Incursion," I said, not fully believing it. But it was the only explanation that even came close to making sense.

"But – but that's not possible!" Connie said.

The Deathmobile's engine revved loudly, as if agreeing with her.

"Only Maelstrom energy bleeding through the barrier between dimensions could cause Jinx and the Deathmobile to assume their Night Aspects," I said. "So unless several million people suddenly fell asleep in the middle of the afternoon, what else can it be *but* an Incursion?"

The thought was far from comforting, though. As far as I knew, an Incursion couldn't happen during the day, and even at night there had never been one strong enough to distort the surrounding area like this. What happened with the Bean at the AT&T Plaza that morning was only a mild hiccup compared to what was happening now.

Connie had continued driving as the local reality shifted around us, but now she cried out, "Oh shit!" and slammed on the brakes. The Deathmobile screeched to a halt – in time to avoid crashing into a mound of rock that had broken through the middle of the street. It stood about twenty feet high, and as we watched, crude facial features formed on its surface – eyes, nose, and most distressingly, a tooth-filled mouth. The eyes glowed red-orange, as if the sockets were filled with roiling magma, and the teeth were uneven stalactites and stalagmites. The mouth opened and closed several times as the creature's magma eyes blazed at us, the stone teeth gnashing with the sound of colliding boulders.

Jinx grinned in delight.

"Showtime!" he cried. The hearse aspect of the Deathmobile had four doors instead of the Pinto's two, and Jinx opened one of the rear passenger doors and jumped out. Muttering a few choice obscenities, I disembarked as well. I wasn't about to let Jinx have all the fun.

I drew my trancer as I ran toward Stoneface, flicking

the selector switch to the highest setting. The weapon would quickly deplete its charge on this setting, but I had a feeling that anything less wasn't going to get the job done. Traffic had ground to a halt in both directions, and there had been a few fender-benders when vehicles came to a stop, but there didn't appear to be any serious accidents. Of course, that was here. Who knew how large an area this Incursion was affecting? A block? Two? More? The thought terrified me, but I thrust it aside. I had work to do.

Some pedestrians stood and stared at the bizarre rock creature that had forced its way up from the earth, but others fled in terror. As far as I was concerned, they were the smart ones. Buildings on either side of the street remained distorted, but at least they showed no signs that they were in danger of collapsing. The air around us continued to shimmer and ripple, which I took as an indication that the Incursion wasn't going to let up anytime soon.

Now that he was back in his Night Aspect, Jinx had access to all his special abilities, and he drew Cuthbert Junior from whatever other-dimensional space he used to store his goodies. He gripped the sledge's handle, spun it around a couple times as easily as if it were a baton, and then ran toward Stoneface, laughing maniacally.

Before Jinx could reach the creature, its mouth opened wide and a stone tongue shot forth. The tongue was covered with sharp spikes, and it lashed toward Jinx like a deadly whip. It happened too fast for me to fire my trancer or shout a warning, but Jinx had it covered. As the spiky length of stone swung toward him, he jumped into the air. As the tongue passed beneath him, he did a somersault in mid-air and brought Cuthbert Junior down in a vicious swing. The sledge's head struck the stone tongue a solid blow, and chunks of stone flew through the air.

Jinx cackled with mad delight as he continued his

somersault on his way to the ground, landing on his oversized shoes with inhuman grace.

"Sorry," he said to Stoneface, "but I don't allow anyone to give me tongue on the first date!"

Jinx had managed to knock a good chunk out of the tongue and dislodge a few spikes, but the rest of it still held together. Stoneface's magma eyes blazed with fury, and a rumbling growl that sounded like an avalanche issued from deep within the creature. Its spiked tongue lifted into the air, paused there for an instant, and then came hurtling down toward Jinx's head. Jinx saw what was happening, and he gripped Cuthbert Junior with both hands and raised the sledge, clearly intending to intercept the rock tongue with a devastating blow.

I decided to give him a hand. I assumed a firing stance, aimed my trancer, and waited.

An instant before the spiked rock-tongue slammed into his head, Jinx swung his hammer. At the same moment, I squeezed my trancer's trigger and Maelstrom energy lanced forth from the muzzle and streaked through the air to strike the tongue near the spot where the sledge impacted. Half of the tongue exploded in a shower of rock fragments, and Stoneface let out a bestial howl in what I assume was pain, and withdrew the remainder of its tongue into its mouth.

"Take that, you stone-faced bastard!" I shouted. I may not have Jinx's talent for groan-inducing repartee, but what I lack in wit I make up for in sheer attitude.

Jinx gave me a grin. "Nice shot, Annie Oakley."

"Nice strike, John Henry," I replied.

We'd only injured the creature, though. The magma bubbling in its eye sockets began to burn hotter and glow whiter, and I knew we had seriously pissed it off.

Behind us, Connie hit the Deathmobile's horn: a spine-chilling sound that was somewhere between a banshee's mournful cry and a pack of howling wolves. Jinx and I both turned to look. She leaned her head out the driver's side window and shouted, "Get out of the way!"

I had no idea what she had planned, but I'd known her long enough to trust her, and I threw myself to the side. Jinx did the same, and the second we hit the ground, the Deathmobile's headlights came on. At first the beams looked like normal light, but the longer they shone, the more green the light became, until twin beams of unearthly verdant energy poured onto Stoneface's surface. The rock creature roared with pain and shook its head back and forth, as if trying to twist away from the beams, but to no effect. Wherever the energy struck, stone began to crumble and fall away from the creature's body, gathering on the street around it in piles of what looked like gray sand.

Still roaring, the creature opened its maw wide and its half-a-tongue lashed out toward the Deathmobile, obviously intending to strike the deadly light at its source. But the Deathmobile adjusted the angle of its headlights so green energy washed over the tongue, and it disintegrated. The Deathmobile trained its greenlights on Stoneface again, and the beams began to blaze even brighter as the hearse poured more power into its attack. It didn't take long after that. Stoneface shrank as its surface sloughed away, and soon nothing remained of the creature but a large gray mound of sand.

The Deathmobile's headlights flicked off.

Jinx and I rose to our feet, keeping our gazes on the sand mound, just in case Stoneface wasn't all the way dead. But the sand made no movement, and I decided the Deathmobile had lived up to its name.

Jinx let out a low whistle. "We have *got* to get ourselves a car like that!"

The idea of Jinx behind the wheel of an Incubi vehicle with as much destructive power as the Deathmobile filled me with dread. It would be like giving an active volcano a nuclear bomb for Christmas.

We started back to the Deathmobile, but I'd only taken a couple steps when the air-shimmer became more intense and a fresh wave of vertigo swept over me. When it passed, the world had more or less returned to normal. The buildings and sidewalks were mostly as they had been before the Incursion began, with only minor damage visible. The mound of sand that had been Stoneface was gone, but the hole in the street it had made when it emerged remained. The Deathmobile had become a piece-of-shit Pinto again, and Jinx was no longer a clown, and Cuthbert Junior was gone.

"Well, that was rather disorienting," Day Jinx said.

"If you think it was bad for us, imagine how it was for *them*." I gestured at the people on the cracked and buckled sidewalk. There were no more Incubi in their midst – none that they could detect, anyway – but they stood quietly, expressions of shocked disbelief on their faces.

"I'd like to see how the M-gineers plan to handle this," I muttered.

SIX

Thankfully, we made it to Perchance to Dream without being attacked by any more Maelstrom-created monsters. The Deathmobile was none the worse – or maybe I should say none the better, in its case – for having experienced the Incursion. But Connie was pretty shaken up, and I have to admit that I was, too. Day Jinx usually plays his emotional cards close to the vest, but I could tell that he was also disturbed by what had happened.

Even during the night, wispers can't transmit between dimensions. Normally, when Jinx and I need to make a report to the Rookery – like we did that morning after fighting Quietus in AT&T Plaza – we rely on a Shadow Watch courier. Couriers are Incubi stationed on Earth. When they receive an officer's report, they record it, haul ass to the first Door they can find, step through, and then once in Nod, they relay the message to the Rookery.

But it was daytime, so in order to report this latest Incursion to Sanderson, we would have to wait until the sun went down. But this news was too important to wait, so on the way to Perchance to Dream, I called David Lindroth, a Shadow Watch officer I knew in London. We'd worked a couple cases together... and we'd done a few other things together that I'd rather not go into detail about, thank you.

Chicago is six hours behind the UK, so it was around 10.30 at night there. I quickly told David what had happened, and he made me repeat it more slowly. I couldn't blame him. A daytime Incursion? I thought it sounded insane, and I'd experienced it first hand. When I finished, David promised to convey my report to Sanderson immediately, and we disconnected.

I asked Connie to drop us off halfway down the street from Perchance to Dream. The business was located in an upper-middle-class suburb, and the Deathmobile's Day Aspect wouldn't make the best impression here. Connie took no offense at my request and did as I asked.

After we got out, she gave us a wave and a wan smile. She hadn't spoken much since the Incursion – I think it had really disturbed her – and she said nothing as she drove off. The Pinto shook and rattled as it went, leaving a trail of noxious exhaust in its wake. If I hadn't known the car was an Incubus, I wouldn't have expected it to last another day.

I'd convinced Connie to hit a Starbucks drive-through along the way so I could get a caramel macchiato with extra espresso, and I took a sip of it as I watched her leave. Jinx frowned. As far as he's concerned, caffeine isn't much different than rev – especially in large quantities – but he didn't say anything about it, for which I was grateful. The way the day had gone so far, I needed it, as much for my morale as for the energy boost.

One good thing about the Incursion: Jinx's shoulder wound had healed when he shifted into his Night Aspect, and it remained healed when he returned to his day self. His tie, while smaller, remained orange and purple, and his shoes, although normal size, were still sneakers. I knew he hated to be seen in public like this, but there was nothing we could do about it right then.

As we started walking toward Perchance to Dream, Jinx said, "There have been only two Incursions in Chicago in the space of twelve hours. Two that we know of, anyway. Doesn't it strike you as odd that we were present when both occurred?"

I frowned. "Now that you mention it, yeah, it does. Are you suggesting *we* caused the Incursions somehow, without knowing it?"

But before Jinx could respond, a man and a black-and-tan dachshund came around the corner. The dog walked at the man's side without a leash, collar jingling and toenails clack-clack-clacking on the sidewalk. I've never been a fan of small yappy dogs, and the doxie must've sensed how I felt, for as it approached it gave me a suspicious look and growled.

"Hush," the dog's owner said softly. He was about my age, maybe a bit older, and dressed in a black T-shirt and jeans. He was brown-haired, with a mustache and beard, handsome, and fit. The man smiled at me as if to apologize for his dog, and then the two of them passed us and continued down the sidewalk. I would've turned to get another look at him, but I didn't want Jinx to tease me about it, so I resisted. It wasn't easy, though.

After calling David in London, I'd called Deacon Booze. He knew about the latest Incursion (of course), but he knew of no others. It was possible he simply hadn't heard of them yet, but I doubted it.

"So, *did* we cause the Incursions?" I asked Jinx.

"Honestly, I don't see how we could have. But think about it: what are the odds that Connie would take us on a route that would coincide with the Incursion's location, and that we would pass through that location at the *precise* moment the Incursion happened?"

"Pretty damn slim."

Jinx and I had reached Perchance to Dream's parking lot, and we headed for the office building. As we drew nearer, I started feeling a cold queasiness in my gut. I put it down to drinking my macchiato on an empty stomach, and I did my best to ignore it.

I went on. "If someone is causing the Incursions on purpose, that someone could've followed us and triggered the Incursion whenever they felt like it."

"Someone like Quietus?" Jinx said.

"We might've lost him in Nod, but that doesn't mean he stayed there. He had plenty of time to get back to Chicago before sunrise."

"I suppose it's possible," Jinx admitted, although he sounded doubtful. "Quietus *was* present during the first Incursion."

There was nothing special about Perchance to Dream, at least not from the outside. The parking lot was full of vehicles, mostly new or newish, nothing too sporty or expensive, but it was clear that none of the employees was starving. There were no signs announcing this as the location of Perchance to Dream. Either the company didn't need to advertise its presence, or it didn't want to. There was a chrome design above the entrance, a shape that made me think of a leaf lying on its side. I wasn't sure what it was supposed to be.

As if reading my mind, Jinx said, "It's a closed eye. It represents sleep."

"Right. I remember now. I saw it on their webpage." I looked at it more closely. "You know, if they positioned it vertically, it would look like this was a gynaecologist's building."

Jinx sighed.

"If it was nighttime, you'd have laughed."

"At that joke? Not likely."

We were halfway across the parking lot by now, and my queasiness surged into full-fledged nausea. My heart started pounding double time and sweat beaded on my skin. I became dizzy, and my vision blurred. I wasn't sure, but I thought I might be experiencing a panic attack. That or I was having a stroke. I almost said something to Jinx, but I was afraid he'd just nag me about forcing myself to have a second backstep. Besides, I didn't want to scare him. I was plenty scared for the both of us. I tried to relax my body as we walked, and I focused on breathing deeply and evenly. But by the time we reached the building's entrance, I was fairly confident I wasn't going to die – at least not within the next few minutes – although I still felt awful.

I wondered if my panic was caused by the thought of seeing Dr Kauffman for the first time in fifteen years. That hadn't exactly been the happiest time of my life. I decided to squash that thought before it could go any further, though. The last thing I needed was to get even more worked up than I already was.

Jinx seemed not to have noticed my spaz attack, and I was grateful. I didn't want to distract him. *At least one of us should have our shit together when we're working*, I thought.

He opened one of the double glass doors and gestured for me to enter. Day Jinx can be a gentleman when it suits him. Night Jinx would've probably just smashed through the glass at a full run, giggling like a lunatic as he went, not caring whether or not I followed. I stepped through and tossed my mostly empty coffee cup into a trash receptacle just inside the large atrium-style lobby. A semicircular reception desk was located on the far side of the lobby, and a round-faced woman in her late thirties with curly black hair sat at the desk, typing on a keyboard.

She was dressed in a stylish business suit, but despite her professional appearance, she didn't look up as we entered. Her attention was completely absorbed by whatever was displayed on her computer monitor.

We walked past a waiting area consisting of several expensive-looking leather chairs and couches. The furniture was arranged around a large-screen TV playing an informational video to empty seats about all the wonderful services Perchance to Dream offered. On the screen, a white-bearded man in his late fifties – wearing a tailored gray suit – was speaking rapidly and at high volume.

"You might be asking yourself, 'Why do I need help sleeping? I sleep just fine!' Well, my friend, the fact is that you only think *you're getting a good night's sleep. But just because your eyes are closed doesn't mean you're getting restful, and most importantly,* restorative *sleep."*

He gave his nonexistent audience a wide, gleaming smile.

"And that's where we come in."

When we reached the desk, I looked at the receptionist and hooked a thumb toward the video monitor.

"You must be sick of listening to that noise all day," I said.

She didn't respond. In fact, she seemed totally unaware of our presence. I leaned forward and waved a hand between her face and the monitor. She gave a start, then looked up at us, an apologetic smile on her face.

"Sorry." She removed a pair of plastic plugs from her ears and placed them on top of the desk.

"No need to apologize," I said. "If I worked here, I'd do the same."

Her smile relaxed. "I wouldn't mind it so much if they'd let me turn the volume down when no one else is here. Oh, well. We all have our crosses to bear, right?"

"That's an interesting pin," I said, nodding toward the

silvery object affixed to her lapel. "It's the company logo, right?"

"Yes. It's supposed to look like a closed eye." She lowered her voice. "I think it's kind of ugly, to tell you the truth, but they make us wear it." She brushed her fingers across her pin as if to give it a quick polish, then said, "How may I help you?"

"My colleague and I are freelance writers," Jinx said. "We're working on an article about your company for *Innovation Today* magazine."

There is, of course, no such magazine. That'll be our little secret, OK?

The woman's smile didn't falter, but her eyes narrowed slightly. "Did you have an appointment to speak with someone? I don't recall seeing anything like that on today's schedule."

She turned to her monitor, worked the mouse for a couple seconds, checked whatever appeared on her screen, then turned back to us.

"I wasn't informed about any interview." She sounded apologetic again, but also a bit guarded.

"We emailed your public relations director last week," Jinx said. He didn't elaborate. He just looked at the receptionist expectantly. Even in his Day Aspect, there's something slightly off-putting about Jinx, and he can stare for a long time without blinking if he wants to. It unnerves people when he does that, and he was doing it now.

The receptionist's smile faded. "I, uh… OK. Just let me check."

She lifted the receiver from her desk phone, punched in an extension number, then lifted to receiver to her ear. After a moment, she said, "Mr Schulte? This is Vivian. I have a man and a woman down here who say they have an appointment with you. They're writers working on a magazine article. They say they sent you an email last week, but I–" She paused as if interrupted, and listened. "Very well. I'll let them know." She replaced the receiver and looked at us, smile firmly in place once again.

"Mr Schulte will be down in a moment."

"Thanks," I said, and then Jinx and I wandered over to the waiting area. We didn't sit down, though. It was bad enough that we couldn't avoid the obnoxiously loud voice of the man in the promotional video. We weren't about to sit where we had to look at him, too.

I still felt queasy and weak, but now that we were actually here and working, I was starting to feel a little better. Maybe I had experienced some kind of physical reaction to the Incursion, I told myself. After all, I normally found passing through Doors disorienting, right? How much more would such an unprecedentedly strong Incursion – one that occurred during the daytime and was capable of distorting a couple blocks' worth of reality – affect me? That's all it was, I told myself.

A few moments later an elevator door next to the receptionist's desk opened with a ding, and who should emerge but the man from the video? He came walking briskly toward us, a used-car-salesman grin on his face.

"Parker Schulte," he said. "I'm the PR guy around here." He spoke just as fast as he did on the video, and his volume was almost as loud.

Like the receptionist, he wore one of the ugly closed-eye pins on his lapel. He looked exactly like his video self, even down to his suit. It was almost as if he'd stepped off the screen to greet us. His white hair was cut short, and his full beard was nearly trimmed, but despite his age, he moved with the energy and vigor of a younger man.

"And you are… ?" he prompted.

"Emmett Kelly," Jinx said. It was his usual cover name,

taken from the famous circus performer.

"Audra Hawthorne." I couldn't give Schulte a false name, not if I wanted Dr Kauffman to recognize me.

"Delighted to meet you both." He shook our hands, mine first, then Jinx's, his grip so firm, it verged on painful.

"Sorry for the confusion," he said. "I must've forgotten to make a note of our appointment time. No worries, though. I'm more than happy to devote the rest of my afternoon to you both."

"Please accept our apologies for arriving so late in the day," Jinx said. "We had several... unexpected delays."

"No problem," Schulte said. "As you might imagine, since our mission is treating sleep disorders, we keep flexible hours around here." His smile increased by a few watts. "So, where would you like to start? With a tour, maybe?"

Jinx and I exchanged glances. The freelance writer bit works every time.

I smiled. "A tour would be lovely."

Perchance to Dream was an impressive operation. They had facilities for conducting sleep studies – a dozen rooms in all – where people suffering everything from sleep apnea, insomnia, and narcolepsy to interrupted sleep patterns and restless leg syndrome could be examined and eventually treated. The company had physicians on staff, of course, but they also had dieticians and physical trainers to help patients with their overall health, along with chiropractors and massage therapists.

"We totally believe in the mind-body connection," Schulte explained.

There was an onsite pharmaceutical research facility as well as what Schulte referred to as their Mental Wellness division. It was this department that Jinx and

I were most interested in, of course, as that's where Dr Kauffman worked.

Jinx had grabbed a camera when he stopped at our place to change clothes, and as Schulte squired us around, Jinx took pictures from time to time to keep up the illusion that we were freelance writers. And I'd brought a small notebook that I pretended to write in. Masters of espionage, that's us.

At one point, Jinx asked, "So what's new at Perchance to Dream? Anything you folks are especially excited about?"

"We're always working on new innovations in sleep therapy," Schulte said. "But one of the things that we're currently researching – that we feel is very promising – is a new sleep aid called Torporian. It's highly effective, non-narcotic, and non-habit-forming. It works in concert with a person's natural body chemistry to produce unparalleled results at a minimal cost with virtually no side effects."

It was the *virtually* part that bothered me. There was probably a long list of "potential" side effects, starting with gastrointestinal discomfort and ending with the usual Big Three: heart attack, stroke, or – in rare cases – death.

"Torporian isn't on the market yet," Schulte said, "but the drug has performed well during clinical trials, and we expect the FDA to approve it any day."

We continued the tour, Schulte maintaining a brisk pace along with a rapid-fire spiel that was, quite frankly, exhausting. At one point we passed by a closed metal door with a keycard lock. A loud, low thrumming noise came from inside, so strong it made my teeth vibrate. When I asked Schulte what was in there, he said that was where they kept the main computer servers. I wasn't aware of any computers that made sounds like that, not outside of old-time science fiction movies, anyway, but Schulte kept going before I could ask him any more about it.

When we finally reached Mental Wellness – which was

located on the third floor – I interrupted his monologue.

"I have to confess that I have an ulterior motive for doing this story," I said.

"Oh?" Schulte's ever-present smile didn't leave his face, but I saw something shift in his eyes, as if he were performing a quick mental recalculation.

I laughed. "I didn't mean that to sound as ominous as it came out. I had severe problems sleeping when I was a child – that's what got me interested in doing an article on your company in the first place. When I was conducting background research on Perchance to Dream, I was surprised to discover the psychiatrist who treated me when I was a child is the director of your Mental Wellness department: Dr Cecelia Kauffman."

My stomach gave a cold twist as I spoke her name, but I managed to keep smiling.

Jinx glanced at me, most likely to check how I was doing, but I ignored him. I didn't want to make Schulte suspicious.

"It's true what they say; it really is a small world," Schulte said. "Well, I'm sure Dr Kauffman would love to see you. I don't know her schedule off the top of my head, so she might be with a client right now, but let's go see." His smile widened a fraction. "I'd love to arrange a reunion between the two of you."

There was nothing special about the Mental Wellness department. It was nothing more than bland hallways with closed, windowless office doors. Some had signs indicating the office's purpose or occupant, but some were blank, giving no indication of who or what lay inside. Dr Kauffman's office was located at the far end of the hall. The sign on the door read simply:

Cecelia Kauffman, PhD.
Director, Mental Wellness.

Now that we were here, I started to feel ill again, like I was going to throw up everything I'd eaten for the last week. I couldn't understand why I was so nervous. I mean, sure, I associated Dr Kauffman with the most painful time of my life, but it wasn't the thought of reliving memories of that time that bothered me. Right now I was afraid of *her*, and I didn't know why. She hadn't been the warmest person, but she hadn't done anything to traumatize me.

That had been Jinx's doing – and my parents', since they refused to believe that I was being terrorized by a living clown that had somehow left my dream and entered the real world. But if I hadn't needed to learn the name of the boy who I was certain became Nocturne, I'd have turned and fled down the hallway, shrieking at the top of my lungs. I tried to tell myself that I just needed rest, needed to cut back on the pharmaceutical assistance I relied on from time to time to get through the day. It was all catching up to me, resulting in what seemed to be panic attacks but were really just my system being completely out of whack.

That's what I tried to tell myself, but I didn't believe it.

Jinx must've sensed what I was feeling – as strong as my anxiety was at that moment, I doubted I was managing to conceal it very well – and he stepped closer and put his hand on the small of my back. The contact made me jump at first, but when I realized what Jinx was doing, I was grateful for his support. The contact didn't make me feel less scared, but it did make me feel less alone, and that was a big help.

Schulte knocked softly on Dr Kauffman's door, then waited. Several moments passed, and I began to hope that either she wasn't in or she was with a patient and was ignoring us. I was about to suggest that we move on when the door opened.

I know my heart didn't stop. That's not possible, right?

But that's what it felt like when I saw Dr Kauffman open her office door and step out into the hall.

She was tall and thin, with straight blond hair that fell to her shoulders. Glasses highlighted her startlingly green eyes, and her makeup was so subtle, you couldn't tell she was wearing any unless you looked closely. She wore a white lab coat over a light green blouse and a dark green skirt. A pair of black flats completed her outfit, and strangely enough, it was those shoes that I remembered most. Maybe because I'd spent so much time with my eyes trained on the floor whenever I'd been in her presence. Like the other employees we'd seen, she wore the company logo pinned to her coat.

The more I saw these miniature company logos, the stranger they seemed to me. What was their purpose? They were too small and generic to serve as ID badges, and they were too cumbersome to swipe through electronic locks like key cards. I supposed it was some sort of rah-rah corporate team-building thing. Working for the Shadow Watch – and babysitting Jinx – can be frustrating at times, but at least I don't have to slave away in a cube farm day after day.

She looked at Jinx and me. A shudder went through me as we locked gazes, and I was sure she was going to recognize me. But then she turned to face Schulte, and I knew she hadn't.

"Yes, Parker?"

Her tone was reserved and professional, but there was a cold undercurrent that said she hoped Schulte had a good reason for disturbing her. A *very* good reason.

Schulte's PR smile didn't falter. "This is Mr Kelly and Ms Hawthorne. They're freelance writers doing an article on the Dream Factory." He looked at us. "My little nickname for the place," he explained. He faced Kauffman once more. "And you might well recognize one of them."

Kauffman frowned and turned to scrutinize our faces. After a couple seconds, her eyes widened. "My God! You're Audra, aren't you?"

She gave me a smile which had the effect of making her seem less intimidating and more human. A bit, anyway. It was that smile more than anything that helped calm me. I began to feel my fear draining away. I took a deep breath – just as Dr Kauffman had taught me so long ago – and stuck out my hand for her to shake.

"It's good to see you again," I said, hoping I sounded like I meant it.

Instead of taking my hand, she stepped forward and enfolded me in a hug. I stiffened at first, surprised and unsure how to react. But then my body relaxed, and I was able to hug her back, although with less enthusiasm. When she stepped back, she kept her hands on my shoulders and looked me up and down.

"You've grown into quite a lovely woman, Audra," she said. "And you're a writer, too. That's wonderful! I remember how much you enjoyed keeping a journal."

She looked at Jinx then and released her hold on me to reach out and shake his hand.

"Nice to you meet you, Mr Kelly."

Jinx gave her a bland smile as he shook her hand. It might've been my imagination, but I thought he seemed jealous. Kauffman gave him a long look, as if she was trying to see into his mind with her psychiatrist ESP, and then she turned back to me.

"It's been how long, Audra? Fifteen years, maybe? I remember it so well, but you were young. You probably don't recall much about that time."

I saw my opportunity – thank the First Dreamer – and I decided to go for it.

"Actually, I remember a lot," I said. "I remember when my parents first brought me to see you, I remember having sessions alone with you, and I remember group sessions, too. Especially with this one boy, Russell..."

"Pelfrey," Dr Kauffman said. "Yes, you and he had a special connection, as I recall."

Pelfrey! That was it!

I gave Jinx a quick look, and he smiled and gave me a slight nod, as if to say, *Well done.*

"Well, this has been a *wonderful* surprise, Audra! But I wish the timing was better. I have a patient coming in shortly, and I really need to prepare for our session. I'd love to talk with you, though – to catch up and to help you with your article. Let me get you one of my cards."

She went back into her office. I stepped forward and glanced inside. It looked basically the same as the office she'd had when I was a kid. Antique desk and chair, brown leather couch, neutral color walls and carpet, file cabinet, paintings of landscapes... In fact, it could've been the *exact* same office, down to the smallest detail. It was more than a little creepy.

Kauffman took a business card from a plastic holder on her desk and brought it to me. It was a Perchance to Dream card, one I assumed all the employees got. It had a bluish-black background with stars sprinkled across it. The silver closed-eye logo was in the upper left corner, and Dr Kauffman's contact information was spelled out in white letters and numbers on the lower right-hand side.

"Call me," she said. "Maybe we can get together for lunch sometime and talk." She gave Jinx a sideways glance. "Your writing partner is welcome too, of course."

Jinx acknowledged her invitation with a less-than-enthusiastic nod.

"I'll call," I said.

She gave me a last smile, told Schulte that she'd be busy for the next couple hours – a clear message that she didn't want him bothering her anymore today. Then she went back into her office and closed the door.

I turned to Schulte. "Thanks for taking the time to show us around, Mr Schulte – especially so late in the day."

He smiled. "It was very much my pleasure. I hope you got enough material for your article."

I assured him we did, and he offered to show us out. I almost told him he didn't have to bother – like Jinx and I couldn't find the front door on our own? – but I didn't want to blow our cover. So instead, I smiled sweetly and thanked him.

He continued yakking as we made our way back to the lobby, further extolling the virtues of the company, as if it were a favored child he loved more than life itself – instead of just a place he worked. The man was an inexhaustible source of words, and I decided he'd been born to work in public relations.

When we reached the lobby, I saw the receptionist was still behind her desk, facing her monitor and typing on her keyboard, even though it was after five by now. Schulte had said they kept odd hours around here. I wondered if they had someone working the desk around the clock. Since they had patients come in for sleep studies and stay overnight, they probably needed someone in the lobby all the time, I decided.

Schulte escorted us all the way to the lobby doors, thanked us for our interest in Perchance to Dream, and asked us to let him know when the article was published so he could buy a copy. He handed me one of his cards in case we had any more questions, and I tucked it into my jacket pocket with Dr Kauffman's. Then he said goodbye – finally! – and headed for the elevator.

Jinx and I went outside before Schulte could think of some last vital piece of information he'd forgotten to tell us and turned to catch us before we left. Dusk was approaching, but a couple hours remained before full nightfall, and I was confident we'd be able to get downtown before Jinx changed. The attention he draws in the city is nothing compared to the reaction he gets in the suburbs. So, the sooner we were back in the heart of the city, the better.

During the time Jinx and I had been inside the building, the parking lot had emptied by two thirds. I didn't want to use my wisper to call for a ride, not so close to the building, so Jinx and I started walking toward the street.

"Can we get a regular cab this time?" he asked. "Please?"

I was about to say sure, even opened my mouth to speak the word, but nothing came out. My vision blurred and my body went numb. I felt my knees buckle, and I started falling to the ground. Jinx caught me before I could hit, though, and he helped me stay on my feet. Whatever hit me passed as quickly as it came, and a few seconds later, I could stand on my own again, although I still felt shaky and weak.

"I..." I didn't have any explanation for what had happened, so I finished by saying, "Sorry."

"I'm sure it was hard for you to see Dr Kauffman after so long," Jinx said. "I imagine it brought forth all kinds of unpleasant memories and emotions. And after experiencing two backsteps today – not to mention not getting the rest you need – something like this was only to be expected."

I knew he was trying to be sympathetic, but it sounded as if he was nagging me again, and I became angry. Partially to spite him, but mostly because I really needed it, I pulled my rev inhaler out of my jacket pocket, and started to take a hit of it. But just as I started to depress the button to deliver the drug into my lungs, Jinx grabbed my wrist and yanked my hand away from my mouth. I pushed the inhaler's button out of reflex, and rev misted the air, the dose wasted.

My anger blossomed into full-fledged fury, and the adrenaline surge wiped away my weakness. I felt energized and beyond pissed.

"Let go!" I said, voice low, jaw muscles tight.

Jinx's expression was stern, and his eyes glittered with an anger that matched mine.

"You can't keep doing this to yourself, Audra. It's not only damaging your health, it's damaging your effectiveness as an officer."

The blaze of fury within me went arctic-cold. "Are you saying that it's *my* fault Quietus escaped?"

Jinx blinked a couple times, and his expression faltered.

"No. I only meant to make a general comment about your overreliance on stimulants." He paused then, and his mouth formed a cruel smile. "But now that you mention it…"

He still had hold of my wrist. I tried to pull free of his grip, but even though he's not as strong during the day as he is during the night, he's strong enough, and I couldn't free myself. As the time draws closer for Jinx to change Aspects, he starts to display traits of his other self, and I was definitely seeing signs of Night Jinx now.

My left hand remained free, so I hit Jinx in the jaw as hard as I could. It hurt like hell, but it was worth it to see that goddamned smile of his vanish. He still maintained his grip on my wrist, and now it tightened, and I thought I could hear as well as feel the bones grinding. If he kept this up, he was going to break my wrist.

My anger started to give way to panic. Ever since I'd

learned that my nightmare clown had become real, I'd been afraid that he would hurt me one day. But after working alongside Jinx for the last few years, I'd thought that I'd gotten over my fear that he would turn on me one day. But now I knew I hadn't. I still had the rev inhaler, and I was able to turn my hand far enough to aim it at Jinx's face. Then I gave him a shot of the drug, right in the face.

Although rev is made for humans, it won't harm Incubi. But getting blasted in the eyes with it hurts, no matter what species you are. Jinx let out a cry that was as much surprise as pain, and released my wrist. Tears flooded from his eyes, and he squeezed them shut and began rubbing them.

"Damn it, Audra! That *hurts!*"

Guilt hit me then, but I fought to keep from showing it. "So does my wrist!" I shot back.

Jinx and I had gotten into fights before, but always when he was in his Night Aspect. He has a completely different view on physical violence then, and never holds anything I do to him against me. In fact, he usually thinks it's hysterical.

But I'd never done anything to hurt Day Jinx before. Hell, not that long ago, I was patching up his wound in the restroom at Wet Dreams. I felt as if I should say something, but I couldn't bring myself to apologize. I was still too angry – and too afraid.

A black van came roaring down the street then. Tires squealed as the driver made a sharp turn into the parking lot and then gunned the engine. The vehicle headed straight for us, and I dropped my inhaler, drew my trancer, and stepped in front of Jinx, who was still rubbing his red and swollen eyes. I had no reason to think the occupants of the van were targeting us, but I'd been a Shadow Watch officer too long to assume otherwise. Mentally kicking myself for disabling my partner – not the brightest move I'd ever made – I shoved aside the emotions roiling inside me and focused on getting ready for whatever was coming next.

I flicked the selector switch on my trancer to its lowest setting. I'd used a lot of power fighting the stone-faced creature earlier, and I wanted to make the weapon's remaining energy last as long as possible.

"What's happening?" Jinx said, frantically trying to blink away tears. He drew his trancer, and that frightened me more than the oncoming van. Until his vision cleared, he was just as likely to hit me with trancer fire as he was any bad guys.

"Don't know," I said. "Stay sharp."

We were only a dozen yards from the building's entrance, and as the van came roaring toward us, I debated telling Jinx to try to get inside the building until his vision cleared. But I knew there was no point. He'd never leave me to face a potential threat alone, just as I would never leave him.

The van didn't slow as it barreled down on us, and I feared the driver intended to run us down. If I fired a low burst of M-energy, it would put the driver to sleep, but that wouldn't stop the van. It might veer off and miss us, but then again, it might not. I could flip the selector switch to high and blast the van with a force beam, but there was still no guarantee the vehicle wouldn't slam into us as it crashed. Of course, we could just jump out of the way, but I wasn't sure Jinx would make it in time. Besides, after the kind of day I'd had, I wanted to cause some damage.

But before I could reset my trancer to high, the driver hit the brakes and the van screeched to a stop less than ten feet away from us. The side door slid open, and men and women began exiting the vehicle, all of them armed with nine-millimeters. There were twelve of them – and my first thought was to wonder how they'd all managed to fit into the van.

They were dressed in black suits and ties, and wore sunglasses. Their features were all strange, exaggerated and distorted – a nose too big here, a mouth too wide there, bushy caterpillar brows, crooked teeth... They weren't grotesque-looking by any means, but they were definitely odd. Now that they were close enough, I could see another black-suited man wearing sunglasses behind the wheel of the van. It didn't escape me that he remained in the driver's seat and that he left the engine running.

The Blacksuits spread out and trained their guns on us. One of them, a guy with overlarge ears, spoke in a toneless voice. "Give us the clown and no one gets hurt."

SEVEN

"Excuse me?" I said.

Instead of replying to me, Big-Ears motioned to a couple of companions – a woman with short, fire-engine-red hair and a man whose nose resembled a vulture's beak. They nodded and moved toward Jinx, keeping their guns pointed at me as they went. I appreciated the implied compliment on my threat level, but I was still trying to wrap my head around the idea that they were apparently here for Jinx. They'd somehow known where to find him, and more importantly, they seemed to know who and what he really was.

I aimed my trancer at the two Blacksuits headed for Jinx.

"I hate to disappoint you, but that's *my* clown. And I'm not about to give him up without a fight."

Redhead and Vulture-Beak hesitated and looked to their boss for instruction. Big-Ears waved them on.

"We're carrying real guns that shoot real bullets," he said. "A *lot* of bullets. If we fire, you'll be dead before you hit the ground."

He continued to speak in a nearly emotionless voice, as if he were having a casual conversation instead of being in the middle of conducting what appeared to be a kidnapping.

I became aware of a tingling at the base of my skull then, and I realized the Blacksuits were all Incubi. Ideators can sense Incubi, although we can't sense other Ideators. Incubi are able to detect the presence of their kind even more strongly, and I imagined Jinx's skull was tingling so hard right now, it probably felt as if his head would explode.

Big-Ears confirmed it for me when his thin lips twitched in what I assumed was an approximation of a smile and said, "And unlike us, you won't heal once the sun sets."

Redhead and Vulture-Beak had reached Jinx by then. They took up positions on either side of him, and with their free hands, each took hold of one of his arms.

"Have no fear, brother," Redhead said. "You'll soon be free."

Jinx's eyes were still sore and swollen, but tears no longer streamed down his cheeks.

"Thanks, but no thanks," he said. He aimed his trancer at the redhead and shot a multicolored beam of concentrated M-energy at her face. He hadn't used his trancer lately – Night Jinx preferred using his personal stock of deadly toys when working – and it had a full charge. Jinx had his weapon set on high, and the force of the beam caused the woman's head to snap back and sent her sunglasses flying. She flew backward several feet and hit the asphalt hard. If she hadn't been an Incubus, there's a good chance a blast that strong would've taken her head off. Incubi might not be at their full strength during the day, but they're still hardier than humans.

Before Jinx could turn and fire on Vulture-Beak, the Blacksuit jammed the muzzle of his 9mm against the underside of Jinx's chin.

"If I splatter your brains all over the ground, you'll still heal when the sun sets, but you know how hard it is to properly regenerate brain tissue. You want to risk living the rest of your life without all your marbles?"

"Why not?" Jinx said. "You lot aren't especially bright, and it hasn't seemed to do you any harm."

"Funny," Vulture-Beak said, and then in a swift motion, he pulled the gun away from Jinx's neck and slammed the butt hard against the side of Jinx's head. Jinx moaned, but he didn't go down. He did lose his grip on his trancer, which fell to the ground.

I aimed my trancer at the Blacksuit and was about to fire when a gun went off, and a chunk of asphalt near my feet exploded.

I turned to see Big-Ears pointing his 9mm at me.

His lips curled slightly in what I think was supposed to be a sneer. "The next move you make will be your last, clown oppressor."

"Me? I'm the best friend a clown ever had!"

I looked to Jinx to back me up, but he was so groggy from the blow to his head, I wasn't sure he'd heard me.

Vulture-Beak hit him one more time for good measure, and Jinx slumped into the man's arms, semiconscious. Vulture-Beak half-walked, half-carried Jinx toward the van while a couple more Blacksuits took hold of the redhead – who hadn't come to yet – and hauled her back to the van. They all piled in, and once more I wondered how they could all fit inside, especially now that they had Jinx with them.

And then it hit me. *Brother. Clown oppressor.* They were all clowns, at least they were in their Night Aspects. And one of the primary clown skills was being able to fit an impossible amount of people into a small car.

"One last thing," Big-Ears said. "Put your trancer on the ground and kick it to me. Then do the same with his."

Crap! So much for trying to shoot out their tires as they tried to make their getaway. I did as he said, and then he had me do the same with my wisper. He crouched down to pick them up with his free hand, keeping his gun pointed at me the whole time. Then he backed toward the van, climbed into the front passenger seat, and slammed the door shut. The van peeled out and roared toward the street.

I didn't know what else to do, so I started running after them. I'd already memorized the license number, not that it would do me any good. The Shadow Watch has operatives working in all the major police departments around the world, but even though I had contacts in the Chicago PD, I doubted they'd be able to locate the van in time to do Jinx any good.

I told myself that if the Blacksuits wanted to kill either of us, they could've done so easily. Besides, they'd acted as if they were rescuing Jinx. But I still couldn't bring myself to just stand there and watch as they drove away with my partner. And so I kept running, but by the time I reached the street, the van was already heading east toward downtown, and I quickly lost sight of it.

I stood on the sidewalk and tried to catch my breath, mind racing. Even though Big-Ears had taken my trancer and wisper, I still had a regular phone on me. But who could I call for help? I couldn't travel to Nod until after sunset, and then I'd need an Incubus' help to locate a Door.

I was so deep in thought that at first I didn't notice the brown-haired man and his black-and-tan dachshund approaching. It was the jingling of the dog's collar that finally got my attention. I looked at the man, and he gave me a smile.

"Rough day?" he asked, as he stopped in front of me.

"You don't know the half of it."

"Actually, I think I do. My name's Russell. Russell Pelfrey. And this" – he gestured toward the dachshund – "is Bloodshedder."

The little dog looked up at me with suspicious eyes and growled.

"Russell?" I said. "*My* Russell?"

"That's right." His smile widened. "It's good to see you again, Audra."

I returned his smile, and then I punched him on the jaw as hard as I could. My hand was already sore from hitting Jinx, but I didn't care. The pain was totally worth it.

The dachshund started barking at me, the sound shrill and piercing, and I was tempted to kick the damn thing to shut it up. Don't look at me like that; I knew it was an Incubus and not a real dog. But Russell waved a hand to call it off.

"It's OK, girl. Stand down."

The dog gave him a look that said she wasn't happy about it, but she stopped barking. She continued glaring at me, though, and growling softly. I had the feeling that come nightfall, she was going to want some payback for what I'd done to her master.

I glared back at her. *Bring it, bitch,* I thought.

So there I was, standing on the sidewalk with an old childhood... I don't know if *friend* is the right word. *Fellow survivor,* maybe. If I'd had my trancer, I'd have rendered him unconscious in a heartbeat. But I didn't. Besides, it was so strange encountering him like this, as if we were two old acquaintances who'd happened to bump into each other during a walk, and I wasn't sure what to do. And it didn't help anything that he was so good-looking. It was more than a little distracting. Yeah, I know. So I can be shallow at times. Sue me.

When in doubt, I decided, go on the offensive.

"What the hell are you doing here? Are you connected with those assholes who kidnapped my partner? Tell me where they're taking him and I'll see what I can do to get you a reduced sentence after I hand you over to the Nightclad Council."

I guess I wasn't as intimidating as I'd hoped. Instead of breaking down and telling me what I wanted to know, he just kept looking at me and smiling.

"What?" I demanded.

"You've come a long way from the little girl who barely said a word in session."

Part of me was pleased that he remembered that detail, but another part wanted to punch him again. I might've, too, but my hand still throbbed, and I didn't want to risk breaking it. I figured I'd be needing it to smack some people around in the near future.

"We need to talk," Russell said. "But we can't do it here." He nodded toward Perchance to Dream. "They're watching."

I frowned. "Who?"

He ignored my question. "The plan is for me to convince you I'm really one of the good guys. The first step is to make contact – which I've done." He rubbed his jaw and smiled ruefully. "Or maybe you made first contact. Then I'm supposed to get you to go with me someplace where we can sit and talk. If you don't come with me, they'll send someone after you immediately. If you come with me, it'll buy you some breathing room to plan your next move."

Even if I'd been at my mentally sharpest – which at that moment I definitely wasn't – I'd have had trouble following what Russell said.

"So you're trying to tell me that you're working with this mysterious *They*, and that *They* want you to pretend to help me for whatever reason, but in reality, you really *do* intend to help me, and you don't want *Them* knowing. Is that it?"

He shrugged. "More or less."

I thought for a moment. "OK."

His eyes widened in surprise. "Really? I mean, I wouldn't blame you for not believing me. It's a pretty weird story."

I sighed. "It's been that kind of day, you know?"

He nodded. "Yeah, I guess it has. I'm parked a couple blocks over."

"Lead the way."

He turned and started walking. The dachshund – I couldn't bring myself to think of the stubby-legged thing as *Bloodshedder* – gave me a last hate-filled look before turning and trotting after Russell. It was official. That dog and I hated each other.

I followed and tried not to worry about Jinx. He was an Incubus and a trained officer. He could take care of himself just fine.

Just fine.

"What's wrong?" Russell asked.

"Nothing. I just never imagined that a dangerous mercenary like you would be such a big fan of grilled cheese."

We were seated in a restaurant called Cheddar's. Actually, *restaurant* is a bit generous. *Greasy spoon* is a better description. *Spoon covered in thick mounds of fattening goo* is even more accurate. Bloodshedder lay curled up on the floor at Russell's feet, eyes closed. She looked like she was asleep, but I doubted it. More likely she was paying close attention to every word we said. After all, she was an Incubus. She only looked like a dog.

Cheddar's didn't serve anything even remotely healthy, so I ordered a grilled three-cheese sandwich, fries, and a soda. Russell ordered the quadruple-decker with eight different kinds of cheese. I was concerned he would have a coronary halfway through the meal.

"What's wrong with grilled cheese?" he asked, before taking a large, gooey bite of his sandwich.

Either he didn't eat like this all the time, he worked out a hell of a lot, or Russell had an extremely high metabolism, because otherwise there was no way he could eat like this regularly and stay in as good a shape as he was.

"Nothing, I guess." I took a bite of my sandwich and was surprised by how good it tasted. Of course, the fact that I hadn't eaten all day might've had something to do with it.

We both ate in silence for a few minutes. I should've been struck by the absurdity of it all. Here I was, eating grilled cheese with a man I'd been trying to track down – for helping a master assassin escape my custody. But instead it felt natural, as if we really were two old friends, who'd gotten together after having been apart for too long.

Russell slowed down when his sandwich was three-quarters finished.

"Sorry," he said. He took a long drink of his soda. "Sometimes it's hard to come by regular meals in this line of work. I can't remember the last time I ate."

Bloodshedder let out a soft woof, and Russell took the remainder of his sandwich and gave it to her. She swallowed it in two bites, licked her mouth, and then closed her eyes and settled back down.

When we'd first come in, the woman at the cash register said we couldn't bring a dog in. But Bloodshedder turned on the charm, wagging her rat-tail and giving the woman an *I'm a cute doggie and I love everybody* look. The woman fell for it and let her stay. Sucker. Despite my dislike for the little beast, I had to admire her skills at emotional manipulation.

"Is all that cheese good for her?" I asked.

"If she was a real dog, no. But she's an Incubus. In her Night Aspect, she can eat just about anything. Or anyone."

From his tone, it sounded like he was joking about his last point. I hoped so, at any rate.

Cheddar's was a small downtown joint with old wooden

furniture, dim lighting, and a musty smell in the air that
spoke of the building's age and bad ventilation. As a city
gal, I felt right at home. The clientele was mostly working-
class folks who'd stopped in after work for a sandwich and
a few beers. I recognized a couple Incubi and Ideators, but
none of them were friends, and they averted their eyes
whenever I looked at them. They did, however, seem
awfully interested in us. They checked us out whenever
they thought we weren't looking. I wasn't worried that
any of them were planning on starting any trouble. I didn't
get that kind of vibe from them.

As if reading my mind, Russell said, "They're probably
wondering where your partner is."

"I'm a bit concerned about that myself. Why don't you
tell me where he is?"

"I don't know where Jinx is. I was just as surprised as
you when he was abducted."

I gave him a look that said I thought he was full of shit.

"Honestly. They think I'm a mercenary. A hired hand.
They only tell me what they think I need to know to get
the job done."

"And did *They* tell you to take me out for grilled cheese?"
I asked.

He smiled. "I added that part. They called me when
you and Jinx arrived. They didn't know that I was out
walking Bloodshedder and that I'd already run into you
before you entered the building. They told me that I was
to approach you after you left and tell you that I knew you
were the same Audra I'd met as a child, that I felt guilty
for freeing Quietus, and that I now wanted to help you get
him back. I was supposed to tell you that Shocktooth hired
me to help her, and then I was supposed to convince you
to let me accompany you when you went to Nod to track
her down."

"The old *mercenary with a heart of gold* routine, eh?"

"That's about the size of it."

"What was supposed to happen when we found Shocktooth? Was she supposed to kill me?"

"No. We weren't going to find her. I was supposed to lead you on a wild goose chase. You *and* Jinx, or so I thought. I guess they had other plans for him."

"This isn't making a whole lot of sense to me, Russell. These people obviously have no compunctions about killing. They've had Quietus kill four people so far. Why not just kill me and Jinx if they wanted us out of their hair so badly?"

He shrugged. "I don't know for sure. My guess is that killing humans is one thing, but killing a couple Shadow Watch officers would cause more trouble than they want right now. Besides, they can always kill you later if they want."

"Let me guess. *They* are the Lords of Misrule."

He nodded. "And as you've probably figured out, the Lords run Perchance to Dream."

"Ha! In your face, Sanderson! I knew I wasn't crazy." I blinked. "Wait? What? I didn't sense any Incubi when Jinx and I were there."

"They've developed some kind of tech that masks the presence of Incubi from both Ideators and each other. It's those pins they wear. They gave me one for Bloodshedder, and I attached it to her collar."

I bent down to look under the table and saw that the dachshund did indeed have one of the closed-eye pins on her collar in place of a tag. When I sat up again, I said, "Dr Kauffman was wearing one of those pins. Does that mean…"

"Maybe. Maybe not. Everyone at Perchance to Dream wears one. They could be Ideators, Incubi, or something else entirely. Who knows?"

I frowned. "Something else? There is no something else. There are humans and Incubi. That's it."

Russell smiled, but he didn't elaborate.

The Lords of Misrule are an ancient order of Incubi, some of them reportedly thousands of years old. The Lords view humanity not as their creators, but more like seeds from which they had sprung, or a spark that touches off a flame. They see Incubi as superior to humans – after all, are they not stronger and, as long as they have periodic access to direct Maelstrom energy, virtually immortal? And if Incubi are a higher form of life, why should they be relegated to spend eternity in a single extra-dimensional city? They should not only rule Nod, but the Earth as well.

At one time, the Lords were a power to equal the Shadow Watch, and the two groups clashed often over the centuries. But as Sanderson had reminded me, the Lords had long ago declined in strength and influence, and now they functioned primarily as a criminal organization, concerned more with profit than with conquering two worlds.

But what if that was only what they *wanted* the Shadow Watch to think? What if they remained as strong as ever? It seemed that was the case – *if* Russell was telling me the truth.

"OK," I said. "Let's back up a bit. If Shocktooth didn't hire you, who did? And what did you do with Quietus after you took off?"

"The Lords hired me through an intermediary. Some man I didn't recognize and who didn't give me his name. He was human, though. Several weeks ago, he put the word out on the streets of Nod that he was looking for me. Well, for Nocturne, anyway. I got in touch with him and we arranged to meet. He said the Lords had heard good things about my work, and that they wanted to put me on retainer. I'd been hoping to get the Lords' attention for some time, so I said yes. They had me do a few jobs for them – nothing too serious," he hastened to add. "Then last night, they called me and told me to meet Shocktooth at the corner of Soma and Stygian streets. I did, and she told me what we were supposed to do. I was surprised. I'd known for some time that you and Jinx were Shadow Watch officers, but our paths had never crossed before. That's one of the reasons I decided to wear a mask when working, just in case we ever did bump into each other."

"You didn't want to see me?" I felt a pang of disappointment at the thought, and I mentally chided myself.

"Your recognizing me would've complicated things."

"What things?"

Once again, he chose to ignore my question. It was really starting to irritate me.

"After Shocktooth and I got Quietus a safe distance away, we freed him from the negators, and then he and Shocktooth left together. That's the last I saw or heard of them. An hour or so before sunrise, I got a call from the man who originally hired me. I was still in Nod, and he told me to go over to Earth and head to Perchance to Dream. It was dawn by the time I got there. I'd never been there before, but Schulte introduced himself to me – man, can that guy talk or what? And then he took me to Dr Kauffman. I was shocked to see her. I was so nervous, in fact, that I almost puked. I felt nauseated the entire time I was there, actually."

I was surprised to hear Russell describe physical symptoms similar to what I'd experienced at Perchance to Dream. Maybe seeing Dr Kauffman had hit him as hard as it had me. Or maybe there was something else. Whatever it was, it seemed too coincidental that both of us had felt sick in the building.

"That's pretty much it," Russell said. "The rest you know."

"Not so fast. There's still plenty I don't know. You've danced around it, but it's clear that you intended to infiltrate the Lords of Misrule. Why?"

Russell just looked at me.

I went on. "If you're not really working for the Lords, then who *are* you working for? Not the Shadow Watch. Sanderson seems to believe the Lords aren't the threat they once were. Besides, I'm familiar with all our officers. I'd know if you were on the force."

Still no response from Russell.

I didn't know what to think. While there are other organizations besides the Shadow Watch and the Lords of Misrule in Nod – the Wakenists, the Dreamtakers, the Somniacs, the Hand of Erebus, and more – most are relatively small-time in comparison. As far as I knew, none of them had the stones to take on the Lords. So, who could Russell be working for? Some group I'd never heard of, maybe even one that was completely unknown to the Shadow Watch? It didn't seem possible. But that didn't mean it wasn't true.

"You know, picking and choosing which of my questions to answer is not a great way to build credibility. It makes me wonder if you're telling the truth about any of this."

"I know. I'm sorry. If I could tell you everything, I would."

"And I'm supposed to take your word and leave it at that."

"You believe what you need to, Audra. Hell, if our positions were reversed, I'd have a hard time believing me, too."

I was starting to get a headache. I could've really used a hit of rev right then, but I'd emptied my inhaler back at Perchance to Dream, and rev wasn't the sort of thing they sold over the counter at the corner drugstore. I'd just have to make do with the caffeine in my soda for now.

"Can you tell me why you wanted to infiltrate the Lords?" I asked.

"We'd gotten word that they were planning something big, as in potentially catastrophic. We needed to find out what."

We. I knew better than to ask again who he was referring to.

"Whatever it is, I bet it has something to do with the Incursions."

"You got it. I'm certain the Lords are causing them, although I have no idea how or why."

"Do you know about the one that happened today?"

He frowned. "You mean that one at AT&T Plaza?"

"Jinx and I were there for that one. Quietus, too. I'm talking about another one." I told him about the Incursion that had happened when Jinx and I were on our way to Perchance to Dream. By the time I was done, much of the color had drained from his face.

"Holy shit. I had no idea something like that was possible! A Day Incursion! Have you told your people about it?"

"I sent word." I had no idea what Sanderson's reaction to the news had been. I hadn't received any word from David Lindroth in London before my wisper was taken by the Blacksuits. I could've called him on my phone, but I was reluctant to do so in front of Russell. I wasn't sure why. I told myself it wasn't because I wanted to avoid talking to a former lover in front of him.

"What about the murders that Quietus committed?" I asked. "How do they fit into all this?"

"I don't know," Russell said. "I assume they're part of the Lords' ultimate plan, whatever that is."

Four murders. All the victims had been human, and

they were all killed in Chicago. But why? After everything I'd learned in the last day, I still had no idea.

"So, do you think whatever is going on at Perchance to Dream is connected to the Incursions?"

"Yes," he said. "But I haven't found any evidence yet."

"Anything else you can tell me?" I asked.

"*Can?*" He smiled. "No. But I haven't kept anything important from you."

I sighed. "I can see we're going to have some serious trust issues to work on in the future."

He raised his eyebrows. "Oh? Are you shipping us already?"

I felt my cheeks burn, and I knew I was blushing. "Just making a joke."

"Sure." But his grin told me he didn't believe it.

I decided to get back to business before this could go any further. Not that I wanted it to. Or maybe I did. Either way, I thought it best to change the subject.

"Where's that ultra-cool sword of yours?" I asked.

"My rapier? It's not the sort of thing I can carry around during the day."

"You keep it stashed in your car?"

He just smiled at me.

"The Shadow Watch has nothing like it. Where did you get it?"

More smiling.

"Fine. Go ahead and play the inscrutable man of mystery. See if I care." I let out a sigh and moved on. "When the sun sets, can you and Bloodshedder help me locate a Door? I need to get to Nod and find Jinx." I was gambling that the Blacksuits would take Jinx to Nod once the sun set, if for no other reason than there weren't many places in the city where a bunch of insane rampaging clowns would go unnoticed.

"No problem. Bloodshedder may be an Incubus, but she has a dog's senses. In her Night Aspect, they're even stronger. She'll have no trouble finding the nearest Door."

"Great. Speaking of Bloodshedder, I was surprised by her Day Aspect. Given what she looks like at night, I was expecting something a bit more..."

"Fierce?" he asked.

I nodded. "And large."

He laughed. Bloodshedder, however, gave me an irritated growl.

"It's OK, girl. Audra wasn't trying to insult you."

Actually, I had been, but I decided not to point that out.

"You know how it is with Incubi," Russell said. "Their Day Aspects are often the opposite of their night ones."

I thought of all the differences between my two Jinxes. I knew exactly what Russell meant.

"But there's another reason that she appears as a dachshund during the day. I talked about it during our sessions with Dr Kauffman. Do you remember?"

"Honestly, I try to remember as little as possible about that time. I remember that she worked with a lot of kids, and that she'd sometimes see us one-on-one, in pairs, or in small groups. She had us talk about a lot of stuff beside our dreams. How things were for us at home and at school, things we fantasized about, and things we were afraid of." I frowned as I tried to recall more detail. "I think I remember you talking about something your family dog did to you when you were really little. It bit you, right?"

"Yeah. I was three. I barely remember it, but my parents told me the story often enough as I was growing up, so that it's almost like I remember every detail, you know? I was playing in the backyard with the dog – a dachshund named Heidi. She loved chewing on rawhide bones, so my mom brought one outside for me to give to her. Heidi and I had been running around the backyard chasing each other up to that point, so she was already worked up. Mom gave me the bone and instead of offering it to Heidi, I ran with it. She chased me. I tripped and fell, and she tried to pull the bone away from me. Unfortunately, one of my fingers got in the way."

"Ouch."

"Dachshunds may look small, but they can bite damn hard. I bled like a stuck pig and wailed as if I was dying. In the end, it only took a couple of stitches to fix. I forgave Heidi and still played with her after that, but I was always a bit wary of her. I knew that even though Heidi was my friend, she could still hurt me if she wanted to. I never was able to forget the sight of her teeth closing around my finger, or the blood gushing from my wound."

"Bloodshedder," I said.

He nodded.

I remembered now. He had told the story during our sessions with Dr Kauffman. More than once. She'd insisted on it, telling us that the more often we spoke about our fears and traumas, the less power they'd have over us. What a crock.

We talked about our lives some more after that. I told Russell about when Jinx achieved full Ideation and how for a time, my life was a living nightmare – in more ways than one – until I'd been recruited by the Shadow Watch not long after graduating high school.

After Bloodshedder reached Ideation – sometime during Russell's first semester in college – he'd run from her, thinking she was going to kill him. She chased after him, merely wanting to make contact with her Ideator, but in doing so, she led him to a Door. He opened it and went through, and Bloodshedder followed. He'd kept running through the streets of the bizarre world he'd entered, until he was so exhausted he couldn't run anymore. He hid in an alley and sat with his back against a wall, eyes closed, gulping air and waiting to die. Before long, he heard Bloodshedder pad into the alley. She stopped in front of him, licked his face once, than curled up on the ground next to him.

After that, he knew he didn't have to be afraid of Bloodshedder anymore. And since he no longer needed to sleep, he spent his days on Earth and his nights in Nod. Eventually, he dropped out of college and took up residence in Nod on a more or less full-time basis.

"It just felt more like home to me, you know?" he said.

Not really. Truth to tell, I don't feel much at home in either dimension. I don't have any human friends – ones that aren't Ideators, I mean – and since I'm an only child, I don't have any siblings. My dad passed away from lung cancer a few years back, and my mom moved to Colorado to be closer to her sister and her kids. About the only time I see her is Thanksgiving and Christmas, and even then I can only see her during the day since I have to get back to whatever hotel I'm staying at by nightfall, when my "platonic friend" accompanying me transforms into a maniacal clown.

Don't get me wrong: I like being a Shadow Watch officer. But it can get lonely sometimes. Which was why, I suppose, that I was enjoying talking with Russell so much. Sure, I didn't know what his true role was in the current mess I found myself in, and for all I knew, he'd fed me a line of bullshit and would turn around and betray me in a heartbeat. But for that short time in a crappy little restaurant, I felt a connection with a human being again, and it was nice.

"Do you ever wonder why?" I asked. "I mean, why *us*? What's so different about us that gave us that power to tap into the Maelstrom and bring our nightmares to life?"

Russell looked at me without expression, and I suddenly felt embarrassed.

"Sorry. I don't really have anyone to talk to about this kind of stuff, and since we were both patients of Kauffman's when we were kids..." I said.

"It's OK," he said. "It's just that no one's ever asked me that before. I've heard that the Somnocologists at the Rookery have some theories."

"But that's all there are," I said. "Theories. No one really knows."

There have been Ideators and Incubi for thousands of years, maybe longer. And still no one knows for certain why one person becomes an Ideator and another doesn't. The power doesn't run in bloodlines, and it's not associated with gender or any particular ethnic or cultural background.

"I guess some people are just born better dreamers than others," Russell said. "Just like some people are born with a talent for music or with a higher IQ."

"Luck of the draw, huh?"

"I guess."

"I don't always feel so lucky," I admitted. "I love my job. It's never boring, that's for sure! And I like to think I've done some good. But it's not always easy being" – I almost used the word *stuck* – "bound to your worst nightmare, you know?"

"Actually, I don't. Bloodshedder and I have become great friends over the years. Haven't we, girl?" He reached down to scratch her head, and I heard her tail thump happily on the floor. "Do you remember how Dr Kauffman used to say that the only way for us to overcome our fears was to confront them? Well, I went one step further than that. I embraced mine. Accepted it. And that made all the difference."

Our conversation had taken an uncomfortable turn – for me, anyway – so I was relieved when Bloodshedder let out a sharp bark.

"That's the signal," Russell said. "It's going to be dark soon. We need to get out of here before she starts to change."

I wondered how the good folks at Cheddar's would react to the sudden appearance of a demon dog in their midst. Too bad I wasn't going to get to find out.

We rose from the table and headed for the exit.

EIGHT

We entered Nod through a manhole. Not the classiest of entrances in my career, but then again, a Door is a Door.

Russell went first. I followed, and Bloodshedder came last, squeezing her bulk through the circular opening in a way no natural creature could. I slid the manhole cover back into place and tried to ignore my usual sense of nauseated disorientation. *At least the voices in between weren't too loud this time,* I thought, and I told myself to be thankful for small favors.

A quick look around told me we were in the Cesspit: neon signs advertising far-less-than-reputable businesses and loud-mouthed hucksters trying to entice passers-by into sampling whatever sleaze they were selling. One good thing about Nod: since you never know where a Door will let you out, the streets are always clearly marked. We were on the corner of Oblivion and Catalepsy.

The Cesspit, as the name implies, isn't exactly Nod's garden district. Incubi are created from the human subconscious, so not only are they drawn to darker pleasures, they don't have inhibitions to prevent them from indulging. Alcohol and drugs – some of the earthly variety, many not – flow freely there, both within various establishments and out on the street. Sex isn't for sale, but it can be rented on the cheap, and it comes in every variety and combination you can imagine, and quite a few that you can't.

Violence is common here, but since Incubi heal swiftly, no one takes it very seriously. Except the humans foolish enough to venture down these filth-strewn streets. Compared to Incubi, we might as well be made of popsicle sticks. And unless you know how to handle yourself – and unless you're willing to shoot first and then run like hell – the Cesspit is an excellent place to meet a swift, if hardly painless, end.

The Nightclad Council tolerates the Cesspit's existence because it gives the more savage Incubi an outlet for their aggressive – and quite often destructive – needs. As long as the mayhem is contained, the Council is content. And who's in charge of doing the containing? The Shadow Watch, of course. Just like all rookies, Jinx and I worked the Cesspit for several years after we finished our training. The theory is that if you can survive the Cesspit, you can survive anything. Sometimes I wonder if Darwin was an Ideator who came up with his concept of survival of the fittest after a visit to the Cesspit.

Russell had donned his pirate outfit before we left Earth – he kept his costume in a suitcase in the trunk of his car and changed in an alley. He had made me turn my back while he changed, but it's possible that I peeked once or twice. And it's possible that Bloodshedder – in full demon dog mode –might've almost bit off one of my hands for doing so. Russell had his rapier, too. I had no idea where he kept it. One moment he didn't have it, and the next, there it was, sheathed at his side. I'd almost asked about it, but I'd decided he'd only smile at me again instead of answer, so I didn't bother. For the record, the rapier really raised the hotness level of his outfit, though.

We'd emerged close to a group of Incubi who were busy trying to see how far one of them would stretch – a male so skinny, he looked like a skeleton covered with a paper-thin layer of skin. Two Incubi had hold of his arms, while another pair had his legs. The two on the hands – a beast that resembled a bipedal rhino and a creature that appeared to be made entirely of loosely connected shards of stained glass – braided the arms as if they were strands of taffy. The two holding the flesh skeleton's feet – a hulking figure whose skin was criss-crossed with jagged scars, and a creature that looked like a weasel on steroids – were twisting the legs. From the sounds of snapping bone, not to mention the victim's screams, it was clear that he was no more pliable than anything else made of flesh. The four Incubi laughed and chanted, "Over, under, over, under!" as they braided the Skin-Skeleton's broken limbs.

The Rhino glanced over at us and said, "Hey, look! A couple humans! How many times do you think we can twist *their* arms and legs?"

The other Incubi grinned and they all dropped the Skin-Skeleton to the ground. He let out a shriek of pain as he hit, and then lay there, moaning in agony.

"Let's find out!" Weasel-Boy said in a chittering voice.

They started toward us, and I reached for my trancer out of reflex, only to remember I'd lost it when the Blacksuits kidnapped Jinx. I still had my M-blade, though, and I drew it now. Russell drew his rapier, and I had to suppress a sudden feeling of weapon envy.

But before the four Incubi could reach us, Bloodshedder jumped in front of us and fixed them with a *Don't fuck with me* glare, bared her mouthful of wickedly sharp teeth, and growled from deep in her chest. The quartet stopped, regarded the huge demonic hound for a moment, and then turned and headed off in separate directions at a near-run.

"You know, I think I'm starting to like her," I said.

She looked back and me and snapped her jaws once, sending flecks of foam flying. The message: the feeling was not mutual.

"She does come in handy," Russell said, smiling.

Bloodshedder trotted over to him, and he scratched her behind an ear. One of her back clawed feet thumped up and down on the asphalt in doggie ecstasy. It might've been cute if Bloodshedder wasn't so damn hideous – and if the Skin-Skeleton hadn't been sobbing in agony close by. I didn't worry about him, though. He was an Incubus and would heal soon enough.

I turned to Russell, but before I could say anything, a glowing red Wild West-style train engine came chugging down the street toward us, flames trailing out behind it as if it were rocket-powered. Everyone in the street – including Russell, Bloodshedder, and myself – hurried to get the hell out of the way. Unfortunately, the Skin-Skeleton couldn't move, not with his pretzel-twisted arms and legs. The Hell-Train roared over the spot where the injured Incubus lay, and everyone lining the sidewalk on both sides of the street let out shouts ranging from, "Dude, that's going to leave a mark!" to "Ten points!"

Incubi aren't known for their empathy.

I didn't look too closely at the burned and mangled body of the Skin-Skeleton. He'd still heal. It was just going to take a *lot* longer now.

"I'm glad that train didn't come through as we were climbing out of the manhole," I said. "Still, it's a lucky thing that Door let us out here. If you want to get the lowdown on lowlifes, there's no better place than the Cesspit."

"That's what Bloodshedder thought, too. In her Night Aspect, her senses are so sharp that she can almost always tell where a particular Door leads. You can thank her for bringing you here."

I turned to look at the demon dog, but she was pointedly looking in the opposite direction. She didn't try to tear my throat out, though, so I took that as a sign of progress.

"I take it you're not planning on going to the Rookery first," Russell said.

"I'm sure they got my report about the Day Incursion by now. And as for Perchance to Dream... well, we don't know much about what's going on there, other than that the Lords of Misrule are involved. And Sanderson won't believe *that* without some serious proof. Maybe if you're willing to turn yourself in and tell my boss everything you know..."

"Afraid not."

"Didn't think so. I'd rather find Jinx, anyway." I glanced at the Skin-Skeleton's ravaged body and felt suddenly queasy. I had no idea where Jinx was or what was happening to him. For all I knew, he might be in as bad a shape as that poor squashed sonofabitch out there. Or worse.

Even with Russell's testimony, I had no direct evidence that Perchance to Dream was connected to the Incursions – just a gut feeling – and although I knew I should still communicate my suspicion to Sanderson ASAP, I didn't want to. I knew it was petty, but I didn't want to hand any info over to Damon and Eklips sooner than I had to. No matter what anyone said, it was still *my* case, damn it! Mine and Jinx's, and I was determined to see it through to the end. Once I got my partner back.

"So if you're not doing anything," I said, "do you want to come with?"

I was surprised to feel nervous, as if I was asking him to go on a date – instead of helping me find my kidnapped partner.

"I was thinking that while you search for Jinx, I should try to track down Shocktooth. It's possible she might not know any more about what's going on than I do, but I figure it's worth having a talk with her." He patted Bloodshedder on the head. "Besides, my girl here loves the taste of reptile, don't you, baby?"

Bloodshedder's morningstar tail slammed into the sidewalk several times, sending cracks fissuring through the concrete.

I couldn't tell if Russell was kidding, and I decided not to ask.

"You know, someone more suspicious than I am might wonder if you want to split up so you can pursue whatever mysterious agenda your *real* bosses have. And someone even more suspicious yet might wonder if you've lied to me all along, and you're really working for the Lords and are just playing some twisted and overly complicated game."

He smiled. "Wheels within wheels, plots within plots, double- and triple-crosses, ad infinitum." His smile fell away. "I can't prove anything I've told you, and there's plenty I've kept to myself for various reasons. You're right not to trust me. Hell, I wouldn't trust me either if I was you. But you want to find Jinx – *and* you'd like to question Shocktooth, right?"

"I'd like to question the scaly bitch upside the head with one of Jinx's sledgehammers."

He nodded. "So it only makes sense to split up. You have no idea how long it will take to track and free your partner. And who knows how long it will take to find Shocktooth?"

"Just look for the nearest swamp," I muttered.

I looked at Russell for a long moment, trying to decide what I should do, and more importantly, what I believed. He had helped me get to Nod, and I knew I couldn't stop him from leaving any time he wanted. Aside from my

M-blade, I was unarmed, while he had his rapier as well as his demon dog Incubus. The fact that he was going to such lengths to convince me we were on the same side – in this situation at least – when he didn't need to, said a lot.

But in the end, it came down to what I saw in his eyes. Sure, they were an adorable milk-chocolate brown, but that had nothing to do with it. I saw no hint of deception in his gaze, just openness, and maybe a touch of fear that I wouldn't believe him. That it mattered what I thought of him.

"How will we find each other? I don't have a wisper, and my phone doesn't get any service here."

He smiled and tapped the side of his nose with a finger. "Bloodshedder will find you."

The demon dog let out a snort, as if to say that while she didn't particularly enjoy my scent, she'd had no trouble tracking me down.

"All right." I reached into my jacket pocket, removed a negator, and handed it to Russell. "For when you find Shocktooth," I explained.

"Take my rapier. I won't need it as long as I have Bloodshedder to protect me."

He started to unbuckle his scabbard, but I held up a hand to stop him.

"Thanks, but I'm strictly a gun-and-knife girl. Besides, I really suck when it comes to using those things, I'd be just as likely to slice off one of my own ears as wound a bad guy."

He didn't look happy about my refusal, but he didn't insist. I appreciated that.

In the end, we didn't gaze longingly at each other, and we certainly didn't kiss. We said goodbye, and Russell and Bloodshedder turned and began making their way edgewise, the crowd of pedestrians parting before them like water flowing around a large rock in a stream.

I watched them go for a moment before turning and heading centerwise.

I had no idea what to do next.

Nod is a damn big place. Shadow Watch officers use their wispers to communicate, but we can also use them like GPSs to get a fix on each other's location. But I didn't have my wisper anymore, and I doubted Jinx did either. His captors would've relieved him of it, just as they'd taken mine. Bloodshedder might've been able to help me track down Jinx, but she was off helping Russell find Shocktooth.

And the fact that Jinx had been kidnapped – or maybe I should say clown-napped – by a group of black-suited men and women who, in their Night Aspects, were mostly likely clowns too, would be no help in locating him. The scary clown is a common nightmare archetype, and Nod is crawling with the greasepaint-covered bastards. They're so ubiquitous, they're practically the nightmare-world version of pigeons. So I couldn't simply walk around asking people if they'd seen a clown lately. All they'd do is laugh at me and walk away.

I wandered through the streets, garish neon signs screaming for my attention: PWN Shop, Self-Surgery Supplies, Brainswapping, You Bet Your Genitals, 3000 Proof Alcohol, Janglers, Adrenalynn's, Live Necrophilia… In the Cesspit, it doesn't take long to grow numb to the sleaze, and when that happens, the signs become merely words.

There was another sign, too, one that hung above most businesses. NO VESTIES. Vesties are Incubi who try to look, dress, and act as much like humans as possible. Some even go so far as to have cosmetic surgery with M-enhanced instruments, especially in the case of the more inhuman-appearing Incubi.

Vesties – a term that's a play on transvestite – believe that since humans created them, humans are therefore a superior life form: the exact opposite of what the Lords of Misrule believe. Because of this belief, they try to emulate humans in the hope of becoming more like them. Most Incubi despise vesties, although Jinx doesn't seem to think anything about them one way or the other. Because of his Shadow Watch uniform, some Incubi tease him about being a vestie, though. The resulting violence is always fun to watch.

At one point in my wanderings, I approached the mouth of a particularly dark and ominous alley. Normally, I give alleys a wide berth, especially in the Cesspit, but I was running on fumes and not thinking straight, and I walked too close to the alley's entrance.

A hand the color and consistency of smoke emerged from the alley's gloom and grabbed my arm. Its touch was cold as winter ice, and despite its insubstantial appearance, the hand fastened on me with an iron grip.

As I was yanked into the alley, a single word screamed through my mind: *Fader!*

There are a lot of dangers in Nod, especially for humans, but Faders are among the most dangerous because they don't discriminate between humans and Incubi. They desperately need life force, and they aren't picky about where they get it. Faders are Incubi whose Ideators have died, leaving them alone and unbonded.

Once they come into full existence, Incubi don't necessarily need to remain connected to their creators to survive. But some become so strongly bonded to their Ideators that when their humans die, these Incubi simply fade away to nothing. The process can take a long time. Years, sometimes decades. But in the end, Faders vanish, never to be seen again.

Unless they can find someone and steal their life energy to stave off the inevitable. Incubus or human, it doesn't matter. Any life energy will do, and tonight this particular Fader had chosen to feed on me.

The Fader dragged me into the alley, and although I pulled and twisted, I couldn't get the damn thing to release me. With my free hand, I drew my M-blade and tried to gut the thing, but the Fader caught hold of my forearm, stopping me. It shoved my arm backward until I could feel the bones grind. My fingers sprang open, and the M-blade fell to the ground.

I was out of weapons. If I'd had my trancer, I could've blasted the damn thing into oblivion. Hell, if I'd had my wisper, I could've activated its holo display. Faders are creatures of darkness, and the light would've driven it off. But now I didn't have anything other than my clothes and my body. But this *was* an alley, and not just any alley, but a *Cesspit* alley.

Faders only have so much energy – which is why they need to feed on others, of course – so I fought to pull both of my arms free, forcing the Fader to expend more energy to hold onto me. By necessity, Faders are loathe to waste energy, and so the creature let go of one of my arms, and continued to pull me deeper into the alley, where it could feed on me without interruption.

I continued to resist as it dragged me, and I bent down in a half crouch, and with my free hand reached toward the ground. My fingers brushed all manner of debris. My eyes hadn't adjusted to the darkness in the alley yet, so I couldn't see what I was touching, which was a very good thing. Too many of the items I touched were wet and spongy, and – if the horrid smells were any indication – I really didn't want to know what sort of trash I was fondling.

I wasn't searching for anything in particular, just

something that I might be able to use against the Fader to wound or at least startle it. I didn't need to kill it. I just needed it to let go of me long enough so I could haul ass out of there.

And I had to hurry. Already I could feel the icy-burning sensation of the Fader's touch spreading into the rest of my arm. It would take only a few minutes for the Fader to drain all of my life force, but the problem was that I'd soon become too weak to fight back, and then I'd be little more than a semiconscious rag doll, and the Fader could consume the rest of my energy without difficulty. If I was going to survive, I had to do something within the next few seconds, while I still had the strength to act.

I continued fumbling in the trash as the Fader pulled me even deeper into the alley. The burning-cold suffused most of my arm now, and I was starting to feel light-headed. I didn't have much time left.

My fingers then brushed against a small disk-shaped object and reflexively curled around it. I could tell by the feel that it was an M-unit. Someone must've had dropped this yoonie coin while passing through the alley. Or, more likely, it had been dropped during a mugging. Either way, someone else's loss was my gain. It wasn't an M-blade – or Russell's rapier, for that matter – but it would do.

My vision had adapted to a degree, and I could make out the Fader's shape. Not that there was much to see. Faders have no distinct features, and there's no way to tell what manner of Incubus they used to be. They're humanoid forms that seem sculpted from grayish-black smoke, although they're solid enough. I had no idea if the creature possessed a mouth anymore, but I was about to find out. I jammed the yoonie toward the Fader's head in what I gauged was the general direction of the thing's mouth, but the coin struck the lower half of the Fader's featureless face and lodged there. I shoved with all my strength – all I had left, that is – and the coin went in all the way.

The Fader stopped pulling me, but it didn't let go of my arm. The creature stood motionless for several seconds, and I feared that my gamble wasn't going to pay off. But then the Fader began shaking all over. Only a little at first, but then more violently. From the center of the thing's body – where its stomach had once been – multicolored light began to glow as the Fader tried to absorb the coin's Maelstrom energy.

A significant amount of power is concentrated in a single M-unit, and the Fader's body was doing its damnedest to metabolize all that energy, and failing. The multicolored light blazing from the creature's core continued to grow brighter, and for an instant, the Fader's smoke-colored body resolved into a more defined shape: an Incubus with a ram's head that sported huge curving horns. It looked at me with sorrowful eyes, and then there was an explosion of light, and I felt the Fader's grip cease.

I managed to turn my head just before the burst of light, but even so, I still saw spots. What I didn't see, though, was the Fader. It was gone, a victim of terminal indigestion.

As I staggered out of the alley, the feeling began to return to my arm, and I vowed to always carry a few extra yoonies with me from now on. Just in case.

Afterward, I wandered the Cesspit for a time, shaken and weak from my encounter with the Fader. I knew I needed to figure out a way to find Jinx, but the more I tried to focus my thoughts, the more they scattered, flying away from me like a flock of frightened birds. My body was weary, but more importantly, my brain felt like it was wrapped in molasses-soaked cotton. Bad enough I was a human walking alone in the Cesspit, but I was far from my sharpest – as getting caught by the Fader testified. The way I felt, a blindfolded toddler could've gotten the drop on me.

My Shadow Watch uniform provided me a certain measure of protection, but without a fully charged trancer and my M-blade – and especially without Jinx – it was only a matter of time before I ended up dead, my corpse discarded in a back alley like so much trash. I really could've used a hit or three of rev right then, but when I pulled out my inhaler and tried to suck on it, I found it empty. I realized I'd wasted the last of it outside Perchance to Dream, when I shot it into Jinx's face.

I was so angry at myself. What the hell had I been thinking? How could I have been so goddamned *stupid?* I threw the spent inhaler to the ground and kept going.

As I walked, the Cesspit's finest street entrepreneurs called out to me, urging me to stop for a moment to examine their wares. I was offered the usual. Tickets to live competitive vivisections. Bizarrely shaped devices that might've been sex toys, torture instruments, or both. Bits of bone reputed to have belonged to the Children of the First Dreamer. But then I heard what I'd been waiting for, at least subconsciously.

"Hey, girl! You look like you're almossst dead on your feet! How'sss about a little rev?"

It was a feminine voice, soft, barely above a whisper. And yet somehow, I heard it above the ever-present din of the Cesspit, as if she was standing right next to me and speaking in my ear. I stopped walking and turned in the direction of the voice.

An Incubus stood on the sidewalk in front of a Scarbucks. It was a sad testament to my current state of awareness that I'd walked right by and hadn't noticed her. Even by

Incubus standards, she was a strange-looking creature. Her form was humanoid, but she appeared to be made of hundreds of serpents, all intertwined to create her body. As I walked back to her, I saw she had no discernible facial features, and her fingers were made of writhing snakes protruding from her wrists, tiny tongues flicking the air and beady black eyes staring at me coldly as I approached.

"I would *not* want to be inside the head of the person who dreamed you up," I said.

She let out a hissing laugh, although I couldn't tell where it came from, since she didn't have a mouth. Not one I could see, anyway.

"Call me Coilsss," she said. "And I've got what you need. For a reasonable prissse, of courssse." She laughed again.

I've never been especially afraid of snakes, and I'd gotten used to seeing all kinds of grotesque beings in Nod, but I found Coils to be more than a bit unnerving. It wasn't just her appearance – although that was bad enough. It was the way the separate serpents that comprised her form were in continuous movement, muscles expanding and contracting, bodies rippling and stretching. The effect was as repulsive as it was mesmerizing.

I tried to put up a tough façade. "I don't see you holding any rev, and it doesn't look like you have any pockets."

Another hissing laugh.

"I've got something better than pocketsss. I've got a medisssine chessst."

The coils covering her chest pulled back to reveal a cavity filled with various drugs: tinglies, stunners, mem, jump juice vials, and – hallelujah! – rev inhalers. Three, to be precise, and the only reason I didn't reach into her chest and grab all three was the knowledge that her coils would close around my hand the instant I tried it, catching me fast. Her snake-head fingers would then be on me before I could free myself. And were they venomous? I didn't want to find out.

"How much for the rev?" I asked.

All pretense of sounding tough or cool was gone. I sounded desperate and eager, and although I hated myself for it, it didn't matter. Not as long as I got some rev. Then one puff on the inhaler, and my strength and energy would come flooding back. I'd be able to think straight again, and I could come up with a plan for finding Jinx. Just. One. Hit.

"Twenty yooniesss," Coils said. "But ssseeing asss how you're in a bad way – not to menssshun you being an offissser and all, I can let you have one for sssixxteen yooniesss. You won't find rev in the Pit for lesss than that!"

That wasn't true. I knew I could find it for fourteen, maybe even twelve yoonies. But I was in no condition to shop around, and Coils knew it. Unfortunately, I had no coins on me. I almost wished I hadn't used the yoonie I'd found in the alley against the Fader, not that one coin would do me any good now.

"Sorry," I said. "I'm tapped out."

Coils said nothing for a moment. Then, "You're an offissser. You could alwaysss threaten to haul me to the Rookery for ssselling illegal drugsss, unlesss I give you freebie."

Now it was my turn to be silent. My mouth was dry, and I trembled all over.

"How about I jussst give you a freebie, and you'll owe me a favor sssomeday?"

I wanted the rev. *Needed* it. But I hesitated. Maybe it was because I could finally admit to myself that Sanderson had been right. I wasn't a machine. I needed rest, even if I didn't need sleep. Maybe it was because I'd used the last shot of rev I had to hurt my partner. Or maybe it was because I imagined the disappointment in Day Jinx's eyes if he ever learned what I'd done to try and save him.

"I... never mind. Thanks anyway."

I turned and started walking away from Coils. She didn't say anything as I departed, didn't urge me to come back, didn't curse me for wasting her time. All she did was laugh that hissing laugh of hers, and all I did was keep walking.

I needed a way to locate Jinx – or at least those who'd taken him. But my tired brain refused to cough up any ideas. I was about to turn around, go find Coils, and attempt to beg some rev off her, despite my earlier decision not to, but then a neon sign caught my eye, and I forgot about the drug. The sign said EAT ME, each letter a different bright color, and I smiled. I'd been so fuzzy-headed that I hadn't realized I'd gone this far into the Cesspit, but I was grateful I had. With any luck, I'd just stumbled across someone who could help me.

The sign hung above an open doorway. No windows, though. Most buildings in the Pit don't have them. Given the level of violence in that section of the city, windows wouldn't last long, so most business owners don't bother with them.

I started toward the doorway, but before I could enter, an Incubus stepped out. His face resembled that of a distorted hairless rat with bulging red eyes and a mouthful of sharp yellow teeth. He was dressed in a top hat and tails, with room for his fleshy tail to stick out. He wore no shoes, and the claws on his feet made clicking noises on the sidewalk as he emerged. But his most striking feature was his hugely distended belly. The protruding mound of tight pink flesh had burst through the rat-thing's shirt and hung almost to his knees. The creature had packed so much into his belly that the mound didn't bounce or jiggle as he walked, and I had the impression that if I still had my M-blade and merely touched the pointed tip to the stretched-tight surface of the stomach, the rat would explode like a too-full water balloon.

"Oh, my!" the rat said in a bad imitation of an upper-class British accent. "I've eaten many things in my time, but I've never had a repast to equal what I have just experienced! I do believe I need to find a spot to rest and digest for a week or two. Bon appétit!"

He doffed his top hat to me and then began waddling at a stately pace down the sidewalk. I felt my gorge rise as I watched him go, but I swallowed, took a deep breath, and stepped inside.

The place wasn't fancy: a dozen round tables with four chairs apiece, featureless walls, and a hardwood floor that looked in desperate need of replacing. The lighting was dim, but there was more than enough illumination to see by. The place was packed. Diners sat at every table, and more customers stood against the walls, holding plates and eating. Most of Eat Me's clientele were Incubi, but there were several humans among the patrons.

With swift, fluid precision, servers delivered fresh plates loaded with candy. Milk, dark, and white chocolate, caramels, gum drops, licorice, peanut brittle, fudge, taffy, hard candy, and more. The servers then removed the empty plates, which were always licked clean. The tables were arranged in circular patterns around a rotating dais in the center of the restaurant. The words "I am what you eat" were printed on the side of the dais in the same multicolored lettering as on the neon sign outside. In the middle of the dais, sitting in a high-backed leather chair, was an Incubus I was very familiar with.

I started toward the dais.

One of the servers, who had a spine-covered head that

reminded me of a sea urchin, tried to stop me. I scowled as I looked into its eyes – or at least where I figured its eyes should be – and said, "Official Shadow Watch business." I pulled out my dream catcher badge and showed it to him for good measure.

Urchin-Head regarded me for a moment, and then its spines quivered once, and it moved off to see to another customer. Wise choice.

I slipped my badge back into my pocket and continued to the dais. The Incubus who owned the joint sat there, breaking off pieces of his body and depositing them on plates the servers held out.

"Hello, Candy," I said.

The Candy Man was bent over, snapping off his chocolate toes. He looked up at me with eyes made of Red Hots, and his red licorice lips curved into a smile.

"Audra!"

He tossed a big toe to me, and I caught it.

"On the house!" he said. His voice was smooth, warm, and honey-sweet.

I smiled but quickly placed the toe on the plate of a server as she hurried by. I then rubbed my hand on my pants leg, not caring if I smeared chocolate on the fabric.

"Thanks," I said, "but as delicious as you are, you know I can't accept."

The dais continued to turn slowly, and I walked with it so I could continue to face Candy, who went back to breaking off chunks of himself and depositing them onto servers' trays as we spoke. I hung back several feet so I wouldn't get in the servers' way.

"I need a favor, Candy."

His gumdrop eyebrows curved into a frown.

The Candy Man's body is formed from a chocolate base, with other varieties of candy covering his skin like bizarre tumescent growths. He wears no clothing, which is more than a little awkward since his genitals are made from a huge peppermint stick and two large marshmallows. I've never seen him break these off before, but the rumor is that he saves them for only the most special of customers.

Whenever he's working, his chocolate flesh is dotted with holes where he's pried off bits of himself, and he's always missing pieces – ears, nose, fingers, toes, sometimes entire limbs. He claims it doesn't hurt to pare himself out as dessert for his customers' enjoyment, and since he lives in Nod and has access to constant exposure to Maelstrom energy, he heals swiftly, so he has an endless supply of goodies to sell.

I've never tasted any of his, uh, offerings. As far as I know, no officer has. One of the first things new Shadow Watch recruits learn is to stay clear of the Candy Man. Jinx and I find him useful, so we visit him from time to time to talk with him. But we never eat.

Abstaining wasn't easy for me, though. I've always had a sweet tooth, and the Candy Man exudes a tantalizingly sweet aroma that's so powerful, your mouth starts watering the moment you walk in, and your stomach rumbles like an angry bear. I've heard rumors that if a diabetic so much as sets foot inside the restaurant, he or she will keel over dead in a matter or moments, just from the smell. I believe it. Word on the street is that Candy was created in the nightmares of a dentist's son. But however he came to be, in his own way – a way not known to most of Nod's citizens – he's one of the most powerful Incubi who's ever lived.

"I'm busy right now, Audra." His voice no longer sounded like warm honey. It was cold and off-putting, like ice cream that had been left in the freezer too long.

He popped out one of his eyes and dropped it onto a plate. Then Candy reached for his other eye.

I lowered my voice. "I'll tell."

He didn't respond, but I knew the threat carried weight with him.

Candy paused in mid-gouge to regard me. After a long moment, he let go of his eye and lowered his hand.

"I can give you five minutes," he said. Then he stood and raised his voice loud enough for the whole restaurant to hear him. "I need to take a short break, ladies and gentlemen!"

A collective groan rose from the room.

"My apologies, but I need a chance to, shall we say, restock?" Candy said.

His skin was mostly picked clean of candy, and he had no toes, and both his left foot and most of his left arm were gone.

The crowd laughed and applauded as Candy stepped off the rotating dais. Since he only had one foot – and his other foot had no toes – I was afraid he might lose his balance as he stepped down, but I didn't reach out to steady him. I didn't know if the candy that formed his body was addictive, but he does get a hell of a lot of repeat customers, and I didn't want to risk any prolonged physical contact with him. I had enough problems with addiction as it was.

Walking like a pirate with a peg leg, Candy made his way toward the back of the restaurant, and I followed. He led me through a swinging door into the kitchen. Since Candy supplies all the eats, the kitchen is primarily for washing and storing plates. A narrow hallway branched off from the kitchen, and Candy headed down it. Again, I followed. We ended up in front of another door, and he gestured toward it with the nub where his left arm had been. It was already regrowing, but slowly.

"Humans first," he said.

I opened the door and stepped inside.

NINE

I expected to enter an office, but it looked more like a dressing room. A mirrored table, a straight-backed chair, and a red satin robe hanging from a hook on the wall. Candy entered, closed the door behind him, and then walked over to the robe. He removed it from the hook, put it on, and then took a seat at the table in front of the mirror. There was no other chair in the room, so I stood.

Candy faced the mirror, his back to me, but I could see his reflection. A new eye was beginning to emerge from the depths of the chocolate socket. Not a Red Hot this time. It was yellow. A lemon drop, maybe.

"Make it quick," Candy said. "I've got a lot of hungry people out there."

"And you have to make sure their bellies don't get too empty, or else you'll lose your psychic connection to them. And if that happens, you won't be able to see and hear what they do."

"I have no idea what you're talking about."

"Of course you don't."

"Even so, I don't like being threatened."

"Duly noted."

He nodded once. With his right hand, he gently touched

his emerging eye, as if he wanted to make sure it was setting up properly.

"So what can I do for you?" he asked.

"I need to find Jinx."

The Candy Man shrugged. "So call him."

"I don't have my wisper, and neither does he."

"Then go to the Rookery and get your people to help."

"That would take too long. I need to find him as soon as possible."

Candy paused, then he asked, "Is he in danger?"

"I don't know. Probably."

He nodded again. "And might you also be reluctant to ask the Shadow Watch for help because you and your partner were ordered off your last case?"

I wondered which of my fellow officers hadn't been able to resist Candy's sweet, sweet charms.

The Candy Man has a special ability. Once someone – Incubus or human – eats a portion of his body, he can see what they see and hear what they hear, at least for a short time. The more someone eats, the longer the effect lasts. This is why Shadow Watch officers are warned to stay away from Candy. Sanderson isn't thrilled by the idea of anyone being able to access his officers' senses, even if only temporarily.

Jinx and I, however, had on occasion found Candy to be a good source of information, not that we let on that we knew how he came by his info. He wasn't in Deacon Booze's league, but he was damn close. If anyone who Candy had a link with had seen or heard anything about Jinx – or better yet, had actually seen Jinx – he'd know it.

"I'm surprised you're asking for my help," Candy said.

"With the psychic connection you have with your customers–"

He waved a chocolate hand to cut me off. "I mean I'm

surprised in *this* case. You're Jinx's Ideator, *and* you work as partners, day in, day out. As closely bonded as you two are, you should have no trouble locating him yourself."

I looked at Candy in amazement for a moment, embarrassed to admit I had no idea what he was talking about. My silence must have clued him in, because he said, "You're not, are you? Bonded. At least not that strongly. That's too bad. If you were, you'd be able to sense where he was. His presence would be a psychic beacon to you, and vice versa. A bond like that would come in handy in your line of work, I'd think."

Candy sounded as if he pitied me, which made me feel even more embarrassed, which in turn made me start to get angry. Especially when I recalled how Sanderson had lectured Jinx and me about this same issue.

"Look, are you going to help me or not?" I asked.

"I will. But not because you threatened to tell my secret. I might lose some customers if the truth got out, but not as many as you might think. I *am* delicious, after all."

A strong chocolate aroma hit me then, and I felt my mouth water anew. I really needed to start carrying some energy bars around with me, I thought. But the smell dissipated as quickly as it had come, and for the first time I wondered if Candy could control it.

"Do you know why I do this, Audra? Sell bits of myself as treats?" he asked.

"I assume it's because you make even more money selling the information you acquire."

Candy laughed, the sound equal parts merriment and sadness. "I provide information as a favor from time to time. To you and to a few others. Don't ask who. I won't tell you. But I never charge money for my services. Have I ever asked you for a payment?"

"No, but I figured that was because I'm so intimidating."

Candy continued as if he hadn't heard my answer. "I'm old, Audra. Much older than anyone knows. I was strongly bonded with my Ideator, and when he died it wasn't long before I started fading. I was lonely – and alone. They're two different things, you know, both just as devastating in their own way. But instead of allowing myself to fade away to nothing, I decided to replace the bond I once had. I couldn't find a new Ideator, of course. That's not possible. But I knew what happened when someone ate a piece of me, so I opened up this place. Now I'm bonded, at least temporarily, to dozens of people at a time. The bonds aren't strong or deep – and to be honest, they aren't nearly as satisfying as the real thing – but they're enough to keep me from fading." He paused before going on. "Enough to keep me from feeling completely alone."

For a moment, I couldn't speak. I was overwhelmed with sadness, compassion, and shame. For years, I had known Incubi, worked alongside them, hell, even lived with one, but I realized that I didn't really understand them.

Candy's left arm had almost completely regrown by now. As if to test it, he reached up with it and broke off a tiny piece of his earlobe. He then offered the bit of chocolate to me.

My stomach gurgled, but I said, "Thanks, but I'm not hungry."

"This isn't a treat. It's my price for helping you."

I frowned. I didn't like where this was going.

"No freebies today, Audra. If you want my help, first you'll need to eat this. It's a small piece, and its effect will last only a short time. I want to glimpse the world as seen through your eyes, Audra. That's my price."

The thought of eating a piece of a sentient being was disturbing enough. Technically, I suppose it wasn't cannibalism since I'm not an Incubus, but it felt like it.

But it was the thought of the intimacy that such a bond, however temporary, would force upon me that made me sick. Candy wanted to get inside my mind, and he was asking me to not only allow it, but to throw the door wide and invite him in.

"Can you guarantee that you'll be able to find Jinx?" I asked.

"No. But if you had anyone else to turn to for help, you wouldn't be here, would you?"

"For a guy with chocolate for brains, you're too damn smart for your own good, you know that?"

Before I could change my mind, I snatched the chocolate earlobe from his newly formed hand and popped it into my mouth. I have no words to describe the sensation that hit me the instant that chocolate touched my tongue. I don't think there are words, not in any language. Imagine the strongest stimulant combined with the most powerful narcotic, and that would be a good start. My head swam and my knees buckled, and it took everything I had to keep standing.

No wonder Candy always has a full house, I thought. If a small piece had affected me this strongly, how much more addictive would a full mouthful be? Or a heaping plate? I was surprised that any of Candy's customers ever left the place. I'd be tempted to withdraw my entire life savings, plunk my ass down on a chair, and keep stuffing my face until I died. It was that good – and that bad.

There wasn't a clear moment when I felt Candy's awareness slipping into my mind, but after a time I became aware of a mild pressure in my head, as if I had the beginnings of a sinus headache. It didn't hurt, but it felt strange and mildly uncomfortable. I looked at Candy, and he looked back at me. He hadn't gone catatonic while we were linked. Candy could still move, but his awareness was – not split, but doubled. He was still inside his own head, but he was inside mine as well.

The connection didn't run both ways. I couldn't see through his eyes or hear through his ears. But I could feel the link between us, a deeper and stronger bond than any I had ever felt with another being before. Including Jinx, who was in a sense my child.

True to Candy's word, the effect didn't last long. I felt the pressure in my head ease little by little, until it was gone, and I knew I was alone inside my own skull once more.

Candy let out a long, soft sigh. "So that's what I look like to you."

He didn't elaborate, and I was glad.

"A deal's a deal," he said. Chocolate lids slid over his eyes – one Red Hot, one lemon drop – as he began concentrating.

He remained like that for several minutes, and during that time I felt naked and exposed in a way I never had before. This person, this *creature*, had been inside my mind, and even though I had allowed it, and Candy hadn't forced his way in, I still felt violated in a way I couldn't define.

Candy's trance, or whatever it was, went on so long that I began to fear he wasn't going to have any luck finding Jinx. But eventually he opened his eyes, smiled, and spoke two words, "Circus Psychosis."

"How many?" a voice asked me.

The Incubus inside the ticket booth was covered with warts, and I mean *covered*. There wasn't an inch of his skin that remained unblemished. The warts were large, each at least the size of a quarter, and they had grown so close together that the Incubus' eyes were sealed shut, as were his nostrils. His mouth remained open enough for him to breathe and speak, but the warts covering his lips made him difficult to understand. I could only see him from the waist up, and since he wasn't wearing any clothes, that was fine by me.

"One," I said.

"Ten yoonies."

I didn't have any yoonies, but I still had some Earth money on me. I took my wallet from my jacket pocket, opened it, and started to pull out a couple bills, but Wart shook his head.

"Yoonies only. We don't take Earth money."

There was a line of customers behind me, and they shuffled their feet and muttered in irritation. The Incubus in line after me let out an exasperated sigh, and I turned to look at her. She was a vegetation-based creature, with thickly intertwined vines for her body, two huge pumpkins for breasts – with protruding stems in place of nipples – and a carved jack-o'-lantern for a head. Slanted triangular eyes and a wide grinning mouth filled with sharp teeth gave her an appropriately sinister appearance. A soft flame burned inside her hollow head, and now it began to glow hotter, indicating her frustration.

"Is there a problem?" I asked sweetly.

"You humans are *always* a problem," she said. Her voice was a combination of rustling leaves and moist pumpkin pulp being squished.

I started to reply, but she cut me off.

"Just because some of you can create us, you act as if you're gods. But you're nothing of the sort! You're weaker than we are as a rule, you have no special abilities to speak of, you take forever to heal – assuming you don't die from your injuries first, that is – and you don't live very long. Only a handful of decades at most."

I tried to cut in, but she kept going.

"*And* as if all that wasn't enough, you don't even have the decency to carry our money! You should go back to your own world, stay there, and leave Nod to us!"

A number of the Incubi in line nodded their heads and offered words of support for Madam Pumpkinhead. A couple even applauded. But several looked uncomfortable, and a few slowly eased out of the line and started walking away, as if they'd changed their minds about seeing the circus. They'd no doubt realized that I was a Shadow Watch officer, and they didn't want any trouble.

I regarded Madam Pumpkinhead for a moment. I considered showing her my badge, but I decided against it. I didn't want to cause any commotion – at least not yet. If Jinx was being held here, I didn't want to alert his captors that I was coming. But there was another reason I wanted to avoid a scene. Despite the fact that I really wanted to put my fist through the bitch's rind, her accusation that humans treated Incubi as inferior struck a chord in me. I like to think of myself as a person who doesn't harbor any kind of bias toward people who are different than me in terms of race, religion, gender, sexuality, politics, profession, etcetera, etcetera. The truth is I'm only human, and I have my share of prejudices, even if they're milder and harder to identify than they might have been if I'd been born in an earlier time. But could I honestly say that I considered Incubi as equal to humans – or even in some ways superior?

And what about the Incubi? Humans give "birth" to them on Earth, but then most of them are shuffled off to live in another dimension. And those that are permitted by the Shadow Watch to visit or stay on Earth must conceal their true nature. How did that make them feel? How did it make *Jinx* feel? It shamed me that it had never occurred to me ask him.

So instead of hitting her or talking tough, I merely said, "I'm sorry."

It was impossible to read her expression since her carved features couldn't move, but the glow inside her head softened, and her plant-tendril body relaxed a bit.

"Well, OK, then," she said, sounding a bit bemused. "How many yoonies do you need?"

I smiled sheepishly. "Ten."

Madam P reached up with both hands, and with her tendril fingers she took hold of the stem on the top of her head and lifted the lid off. Then with her other hand, she reached inside her head and pulled out a large handful of yoonies. Whatever caused the glow in there, it must not have been literal flame, for her vine fingers were undamaged. Madam P replaced her lid and then gently nudged me aside and stepped up to the ticket booth.

"We'll take two," she told Wart.

He didn't look happy about letting me in, but money was money. He took the yoonics and handed Madam P two tickets. She in turn handed one to me.

"Thank you," I said.

"It was my pleasure, dear. Sorry I got so huffy. My rind has a tendency to go off a bit now and then. Makes me cross."

Then she slipped a viney arm through mine.

"Shall we?" she asked.

I smiled and accompanied her inside the tent.

The Circus Psychosis was located in the Arcade, the main entertainment district in Newtown. You can find any sort of amusement there, from all the usual diversions to be found on Earth to ones invented by the Incubi, to strange combinations of the two. My favorite is Noddian soccer, where the players are allowed to arm themselves with whatever weapons they choose, and the balls are set to explode at random times. Fun for the whole family.

Circus Psychosis was housed inside a gigantic rainbow-striped tent that covered an entire block. I'd seen the tent before, of course, but I'd never been inside and had barely paid attention to it. I'd been busy with other cases at the time, and given how I feel about clowns, I'm not big on circuses. But now I was here, walking arm in arm with a pumpkin-headed Incubus that only a few moments ago acted like she couldn't stand my entire species. Life is weird, but life in Nod is ultra-weird.

Wooden bleachers were set up around the circumference of the tent, and they were filled with Incubi and more than a few humans. More people were streaming in from three other entrances beside the one we'd used, and from the looks of things, I guessed the circus was going to have a sold-out performance.

I was even more grateful then for Madam P's help. Without her, I would've had to find another way in and risk alerting Jinx's captors to my presence. A big crowd meant that I could hide in plain sight. Of course, it also meant a lot of people might get in my way if I had to act. I didn't have to worry about Incubi getting caught in the crossfire, since they could heal swiftly. But the same wasn't true for my fellow humans, so weapons or no weapons, I'd have to do my best to be careful when it came time to make my move.

Madam P wanted to sit up high, but I convinced her that it would be more exciting to sit closer to the performers, and we managed to find a couple seats in the third row. Not quite as close as I would've liked, but it would do. We sat, and Madam P began telling me about the last time she'd been here and how much fun she'd had, peppering her monologue with the occasional *darling* and *sweetie*. I started to think I'd liked her better when she'd been a bitch.

A cacophony of noise filled the tent – circus music

blared from speakers set at regular intervals throughout the tent, and everyone in the crowd was talking, shouting, and laughing, creating waves of sound that rose, crested, and dipped, only to rise again. Food and souvenir vendors made their way through the bleachers, calling out their wares and urging people to buy. Peanuts, popcorn, cotton candy, and hot dogs were popular snack items sold, but they had Noddian touches. The peanuts screamed when their shells were broken, and the cotton candy was pink fiberglass insulation wrapped in gleaming barbed wire. The hot dogs were the same as those on Earth, but they're disgusting in any dimension. The souvenirs ranged from the charming dead-rat-on-a-stick to the unsettling death-scream-in-a-jar. So far, the Circus Psychosis was living up to its name.

The circus had the traditional three rings; the floors inside the rings were covered with fresh sawdust, and there was also rigging set up for trapeze and high-wire acts. While the crowd filed in, a number of performers were walking around, providing simple entertainments to keep the audience happy while they waited for the show to begin.

A clown – who was *not* Jinx – juggled a trio of decapitated heads that were reciting soliloquies from Shakespeare, each head speaking a word in turn. A human-sized poodle was making tiny naked humans jump through hoops, and a skeleton artist had slipped off his skin and was tying it into different shapes resembling balloon animals in response to suggestions called out by the crowd.

Madam P commented on each of the performers, punctuating her responses with copious oohs and ahhs, but I ignored her. I slowly swept my eyes around the tent, looking for Jinx. I didn't see any sign of him, and I was beginning to wonder if the Candy Man had been mistaken – or, worse, had lied to me. I considered leaving my seat and going in search of my partner, when the ringmaster stepped in from behind a flap in the tent and strode to the middle of the center ring.

I could tell he was a ringmaster by his sequin-covered top hat and red swallowtail jacket. But even though he had a human face – thin mustache, Van Dyke beard – the octopus tentacles he had in place of human arms and legs caused him to move in a distinctly alien fashion. His gait was at once smooth and awkward, and I had no trouble imagining him once starring in someone's nightmares. When he reached the center of the ring, he stopped and raised his arm tentacles into the air to get the audience's attention. He wore a microphone headset, and when he spoke, his voice issued from the tent's sound system.

"Ladies and gentlemen! Welcome to the strangest show *off* Earth!"

Laughter and applause.

I decided to remain seated for the time being. Once the show was underway, everyone's attention would be on the performers, allowing me to sneak around more easily. At least, that was my hope.

The ringmaster continued.

"We've got chills, we've got thrills, but most of all" – his voice lowered to a whisper – "we've got *madness!*"

The tent lights cut off at his cue, plunging the audience into darkness. The crowd cheered, roared, and stamped their feet so hard, I feared the bleachers would collapse. A spotlight came on and shone on the center ring, illuminating a tall, blue-skinned Incubus who wore only black Speedos. He had large black eyes, a bald head, and large ears that tapered to points.

Blueskin wasn't alone, however. Next to him in the ring crouched a huge beast that looked like an amalgamation of various big cats – lion, tiger, leopard, panther, and cougar. The creature was obviously an Incubus of some sort, but even if that hadn't been obvious from its appearance, I could've guessed its true nature from its demeanor. There was no hint of restlessness or nervousness from the beast. It looked relaxed, casual even, and intelligence shone in its gaze.

Blueskin wasn't wearing a microphone, but the ringmaster's voice came over the sound system again. I couldn't see him, so I assumed he was backstage somewhere.

"Azul the Amazing, the Astounding, the Astonishing is here to answer the question: how much pain can a single Incubus endure? A warning for those of you in the audience who are squeamish, you may wish to avert your eyes for this next part!"

The crowd roared with laughter. Incubi aren't known for their squeamishness.

I had a bad feeling that I knew what was coming – a variation of the animal tamer putting his head into a lion's mouth. Only in this case, because Incubi could heal all but the most catastrophic of injuries, the gimmick here was to watch the lion bite Azul and see how much pain he could withstand.

The cat-beast crouched lower to the ground and fixed its gaze on Azul. Azul faced the creature, seemingly unconcerned. The cat-beast's leg muscles tightened in preparation for an attack, and a low growling sound came from deep within its throat. Azul showed no reaction. The cat-beast let out a deafening roar and leaped toward Azul.

In that instant, I understood that this act was intended to be a far more savage variation on the classic circus bit. I was right about that, but I was wrong in how I thought it would turn out. Azul – who up to this point had stood motionless – blurred into action. He sped forward and met the cat-beast in the middle of its leap. Even though Azul appeared lean and not especially strong, he plucked the cat-beast out of the air as if it were no more than a stuffed animal and slammed it to the ground.

Bones cracked, the cat-beast howled in pain, and Azul opened his mouth impossibly wide to reveal three-inch-long needle-sharp teeth. Curved talons extended from Azul's limber fingers, and with a high-pitched shriek, Azul fell upon the cat-beast. Flesh tore, blood sprayed the air, and the audience roared approval. It only took a few moments for Azul to strip most of the cat-beast's meat from its body and swallow it down.

I had no idea where the meat went. Azul's stomach didn't expand so much as an inch Despite how sickening the display was, I couldn't help feeling a bit envious. I wish I could eat like that and not gain any weight.

Almost as fast as Azul could eat, the cat-beast regenerated its lost mass, and once it was whole again, Azul went back for seconds. Then thirds. It was an impressive spectacle in its own savage way, and extreme even by Noddian standards.

The cat-beast called it quits after the fifth time it was devoured by Azul, and the act ended. Then a large bull-headed Incubus dressed in a tuxedo wheeled a stainless steel table upon which a half-dozen other Incubi who looked like demon babies were strapped down. He stepped into one of the other rings as circus hands carrying shovels moved wheelbarrows into the center ring to start cleaning away the blood-soaked sawdust. The minotaur removed a pair of claw hammers from his pants pockets, bowed, and then began to play his hideous instrument. Demon babies shrieked as hammers pounded their scaled flesh, their cries creating an atonal symphony of agony.

I figured the crowd was sufficiently distracted, and I wasn't confident that I could sit through another violent blood-soaked act without losing the grilled cheese I'd eaten earlier. I started to stand, but Madam P grabbed my arm and stopped me.

"You can't go now, sweetie! The clowns are next. They're always *so* amusing!"

I sat back down and did my best to tune out the demon infants' screams.

I don't think I've ever been as grateful for anything as I was for that act's conclusion, and I let out a shaky sigh as the audience applauded and the minotaur maestro wheeled his table away. None of the demon babies moved. None of them looked much like babies anymore, either.

The ringmaster's voice came over the sound system once more.

"And now, ladies and gentlemen, *Damen und Herren, mesdames et messieurs*, the Circus Psychosis is proud to present those Masters of Disaster, those Mavens of Mayhem, those Barons of Butchery... the Bedlam Brothers!"

The crowd went crazy. Well, *crazier*. They shouted and cheered, hooted and hollered. Clearly, the Bedlam Brothers were a favorite act.

Several spotlights came on, and their beams began circling and criss-crossing the tent, as if searching for the clowns. From somewhere in the bleachers behind me came the roar of an engine. I looked back just in time to see a small car drop through a flap in the tent's roof. It was an exceptionally small vehicle, only large enough for a child to drive, but it was more than big enough to cause some serious damage as it plunged into the crowd. Incubi cried out in pain as the car landed on them, and when the driver floored the accelerator and the vehicle's tires began spinning on flesh, those cries begot shrieks of agony. People scrambled to get out of the car's way as it roared toward the circus floor. Those who didn't move fast enough were mowed down or knocked aside. Despite its size, the little vehicle packed a hell of a wallop.

The car was painted white, but patterns of multicolored dots, stripes, and various geometric shapes flowed across its surface like liquid as it went. Of course, it also picked up a good amount of blood-red on its journey toward the circus floor.

As the vehicle came bouncing and juddering toward where I sat, I was able to catch a glimpse of the driver. It was a clown, and at first I thought it was Jinx. I'd seen him drive before, and vehicular homicide was the least of the damage he'd caused.

But I quickly saw that the driver was a different clown. He wore a bowler hat on his round head and he had different markings. But his most distinctive features were his huge, almost elephant-like ears. Big-Ears: the leader of the Blacksuits. I recognized the insanity blazing in his eyes, as well as the far-too-wide lunatic smile spread across the bottom half of his face. It was the clown version of berserker rage, and once a clown was caught up in it, the only thing to do was get the hell out of the way.

The crowd around me was panicking as they attempted to remove themselves from the vehicle's path, which of course meant that people were falling over one another and not getting anywhere. Those Incubi who had other ways of getting around besides walking fared better. They took to the air or simply vanished. One turned intangible and the maniacal clown drove right through her.

Madam P laughed in delight as she watched the car come toward us, as if she didn't realize – or didn't care – about the danger we were in. I grabbed hold of one of her vine hands and tried to pull her with me, but she didn't budge. I pulled harder, but all I succeeded in doing was breaking her hand off at the wrist. I fell backward just as the clown car slammed into Madam P, cutting off her laughter. Pumpkin rind, pulp, and seeds exploded into the air, and her vine body came apart like dried straw. The car continued until its gore-smeared wheels at last reached the ground.

The vehicle didn't stop there, though. It picked up speed and began going around the circumference of the tent, as if it were in a race with opponents that only the driver could see. Halfway through the first lap, the passenger door sprang open and a clown came tumbling out. That one was followed by another, and another, and so on, until a dozen different clowns – mostly male, but several female – were running around and laughing like lunatics. All of them were dressed in colorful, outlandish outfits, but Jinx wasn't among them.

Now that its passengers had disembarked, the clown car veered toward the center ring, drove into it, and slid to halt in a shower of fresh sawdust. Big-Ears hopped out and the Bedlam Brothers (and Sisters) gathered around their vehicle. Along with his bowler, Big-Ears wore a yellow suit with black criss-crossing stripes, and brown hobo shoes open at the toes. With exaggerated motions, he reached into the inner pocket of his jacket and withdrew a square metal box with a short antenna protruding from one end.

He then pointed the box at the car and thumbed a red button on the front. There was a loud bang, a burst of smoke, and the roof of the tiny car flew into the air and landed on one of the clowns. I recognized her as the redheaded woman from the parking lot at Perchance to Dream. The roof slammed her to the ground, and she lay there, unmoving. *Stupid bitch gets knocked unconscious in both dimensions,* I thought. The crowd laughed. I brushed bits of Madam P off my shirt and kept my gaze focused on the car.

The vehicle began to shake and a metallic ratcheting

sound came from within. A pair of impossibly long metal rods rose from within the car, extending fifty feet into the air. Between the rods, bound to them by lengths of wire coiled around his bleeding wrists, was Jinx. He was in his Night Aspect, but he was bruised and bloody, and his head hung forward, chin on chest, and I couldn't tell if he was alive or dead. His gigantic shoes were gone, revealing equally gigantic ivory-colored feet. I'd never seen Jinx without his shoes, and I'd always wondered whether they were just an affectation. Now I knew.

The crowd went crazy when they saw Jinx, howling with bloodthirsty excitement that wouldn't have been out of place in an arena in ancient Rome.

The sight of Jinx – my personal childhood boogeyman – brought low like this and displayed like some sort of trophy came as a profound shock. I'd never seen him beaten and weak before. He was Mr Jinx, the Dark Clown, the Phantom Prankster, the Thing That Laughed in the Dark. He was a fierce, terrifying lunatic, the very definition of the word *nightmare*. That's what he was supposed to be, what I'd *created* him to be.

Sorrow and rage battled for dominance inside me, and while it was a near thing, rage won.

Big-Ears pulled a headset mic from somewhere within the car and slipped it on. His voice was more guttural, but it definitely belonged to the leader of the Blacksuits that had abducted Jinx.

"All right, my brothers and sisters... pree-sent arms!"

In unison, the clowns reached into their pockets and withdrew weapons, most of which – like Jinx's beloved sledgehammers – were far too large to fit where they'd been stored. Pistols, shotguns, rifles, automatic weapons, crossbow, shuriken, and in one case a flamethrower were removed and aimed at Jinx.

"We have here a brother clown," Big-Ears said. "One who not only remained bound to his Ideator–"

The crowd booed.

"He also works for the Shadow Watch!"

The boos became shouts of outrage. I'd known the Shadow Watch wasn't exactly popular among the Incubi, but I hadn't realized it was this bad.

Big-Ears continued. "When my family and I received word that poor, misguided Jinx here" – Big-Ears dropped the remote control to the sawdust and drew a double-barreled shotgun from his pants pocket – "was in need of rescue, we raced to his location and liberated him from his *Ideator!*" He almost spat the word this time, and the crowd's roar of outrage grew louder. "Then we brought him here, to the Circus Psychosis, and we tried to get him to see that he was an *Incubus*, not a *servant!* More, that he was a *clown* – a creature of anarchy and chaos! How could such a being belong to an organization dedicated to" – he shuddered – "order?"

The rest of the clowns grimaced at the word, and one turned and vomited colorful paper streamers onto the sawdust.

"We offered him a place in our family," Big-Ears said. "A new, glamorous life as a member of the Bedlam Brothers! And do you know what his reply was?"

The crowd grew quiet and listened closely. But before the clown could speak again, I stood.

"He told you to go fuck yourselves with a chainsaw."

The clowns gaped at me, as did the surviving audience members. I ignored them all as I made my way to the front row, picking my way carefully through the carnage the clown car had left behind. I jumped onto the floor and started walking toward the center ring, my gaze fastened on Big-Ears. I had no weapons – no trancer, no M-blade – and I didn't give a damn.

I glanced up at Jinx. He still hung limply, his head lowered. Not a good sign.

Big-Ears regained his composure. He lowered his weapon and grinned at me. "That's precisely what he said."

I shrugged. "We know each other pretty well."

"And do you know what we did to him after he said that?" Big-Ears asked.

"Looks like you beat the shit out of him."

Big-Ear's grin widened to the point that the flesh at the corners of his mouth began to tear. "Oh, that's the least of the fun we had with him. Since he wouldn't join our act willingly, we decided to force the issue." He gestured toward Jinx. "We were about to start target practice. We were going to let the audience choose which of us gets to take the first shot, but now that you're here, I think we'll extend that honor to you. So which one of us will it be? Personally, I hope you go for the flamethrower. We brought marshmallows."

"No one's going to shoot him," I said calmly.

By this point I'd crossed two-thirds of the distance to the center ring.

"Really?" Big-Ears said. His grin turned into a sneer. "Maybe that's because we're going to be too busy shooting you."

He raised his shotgun and drew a bead on me. Taking their leader's cue, the other clowns also aimed their weapons at me. I knew I was helplessly outnumbered and outgunned, but I didn't care. I was too damn angry to care.

I kept walking.

Big-Ears' body tensed, and I knew he was going to fire. Without thinking, I started running toward him as fast as I could. I had no illusions that I could reach him before he fired, but at that moment, I didn't really give a shit.

I didn't look at the shotgun as I ran. I kept my gaze

focused on Big-Ears' eyes. In them I saw a mixture of glee, lunacy, and bloodlust that was nearly sexual in its intensity. I hoped this meant Big-Ears would want to extend our "foreplay" as long as possible, giving me a chance to try to take the shotgun from him. And I did manage to reach him, but when I was close enough, he spun the shotgun around in his hands, grabbed hold of the barrel, and wielding it like a club, swung the stock toward my head.

I saw the blow coming, and if it had been a human attacking me, I might've been able to avoid getting hit. But Big-Ears was an Incubus, and he moved so swiftly that there was little I could do. I was able to move sideways enough so the stock clipped me instead of hitting me straight on, which probably saved my life. Even so, it felt as if I'd been hit in the head with a block of concrete. Bright light exploded along my optic nerves, and I felt the world spin around me. The next thing I knew I was lying in sawdust with one hell of a headache.

I heard the soft shuffling sound of someone walking toward me. Then Big-Ears knelt down beside me, grabbed a handful of my hair, and lifted my head off the sawdust. That made my head hurt even worse, and I almost started to cry.

Big-Ears leaned his face close to mine.

"Nice try, bitch. Now we're going to have some playtime with you before we take care of your *partner* up there."

The crowd, which had been watching our little drama play out with silent, rapt attention, now burst into wild applause and cheers. But soon I detected another sound, soft at first, but quickly increasing in volume. The crowd heard it too, and they grew quiet once more.

It was the sound of laughter. Dark, dangerous, batshit-crazy laughter.

I managed to tilt my head enough to look up and see

that Jinx was awake. It was his laughter I heard – that we all heard – and his eyes gleamed with a level of madness I'd never seen in him before, that I'd never imagined was possible. In that moment, I should've been terrified. But I wasn't. I was relieved. Jinx was alive, and better yet, he sounded pissed.

"It was fun *hanging out* with you clowns for a while," he said, his voice low and filled with menace. "But no one – *no one* – hurts my mommy."

I couldn't hold onto consciousness any longer, and as my mind fell into darkness, I heard the sound of wire snapping, followed by screams of agony and terror. And then I heard no more.

TEN

"Audra? Can you hear me?"

Jinx's voice was muffled, as if I was hearing him through yards of cotton. I tried to open my eyes, failed, and tried again. This time I was successful. I saw Jinx's clown face looking down at me, concerned. He was a bit blurry, but otherwise I could make him out just fine.

"Yeah," was all I could manage to say. The word came out as little more than a croak, and I wasn't confident that Jinx could understand it. He must have, though, for he smiled and nodded.

"Good."

As my head started to clear, I realized I was lying on Jinx's lap, and he was cradling me in his arms. During the entire time that we'd been together – from the moment of his full Ideation, really – I'd rarely touched him, and I'd never touched him like *this*. There was nothing romantic or sexual about it, but there was a powerful intimacy to it all the same.

I let Jinx hold me for a moment or two longer as I waited to see if I would remain conscious. When I was confident I was in no immediate danger of slipping back into nothingness, I asked him to help me stand. He did so, gently, and when I thought I was capable of standing on my own, I motioned for him to step back. He did, but he didn't move far, in case I started to fall.

I looked around. My head felt like a bass drum being pounded on by Godzilla, and I had to move my head slowly to keep it from hurting even more. We were standing near the bleachers. The tent was empty, except for scattered food wrappers, uneaten snacks, and dropped souvenirs that people had left behind in their panic to escape. The clown car remained in the middle of the center ring, but the long metal rods Jinx had been bound to were bent and twisted, as if they'd been subjected to hurricane-force winds. Scattered through the center ring were blood-soaked bits of clothing, chunks of meat, bone, and viscera that I took to be pieces of the Bedlam Brothers. Jinx was covered in gore, and since he'd been holding me, so was I.

I glanced down at Jinx's wrists. The wounds he'd suffered from being bound with wire were in the process of healing.

I nodded toward a particularly large piece of clown lying on the blood-soaked sawdust nearby.

"Remind me never to make you mad."

Jinx grinned, and despite the fact that at that moment he was a nightmare clown with a blood-stippled face, his grin didn't look sinister to me in the slightest.

"So..." Jinx said. "Took you long enough to get here. What did I miss?" He looked around at the carnage he'd wrought, and his grin took on a darker edge. "And who else can I hurt?"

Another good thing about Nod: the residents are so used to seeing bizarre shit that they barely gave Jinx and me – and our blood-stained clothes – a glance. We headed centerwise, toward Oldtown and the Rookery. The Bedlam Brothers had taken Jinx's acid-spraying flower, but they hadn't been able to find Cuthbert Junior in whatever hidden dimension Jinx stores it in, so at least we had one weapon.

Jinx had healed enough by this point that outwardly he appeared uninjured, but he walked more slowly than usual, and he favored his left leg. But what really told me that he was still hurting on the inside was how quiet he was. He had to be pretty bad off not to talk. Normally, I might've been glad to have a break from his nonstop chatter, but now his silence worried me. I hoped he would continue to heal as time wore on.

"Did you learn anything from the Bedlam Brothers?" I asked.

Jinx rubbed his abdomen and grimaced. "I picked up a few more tricks for rearranging someone's internal organs without removing them first, if that's what you mean."

"Anything *useful*," I clarified.

"Only that they work for the Fata Morgana."

I stopped walking and stared at him. "What did you say?"

"They wouldn't stop going on about her, especially the big-eared guy in the bowler hat. 'The Fata Morgana will bring about a new order.' 'Both Earth and Nod will be forever changed once the Fata Morgana is finished with her great work.'" He made a face. "If my wrists hadn't been wrapped in wire, I'd have jabbed knitting needles into my ears so I wouldn't have had to listen to his blathering anymore."

The Fata Morgana was one of the oldest known Incubi. Just how old, no one was certain. I didn't know much about the Fata Morgana – I'd never met her, in fact – but Sanderson seemed to have a great deal of respect for her. She'd served on the Nightclad Council sometime in the past, but she'd had nothing to do with them for at least a century, probably longer. As far as I knew, she had no known connections to the Lords of Misrule, but anything was possible.

"Let's keep going," I said. "The sooner we can report to Sanderson – *and* get a shower and change of clothes – the better."

Our boss wouldn't be thrilled that we – all right, mostly *me* – had decided to disobey his orders to stay off the case, but he needed to know what we'd learned so far. Even if in the end it helped out those two divas, Damon and Eklips. Whatever was going on, it was way more important than any grudge I was carrying against them.

We continued walking, and I filled Jinx in on everything that had happened to me since his abduction by the Blacksuits/Bedlam Brothers. With each block we traveled, Jinx became stronger, until he'd returned to his normal obnoxious self. My head began to hurt less, but I was still dragging ass big-time. It must've been obvious as hell, because at one point, Jinx said, "Do you want to try and score some rev somewhere?"

I was tempted. First Dreamer, how I was tempted! And I knew that Night Jinx wouldn't give me grief about using the drug, unlike his Day Aspect. But I'd come this far without any chemical help, and I decided to keep it up as long as I could.

"I'm fine," I said.

Jinx looked as if he might argue the point, but he didn't push the matter.

Newtown isn't as dangerous as the Cesspit, but no place in Nod is entirely safe. During our trip, we encountered our fair share of tough guys and gals who thought it would be fun to rough up a pair of Shadow Watch officers who looked as if they weren't, shall we say, at their best. Trying to attack us wasn't the best decision they ever made.

Eventually, we crossed over to Oldtown, and as we

approached the Rookery, I knew something was wrong. At first I couldn't figure out what it was, but then Jinx put it into words for me.

"There's nobody standing guard."

The main gate was open, as it always was except in the most dire emergencies, but there were no guards posted. A minimum of two guards – one human, one Incubus – are on duty at all times. I had never in my years as an officer seen the gate unguarded. If I hadn't been so sludge-brained, I would've noticed the missing guards right away.

"Better get Cuthbert Junior out," I said.

"Way ahead of you." Jinx giggled as he reached into his jacket and pulled out his sledgehammer. The hammer's head was smeared with tacky blood, strands of hair, and bits of what looked like brain matter.

But before we could pass through the unguarded gate, I saw a trio of figures coming down Chimera Street toward us. It was Russell and Bloodshedder, and between them – her wrists bound together with a negator serving as handcuffs – was Shocktooth.

Since I'd brought Jinx up to speed, he knew that Russell wasn't an enemy, if not exactly a friend yet. But either Jinx had forgotten, which was entirely possible – given the chaotic nature of his mind when he's in his Night Aspect – or he didn't care. He let out a deafening bellow of rage, raised Cuthbert Junior over his head in a two-handed grip, and started running toward Russell and Bloodshedder, his giant bare feet making meaty slapping sounds as he ran.

Russell showed no reaction to Jinx's charge, but Bloodshedder growled and sprang forward.

The demon hound slammed into Jinx before he could swing his hammer, and she knocked him to the ground and pinned him with her front paws. Then she lowered her head to Jinx's body and began devouring him. Jinx shrieked

in agony, and I dashed forward, praying I could reach him
before Bloodshedder did too much damage. Russell stood
next to Shocktooth and kept hold of her while he watched
his Incubus savage mine, seemingly unconcerned.

As I drew closer to Jinx, I realized that Bloodshedder
wasn't hurting him. She was *licking* him, and his shrieks
weren't caused by pain, but laughter.

"That tickles!" he shouted. "Stop it!"

I looked at Russell and he shrugged. "What can I say?
She likes blood. It's part of her name, after all."

I looked down at Bloodshedder as she cleaned the gore
off Jinx's skin.

"That's disgusting," I said.

"Doesn't your partner do disgusting things sometimes?"
Russell asked.

"Last week he made a salami and toenail-clipping
sandwich – with extra toenails."

"I rest my case."

Still laughing, Jinx managed to extricate himself from
Bloodshedder's hold and stand up. I was shocked to see
him pat the demon dog on the head, and shocked again
when Bloodshedder wagged her spiked tail a couple times.
Incubi. You never know what the hell they'll do.

"How did you find us?" I asked Russell. "Bloodshedder
track us down?"

"Not this time. I figured once you found Jinx, you'd
most likely head to the Rookery, to get your hands on new
weapons if nothing else."

"Makes sense." I nodded at Shocktooth. "So what rock
did you find her under?"

Before Russell could answer, Shocktooth said, "The
bastard snuck up on me while I was playing a game of
mega-roulette at Last Chancers. He stuck me in the shoulder
with that sissy-boy sword of his, and then he slapped the

negator on me while I was bleeding all over the damn floor! And I had a streak going, too," she added sullenly.

Last Chancers was the most popular casino in Nod. Located in the Arcade, Last Chancers was known for its extreme – and often fatal – forms of gambling. Mega-roulette was played on a gigantic table that could've filled a stadium, and instead of balls, it used down-on-their-luck gamblers – who owed the casino money – as game pieces. They keep the music turned up loud at Last Chancers to cover the screams. It doesn't help much.

"Gambling away your payment for helping Quietus escape?" I asked.

"What the hell else would I be doing there?" Shocktooth said. "And the worst part was he made me leave my winnings! Lousy bastard." She sounded as if she might cry. Good thing her electrical powers were negated, or she might've short-circuited herself once tears started flowing.

"Tell her what you told me," Russell said to Shocktooth.

She didn't respond right away, and Bloodshedder took a step closer to her and began growling. Jinx gripped Cuthbert Junior's handle tight.

"Let me interrogate her, Audra," he said. "Pleeeease? I do *so* love a good interrogation!" He grinned. "The messier, the better."

Shocktooth glared at us all defiantly a moment more, but then the anger seemed to drain out of her. With her powers negated, there was no way she could heal whatever injuries we inflicted on her, at least, not any faster than a human, and she knew it.

"Fine. The Lords of Misrule have me on retainer. They have a lot of people working for them, Incubi *and* humans. They removed the negator collar the Council slapped around my neck after you two busted me." A little fire returned to her gaze as she looked at Jinx and me. "The

Lords contact me whenever they have a job they want me to do. It could be something as simple as delivering a package. Sometimes they want me to lean on someone." She grinned, displaying her sharp crocodilian teeth. "I'm real good at the rough stuff, you know. Anyway, yesterday I got a call from the Lords – but I never know who it is. Sometimes it's a guy, sometimes a woman. This time it was a woman. She told me you two had captured Quietus, and she wanted me to help him escape. The fact that I'd get to stomp on you two was a bonus." She glanced at Russell. "She told me someone else would meet me, and that he'd help make sure Quietus got away. She didn't tell me he'd actually be a fucking backstabber, though! Literally!"

I looked at Russell. "So the two of you hooked up, found us, and freed Quietus. Which you totally couldn't have done if Jinx and I hadn't been so worn out from capturing him in the first place," I pointed out. "The question is, how did you find us? Did Quietus have some kind of tracing device on him?"

Jinx had been quiet as we talked, but now he said, "They were told where to find us."

I frowned. "But no one knew where we'd enter Nod. *We* didn't even know."

"Jinx is right," Russell said. "No one told me where to find you, but Shocktooth knew. Or at least she had a good idea. She told me which street we'd most likely find you on."

We all looked at Shocktooth, Bloodshedder included.

"The woman – I assume the same one – told me where you'd be," Shocktooth said.

I thought about this for a moment. "Do the Lords have some way of identifying which Doors lead where each night?"

As far as the Shadow Watch knew, the Lords didn't

possess any advanced tech, but after everything Jinx and I had experienced over the last couple days, I knew differently. Hell, whoever Russell really worked for had the capability of making weapons out of pure M-energy in ways the Shadow Watch's M-gineers could only – pardon the pun – dream about.

Shocktooth shrugged. "How the fuck should I know? I'm just a hired hand."

I looked at Russell.

"I don't know much about their tech, either," he said. "Though I wouldn't be surprised if they can communicate directly between dimensions without having to rely on couriers. I mean, my people can–" He broke off. "Well, let's just say I know that such communication is possible."

I looked at Shocktooth. "What happened after you freed Quietus?"

"Not much. We got the negators off him, and he took off. Asshole didn't even say thanks. Backstabber and I went our separate ways after that. When I got back to my place, I found a stack of yoonies on my kitchen table, same as usual after I finish a job for the Lords. As far as I was concerned, I'd been paid and the job was over."

I had no idea whether Shocktooth had told us the whole truth. The less humanlike an Incubus is, the more difficult it is for me to read their facial expressions and vocal tones. I thought there was a decent chance she wasn't lying to us, but I really didn't know. I figured Jinx and I had learned enough for the time being, though. While we'd been talking, I'd kept an eye on the Rookery's main gate, hoping to see a pair of guards emerge and take up their accustomed positions. But no one had exited the building the entire time we'd been standing there, and I was rapidly transitioning from nervous to alarmed.

"Let's go inside," I said. "We need to report in to

Sanderson. And the sooner Shocktooth is behind bars, the better. You're going to get more than a binding this time," I told her. "You're going to get an all-expense-paid trip to Deadlock."

Shocktooth groaned. Deadlock was often referred to as the Roach Motel, because Incubi went in, but they never came out.

I looked at Russell. "This is your chance to duck out. Sanderson's going to have a lot of questions for you, and you might not want to answer them."

He didn't even pause to think about it. "Bloodshedder and I'll go with. My cover's blown with the Lords now anyway, and as for who I really work for..." He did pause now. "Commander Sanderson won't be surprised."

I raised an eyebrow, but as usual, Russell didn't elaborate. I felt like punching him really hard in an especially sensitive area, but I resisted the urge. We had work to do.

Jinx chose that moment to speak to Bloodshedder. "Did you know your initials are BS?"

Bloodshedder growled, Russell grinned, and I sighed.

"Let's go," I said.

I knew something was wrong before we were even halfway across the courtyard. The Rookery is usually a quiet place on the outside. Shadow Watch patrol officers are almost always out in the field, whether on Earth or in Nod, and most of the time we receive our orders via wisper. The only times we go into the Rookery are when we're bringing in a suspect or – as is often the case for Jinx and me – when we're in trouble and summoned to appear before Sanderson.

But the Shadow Watch has other divisions beside Patrol: Dispatch, Processing, the Armory, and Detention, all located on the ground floor. The upper floors house the Rookery's Central Administration, Permissions (for passports and licenses), the courtrooms of the Judiciary, Somnocology, M-gineering – and at the very top, the Bower. That's where the Unwakened eternally slumber, their powerful dreams maintaining Nod's existence and keeping the Maelstrom's violent energies at bay. So even though it's quiet, the Rookery still has the feeling of a place that's inhabited and alive. But I didn't feel that now. All I felt was emptiness.

Jinx still held Cuthbert Junior in a one-handed grip, but he now spun the hammer around and took hold of it with both hands. Which told me he also felt something wasn't right. Russell had grabbed Shocktooth's arm with one hand, and with his other he drew an M-blade from his belt.

"I made a stop along the way," he said, as he handed it to me. "Sorry I wasn't able to score you a new trancer. This was the best I could do."

It wasn't a normal M-blade. They're made from steel blended with threads of Maelstrom energy. The entire blade of this weapon was multicolored, like Russell's rapier. It was fashioned entirely from M-energy, and I assumed Russell's "people" had made it. If it was anything like his sword, it would probably deliver a hell of a strike.

"Thanks," I said.

Russell nodded, then drew his rapier. Bloodshedder began growling softly.

Shocktooth looked at each of us in turn.

"What's wrong with you people?" she asked. "You're acting like you're heading for a fight or something."

I glanced sideways at her. "Seriously? How the hell have you survived on the streets so long if your instincts are so bad?"

Shocktooth looked puzzled, but she didn't say anything

more, and I was grateful. The last thing I wanted to do was head into danger with her yakking like an idiot. I get enough of that from Jinx.

The Rookery's main entrance is a large wooden door that wouldn't have been out of place on a medieval Earth castle. There were torches on either side of the door: horned demonic skulls with huge incisors, wreathed in scarlet flame.

As we drew close to the door, I said, "What's up, boys?"

The skulls didn't answer. That was a bad sign. The fireskulls are part of the Rookery's security system, and if they weren't working...

"I'll get the door," Jinx said.

I can open it myself, but it's a heavy bastard, so Jinx usually does the honors. I raised my new weapon, ready to slice anyone who tried to attack us. Jinx pulled the door open without a sound. Another bad sign. Incubi are born from humanity's fears, so they're theatrical by nature. The door was built to make an ominous creaking sound when opened. But it hadn't. I was beginning to suspect someone had deactivated the Rookery's security system.

Bloodshedder sniffed the air, her nostrils flaring wide as she drew in the scents around her. She began to whine, and I went cold at the sound. No one came running out to kill us, though, which was encouraging. I started to tell Jinx to go in slowly, but before I could, he raised Cuthbert Junior over his head and ran into the building, roaring a challenge. Jinx does not do stealthy.

Ah, what the hell? I thought and dashed in after Jinx. I heard Bloodshedder follow after me, and I assumed Russell brought up the rear, hauling Shocktooth along with him, but I didn't look back to make sure. The main entrance opens onto a short corridor, which leads to Level One, where the Shadow Watch divisions are located. I ran down the hall at my top speed, ignoring the protests of my sore head and my tired, aching muscles.

Despite its outward appearance, the Rookery is thoroughly modern inside, and the Shadow Watch's level looks like a standard corporate office. The only anachronistic touch is the stone column in the center of the level which houses the building's elevators.

The first time you enter the Rookery, it's actually more than a little disappointing, considering how much more... colorful the rest of Nod is. Normally, it's a beehive of activity, but now it was deathly quiet. Emphasis on *death*. Bodies of both Incubi and humans were scattered throughout the area. Some still sat at their desks, while others lay on the floor, struck down where they'd stood. Some of the people held trancers or M-blades, while others looked like they'd been trying to flee. Patrol officers or support staff, none had been spared.

The air had a faint sickly-sweet odor to it, like rotting apples. It was nauseating, and my stomach gave a lurch.

"Wow!" Shocktooth said as she gazed upon the bodies. She was obviously thrilled to see so many members of the Shadow Watch dead.

The sight of so many bodies was so overwhelming that I didn't feel anything at first, not even shock. As a mental defense, I went into professional mode and began logically assessing the scene.

"We need to check for survivors," I said. My voice was strong, my tone commanding. I sounded calm and confident, but inside I was screaming in despair.

"They're not dead," Jinx said.

"We'll need to split up," I continued. "Jinx, you take the left side of this level, I'll take the right, and Russell, you and Bloodshedder take the middle."

"They're not dead," Jinx repeated.

I went on. "If you find a survivor, call out. Any questions?"

Jinx placed Cuthbert Junior on a nearby desk, then pulled a rubber chicken from one of his pockets. With a swift motion, he wacked me in the side of the head with it.

My head started throbbing again, and anger welled up inside me. I pointed my new M-blade at him and took a step forward. "Why the hell did–" And then I realized what Jinx had been trying to tell me.

"They're not dead?"

"Not even a little," he said, tucking the rubber chicken away. "They're sleeping."

"*All* of them?"

"Well, that's what Bloodshedder says," Jinx added.

"You can understand her?"

"Sure. Can't you?"

I looked at Bloodshedder. "Is that true? They're just asleep?"

She barked once and wagged her spiked tail.

"Well, shit," Shocktooth said. "That sucks."

Jinx's rubber chicken made a fast reappearance, only now a large rectangular object lodged in its bulging belly. Jinx smashed the chicken into Shocktooth's head, and there was a loud crunching sound as the brick inside the chicken shattered. With the negator wrapped around her wrists, Shocktooth was no stronger or tougher than a human. Her eyes rolled white, and she collapsed to the floor, unconscious. Grinning, Jinx put the chicken away once more.

I was relieved no one had died, but I needed to be sure. I checked a couple of the bodies and found they both had pulses. I tried to rouse them, shaking their shoulders, lightly patting their cheeks, but nothing worked. I know everyone who works for the Shadow Watch, and although most of them are more acquaintances than friends, I was happy they were all alive and apparently unharmed. But my relief quickly gave way to puzzlement.

"Wait a minute. Incubi and Ideators *can't* sleep!"

"Looks like someone found a way to make them," Russell said.

Bloodshedder suddenly ran off, nose to the floor. She weaved between several desks, and then came trotting back, carrying a small object in her mouth. She dropped it in Russell's outstretched hand, and he patted her head. He then held up the object to examine it. It was round, about the size of a tennis ball, and its silver surface was shot through with multicolored threads of M-energy. A small nozzle protruded from the sphere. Russell looked at it closely, but he was too smart to touch it.

"It looks like some sort of grenade," I said.

"Designed to release a gas of some kind," Russell said. "If we look around, we'll probably find more. A lot more."

Gas. That explained the strange smell in the air.

"The Lords of Misrule," I said.

"Perchance to Dream," Jinx put in. "Advanced Sleep Solutions, remember?" He gestured at the unconscious Incubi and humans all around us. "I'd say this qualifies as pretty damn advanced, wouldn't you?"

I remembered the wonder drug Perchance to Dream had developed. "Do you think they used Torporian, maybe found a way to deliver it as a gas? But why would they attack the Rookery? What could they–" I broke off as a horrible realization came to me. "The Unwakened!"

I started running toward the elevators, weaving through the mass of unconscious bodies and, when necessary, leaping over them. I was dimly aware of Russell shouting to me, wanting to know what was wrong. I thought maybe he and Bloodshedder followed after me, but I wasn't sure.

I knew Jinx was close behind me, not only because I

could hear his gigantic bare feet slapping the floor, but because I could feel his presence in a way I never had before. Something had happened between us. I wasn't sure when or how it had occurred, but it seemed Jinx and I were more closely connected now. It wasn't as if we could read each other's thoughts, but we were more *aware* of one another in a way that's hard to describe. It's kind of like how you're aware of one of your arms. You just know it's there and what's more, you know what it's capable of.

When I reached the elevator, I stabbed the UP button and the door slid open with a ding. The car had been sitting on the ground floor. Without waiting for Russell, I ran in and hit the button for the Bower. I knew Jinx would slip inside before the door could close, and he did.

The Bower – where the Unwakened sleep and dream – is located on the top level of the Rookery. If something bad had happened to the Unwakened, it could prove cataclysmic, if not downright apocalyptic for Nod.

For all we knew, the Unwakened had been neutralized – I couldn't bring myself to think the word *killed* – in which case even now, the Canopy could be on the verge of collapse, and the Maelstrom would rush in like a variegated tsunami to engulf the city, breaking down its substance, along with everyone and everything in it, absorbing all that energy into itself until nothing and no one was left.

The elevator stopped at the top level, but the door didn't open immediately. No one could enter the Bower without authorization, and there was a keypad next to the elevator buttons on which to input an access code. Hardly anyone at the Rookery possessed the code. Sanderson did, along with the members of the Nightclad Council. As a lowly officer, I didn't have the code, but I did have something just as good. I had Jinx.

"Your move," I told him.

I had no idea how he could get the door to open, but he's a master of destructive mayhem, and I was confident he'd find a way. I just hoped I survived it.

He examined the keypad for a moment, his fingers tightening on Cuthbert Junior's handle. I thought he might swing the hammer into the keypad and destroy it, but instead he handed it to me, and then in the blink of an eye, he vanished. I'd never seen him do that before, and for a second I worried that something bad had happened to him. But I could still feel his presence through our new link, and I knew he was OK, wherever he was. A few moments later, sparks flew from the control panel, and Jinx sprang back into existence. An instant later, the elevator door opened with a soft ding.

Jinx reached out for his hammer, and I returned it to him.

"I got small and hopped inside the panel," he explained. Then he grinned. "I broke it."

"Um… you can shrink?" I asked.

He shrugged. "Sure. All clowns can. How do you think we fit so many of us into those little cars?"

"Good to know," I said.

I tightened my grip on my M-blade, Jinx squeezed Cuthbert Junior's handle, and we stepped out of the elevator, ready for whatever we'd find.

The Bower is protected by thick layers of stone threaded with solidified M-energy. The only access to it was via a gleaming white corridor lit by fluorescent ceiling lights. The corridor was lined with security cameras and alarm sensors, all of which appeared intact, as far as I could tell from where we stood. We moved down the corridor quickly but cautiously.

I listened, and I heard the sound of soft, gentle music coming from the other end of the corridor. I'd never been to the Bower before – as far as I knew, no officer had – but I'd heard that soothing music was played nonstop in the Bower to help the Unwakened remain asleep. In the old days, live singers and musicians had performed for the master dreamers, but now the music's recorded. Light classical and smooth jazz, from what I'd heard.

The music increased in volume as we made our way down the corridor, which opened on a domed chamber. The floor was stone, but the walls and ceiling were fashioned from some sort of crystalline substance I was unfamiliar with. It was cloudy and seemed to pulse softly with an inner light. The Unwakened slumbered on narrow beds encased in rounded glass boxes. There were twenty of them, all humans of different races and ethnicities, all extremely old, all dressed in white robes, hands clasped over their chests. Their biers lined the circumference of the Bower, their feet pointed toward the wall, their heads toward each other.

Jinx and I walked into the middle of the chamber. None of the cases appeared to have been tampered with, and there were no signs that anyone besides us had been here recently.

I relaxed a little. "I guess they're OK."

"How can you tell?" Jinx asked. "They all look like they're dead."

He had a point. I walked to the nearest case, which contained a woman with long white hair splayed out on her equally white pillow, and examined her closely. I couldn't tell if she was breathing, but I could see her eyes moving behind her eyelids as she dreamed.

I let out a relieved sigh. It seemed that Nod wasn't in danger of being destroyed anytime soon.

"Come on," I told Jinx. "We need to check on Sanderson."

We left the Bower and headed back down the corridor to

the elevator. Sanderson's office was located on Level Two, in Central Administration. Jinx's shorting out the security keypad hadn't affected the elevator's other functions, and when I pressed the button for Level Two, the door slid closed and the car descended. I hoped that we'd find Sanderson asleep like the others downstairs, but I feared we'd find him injured or dead. There had to be a reason for the attack on the Rookery, and if it hadn't been to go after the Unwakened, the only other target I could think of was Sanderson.

When the door opened, we headed down a curving hallway that wouldn't have been out of place in a modern office building on Earth. Just as we'd done in the Bower, we moved swiftly and silently, our motions perfectly synchronized. When we reached Sanderson's office, we found the door closed. I gave Jinx a nod, he grinned, and smashed the door down with Cuthbert Junior. I jumped into the room, blade in hand, ready for trouble.

But Sanderson wasn't in his office. Damon and Eklips were, though. Damon's throat had been cut and a large pool of blood had spread out around him. A pair of M-blades had been thrust into Eklips' eye sockets and into her brain. She'd bled, too, although not nearly as much as her partner. Incubi are hard to kill, but a pair of M-blades in the brain will do the job.

"Well," Jinx said. "Looks like the case is ours again."

ELEVEN

A half hour later, we had the situation at the Rookery under a rough semblance of control. I'd gone to Dispatch and put out a call for all available officers in the city to come in, and six teams – three Incubi and their Ideators – showed up. They regarded Russell and Bloodshedder with suspicion at first, but I'd vouched for the pair, and the officers accepted my word, if grudgingly.

Now two officers stood guard at the main gate, while the rest were checking the vital signs of the sleepers and doing their best to arrange their bodies in comfortable positions – which basically meant stretching them out on the floor. Jinx, Russell, Bloodshedder, and I made a quick search of the building, but we found no other casualties, only a lot more sleepers. And, as Russell had surmised, a lot more empty torporian grenades. We didn't find any sign of whoever had mounted the attack on the Rookery, though.

I hated to leave Damon and Eklips lying where they'd fallen, but I didn't know what else to do with them. Normally, forensic M-gineers would've examined the bodies for evidence, but – like everyone else who'd been in the Rookery during the attack – they were all sleeping. I decided we'd just have to preserve the crime scene for the time being and worry about it later. Damon and Eklips had been officers. They would've understood.

We might not have known who killed them, but we had a good idea how it had been done. Once Damon and Eklips had been knocked out by torporian gas, it would've been child's play to kill them. They wouldn't have been able to put up even token resistance. The cold-blooded nature of their murders filled me with rage and disgust, and I vowed to bring their killers to justice – or better yet, let Jinx have his fun with them.

We put Shocktooth, who by this time had regained consciousness, into a holding cell in Detention, and Jinx and I picked up new trancers and wispers from the Armory. Russell let me keep my new M-blade, which I appreciated. Jinx and I were also able to clean up a bit and put on a fresh change of clothes. The latter entailed "borrowing" uniforms from a pair of sleeping officers. Not one of my prouder moments on the force, I must admit. Jinx also somehow managed to find – or more likely generate – a new boutonnière and a pair of oversized shoes.

The Shadow Watch keeps med kits around for its human officers, and I grabbed some pain pills and swallowed them with some lukewarm coffee I found in the break room. My head didn't hurt as much as it had when we arrived, but I didn't want any distractions. Plus, I needed the caffeine badly. So much so that I downed the rest of the pot.

I told the other officers to stay behind, guard the Unwakened, and wait for everyone else to come out of their torporian-induced comas. I wasn't a senior officer, and I couldn't order them, but they agreed, probably because the situation was such a clusterfuck, they didn't know what else to do. Afterward, Jinx, Russell, Bloodshedder and I hauled ass out of there.

The four of us hurried through the streets of Oldtown,

looking for a Door. Not just any Door, though. We needed one that would take us back to Chicago. Actually, only Jinx and Bloodshedder were searching for a Door. Russell and I, with only our dull human senses to guide us, were just along for the ride.

"Sanderson could be anywhere," Russell said as we jogged after our Incubi. "In Nod *or* on Earth." He paused. "Unless he wasn't abducted at all."

I frowned. "Are you implying that Sanderson was behind the attack on the Rookery? That he's an ally of the Lords of Misrule?"

"Or a full-fledged member. How much do you – or anyone at the Shadow Watch, for that matter – know about him?"

I wanted to defend Sanderson, but Russell was right. I knew next to nothing about the man who was my commander. Hell, I didn't even know if he was human, Incubus, or something else altogether.

"Until I find out otherwise, I'm going to assume Sanderson was abducted, and I'm going to do everything I can to find him. If you've got a problem with that, you're free to go back to your mysterious employers – whoever they may be – and see if they have any other errands for you to run."

Russell gave me a hurt, angry look, but he said nothing more.

We'd come to Hearthstone, one of the oldest neighborhoods in Oldtown, little more than a collection of wattle-and-daub huts with thatched roofs. What light there was here came primarily from Espial above, although there were cook fires burning outside some of the huts. The Incubi here dressed in coarsely woven plain tunics and dresses, and they eyed us with suspicion as we passed. Most of the elder Incubi had long ago moved to the Aerie or to Newtown, but these were the diehards – the Incubi determined to live exactly as they had during their time on Earth – and they didn't take too kindly to outsiders.

Bloodshedder let out a yip, and Jinx groaned. "You found one? All right, you win."

Bloodshedder wagged her tail in victory as she bounded forward, tongue lolling out the side of her mouth. I had to admit, she was kind of cute in a terrifying way. She ran to a hut, sniffed at the simple wooden door, snorted, then ran around to the side. We followed, and although we only had Espial's light to see by, the outline of a Door was clearly visible in the outer wall. It was a modern door, with a chrome frame and square panes of glass. Nothing was visible behind the glass, only darkness, as if the panes were coated with thick layers of black paint. The Door had a vertical metal handle.

Jinx looked at Bloodshedder. "Better leave this to someone with opposable thumbs." He stuck his tongue out at her, then stepped forward, took hold of the anachronistic handle, and opened the Door to reveal black Nothingness.

Jinx grinned at me and made a sweeping gesture to the open doorway and the darkness that lay beyond. "After you, Audra."

Not *Mommy*.

Despite my discomfort at traveling between dimensions, I returned Jinx's smile.

"Thank you, good sir."

I took a deep breath and stepped through the doorway. I experienced the same sensations I always do – the long period of floating in a lightless limbo, the dizziness, the nausea... And I heard the same eerie whispers. Only now, I thought I was able to make out what they were saying. It sounded like *Hurry, hurry, hurry...*

And then I stepped through another Door and into the

Chicago night. A breeze was blowing – big surprise – and I could smell Lake Michigan. As the others came through behind me, I tried to get my bearings. Narrow streets, small buildings, fast food joints, convenience stores... I recognized this area. We weren't that far from the Lincoln Park Zoo.

The Door – which Russell closed after he stepped through – was set into the outer wall of a souvenir shop, the kind of place where tourists can buy replicas of the Sears Tower, and Bears and Cubs T-shirts and hats. I checked the time with my wisper and saw it was almost 1.30 in the morning. The sidewalks were empty, which is good when you're traveling with a six-and-a-half-foot clown, a guy in a pirate outfit, and a huge demonic canine.

"So, what's the plan?" Russell asked. "You want Bloodshedder to try and track Sanderson?"

She looked at Russell and whined.

"I know it's a long shot," he said. "But your sense of smell is stronger than any Earth dog. If we criss-cross the city long enough, there's a chance you might pick up his trail."

I shook my head. "They've taken him to Perchance to Dream. Where else could they go?"

"Anywhere on Earth or Nod," Jinx said.

I scowled at him.

"What? It's true, isn't it?"

"Technically," I allowed. "But the Lords of Misrule wouldn't have abducted Sanderson unless they had a use for him. If they just wanted him out of the way, they could've killed him, just like they did Damon and Eklips."

"Maybe," Russell said. "But what if you're wrong? If we hightail it to Perchance to Dream and Sanderson isn't there, all we'll do is alert the Lords that we're on to them, and wherever Sanderson really is, they'll move him. We might lose our only chance to get him back. I say we let Bloodshedder take a shot at finding him."

I knew what Russell proposed was logical, but I couldn't stop thinking about those voices in the void, whispering for me to hurry, hurry.

"That would take too long. I can't explain it, but I've got a gut feeling that whatever move we're going to make, we have to make it fast."

Russell started to protest, but before he could get a word out, Jinx stepped close and put an arm around my shoulders.

"If there's one thing I've learned during my years of working with Audra, it's to pay attention when her gut starts talking. It makes the most interesting sounds. Squishy, rumbly, gurgly sounds mostly, but every once in a while, it makes these cute little high-pitched noises that sound like whale song. It's really quite—"

I elbowed him in the ribs, cutting him off.

"Thanks for the vote of confidence."

I lifted my wisper to my mouth and spoke a command. "Search for phone number. Name: Connie Desposito." I hadn't had time to program any numbers into my new wisper, but I knew her name was in the Shadow Watch database that lists all registered Incubi and Ideators on Earth.

A soft chime sounded, indicating her number had been found.

"Call," I said. She picked up after the second ring.

"Yeah?"

"Hey, Connie. It's Audra. Jinx and I need a ride. It's an emergency. Big time."

There was a second's hesitation, but then she said, "No problem. Where are you?"

I checked the nearest street sign, told her our location,

and she said, "Be there in a few minutes."

I thanked her and lowered my wrist. The wisper, sensing the movement, disconnected.

"Before she gets here, there's something we need to take care of," I said. "Jinx and I experienced two Incursions in a row, almost as if they were targeted on us. I think they were. We need to make sure that doesn't happen again."

"*Targeted* Incursions?" Russell said. "How is that possible?"

"Your people have better toys than the Shadow Watch," I said. "Maybe the Lords have better than both." I smiled. "*And* I have a theory. Jinx was struck by a number of Quietus' dark shards when he attacked us last night. What if one of those shards did more than just cut Jinx? What if it *implanted* something inside him?"

"Without even buying me dinner first?" Jinx said. "How rude!"

"Like some kind of targeting device?" Russell asked. He thought for a moment. "Yeah, I suppose that's possible."

I turned to Jinx. "Strip."

His features twisted into an exaggerated expression of horror. "Audra! You're my partner, and I respect you immensely, but you are in a very real sense my creator. I appreciate your… uh, interest. I can't blame you. After all, I *am* one hundred percent, grade-A, prime clown beefcake. But I don't think a relationship of an, er, intimate nature between us would be appropriate. In other words – *eew!*"

"You're not funny," I said. "Now take your clothes off. For the First Dreamer's sake, most of the time I have trouble convincing you to keep your damn clothes *on*."

Jinx removed his jacket, tie, shirt, pants, and shoes, until his lean but well-muscled chalk-white body was revealed. Not counting the bits still concealed by his Bozo the Clown boxers.

"Now *there's* a sight I could've gone to my grave without seeing," Russell said.

Jinx's lips curled away from teeth suddenly grown sharp. "I can arrange your trip to the afterlife any time you want."

Bloodshedder started growling.

I held Jinx's clothes, and I made sure to keep my hands away from his pockets. I didn't want to risk any of his murderous novelty items taking my fingers off.

"Knock it off, you three. Bloodshedder, give Jinx a good all-over sniff and see if you can find any foreign objects in his body."

"I had Chinese the other day," Jinx said. "Does that count?"

Bloodshedder glanced at Russell, and he nodded. Looking none too happy about it, Bloodshedder padded over to Jinx and began sniffing him.

"Careful there, Lassie!" Jinx said. "You and I barely know one another!"

Bloodshedder snorted to show she didn't think he was funny either, and continued with her work. After a few moments, she jumped up, put her front paws on Jinx's shoulder, and with a swift, savage motion she bit a hunk of flesh out of Jinx's chest. Jinx shouted a word that's probably frowned upon even in nightmare clown society, and clapped a hand to the wound to stop the bleeding.

Bloodshedder – who'd once again lived up to her name – jumped down and spat a gore-smeared piece of clown meat onto the sidewalk. Then she grimaced.

"Sorry," Jinx said. "It's the chalky aftertaste."

Russell and I knelt down, and I drew my new M-blade and prodded the flesh. I saw a small metallic sphere the size of a BB embedded in the meat. I pried it loose with the tip of my blade and then took hold of it between my thumb and forefinger. It was slick with blood, so I cleaned it on Jinx's pants.

I looked at Jinx then. "You need a bandage?"

He removed his hand from his wound. His fingers were bloody, but his chest wound was already sealing itself.

"I'm good," he said. He then glared at Bloodshedder. "Better watch out. Next time, I'll bite *you*." He once again flashed a mouthful of sharp teeth.

Unimpressed, Bloodshedder yawned.

I tossed Jinx's clothes to him. By this point, his body had reabsorbed the blood on his hand, and he was able to handle his clothing without staining it. He started to get dressed while Russell and I examined the tiny sphere.

"Looks awfully small to be a targeting device," Russell said.

"If the Lords can create Incursions at will – including during the day – then they should be able to handle a bit of miniaturization," I said.

"Point taken."

Jinx dressed quickly. Since whatever clothes Night Jinx wears become a part of his substance in ways I've never understood, they practically flowed onto him. He then stepped over and examined the sphere.

"You want me to smash it?" he asked.

"No. If we do that, the Lords might know we found and removed it."

"We can't just toss it into a Dumpster or the sewer," Russell said. "If it also functions as a tracking device, the Lords will get suspicious if it looks like Jinx is remaining in one place the rest of the night."

"No worries," Jinx said. He reached into his pants pocket, rummaged around for a couple seconds and then pulled out a white rat. Well, most of its fur was white. On its head were blue and red markings that matched the color design of Jinx's face. Jinx made some squeaking sounds to the rat, and the rat answered him back in kind. Jinx then took the sphere and held it out to the rodent. The rat swallowed it, and then Jinx knelt and placed the animal on the sidewalk.

As he straightened, he said, "Try not to poop it out too soon, Itchy. Clench if you have to."

The rat squeaked once more and then scurried into a nearby alley.

Russell looked at me, and I shrugged.

"You have to admit, he's not boring," I said.

Jinx grinned.

Connie arrived soon after that, and Russell, Jinx, and I climbed into the Deathmobile, which was in its hearse Aspect. Russell and Jinx sat in the back, and I sat in the front next to Connie. Bloodshedder remained on the sidewalk.

"She'll be able to get to where we're going faster on her own," Russell said.

"We're going to Wet Dreams," I told her.

Bloodshedder yipped once, and then turned and bounded off down the sidewalk, moving like a shadow, swift and silent.

I closed the passenger door and looked at Connie. "Let's go."

"You got it, Audra." She put the hearse in gear, and the Deathmobile glided away from the curb.

"You said this was an emergency?" she asked.

"It sure as hell is."

She grinned. "Then you three better buckle up."

We quickly did as Connie suggested. She then reached out, patted the dashboard, and spoke a single word. "Engage."

The Deathmobile's engine rumbled, the sound building

in volume and intensity, and then we were thrown back against the seats as the unearthly vehicle surged forward like a rocket.

"Hope you guys can handle some extra Gs!" Connie shouted over the engine's roar.

I closed my eyes, gritted my teeth, and did my best to hold onto consciousness as the Deathmobile hurtled through the streets of Chicago.

The Deathmobile decelerated as we approached Wet Dreams, which I was very grateful for. If the hearse had slammed on the brakes, I probably would've gone flying through the windshield, seatbelt or not. When the vehicle stopped, I told Connie to wait for us.

"And keep the engine running," I said.

Connie looked at me. "You weren't kidding when you said this was an emergency, were you?"

"Nope."

She nodded. "We'll be waiting."

Jinx, Russell, and I started toward Wet Dreams' entrance, but before we reached it, a pair of figures stepped out of the alley. One was an emaciated bald man in jeans and a leather jacket, a smoldering cigarette in his mouth. His face was little more than a flesh-covered skull, and his eyes were a glowing fiery orange. Instead of fingers, he had cigarettes for digits, each one lit, smoke curling from the burning tips. The other figure, a female, wore a tank top and shorts, and her blond hair looked frizzed out as if she'd been subjected to an electric shock. There were dark circles around her eyes, and her lips were a harsh, cruel red. But her most striking feature was her legs. They were impossibly long and multi-jointed, like those of some hideously mutated insect.

The male flexed his cigarette fingers and flames sprouted

from the tips, but no matter how much they burned, his fingers didn't decrease in length. The female flicked her wrists and from nowhere a pair of curved steel daggers appeared in her hands.

The male smiled, and when he opened his mouth to speak, gray smoke wafted forth.

"We were hoping you'd stop by tonight," Cancer Jack said, his voice crackling like burning paper.

Lizzie Longlegs smiled sweetly as her bizarrely angled legs quivered in excitement. "Payback's a bitch, and so am I," she said.

I grinned at them. "I'm so glad to see you two!"

Jack and Lizzie glanced at each other, then turned back to look at us.

"Um, you realize we're here to kick your asses, right?" Lizzie said.

"You can do that later," I said. "Right now we have bigger problems. Come on."

Without waiting for either of them to reply, I opened the door to Wet Dreams and stepped inside. A blast of noise hit me the instant I walked in – a mix of conversation, laughter, shouting, and music. The place was packed wall to wall, mostly with Incubi, but there was a scattering of humans in the crowd. It was hot as a blast furnace inside, and when I took a breath, it felt as if I were sucking in wet sand. I pulled my dream catcher badge from my jacket and held it high over my head.

"This is a raid!" I shouted.

Everyone got quiet.

"Seriously?" someone said.

"Not really," I admitted. "I just need to get to the bar."

With much grunting and complaining, people made a path for us. I put my badge away and charged forward, the others following after me, including Jack and Lizzie, who had put their weapons away – or in Jack's case, extinguished his finger-flames – for the time being, at least.

Abe was in his usual seat at the bar, and I wondered if he'd gone home since the last time I'd seen him. Despite how crowded it was tonight, there were a number of empty seats at the bar, and I realized why when I saw Maggie sitting next to a tall, broad-shouldered figure garbed in a hooded black robe. Given how terrifying the Darkness can be in his Night Aspect, I was surprised that anyone was still in the bar. I figured Deacon must've been pouring the drinks extra-strong tonight.

Speaking of Deacon Booze, he was, as always, behind the bar. He was in his Night Aspect, which is truly a sight to behold. He's a large humanoid garbed in his usual clothing, albeit several sizes larger to fit this Aspect's frame. But while his body resembles a human's, his head is that of an elephant with long ivory tusks. A *pink* elephant.

I don't know what alcoholic dreamed up Deacon or how long ago it was, but every time I see him in his Night Aspect, it takes everything I've got not to burst out laughing. Don't tell him, though. I don't want to hurt his feelings. Or worse – piss him off so he won't pass along info to Jinx and me anymore.

I moved to the empty spot near Maggie and the Darkness, and gestured for Deacon to come over. Jinx, Russell, Jack, and Lizzie gathered behind me.

"Hello, Audra," Maggie said. "It's good to see you again so soon!" She glanced at Russell. "I see you found the young man you were looking for. He fills out that pirate costume quite well, don't you think?"

Deacon joined us. "Two nights in a row, Audra? It must be my lucky week."

His trunk hung down slack on his chest, partially covering his mouth and muffling his voice. He stood several feet back from the bar's edge to keep his tusks from spearing his customers.

I skipped the small talk. I drew my trancer, flicked the selector switch to the highest setting, and pointed the muzzle at a spot right between his eyes.

"Cut the master-of-the-house routine. I want you to tell me everything you know about the Lords' plan – and don't leave out a single detail."

Deacon's elephant eyes flashed with anger, but when he spoke, his voice remained calm.

"You know I don't work that way, Audra."

"I don't care about your stupid rules. The Lords have abducted Sanderson – as you probably know by now – and they've got some kind of tech they've been using to create Incursions. I intend to get my boss back and shut down the Lords' operation. And you're going to help me do that, whether you like it or not."

The anger in Deacon's eyes blazed hotter, and his pink complexion edged toward crimson. When he spoke this time, while his tone remained calm on the surface, I could hear the tension beneath.

"Go ahead and shoot. I'll recover much faster than you think. And in the meantime, you'll have to deal with a lot of angry customers who are wondering why I'm not serving them."

I'd been so focused on Deacon that I hadn't noticed all conversation in the bar had ceased. I didn't take my gaze off Deacon, but I could imagine Wet Dreams' clientele all staring at me silently, trying to decide what, if anything, they should do. I might've been an officer of the Shadow Watch – which for a lot of people here was more than enough reason to hate me – but I was also a human. Incubi, especially those who are no longer bonded to an Ideator, didn't appreciate a human giving orders to one of their kind. Especially when the Incubus being ordered is someone as beloved as Deacon Booze. Even with Jinx and Russell backing me up, I knew I wouldn't stand a chance against everyone in the bar.

The tension in the air grew thicker by the second, and I knew that something was going to have to break soon.

When Maggie spoke next to me, I was so surprised, I nearly jumped.

"Now, dear, you really don't want to shoot Deacon, do you?"

I didn't answer and my gun hand didn't waver.

Maggie looked at Deacon. "Yes, you'll heal from a trancer blast, even one at full power. But doing so would be awfully inconvenient, wouldn't it? Not to mention painful."

Deacon didn't respond to her, either.

Maggie turned around on her seat to face the rest of the bar. She raised her voice so everyone could hear her.

"And you've all been talking and fretting about the Incursions most of the night. I've heard the questions you've been asking one another. What's causing them? Are they going to get worse? What will happen if they don't stop? If Deacon knows anything that could help Audra stop the Incursions, don't you think he should tell her?"

Deacon and I continued our staring contest, while his patrons murmured uncertainly among themselves. No one did anything for several moments, and then – without lifting his head or raising his voice – the Darkness said, "You should all listen to Maggie."

His voice didn't drip with menace, nor did it echo eerily throughout the bar. In fact, he didn't sound much different than he did in his Day Aspect. But the effect of the Darkness' voice was profound as it was instant. The Darkness was one of the most powerful types of Incubi – a fear-caster. And his ability to evoke terror in those around him worked on humans and Incubi alike. So when the Darkness spoke, everyone listened. I felt a surge of momentary panic wash over me like a cold wave, and I gritted my teeth and tensed my muscles until it passed.

I sighed and holstered my trancer. "We really need your help, Deacon." I tried not to sound as desperate as I felt. "All of us do – Incubi and human, Earth and Nod."

He continued to stare at me for another few seconds before the tension left his body and he relaxed.

"Very well, I'll help. On the house, even. But don't think you can take advantage of me like this in the future," he warned.

"Noted," I said, smiling with relief.

I turned to Jinx. Now that the threat of violence had ended, he looked like a kid who'd just been informed that Christmas was canceled this year.

"I'm not going to get to hurt *anyone?*" He made a pouty face.

"Cheer up," I told him. "I have a feeling you're going to get your chance to wreak maximum havoc soon."

He grinned. "It's about damn time."

"Could you scoot over a little, please?" Abe asked.

Lizzie glared at him, but she did as he asked, although it wasn't easy, given the way her legs were folded.

The Deathmobile might be larger in its Night Aspect compared to its day form, but it was still a tight fit for all of us. Jinx, Russell, and I sat in front with Connie. I sat on Russell's lap – purely out of necessity, of course. Jack, Lizzie, Maggie, and Abe were jammed shoulder to shoulder in the backseat, and Bloodshedder – who'd been waiting for us in the alley – lay half on, half off the closed casket in the rear of the vehicle. I had no idea if there was something in the casket; up to that point, I hadn't had the courage to ask Connie.

The Darkness wasn't with us. As soon as we were on the street, he simply disappeared into the shadows.

"He'll meet us there," Maggie had explained.

I didn't ask her how the Darkness traveled; I figured the less I knew about him, the better.

Connie drove at the Deathmobile's top speed, and we were all pressed back against the seats – or in my case, against Russell – as the vehicle rocketed through the streets. I thanked the First Dreamer that it was so late; otherwise, the traffic would've been too thick even for the Deathmobile to maneuver at this speed.

I wasn't comfortable that Maggie and Abe had insisted on joining the rest of us for our assault on Perchance to Dream. Maggie's presence was a necessity because the Darkness wouldn't have agreed to help us without her. But Abe didn't have an Incubus – and probably never had – and he wasn't trained for combat, at least as far as I knew. I was surprised when he insisted on accompanying us, and I'd almost told him he couldn't, but then the Darkness had said, "Let him." So, to keep the Darkness happy, I agreed.

Besides, Abe was probably holding, and while I'd gone without pharmaceutical help for half a day – not counting the headache pills I'd taken at the Rookery – there was a chance I might need a boost before this was all said and done. None of the Incubi seemed to care that Maggie and Abe were coming with us. They were used to doing crazy things.

"I'm still not clear on why we're helping you instead of beating the holy living shit out of you," Jack said. Smoke curled out of his mouth as he spoke.

Abe coughed and Maggie cracked open a window.

"Mayhem, remember?" Lizzie said. "Lots and lots of it."

Jack smiled, revealing nicotine-stained teeth. "That's right! Bring it on, baby!"

The stink of tobacco on his breath was fierce, but Jinx can produce some nasty smells of his own when he wants to, and Jack's stink-breath was like roses in comparison.

As the Deathmobile raced toward our destination, I couldn't help fearing that we'd be hit with another Incursion along the way, but removing the tiny metal sphere from Jinx seemed to have done the trick – because nothing happened.

Our grand plan? We didn't really have one. Look, I'm a cop, not a military strategist. And it's almost impossible to strategize when your enemy isn't human and doesn't always think rationally – or at least in ways humans recognize as rational. Plus, I kept hearing the voices in the void whispering for me to hurry, hurry, hurry. Regardless of whether those voices were real or imaginary, I couldn't escape the feeling that it was more important that whatever we were going to do, we did it fast. And yes, it did occur to me that I wasn't acting anymore rationally than an Incubus. So what?

After a bit, Abe spoke. "I wish Budgie were here. I'm sure he'd be a big help."

"Budgie?" Russell said in my ear.

"His Incubus. It left him a long time ago." I lowered my voice to a whisper. "At least, that's what he likes to pretend."

Abe whistled a trio of notes: one high, one low, one high. "That's how I used to call him. He loved to fly. He was a bird, you know. He'd take off and sometimes I wouldn't see him for hours. But he always came back when I whistled. Until one day he didn't. I was afraid he'd gotten lost somehow, and I went all over town whistling for him. I kept searching for days, but I never found him.

I hope nothing bad happened to him. I like to think that he fell in love with the freedom of flying so much that he couldn't bring himself to be tied down by me. I hope that's all it was. I hope I didn't do anything to drive him away."

I turned to look at Abe and saw Maggie patting his hand in sympathy. I wondered if she believed his story, and then I decided it wouldn't matter to her if he was telling the truth or not. Either way, she would've comforted him. I turned back around, and we continued driving in silence.

It seemed to take only a few more moments for us to leave the city and enter the suburbs. As we turned onto the street where Perchance to Dream was located, Russell shifted beneath me, and I felt something hard poke my behind.

I looked at him. "I could make a joke and ask if that's your rapier or if you're just glad to see me – but I won't."

His cheeks colored a bit as he replied, "I appreciate your restraint."

Despite our attempt to fool the Lords by giving the targeting device to Itchy, I had to assume they knew we were coming. There was an excellent chance that someone who'd been in the crowd at Wet Dreams was on their payroll, just as Shocktooth had been. Probably multiple someones. The moment we'd walked out of the bar, those someones had been on the phone to Perchance to Dream. And if that was the case, then the Lords would be ready and waiting.

As we approached the building, I said, "Get ready, everyone. And as Jinx always says..."

He grinned. "It's showtime!"

Connie yanked the Deathmobile's wheel to the left, its unearthly tires quite literally shrieked, and we shot into the parking lot. Fluorescent light from the streetlamps in the lot provided sufficient illumination, and we could see rows of parked cars. Parker Schulte had told us Perchance to Dream operated around the clock, which only made sense as it was staffed by Incubi who never needed to sleep.

Our plan was a simple one, so much so that it didn't really deserve to be called a plan. More like a half-assed idea. We were going to drive right up the building's entrance, get out, rush inside, and start fucking shit up. Like I said, not much of a plan, but when you've got powerful Incubi on your side, you don't need much more. Or so I hoped.

But before we could make it halfway across the parking lot, the air outside the Deathmobile shimmered, and I experienced a too-familiar sensation of vertigo and nausea.

"They're throwing an Incursion at us!" I shouted. "Be—"

My words were cut off as a dozen of the cars in the parking lot began to twist and reform, – their bodies, frames, engines, transmissions, tires, and interiors merging and rearranging in seconds to form a trio of mechanical monsters, each of which stood twenty feet tall. The makeshift creatures had multiple headlights for eyes, grills for mouths, engines for chests, and tires for hands and feet. The light glowing in their eyes was a roiling mix of colors, and I knew we were seeing the Maelstrom energy that animated them. The creatures looked exactly like what they were: nightmares made real.

One of the metal giants rolled forward on its wheeled feet to block our path. Connie stomped on the brake pedal, although it was obvious she didn't have enough room to stop. She shouted, "Hey, DM! A little help!"

The Deathmobile's headlight beams turned green, and it trained the light onto the car-bot as we skidded toward it. The verdant beams struck the creature's engine-block chest, and the metal began to rapidly corrode. But not, however, rapidly enough to prevent the car-bot from stepping forward and slamming its tire hands down on the

Deathmobile's hood. The car-bot struck the hearse's hood off-center, and the impact sent the Deathmobile into a spin. Connie swore, Maggie screamed, Abe remained silent, Bloodshedder started barking – and Jack, Lizzie, and Jinx whooped with delight like they were on a carnival ride.

Incubi...

Russell grabbed hold of me – or maybe I grabbed him. I can't remember. Connie worked the steering wheel furiously, trying to keep us from flipping over. The Deathmobile's spin came to a sudden, jarring halt when the driver's side slammed into one of the light poles. We sat there for a moment, stunned. The Deathmobile's engine was still running, but the sound was softer, intermittent, as if the hearse was in pain. And since the Deathmobile is an Incubus instead of a true machine, I suppose it really was hurting.

Speaking of hurting, my head was throbbing again, and when I turned to see Russell, I saw why. Blood ran from his nose like a faucet, and I realized the back of my head had slammed into his face when we hit the streetlamp.

"We need to get out of here!" Maggie said. "They're coming!"

She didn't have to tell me that *they* were the car-bots.

Jinx opened the passenger door and hopped out, and I scooted off Russell's lap and followed. Connie was groggy. Her forehead had bounced off the steering wheel during the wreck. I guess she didn't dream the Deathmobile with airbags. Russell took hold of her arm and pulled her out of the car. Jack, Lizzie, Maggie, and Abe followed. Bloodshedder kicked open the Deathmobile's back door and wriggled out tail-first.

The three car-bots rolled toward us, headlight eyes blazing with Maelstrom energy, arms raised, tire hands ready to smash down upon us.

TWELVE

I wasn't worried about the Incubi having been injured in the crash. If they'd been hurt, they'd heal eventually. Despite Russell's bloody and possibly broken nose, he seemed OK, and I felt all right aside from a renewed headache. I wasn't certain about Connie, Maggie, and Abe, but there wasn't time to check them over. I'd just have to hope they weren't seriously injured.

Jack and Lizzie didn't waste any time. The couple ran forward to meet the car-bots' attack, savage grins on their faces.

"Wait for me!" Jinx called. Cuthbert Junior appeared in his hand as if by magic, and he went running after his fellow Incubi, eager to cause some damage at last.

I heard Connie say, "Oh, my poor baby! Look what they did to you!"

I hadn't had time to do more than glance at the Deathmobile, but I knew it too would heal, so I wasn't concerned about it. Instead, I focused on the immediate and rapidly approaching threat: the car-bots. I drew my trancer, flicked the selector to high, and aimed it at the advancing machine-golems.

Each of the Incubi chose one of the car-bots and headed for it. Lizzie reached hers first, scuttling toward it swiftly on her multi-jointed insect legs. She leaped onto its body and skittered upward, hacking at the creature with her unnaturally sharp knives as she went, slicing hoses and belts, and cutting jagged furrows in its metal.

Streams of fire shot forth from Jack's cigarette fingers to engulf the tire feet of his car-bot. Rubber and asphalt melted together, and the car-bot was stuck fast. Its feet might have been sealed in place, but its momentum caused its body to pitch forward, and the car-bot smashed face-first into the ground, metal tearing and crumpling.

Springs shot out from Jinx's gigantic shoes, propelling him into the air and toward the third car-bot. Bloodshedder – not to be left out – bounded after him. Jinx raised Cuthbert Junior high over his head as he hurtled toward the car-bot. The springs retracted into his shoes an instant before he landed on the machine-monster's left shoulder.

Jinx slammed his sledgehammer into the side of the car-bot's head, the impact making a tremendous sound and causing a number of the creature's headlight eyes to explode outward. The car-bot's head bent to the right so far that I thought it would fall off, but it managed to remain attached, although it didn't straighten. I didn't know if the metal giant had enough sentience to be angry at Jinx, but it reached for him with one of its tire hands, as if he were an irritating bug that needed to be swatted.

But before the car-bot could strike Jinx, Bloodshedder leaped into the air and sank her diamond-hard teeth into the creature's wrist. The car-bot let out a shrill honking sound, as if it were in pain, and tried to shake Bloodshedder loose. The demon dog was flung around like a rag doll, but she refused to release her grip on the monster's arm. Jinx took advantage of the distraction Bloodshedder had created. With an insane cackle that would've given insomnia to an asylum full of lunatics, Jinx slammed Cuthbert Junior into the car-bot's head, over and over again.

I could feel the savage joy he took in the destruction he was causing, and I didn't want to spoil his fun, but as the saying goes, we had bigger fish to fry. I aimed my trancer at his car-bot, preparing to unleash a blast of M-energy at the creature's chest, hopefully finishing it off. Before I could fire, I heard Maggie cry out, "Abe!"

I spun around to see that the streetlamp the Deathmobile had hit had become animate, and like a constricting serpent, it had wrapped around Abe and lifted him into the air. Like the car-bots, its bulb shone with Maelstrom energy.

I wanted to shoot the damn thing, hoping to overload it with enough Maelstrom energy to at least stun it into releasing Abe. But he was held in the lamp's metal coils fifteen feet off the ground, and I was afraid the fall to the hard asphalt would injure him as severely as the lamp would. Then I saw his bulging eyes and gaping mouth as he struggled for air. His face began to turn purple, and I knew if I didn't do something immediately, he would die.

Maggie and Connie stood beneath Abe, shouting for him to hold on. Russell ran toward the base of the lamp and began stabbing it with his rapier. The lamp-serpent ignored the strikes from Russell's sword and continued waving Abe back and forth as it squeezed the life out of him, making it difficult for me to get a good shot. I knew Abe couldn't afford for me to wait for the perfect opportunity, though, so I started firing, trusting to luck and skill – but mostly luck. A beam of multicolored energy lanced forth from my trancer, but it missed. My second shot came close, but not close enough. My third shot did the trick, though. The beam clipped the edge of one of the coils encircling Abe, and although it was a glancing blow, it was enough. The coils slackened and Abe slipped free.

Russell dropped his sword and moved beneath Abe, as if to catch him, or at least break his fall with his own body. But just as Abe started to fall, a figure emerged from a pool of shadow on the ground. Then the Darkness stepped in front of Russell and caught Abe as easily as if the man weighed no more than a child's balloon.

The "head" of the lamp-serpent lunged toward them, but I fired once more, this time hitting the lamp's bulb. It shattered, the Maelstrom energy winked out, and the lamp's movement ceased, leaving it nothing more than a looping, curved statue.

I turned and shouted to the other Incubi. "Put out their eyes!"

None of the Incubi questioned me, and why would they? As far as they were concerned, I'd just said, "Let the good times roll."

Lizzie crawled around the side of the car-bot, up its spine, onto its head, and then hung down in front of its face. She thrust her curved blades into its multiple headlight eyes, one after the other – *pop-pop-pop!* – as fast as she could. Jack thrust his hands toward the car-bot he'd downed, which was busy attempting to pull its legs free of the melted asphalt that held it fast. The cigarettes that formed his fingers flew off like ten small white rockets, trailing lines of flame as they flew toward the car-bot's eyes and shattered them.

Jinx kept pounding on his car-bot's head, taking out more headlights with each blow, until finally all the headlights were out. The creature stopped moving, and Bloodshedder's weight finally pulled it to the ground. Both Jinx and Bloodshedder leaped free as the car-bot crashed into a half-dozen untransformed vehicles, crushing them. A moment later, it was joined by Lizzie's car-bot, which also crashed into a number of parked cars. Jack's car-bot was already on the ground, and it simply stopped moving once its headlights were out. The monstrous metal creatures were now nothing more than scrap.

The Darkness was still holding Abe. He put him down gently, and Maggie ran over to check if Abe was all right. I realized that Maggie and Abe, while perhaps not a couple per se, were at least sweet on each other. I wondered if they'd been aware of that themselves until this moment. I understood then why Abe had wanted so badly to come along with us. He hadn't been able to stand the idea of Maggie going into danger without him. He'd wanted to protect her. Instead, she – or at least her Incubus – had been the one doing the protecting.

Jinx came toward me, grinning and spinning Cuthbert Junior in one hand as if it were a baton.

"That was a nice warm-up," he said.

"Warm-up?" Maggie asked. She, the Darkness, and Abe joined us in the middle of the parking lot, as did Russell, Bloodshedder, Jack, and Lizzie. Connie remained with the Deathmobile, stroking its hood softly as the car worked on repairing itself.

"There's more to come," Russell said.

"A lot more," I added.

"One can only hope," Jinx said, still grinning. As long as there was violence in the offing, that grin wouldn't leave his face.

The Deathmobile, though still damaged, was now in a hell of a lot better shape than it had been when the fight with the car-bots had started. It was more or less in good shape again, although it still had a multitude of dents and scratches across its surface, and its windshield and windows were still spiderwebbed with cracks. But its engine sounded stronger, if still a bit unsteady, and its right headlight gleamed with life, although its left remained broken and dark. Connie continued to stroke the vehicle's hood, and the Deathmobile's engine seemed to purr in response.

"What should we do next?" Abe asked.

Before I could answer, the door to the building burst open, and Incubi flooded into the parking lot, bellowing with rage and bloodlust as they ran toward us. None of them were armed from what I could see, and most were dressed in work clothes – suits and ties, blouses with slacks or skirts. But that's where the similarity to normal office workers ended.

Some resembled animals – mammals, reptiles, avians, sea creatures, insects, or bizarre combinations thereof. Others looked as if they'd started life as inanimate objects – wood, stone, metal, glass, plastic... Some defied easy description, forms and faces so distorted, the human eye could barely make sense of them. They shouted, roared, and shrieked as they came rushing toward us, hands, talons, claws, paws, and assorted other appendages raised and ready to do some damage.

Jinx gripped the handle of Cuthbert Junior so tight I feared the wood would splinter. He looked at me, and his grin should've turned my guts to ice, but it didn't.

"Now *this* is more like it!" he said.

I was already holding my trancer, and with my other hand, I drew my M-blade. I grinned back.

"First one to draw blood wins," I said.

Russell shook his head. His mustache and beard were tacky with blood, but his nose had stopped bleeding. "I swear, sometimes I don't know which one of you is scarier."

Bloodshedder gave a snort of agreement.

I turned to Abe, Maggie, and Connie. "You three should get in the Deathmobile. You'll be safer there." *I hope*, I added mentally.

The hearse was almost completely repaired by now, and Connie climbed into the driver's seat.

"Lousy bastards think they can hurt my baby," she muttered. She revved the engine a couple times, her face a mask of anger and determination.

Before Abe and Maggie could get in, the Darkness said, "Don't worry. I'll protect them."

I nodded. I wasn't about to argue with the Darkness.

Jinx and I exchanged a last look, and then we sprinted toward the oncoming Incubi, with Russell, Bloodshedder, Cancer Jack, and Lizzie Longlegs at our sides.

What happened after that was a blur. I fired my trancer and cut with my M-blade, while Jinx swung his sledgehammer like a berserker in clown-white makeup. Acid sprayed from his boutonnière as if of its own accord, striking attacking Incubi in the face and causing them to back off, screaming in agony. My earlier weariness and muzzy-headedness were gone, swept away by surging adrenaline. I felt strong, fast, and, most important of all, focused.

Russell wielded his rapier to devastating effect, the M-sword far stronger and sharper than any steel blade could ever be. For good measure, he held a trancer in his other hand and blasted those Incubi his sword couldn't reach.

Bloodshedder did what she specialized in, tearing into Incubi with teeth and claws and swinging her spiked tail like a mace. Cancer Jack shot jets of fire from his newly grown cigarette fingers, setting Incubi aflame, and he spewed toxic smoke from his mouth, causing Incubi to gag and choke. Lizzie Longlegs was putting her curved blades to good use, slicing and dicing opponents with maniacal glee.

Maggie and Abe stood close together, Abe with his arm around her shoulders. The Darkness stood in front of them, broadcasting waves of terror at anyone who approached. Whenever an Incubus managed to resist his fear-casting and came rushing toward him, he opened his robe to reveal an endless expanse of Nothingness inside. The lucky Incubi were able to turn aside at the last instant, fall to the ground, and curl into a fetal position, sobbing and shivering. The unlucky ones were unable to stop – and they fell into the void contained within the Darkness, their screams growing fainter the farther into Nothing they traveled.

Connie and the Deathmobile were perhaps the most deadly of us all The hearse's headlights – now both restored – blasted attacking Incubi with their rapid-aging beams. Normally, Incubi are immune – or at least resistant – to the passage of time. However, in the green wash of the Deathmobile's energy, they grew wrinkled, stooped, and weak.

But that wasn't Connie's and the Deathmobile's only contribution to the fight. The hearse's rear door was open, as was the lid of the coffin housed inside. A legion of moaning wraithlike forms poured forth from the casket, and they darted and swirled through the crowd of Incubi, passing intangibly through their bodies. Whenever they did so, the victim stiffened as if struck a painful blow, but instead of falling to the ground, they remained standing but immobile. I didn't know if they were dead or just in some kind of suspended animation, and right then I didn't care.

So, Connie kept an army of ghosts in that coffin. Cool.

At one point during the battle, a large figure came rushing toward us. Jinx and I were fighting side by side, each moving in a comfortable rhythm with the other. Neither of us paid much attention to the figure at first, as we were too busy dealing with other Incubi.

But once the others were out of the way, the newcomer loomed before us, a grotesque mound of flesh with multiple arms and legs, as well as heads, all protruding haphazardly from the flesh-mound wherever they could fit. The body parts came from both males and females, and they were held together by what looked like miles of duct tape. So much of the stuff had been needed to hold the thing together that it looked like some kind of bizarre hardware-store mummy. Oh, and one more thing: the flesh of all those parts was ivory white, and the faces had individualized patterns of color around their eyes and mouths.

It was the Brothers (and Sisters) of Bedlam, the clowns that had kidnapped Jinx. Or what was left of them, anyway.

"Well, *that's* something you don't see every day," Jinx said.

"Thank the First Dreamer," I added.

The clowns spoke in unison, their voices seeming to merge as one, as if they had become a single being operating with a combined intelligence. The loudest voice of all belonged to the head on the very top of the mound – the one that had once been on Big-Ears' body.

"We didn't have time to heal properly. It didn't help that we couldn't find all our pieces."

Jinx let out a loud burp. He picked a piece of meat from his teeth with a thumbnail, then flicked it away.

The Clownglomerate ignored him and continued.

"So, we got ourselves together as best we could and hurried to Earth to join the party. The Fata Morgana summoned us to deal with Jinx in the first place because she figured she'd fight clown with clown, as it were. We decided to take you back with us to the Circus Psychosis because those of us of the clownish persuasion should stick together. As scary as we are on our own, together we're absolutely *terrifying!*"

The heads broke out in lunatic laughter, and I had to

admit they had a point. They were pretty damn scary like this. But they were even more annoying.

"Come back with us willingly, Jinx," they continued, "and your partner lives. Refuse, and we'll kill her, subdue you, and take you anyway. Your choice."

Jinx and I exchanged a glance.

"You thinking what I'm thinking?" I asked.

"I believe so," Jinx said.

We turned to face the Clownglomerate.

"Fuck you," we said in unison. Jinx swung his hammer at the same time I fired my trancer. They say duct tape will hold anything together. They're wrong.

The Clownglomerate exploded apart in a spray of blood, organs, and bone shards. I squeezed my eyes shut and turned my head to keep from getting splattered in the eyes. I knew from experience that Jinx didn't bother averting his face. As far as he's concerned, getting sprayed by blood is like walking in a warm spring rain.

After that, we went back to fighting whatever came at us.

It appeared not all of the Incubi were fanatically devoted to the Lords' cause, for as soon as they realized the tide of battle had turned against them, many fled. Some ran for their cars, got in, cranked the engines, and got the hell out of there as fast as they could. Others just ran for the sidewalk and headed down the street at full speed.

After what seemed like hours but was surely only minutes, there were no more Incubi to fight. Our opponents – those who hadn't headed for the hills, that is, or been frozen by the wraiths' touch – lay scattered across the parking lot. Some lay on the ground, some atop smashed vehicles, and a few hung from light poles. The fortunate were broken, bleeding, or burned. The unfortunate had been aged to desiccated scarecrows – or torn into pieces of various sizes, from large chunks to tiny shreds. The wounded who remained conscious groaned, wailed, and cursed us, but I ignored them.

All of us had blood on our clothes, but Jinx, Jack, and Lizzie had been drenched, and Bloodshedder wasn't much better. Even though I'd contributed to the carnage that surrounded us, I still found the aftermath of our battle to be a stomach-churning sight. I consoled myself with the knowledge that these were Incubi and thus capable of recovering even from injuries this severe. Although from the look of many of them, their recovery was going to take quite some time.

"Let's go," I said. "We still have work to do."

It was an effort to get the words out. My adrenaline rush had run its course, and now all I wanted to do was go find somewhere soft and quiet to lie down. Jinx looked as if he might say something, and I noticed Abe reach into his pocket, probably intending to offer me something from his portable pharmacy to keep me going.

I was tempted, but I turned away and started jogging toward the building. My legs felt like lead and my lungs burned with every breath, but I forced myself to keep going. An instant later, Jinx was by my side, and although I didn't turn to look, I could hear the others, including Connie and the Deathmobile, following.

I felt another wave of dizziness and nausea hit me, and I knew we were about to experience another Incursion. This one was subtle, though, and at first I didn't realize what was happening. The asphalt beneath our feet began to grow soft, assuming the consistency of thick batter.

We were lucky. The change occurred slowly enough that we had time to slow down. If the transformation had taken place instantly, we'd have fallen face-first into the goo and risked suffocation. We were two car lengths from the entrance when we began to sink. Jinx and I managed to keep our balance as the soft black asphalt rose over our ankles, then halfway to our knees. Russell maintained his balance, too, and Bloodshedder's four legs helped keep her steady.

Jack and Lizzie both fell backward onto their butts, though, and immediately sank up to their waists, the tops of their knees peeking out from the black muck. Abe held onto Maggie, so they remained upright as they sank. Next to them, the Darkness sank, too, but he appeared undisturbed by this. He made no move to assist Maggie, so I assumed that despite how powerful he was, there was nothing he could do in this circumstance.

Connie and the Deathmobile had it worst of all. The heavy vehicle rapidly sank into the liquefied asphalt, and the wraiths that had been released from the coffin could only circle in the air above the Deathmobile, wailing impotently. It seemed they really were wraiths, creatures without substance, and whatever unearthly attributes they possessed, grabbing hold of physical objects and pulling them out of quicksand-like muck was not among them.

I looked at Jinx.

"Anything in those bottomless pockets of yours that'll get us out of this crap?" I asked.

"You mean like a grappling gun?"

I felt a surge of hope. "Yes, *exactly* like a grappling gun!"

"Nope. I've got a squirt gun, though. Does that count?"

The asphalt was over our knees now, and if we hadn't been in danger of imminent death, I'd have punched Jinx in the jaw as hard as I could.

I turned to Russell. "How about you? You got any fancy tech that'll help us get free?"

"Afraid not," Russell said.

I thought furiously, trying to come up with some way

out of this mess, but nothing came to me. It looked like we were headed to gooey black graves. Well, we humans were. The Incubi would likely survive, and maybe in time they would be able to dig their way free. A fat lot of good that would do me, Russell, Abe, Maggie, and Connie, though.

I looked at Russell again. "Too bad we didn't get to know each other better."

He smiled. "I was just thinking the same thing."

"Were you imagining the two of us naked and in bed? Because I totally was."

His smile widened. "No comment."

"Chicken," I said. I then turned to face Jinx once more. The asphalt was up to our waists now.

"We had a good run, didn't we?" I said.

For once, he didn't grin at me like a maniac. "Yeah. It sure would've been nice to disembowel the bastards inside that building before we checked out, though."

"Sure would've," I agreed. "But I'm the only one checking out tonight. You'll just be stuck at the bottom of an asphalt-goo lake until you can find a way out."

He shook his head. "You go, I go. Incubi only fade slowly if they try to fight it. I won't."

I didn't know what to say to that. I found myself wishing that his Day Aspect could also be present, so I could have a chance to say goodbye to him, too. Both Jinxes had been a part of my life since my late teens, and even though they could both be pains in the ass, leaving them was the worst part about my dying.

The asphalt rose up to our chests – and Russell, Maggie, Abe, and the Darkness had sunk to the same level. Bloodshedder was in up to her neck, and she held her head as high as she could, straining to keep it out of the asphalt for as long as possible. Jack and Lizzie were up to their chins, but Connie and the Deathmobile had fared even worse. The hearse was almost completely submerged, with only a foot or so still showing. The circling wraiths, still moaning in despair, dove toward the hearse's roof one by one and passed through the metal and back into the vehicle. I suppose they intended to go down with their ship.

"Fuck you for getting us into this mess!" Lizzie said.

"You're lucky you're going to die," Jack added, "or we'd kill you!"

"It's too bad Budgie isn't here," Abe said sadly. "He'd be able to get us out of this." Then Abe whistled the simple melody he'd shared with us on the drive here. One high note, one low, one high. "I so would've liked to see him one last time."

Maybe it was the stress coupled with the fact that I hadn't gotten decent rest in who knows how long, but I looked over my shoulder at Abe and shouted, "Damn it! Budgie isn't real! Everyone's just been humoring you all these years!"

Maggie shot me a venomous look, but Abe's expression didn't change. I wondered if he'd heard me. But then I realized he wasn't looking at me. He was looking up. A wide smile spread across his face.

"Budgie! You came back!"

I heard a sound like burlap snapping in the wind, and I understood that I was hearing the flapping of wings. *Big* wings.

The creature that descended from the night sky resembled a pterosaur – long, pointed mouth, bony-crested head, saucer-sized eyes, wide wings, and sharp-clawed feet. Budgie lowered those feet and took hold of Abe by the shoulders, and then the dinosaurian beast flapped harder and lifted Abe – and Maggie, whom Abe still held tight – out of the black mire, liquid asphalt dripping from their clothes. Abe laughed with delight as they rose into the air.

"Take us to the roof!" Maggie shouted.

"Yes, Budgie!" Abe said. "That's a great idea! Please do as she says!"

Budgie let out a loud squawk that sounded like a cross between Godzilla and a chicken. He then angled toward the building's roof, lizard-skin wings flapping. I'd read somewhere that pterosaurs didn't so much fly as glide on warm air currents, but Budgie was Abe's Incubus, and his body worked the way Abe had dreamed it would. So, regardless of how real pterosaurs had flown, Budgie flew like a bird, and he did so with the same speed and skill, despite his immense size. He deposited Abe and Maggie on the roof and then, at Abe's request, returned for the rest of us.

As Budgie approached, I shouted for him to save Connie first, but it was too late. The Deathmobile had disappeared beneath the rippling black surface, taking Connie with it. I then looked for Lizzie and Jack, but I couldn't see them either.

"They're gone," Russell said.

The Darkness hadn't sunk all the way yet, but he was as badly off as the rest of us. He hadn't said a word when Budgie had rescued Maggie and Abe, and since I couldn't see into the shadows within his cowl, I couldn't tell what, if anything, he was thinking.

Like Jinx and I, Russell had sunk up to his neck by this point, but Bloodshedder fared worse. Her muzzle was all that protruded from the asphalt. Russell had hold of her spiked collar, trying to keep her from slipping all the way under, but it was useless. She was too big and heavy, and Russell didn't have any leverage. But he'd die before he let go of her collar. I could see it in his eyes.

As Budgie approached, I told him to rescue Bloodshedder first. The pterosaur dipped low enough to reach into the asphalt and take hold of her collar. Budgie's wings beat the air furiously, and with an effort, he dislodged Bloodshedder from the black muck and transported her to the roof. She growled softly as Budgie carried her, probably because she was irritated at having to be saved by a giant flying lizard.

By the time Budgie returned, Jinx, Russell, and I were up to our chins in liquid asphalt. Jinx dipped his mouth toward the goo, stuck out his tongue, and tasted it. His tongue flew back into his mouth with the speed of a frog catching an insect. He swished his tongue around in his mouth, a thoughtful expression on his face. "Not enough tar for my taste, but overall, not bad."

As Budgie lowered to rescue us, Jinx reached out to grab both my hand and Russell's. As an Incubus, he was stronger than both of us combined, and if Budgie's claws had to sink into his flesh to maintain their grip, he'd heal a hell of a lot faster than we would. Budgie's clawed feet dipped into the asphalt and fastened on Jinx's shoulders, and the pterosaur flapped hard, not only trying to pull us free but attempting to keep from getting stuck himself. At first, Jinx didn't move, and I feared it was too late for us. I felt myself sink even further, the asphalt rising over my cheeks, and I tilted my head back so I could get a few more precious breaths of air before I went down.

But then there was a loud sucking sound, and Budgie pulled Jinx free, bringing Russell and me along for the ride.

Budgie might have been an Incubus, but that didn't mean the creature's strength was inexhaustible. His flapping slowed, and he started losing altitude. Budgie had carried a lot of weight over the last few minutes, and it looked as if he was running out of energy. But then Abe called out, "You can do it, boy! You can do it!"

Budgie sank another few inches, until my feet nearly touched the asphalt quicksand again, but then he redoubled his efforts and started gaining altitude once more. As he'd done for the others, he deposited us on the building's roof, then landed and folded his wings against his body.

"Wait a minute!" I said. "What about the Darkness?"

"What about me?"

I nearly jumped when I realized the Darkness stood next to me. Unlike our clothes, his robe was free of black stains. At least, I think it was. As black as the Darkness' robe was, it was hard to tell.

"If you could get out of there on your own," I said, "why didn't you rescue Maggie and Abe yourself?"

The Darkness turned to look at Abe, who was laughing and stroking Budgie's long beak-mouth. In response, the pterosaur was making a sound like a cooing pigeon.

"If I had, Budgie wouldn't have come," the Darkness said.

I was about to ask how the hell he'd known that, when Maggie said, "We have to do something to help the others!"

"I'm not sure there's anything we can do," Russell said. "We barely got free of that goop as it was."

I turned to the Darkness, but he shook his head. "There are no shadows within the asphalt. Without shadows, I cannot travel."

I looked at Maggie. "Jack and Lizzie will be OK, although they'll probably be so pissed off at our leaving them that they'll want to eviscerate Jinx and me the next time we meet."

"What else is new?" Jinx said.

"What about Connie?" Maggie asked.

"I don't know," I admitted. "She's in the Deathmobile, and that should protect her for a while."

"Until her air runs out," Jinx said cheerfully.

I shot him a dark look, but he only smiled at me.

I'd managed to hold onto my trancer while stuck in the asphalt, although it didn't have much juice left by this point. I'd lost the M-blade Russell had given me, though, which was a damn shame. It had been a hell of a weapon. Russell still held his rapier, although he'd lost his trancer. Jinx reached into his inner jacket pocket and pulled out Cuthbert Junior, or a replacement. Either he'd managed to store the hammer before he'd sunk too far, or he'd lost it and pulled out a new one. I didn't want to ask. The last thing we needed was for Jinx to start mourning the loss of one of his beloved Cuthberts.

I turned to look out over the parking lot. Broken carbots – dozens of frozen, wounded, maimed, and mutilated Incubi – and a patch of asphalt that might or might not remain liquefied. It was an impressive amount of damage for a single night, even by Jinx's and my standards. But we weren't finished yet.

"Whatever we're going to do next, we need to get on with it," Russell said. "It won't be long before the Lords make their next move."

Bloodshedder woofed in agreement.

"Do you think they might do something to the building?" Maggie said, clearly nervous. "Like they did to the parking lot?"

"I doubt it," I said. "I don't know how much control they have over the effects of the Incursions they create, but regardless, I doubt they'd risk bringing the entire building down on top of them."

"Then again," Russell said, "these *are* Incubi we're talking about."

"Hey!" Jinx said. "That's racial profiling!"

Russell had a point, but his remark didn't make Maggie feel any better. She kept glancing nervously back and forth between the parking lot and the rooftop, as if she expected it to go soft beneath us any moment, or perhaps burst into flame.

The Darkness took note of her emotional state and stepped close to her.

"You are distressed," he said.

"Yes, dear," she said, "but I'll be OK. Don't worry."

The Darkness cocked his head to the side. "Your pulse is elevated and somewhat erratic. I think it's time that we go." He turned his hooded face toward us, and I had a momentary impression of human features shrouded by the blackness within. "Good luck."

Maggie's expression became stern. "Now, see here, we are *not* going to abandon our friends when they need–"

That's as far as she got before the Darkness took a step toward her, wrapped his shadowy robe around her, and then they both vanished.

"Maggie?" Abe said. Then he sighed. "Oh well, I suppose it's for the best."

We could've used the Darkness' help, but I agreed with Abe. I felt better knowing that Maggie was somewhere safe.

The roof had an exterior door, but there was no way I was going to use it as an entrance into the building. Too obvious. I turned to Abe.

"Do you think Budgie has enough strength left to lower us to one of the windows?" I figured that since so many Incubi had raced out of the building to attack us, there was almost no one left inside. So if we could break one of the upper-floor windows, we could get inside without the Fata Morgana realizing it.

Abe patted the pterosaur's leather-skinned neck. "I'm sure he's recovered sufficiently by now – especially if he can carry us one at a time."

Russell grinned. "That's an excellent idea, Audra!

Bloodshedder will be able to crawl down the building on her own. She can go first and break the window for us."

"Great!" I said. "Let's get–"

I was about to say *going*, but then the roof door burst open and Quietus stepped out. He was followed by an Incubus I didn't recognize – a thick, squat, greenish creature with stubby arms and legs covered with wickedly sharp spines. Some kind of cactus-thing, with two black holes for eyes and a wide slit for a mouth.

After the two Incubi, a human-looking woman stepped through the open doorway. It was Dr Kauffman, looking exactly the same as she had when I'd seen her earlier that day. She smiled coolly at us, and although her expression remained professionally neutral, I had the sense that she was amused.

When I saw the next person come through the doorway, I felt both joy and relief. It was Sanderson, and he looked unharmed. I almost called out to him, but then I noted the vacant look on his face, and his dull glassy eyes. I saw then he had a rainbow-colored collar around his neck, but it wasn't a negator. It was wider and thicker than that, and it was fashioned from solidified M-energy.

And when the next person stepped through the doorway and onto the roof, I wasn't surprised. But that was only because of my little chat with Deacon Booze. I'd learned all kinds of interesting tidbits from him, such as the fact there was a traitor in the Shadow Watch. I'd even learned his name. Neil Gonnick, the M-gineer Jinx and I had run into on our way to take Quietus to Nod.

Neil smiled. "Hello, Audra. Good to see you again."

Jinx sighed. "So much for our sneak attack."

THIRTEEN

But then Jinx brightened.

"Hey, this means I don't have to wait to bash your heads in! That's great!"

"You're not going to bash anything," Cactus-Face said in a woman's voice. It took me a second to recognize it as belonging to the receptionist Jinx and I had encountered when we'd first visited Perchance to Dream. It seemed like everyone who'd worked here was an Incubus. I tried to remember her name. Valerie? No, Vivian.

"If you want to get to the Fata Morgana," she said, "you'll have to go through me first!"

She started running toward us on her stumpy green legs, flicking her arms and shooting needles toward us as if they were fléchettes. Jinx stepped in front of me to shield me from the worst of the attack, but I still caught a couple needles, one in my shoulder, and another in the back of my hand.

Bloodshedder leaped in front of Russell, planted her feet, and growled at Vivian. Russell half-turned away from her and raised his cape as a protective barrier. Up to now, I'd assumed the cape was only an affectation, part of his Nocturne cover. But the cactus needles bounced off the cloth without penetrating it. I wondered if I could get one for myself, except in gray.

The barrage of needles struck Budgie, and the pterosaur let out a pained squawk. He launched himself into the air, grabbed hold of Abe – who'd caught a few needles himself – and flapping furiously, he quickly gained altitude.

As Vivian came closer, I could sense what Jinx planned to do, so I waited for just the right moment, and then I moved out from behind him to give him room to maneuver. Vivian stopped firing needles as she drew near Jinx. Instead, she spread her arms wide, and it was clear she intended to give him one extremely painful bear hug. But before she could reach him, Jinx stepped to the side, and I saw that the front of his body was covered with cactus needles from head to toe, thin trails of blood trickling from dozens of tiny wounds.

Vivian tried to stop, but she was moving too fast, and her body wasn't designed for quick course corrections. As she passed Jinx, he swung Cuthbert Junior with a two-handed grip and the sledge struck Vivian on the back with a sickeningly hollow thump. Chunks of cactus flew as a result of the blow, but far more spectacularly, the impact sent Vivian flying over the side of the building. She arced through the air, screaming in rage and frustration, only to land in the liquefied asphalt with a loud *kerplunk* and disappear beneath the surface.

"Hot damn!" Jinx said. "Hole in one!"

He grinned savagely, and if he was frightening before, seeing him grin like that while bleeding from dozens of wounds from Vivian's impromptu acupuncture treatment made him look almost demonic.

While we'd been dealing with Vivian, Budgie had continued flying away with Abe.

"Go back!" Abe shouted. "We have to help them!"

But Budgie refused to listen to Abe's pleas. Just as with Maggie and the Darkness, Budgie was determined to protect his Ideator. Good. I didn't want Abe to get hurt any more than he already had. He and Budgie had helped us get to this point. We'd take it from here.

Jinx and I turned around to face Dr Kauffman and the others. Russell lowered his cape. He'd caught a cactus needle in his cheek, but that seemed to be the extent of his injuries. He plucked it out and dropped it to the roof. Bloodshedder's hide was far tougher than Jinx's, and although a number of needles were embedded in her skin, none appeared to have penetrated very far, and the tiny wounds weren't bleeding. A quick shake of her body dislodged most of them.

Jinx took in a large breath of air, stuck his thumb in his mouth, and blew. The needles sticking in his flesh popped out and showered down onto the roof. As soon as they were out, the pinpoint wounds began to heal. Like Russell, I removed my needles by hand.

"Vivian always was something of a hothead," Kauffman said. "Must've been the desert climate."

I took a step toward her, but Quietus flicked his hand toward me, and a shard of darkness flew through the air to *thunk* into the roof near my feet. I got the message loud and clear, and I stayed where I was.

"Hello, Quietus," I said. "Or should I say Parker Schulte?"

The assassin didn't say anything, of course, but he inclined his head.

"It figures," I said. "Day Aspects are often opposite to Night ones. You don't speak a word at night–"

"–and you can't shut the hell up during the day," Jinx finished.

"He serves the cause in many ways," Kauffman said.

"Serves?" Russell said. "He's a hired assassin. He does what he does for pay."

"True," Kauffman said. "But we compensate him very well. In all kinds of ways."

She reached out to stroke Quietus' arm, and I felt my gorge rise. I did *not* want to imagine the two of them having sex.

Kauffman went on. "I must say, Russell, I'm surprised to discover that you're aiding Audra and her... *pet*." She glanced at Jinx and curled her upper lip in disdain. Jinx gave her the finger.

Kauffman turned back to Russell. "You had me believing that like Quietus, it was all about the money for you. I must say that I'm impressed. I'm not easy to fool."

Russell shrugged. "I took a couple acting classes in college."

"They obviously paid off for you. Kudos."

Kudos? I thought. *Who the hell talks like that?*

"So are you an officer of the Shadow Watch like Audra, albeit an undercover one?" Kauffman asked. "Or did they just pay you more than we did?"

"Neither," Russell said.

"So we have a hero among us?" she said. "How romantic."

Quietus seemed to be focused on Russell, so I tried taking a step forward to see if he was paying attention.

"Nice try," Neil said.

He pulled a familiar silver sphere from one of his many pockets. He thumbed the nozzle on the side and hurled it toward us. Yellowish gas began spraying out of the sphere, but just as the toporian grenade reached us, Jinx swung Cuthbert Junior. The hammer's head hit the sphere with a metallic clang, and the grenade arced away from the rooftop, trailing streams of torporian gas behind it.

"Home run!" Jinx yelled.

There was a sickly-sweet smell in the air like rotting apples, but not enough toporian had been released to do us any harm.

"That was my last grenade," Neil said. He sighed. "Guess

I'll just have to rely on this."

He wore a side holster, and from it he drew what I thought at first was a trancer. But then I saw that the pistol's design was different than Shadow Watch standard issue. Instead of being silver, it was flat black, and it had a thick nozzle resembling a silencer on the end of the barrel.

"This gun also releases torporian gas," he said, "but in more focused, controlled bursts. I call it a torpion."

Jinx, Russell, Bloodshedder, and I just looked at him blankly.

"*Torpion*," Neil said. "It shoots *torporian* gas, and it strikes as swift as a *scorpion*. Tor-pi-on. Get it?"

"That's a *terrible* name!" I said.

"Dreadful," Jinx agreed.

"*Sleeper* might work better," I said.

"Not bad," Jinx said. "How about the *Zzzapper?*"

"Maybe... the *Dozer?*"

"The *Hibernator?*"

"The *Slumberizer?*"

Neil's face had turned a bright red during our exchange. "Shut up!" he shouted.

Jinx looked thoughtful for a moment, then he said, "No, that definitely won't work."

"Its name is irrelevant," Kauffman said. "For centuries, the Lords have sought a weapon that would be effective not only on humans, but on Incubi and Ideators as well. With torporian, we now have that weapon."

"The attack on the Rookery was its first large-scale test," Neil said. "And it exceeded our expectations. It even worked on Sanderson."

Neil patted Sanderson's shoulder, but Sanderson didn't respond.

I knew then who had deactivated the Rookery's security system.

"If you have a weapon that can put people to sleep," I said, "then why kill Damon and Eklips?"

"They were too much of a threat," Kauffman said.

"They were *real* officers," Neil added. "Legends, really. Unlike you and Jinx. You're not dangerous." He sneered. "You're merely annoying."

Jinx gritted his teeth, the sound like metal screeching on metal. "Why don't you put the fucking gun down, and I'll show you how dangerous I am?"

"It doesn't seem like that much of a weapon to me," Russell said. "All any of us have to do is hold our breath."

"Torporian is a very versatile drug," Kauffman said. "It can be administered orally, as an inhalant–"

Bloodshedder – probably tired of all this talk – chose that moment to spring forward and rushed toward Kauffman. Kauffman showed no reaction as the demon dog bounded toward her. Neither did Quietus. The assassin simply stood motionless as Neil aimed his gun and squeezed the trigger. A stream of yellow gas struck Bloodshedder in the face, and she managed to continue running a couple more feet before her eyes closed and she collapsed, her momentum causing her body to slide until her muzzle almost touched Kauffman's shoes.

"Or it can be administered topically," Kauffman said. "And as you can see, it's extremely fast-acting."

Bloodshedder wasn't dead. I could see she was still breathing, but she wasn't going to be any help for the foreseeable future.

Russell gripped the handle of his rapier more tightly, and his jaw clenched in anger. He started to take a step forward, but then he stopped himself. If Neil could take down Bloodshedder that easily, he could certainly do the same to us. The best we could do right now was to keep Kauffman and Neil talking and wait for some kind of advantage to present itself.

"Why publicize torporian as a regular sleep aid?" I asked. "For that matter, why bother with establishing Perchance to Dream at all?"

"We needed test subjects," Kauffman said. "I suppose we could've abducted them, but why not have willing ones? It makes things less complicated. And as far as our business front, it's a matter of hiding in plain sight. The Shadow Watch is always on the lookout for any of our... projects. So instead of concealing our activities, this time we camouflaged them. It's why our employees wear these." She reached up and tapped the Perchance to Dream logo pin on her jacket. "It prevents Incubi and Ideators from sensing what we really are."

"Another little innovation of mine," Neil said.

I wanted to snatch Cuthbert Junior out of Jinx's hand and smash the sledgehammer into Neil's face.

"Our ruse worked," Kauffman said. "For years, the Shadow Watch has believed that we are an organization in decline, our influence and power diminished. It's how we've been able to keep this operation secret." She gave Quietus a dark look. "Until recently, that is."

"Quietus' murders," I said. "They were connected to all of this. The people he killed were a threat to you." When Kauffman looked surprised, I added, "Deacon Booze told us."

"Really? So much for his vaunted neutrality. But yes, those humans were threats, if not direct ones. There was a possibility that each could've passed on information that might've caught the Shadow Watch's attention. One was a newspaper reporter who was skeptical about torporian. Another was a lawyer who'd come here as a patient and sensed that something wasn't quite right about our business. And yet another was a too-curious physician who had a patient participating as one of our test subjects. And the last was a college student with a long history of sleep disorders who kept a blog about his life –including his participation in torporian trials. I decided to silence them solely as a precaution. Nothing more."

Four lives. Snuffed out as easily as – and with no more thought than – someone blowing out a candle flame.

"Quietus was supposed to avoid drawing attention to his... removals. But you and Jinx realized who was responsible for the killings. Quite frankly, we didn't expect you to catch on so fast."

"Thanks," I muttered.

She went on. "You alerted the Shadow Watch and were assigned to track down Quietus. I had already taken steps to accelerate our timetable, and then yesterday happened. Quietus tagged Jinx with an M-focuser–"

"Another of my little contributions," Neil interrupted.

Kauffman scowled but continued without rebuking him. "The device allowed us to center an Incursion on your location. We'd hoped to destroy you, but instead the Maelstrom energy brought the Bean to life. And that definitely made the Shadow Watch sit up and take notice."

I looked at Neil. "So all that stuff you said to us about how irritated you were to have to clean up our mess was bullshit?"

He smiled. "I had to keep playing the part of a loyal Shadow Watch employee. Once my fellow M-gineers got busy repairing the damage to the Bean, I slipped away and came here. I've been here ever since, working to get things ready for tonight."

"We know what you intend to do," I said. "Deacon told us everything. You have a machine here capable of creating Incursions, and you plan to use it to break down the barriers between Earth, Nod, and the Maelstrom in order to create your twisted version of paradise."

"Earth is an incubator," Kauffman said. A place where people like you and Russell can be born so that you, in turn, can give birth to Incubi.

"Now imagine a world where any human, any Incubus, could tap into the energies of the Maelstrom to create whatever they wanted. Where they could satisfy any whim, any desire, with the merest thought. A world where everyone would have the power of a god. That's the world the Lords of Misrule wish to create. And now – at long last – we will succeed, thanks to Neil's genius."

"Reality is a prison," Neil said. "We all know this subconsciously. Why else would humanity dream? We long for release from the mundane; we hunger for *true* freedom. M-gineers work more closely with Maelstrom energy than anyone else. Because of this, we understand it better than Incubi or even Ideators. That's why years ago, I sought out the Lords of Misrule and offered them my services. That's why I created the Incursion Engine: so we could all be free at last."

I turned to Jinx. "Sounds like someone skipped a few safety protocols over the years."

Jinx nodded. "They do say too much exposure to Maelstrom energy does funny things to a person's mind."

"I am *not* crazy!" Neil said, eyes wide, mouth twisted into a snarl.

"Yeah, that's convincing," Russell said.

"So the Lords get their hands on an insane M-gineer," I said, "and he develops new tech that allows you to create Incursions. You test it out several times, including an attack on us during the day…"

"Two birds, one stone," Kauffman said. "Unfortunately, you survived. Again."

"And after Jinx and I came sniffing around here, you

decided to speed things up even more. We might only be *annoying*, but we could bring the whole Shadow Watch down on you."

"But the Incursion Engine wasn't ready," Russell said. "You needed some kind of focus or power boost or something."

"So you kidnapped Sanderson," Jinx finished.

Kauffman reached out and stroked Sanderson's cheek. I thought I saw him shudder slightly in response, but it could've been my imagination.

"You have no idea what he really is," she said. "Or what I am, for that matter. Oh, I'm sure Deacon told you I'm the Fata Morgana, but that's merely a name. Beings such as Sanderson and I are far, far older than we seem. And far more powerful."

Neil grinned. "Unfortunately for him, not powerful enough to resist a blast of torporian."

"So, why didn't the great Fata Morgana offer to power the Incursion Engine herself?" I asked. "Wait, let me guess. Sanderson won't survive the process, will he?"

Kauffman simply smiled.

"There's nothing you can do to stop us," Neil said. "By now, the Incursion Engine is online and functioning at full capacity. All we have to do is activate it."

I thought of the room Jinx and I had walked past during our tour, the one from which I'd heard a loud, powerful thrumming. I felt certain that's where the Incursion Engine was housed. And now I understood why I'd felt so anxious and nauseated at Perchance to Dream earlier. As an Ideator, I was sensitive to Maelstrom energy, and the power given off by Neil's machine was too much for me to handle comfortably, especially when it was operating and warping reality.

"Have you ever really thought about your role as an officer of the Shadow Watch, Audra?" Kauffman asked.

"Have you considered what it is that you really *do?* You've sworn to keep the worlds of the Incubi and humanity apart. Do you truly think that's fair? Who gave the Shadow Watch the authority to decide the destiny of others? Incubi like *him?*"

She nodded to Sanderson. "Earth is our home, too. We're the children of humanity, and we deserve to live and walk among you freely. For a long time, that was the goal of the Lords of Misrule. And for some of us, it still is. But over the centuries, I've come to the conclusion that humankind will never accept us. To them, we'll always be nightmares, best locked away and forgotten. But once our worlds are merged, that will change." She smiled. "Permanently."

I didn't want to admit it, but Kauffman's words had hit a nerve with me. I'd never considered that instead of a cop, I was really more like a border patrol officer, keeping two groups of people apart simply because someone in power thought they shouldn't mix. The idea didn't sit well with me.

"There's one thing I still don't understand," Russell said. "Why bother to pose as a human psychiatrist? Why treat young children with sleep disorders?"

"What better way to identify possible Ideators and sway them to the Lords' cause before the Shadow Watch – those noble defenders of the status quo – could get to them? Many of our earliest test subjects for torporian were Ideators I recruited. And most of the Incubi who worked here were created by them. Sometimes, it's easier to grow your own instead of stealing from someone else's garden. This way, there was less chance of the Shadow Watch discovering what we were up to."

"You didn't try very hard to recruit Russell and me," I said. "Not that either of us is complaining."

"Damn straight," Russell said.

"I *did* try, although neither of you were aware of it at the time. You only remembered what I wanted you to."

Her eyes flashed yellow, and my gut clenched as if I'd been punched in the stomach. I remembered those eyes. Remembered seeing them as Kauffman told me things: strange, dark, disturbing things. Things she'd later tell me to forget.

Right then I found it ironic that as a child, I had been afraid of what, at the time, had been an imaginary nightmare clown, when all the while my mom and dad had been taking me to see a *real* monster.

Kauffman's eyes returned to normal. "Unfortunately, neither of you were pliable enough to make suitable candidates for conversion. You're too… *independent.*" She made a face as she said the word, as if it left a bad taste in her mouth. "I continued to keep an eye on you both as you grew up and your Incubi became fully Ideated. Just in case you might prove useful one day. I thought that day had come, at least in part, when we hired Russell and his canine friend to help us. Unfortunately, I was wrong."

She looked at me then. "Neil wanted me to give you the chance to join us, Audra. He truly believes that once you understand our goals, you'll see the beauty of the world we're trying to create. But I doubt there's anything I can say that will convince you and your clown, is there?"

"Oh, I don't know," Jinx said. "I *am* batshit crazy, you know. I might come on over to the dark side just for shits and giggles."

Kauffman scowled. "Please. I am the Fata Morgana, and I see that which is hidden to all others. You're simply attempting to lull us into thinking you've turned traitor so that you can then attack us. It's a pathetic ploy from a pathetic creature."

Jinx shrugged. "Can't blame a clown for trying." He turned to me. "Your curiosity satisfied?" he asked.

"Yep," I said.

"How about you?" he asked Russell.

"I'm good."

Jinx nodded. "Then let's get this road on the show."

Jinx made no obvious move, but a stream of liquid shot forth from his oversized lapel flower, and arced through the air toward Neil. Quietus hurled a pair of dark shards which *thunked* into Jinx's chest, but the assassin was too late. The acid struck its target: the nozzle of Neil's torporian gun. The metal hissed and sizzled, and the nozzle melted shut.

"Fuck!" Neil shouted and threw his useless weapon to the rooftop.

I fired my trancer at the Fata Morgana, and the multicolored beam struck her in the chest. My gun didn't have much charge left, but I poured every ounce of remaining power into the ancient Incubus. Raw Maelstrom energy slammed into her, wreathing her in swirling, multihued light. For good measure, I pulled Jinx's trancer from its holster and fired it at the Fata Morgana, adding its power to my own.

Without bothering to remove the dark shards protruding from his chest – and ignoring the blood oozing from the wounds they'd made – Jinx hurled Cuthbert Junior toward Quietus. The sledgehammer tumbled end over end toward the silent assassin with such speed that he couldn't avoid it. The hammer struck him a devastating blow right between the eyes – or at least where his eyes would've been if he'd had any visible.

Neil let out a stream of foul language as he began rummaging through the numerous pockets of his gray jumpsuit, searching for another weapon, I assumed.

"Fuck-shit-damn-cunt-suck-hell!"

Russell, rapier in hand, ran forward to attack him. Before Russell could run him through, Neil pulled out a two-pronged device from one of his pockets and activated it. It began vibrating and humming, like a tuning fork, and a barrier of M-energy sprung up in front of him like a wall. Russell tried to thrust his rapier through the barrier, but his blade was turned aside. Russell attempted to maneuver around the barrier, but it moved with Neil, who kept it between himself and Russell.

Sanderson continued to stand motionless and expressionless, eyes dull and unseeing. Bloodshedder remained asleep, snoring rather loudly.

The hammer strike sent Quietus flying backward, and if he'd been human, the blow would've splattered his head like rotten melon. But he was an Incubus, and a strong one at that. He landed on his back and slid a few feet. Cuthbert Junior landed only a foot away from his outstretched hand, and he grabbed hold of the hammer and sprang to his feet, uninjured.

I continued putting the heat on the Fata Morgana, but both my trancer and Jinx's were rapidly running out of power. The energy output was dwindling, and the beams were thinning out. The Fata Morgana remained encased in a cocoon of roiling M-energy, but I had no idea what, if any, effect it was having on her. All I could do was keep firing and hope.

Quietus started running toward Jinx, Cuthbert Junior raised over his head, clearly intending to give Jinx a taste of his own medicine. But Jinx wasn't about to stand and wait for it. Springs shot out of his shoes and propelled him toward Quietus.

Jinx held his hands out before him – and although I only caught a blurred glimpse of silvery-gray on his fingers, I knew that he now wore high-voltage joy buzzers, like he'd used on Shocktooth in Nod, on each of his fingers. He slammed into Quietus and grabbed hold of the assassin's throat as they both went down in a heap. Before Quietus could swing Cuthbert Junior, Jinx moved into a crouching position over Quietus, his rubber-soled feet firmly planted on the rooftop. He then activated his joy buzzers, and electrical power coruscated over them both.

Quietus jerked and spasmed as Jinx maintained his double grip on the assassin's neck. Coils of smoke rose from Jinx's hands, and his face was contorted into an expression of homicidal ecstasy that would've caused any bystanders to piss themselves in terror if they'd been present.

"Just call me the Electro-cutioner, baby!" he cried. He followed this with one of his earsplitting hyena laughs.

Russell, who continued his shuffling dance with Neil, called out, "How the hell can you stand to work with him?"

"He grows on you," I called back. "Kind of like a clown-white tumor!"

My trancer finally came up empty, the energy field surrounding the Fata Morgana winked out, and a different being now stood in her place. I don't know if she'd been able to maintain her Day Aspect even at night or if she was able to shift between them at will. Whichever the case, she now appeared to be a tall woman – almost inhumanly lithe – with alabaster skin and long raven-black hair that fell all the way to her feet. She wore a dark green Renaissance-festival-style dress that glinted in the parking lot lights as if the fabric contained flecks of diamond.

All of that made her an imposing figure, but the most disturbing feature of this Aspect was her face. It appeared to be made from uneven pieces of crystal that constantly shifted like a kaleidoscope. And set in the midst of the seething crystalline shards was a pair of gleaming yellow eyes.

The sight of the Fata Morgana's true appearance startled me, as it did Russell. I lowered my useless trancers, and he broke off the attack on Neil. Both of us stared at her.

"I remember her," Russell said. I could barely hear him over Jinx's mad laughter and the sound of crackling electricity.

"Me, too." When Kauffman closed her office door, day or night, she would shed her illusion of humanity and reveal this creature, her true self – the Fata Morgana.

If my trancer fire had done her any damage, I couldn't tell by looking at her. She stood tall and steady, and exuded a palpable aura of strength.

"A for effort," she said in a voice like tinkling wind chimes.

While Russell and I were distracted, Neil deactivated his tuning fork, tucked it away in a pocket, and then from another pocket withdrew a new object. It was made of M-energy and was roughly the size and shape of a yo-yo. He pointed it at Sanderson and thumbed a button on the side.

Sanderson stiffened as the collar around his neck began to pulse with white light. His eyes gleamed with the same light, and they pulsed in time with the collar.

Pain lanced through my skull as if someone had taken a white-hot iron spike and driven it into one of my ears and out the other. Crippling nausea twisted my insides, and I dropped my spent trancers, fell to all fours, and began retching uncontrollably. It took me several moments to get my body under some semblance of control. When I did, I looked at Russell and saw he was as bad off as I was.

I looked for Jinx, and I saw he was now on his back. Quietus was straddling him and plunging deadly shards into Jinx's body, one after the other, in rapid succession. Tendrils of steam rose from the assassin, but there was no more electricity. Like the trancers, Jinx's joy buzzers – all ten of them – had run out of power, and now Quietus was fighting back.

The Fata Morgana turned to Neil. "You took your time activating the Engine."

It was difficult to read the Fata Morgana's expression, given her constantly shifting features, but I was fairly certain she was displeased with Neil. He lowered his gaze, as if unwilling to meet her glowing yellow eyes.

"Sorry. I was busy trying to avoid getting skewered by Nocturne."

Despite the agony that continued to explode in my skull, I was able to think clearly enough to wonder why Neil was unaffected by the energies being given off by the Incursion Engine. A resistance built up from years of exposure to M-energy? Some protective device he carried? Not that I cared much at that moment. As horrible as I felt right then, all I wanted was for some kind soul with a shotgun to come along and put me out of my misery.

I turned my face skyward and saw streaks of multicolored Maelstrom energy rippling in the air above us. Only a few at first, but more appeared with each passing second.

I lowered my gaze to check on Jinx. The activation of the Incursion Engine seemed to have had no effect on him, or for that matter, on Quietus. Jinx had turned the tables on Quietus, and now the assassin lay facedown on the rooftop, while Jinx – with a dozen dark shards sticking out of his chest – straddled Quietus' back. He was repeatedly slamming the assassin's face onto the roof, making a sound like a bag of cement being slapped against concrete.

I then looked at the Fata Morgana, and drawing on whatever reserves of strength I had left, I fought to concentrate past my pain and speak. I did so, but haltingly, each word an effort of will.

"It won't… work. Deacon said… so. An Incursion this…

large will only... destroy both worlds." My vision went gray for a moment, and I thought I would pass out. I almost did, but somehow I managed to hold onto consciousness, or at least some semblance of it.

"He's wrong," Neil said, without the slightest hint of uncertainty. "Thanks to Sanderson, this Incursion will be completely under our control. It will create an opening between dimensions that will become increasingly larger, until the barrier between Earth's universe and the Maelstrom's collapses once and for all. And then a new world will be born. A free world!"

The Fata Morgana looked at him. "Take it easy on the rhetoric, will you, Neil? It gets tiresome after a while."

Ribbons of Maelstrom energy now filled the sky above the building, their multicolored light illuminating the area in a panoply of ever-shifting hues. If I hadn't known it meant the end of all existence, I would've thought it was beautiful. I could still see some stars, but not many. Soon, the night sky would be blotted out completely. I knew we didn't have much time left. I had to stop this, whatever the cost.

I struggled to my feet, nearly blacking out for real this time. My brain still felt as if it were being devoured by fire ants, and my weak legs shook and threatened to give out any moment, but I was standing, and that alone was a victory, if only a small one.

Jinx was still slamming Quietus' face onto the rooftop, the assassin's arms and legs flailing as he tried to get out from under Jinx. The dark shards in Jinx's chest had faded away, leaving behind rapidly healing wounds. It looked like Jinx had things under control on his end. At least I didn't have to worry about him.

Sanderson, however, was a different matter. His eyes still pulsed with white light, only more rapidly now, and his body seemed to be shrinking in upon itself. He'd lost weight, and his skin was drawn tighter to his frame. Neil's collar was draining Sanderson's power to fuel the Incursion Engine – and it was killing my boss.

The trancers lay on the rooftop, spent and useless. Russell was struggling to rise, but he was having a harder time of it than I had. Maybe the Incursion energies had hit him harder than they had me, or maybe he wasn't as used to functioning when he felt like shit. He lay on the roof only a few feet from Neil – and not too far from Bloodshedder, either – his rapier still clutched in his hand. I considered trying to reach him and grab the sword, but even as transfixed as Neil and the Fata Morgana were by the spectacle taking place above us, I doubted I'd be able to get the rapier without at least one of them noticing. Still, I had to try.

I ran – actually, *stumbled awkwardly* is a better description – toward Russell. A strong wind had risen, maybe as a side effect of the Incursion, and weak as I was, it threatened to knock me over. The Fata Morgana and Neil remained mesmerized by the multicolored lightshow above us, and I realized I could no longer see any stars. I reached Russell, knelt down, and pulled the rapier from his grasp. He struggled to hold onto it for a second, but then he released it and gave me a weak smile before closing his eyes and falling still.

He just passed out, I told myself. *That's all.* But I didn't pause to check his pulse. There wasn't time.

I straightened and, Russell's sword in hand, started toward Sanderson.

I knew killing Neil wouldn't do anything at this point, and neither would killing the Fata Morgana. But Sanderson was powering the Incursion Engine, and if I could sever his link to the machine, the Incursion would stop. I hoped. As I approached Sanderson, I couldn't look him in the eyes – the white light blazing forth from them made that impossible.

I didn't know if he was aware of what was happening, but I hoped the light worked both ways, and he didn't see me coming toward him, gripping Russell's sword. Its blade was fashioned from Maelstrom energy – and if a strike from a simple M-blade could kill an Incubus, how much more damage could a weapon like this do? Especially if the blade were thrust through the heart. If Sanderson had known what I was about to do and could speak to me, he might well have told me I was doing the right thing. But that thought didn't make me feel any better about what I was about to do.

I don't know what happened, whether I was clumsy in my approach and made too much noise, or if my luck simply ran out – but both the Fata Morgana and Neil lowered their eyes to look at me. I was within striking distance of Sanderson, and I thrust the rapier forward, point aimed at his heart. But the blade was stopped by a small flash of white light, no larger than the rapier's tip. I tried thrusting the blade into Sanderson a couple more times, but with the same result.

Neil gave me a satisfied grin. "The collar has a built-in force field."

The Fata Morgana gestured, and the sword flew out of my hand and into hers. She took hold of the blade with both hands and with a single – almost contemptuous – motion, she snapped it in two.

I'd known she was strong, but I couldn't believe what I had just seen. Neil's rapier had been made entirely of solidified M-energy. It should have been, for all intents and purposes, unbreakable. But the Fata Morgana had snapped it like a twig. Evidently, Neil was surprised, too, for he gaped at her as she dropped the pieces of the broken sword onto the roof.

The Fata Morgana looked at me, sadness in her eerie yellow eyes.

"I truly regret that I wasn't able to bring you into my fold, Audra. But I think in time, you'll come to appreciate the new reality we're going to create. Who knows? You might even enjoy it."

Jinx had been so busy fighting Quietus that I thought he hadn't been paying attention to anything else. But at that moment, he stopped pounding Quietus' face onto the rooftop.

"Sorry, Q, but I can't play anymore," he said. "I've got work to do."

He still had hold of Quietus' head, and he gritted his teeth, pulled, and twisted. Quietus' head tore free from his body with a snapping sound. There was no blood, just a spray of black ichor that resembled thick ink. Quietus' body spasmed once and then fell still. Holding onto the head, Jinx stood, turned to face the edge of the roof, and with one of his enormous red shoes, he punted Quietus' head as if it were a football. The head flew through the air in a high arc until I lost sight of it in the swirls of Maelstrom energy.

Jinx's hands were covered with black goo, and he rubbed them on his pants before bending down to pick up Cuthbert Junior. He moved easily, as if the battle with Quietus hadn't taken anything out of him, but I could feel that it had. He'd been wounded – and healed – a hell of a lot tonight, and I knew that despite appearances, it had taken a toll on his system.

The sky was completely filled with Maelstrom energy now, and it blazed so brightly that it was difficult to see. How much longer until it was too late to prevent the dimensional barrier from collapsing? Was it already too late?

I didn't have any weapons left, but I didn't care. If I couldn't stop the Maelstrom from flooding into Earth's dimension and altering it forever, I was determined to make sure the kaleidoscope-faced cunt wouldn't live long enough to enjoy the new world she created. I walked over to her, careful to avoid stepping on Russell and Bloodshedder, of course, and Jinx joined me.

"You might not believe this, Audra," the Fata Morgana said. "But I'm glad you're here. Out of all the Ideators-in-the-making that I've worked with over the years, you were the one who had the most potential. The fact that you've gotten as far as you have in stopping me is a testament to–"

My hand snatched out, and I grabbed hold of her throat.

"Hey!" Neil said. "You can't do that!"

He tried to grab my arm in an attempt to stop me from choking the living shit out of the Fata Morgana, who – curiously enough – was making no attempt to do so herself.

Jinx's fist pistoned out in a blur of motion, and Neil's nose exploded in a burst of blood. There was also a sickening cracking sound as his jaw broke in several places. He flew backward, hit the rooftop, and didn't get back up.

I maintained my grip on the Fata Morgana's throat until my hand and arm shook from the effort. But even though I could feel my fingers digging into her soft flesh, she didn't react.

Jinx's shoulders slumped slightly, and his head drooped a bit. I knew he was nearing the last of his energy and wouldn't be able to go on much longer.

"The collar around Sanderson produces some kind of force field," I said. "See if you can break through it!"

Jinx ran over to Sanderson and began pounding on him with Cuthbert Junior, but with no more success than I'd had before. The collar's force field stopped the hammer a few inches from Sanderson's body, white bursts of light flaring from the point where Jinx's hammer made contact with the field. Jinx kept at it, slamming the hammer into the force field again and again. But with each strike, his blows became weaker.

I continued choking the Fata Morgana, but her yellow eyes locked onto mine, and her lips stretched into a cold smile. Then light blasted forth from her amber gaze, and I felt like I was falling...

I was sitting in my bed, the covers pulled up to my chin. It was dark, and I was ten years old. At least, my body was ten. My mind was still that of the adult Audra.

"Jinx?" I whispered. "Are you here?"

A few seconds of silence, and then, "Yes. I'm crouched at the footboard."

My eyes were beginning to adjust to the darkness, and I could make out the silhouette of a head and shoulders at the end of my bed. Despite myself, I felt a thrill of fear at seeing that shape. It brought back too many memories, none of them good.

"Is it you?" I asked. "The *now* you, I mean. The one that's my partner."

"Yes."

The shape stood and came around to the side of my bed. I was physically smaller than my adult self, and Jinx's silhouette looked so much larger than what I was used to. Like a giant sculpted from darkness. As if sensing my discomfort, he knelt down so he wouldn't be looming over me. Was he wearing his old hobo outfit? Probably.

"What happened?" he asked. His voice was odd. It didn't belong to either of his Aspects, but seemed rather to be a mixture of the two, as if both sides of his personality were speaking to me.

"I'm not sure." I lowered the covers and sat up straighter. "I think the Fata Morgana did something to our minds."

"*Fata Morgana* has two meanings," Jinx said. "A sorceress in Arthurian legend, and also a type of mirage."

Now I knew for certain that Day Jinx was present alongside Night Jinx. No way would the latter have known that tidbit of information.

"So she's trapped us in some kind of mental illusion?"

"I believe so."

"So are you really here or are you just part of one of my memories?" I asked.

"Funny. I was wondering the same thing."

That took me aback. "You have memories of... scaring me?"

"Of course. They're my earliest memories. I was only partly real then, but I was real enough. It was so confusing. I only existed when you dreamed about me, so for me, life consisted of perpetual darkness in a small enclosed space – your bedroom – with a little girl whose attention I was supposed to try and get. But for some reason, I was supposed to catch her attention in a certain way. I couldn't just walk up to her and say, 'Hi! My name is Jinx and you created me.' I was supposed to be *scary*. It was almost like being an actor performing for an audience of one – the playwright herself."

"So you didn't enjoy scaring me?"

His voice took on the lighter, goofier tone of his Night Aspect. "I wouldn't go that far! After all, I was damn good at it, wasn't I?" He then let out one of his lunatic giggles.

In the darkness, I smiled. I reached up and touched his cheek. "Yes, you were. The best."

We were quiet for a few moments after that. Jinx broke the silence first.

"So, what do we do? Stay in this memory until the Fata

Morgana's glorious new world is born?"

"Or we could force ourselves back to awareness. If we're both here together, maybe we can combine our psychic strength and bust out of this joint."

"But even if we manage to return to full consciousness, what can we do to stop the Fata Morgana?"

I reached out and touched Jinx's wrist. Here in the memory, it was bare. But in the real world, he wore a bracelet around it.

"You can ask yourself a very important question," I began.

"'What Would Joker Do?'" he finished.

He started laughing then, softly at first, and then louder and louder, and I realized that I was laughing, too.

My eyes opened and I was on the roof again, only now I was lying on my side, looking up at the Fata Morgana, who once again was gazing at the blazing multicolored sky. I realized that when she mind-zapped me, I must have literally lost consciousness and fallen. But I was awake now, and Jinx was lying next to me. His eyes were open, too, but he put a finger to his lips in a signal for me to be quiet. He then slowly and silently moved into a crouching position, and I did the same.

Sanderson remained standing in the same position, his glowing eyes flickering rapidly. His body had lost much of its mass, and he was so very thin. He'd be dead soon, if he wasn't already. Russell was still unconscious, as was Neil. Bloodshedder was still snoring. Quietus remained headless.

Jinx straightened to a standing position, and I followed. I had no idea what he had planned, but whatever it was, I wanted to be ready. He reached into the inner jacket pocket of his suit, digging deep, his arm disappearing all the way up to the elbow. His face scrunched up in concentration, but then his expression brightened. He leaned close to me and whispered, "I've been saving this for a special occasion."

He withdrew his hand from his pocket and showed me what he held. It was a black sphere about the size of a grapefruit. A fuse extended from the top and sparks flew off as it burned. Did I mention it was a very short fuse?

Jinx turned to face the Fata Morgana.

"Hey, Doc! Catch!"

Startled, the Fata Morgana looked at Jinx as he lobbed the bomb toward her. She caught the cartoonish explosive and stared at it, as if she had no idea what the thing was.

Jinx then spun around, grabbed me, and – carrying me as if I weighed nothing – he ran toward the edge of the roof, his gigantic shoes *slap-slap-slapping*. Just as we reached the roof's edge, Jinx's shoe-springs activated and launched us into the air.

The world disappeared in an explosion of noise, light, and fire, but all I could hear was the sound of Jinx's mad laughter.

FOURTEEN

"You haven't touched your omelet."

"I'm not hungry."

Jinx – Day Jinx, that is – and I sat at a corner table in small greasy spoon downtown. We looked as if we'd fought our way here through a war zone, which was pretty much the truth, I suppose. Our clothes were dirty, torn, and stained with blood, asphalt, and who knew what else. The manager on duty at the diner hadn't wanted to let us in, but Jinx had slipped him a couple twenties, and the man had been only too happy to change his mind. I think it helped that there were hardly any other customers in the place.

Jinx had ordered a fruit plate and a yogurt, and since I hadn't been in the mood for anything, he'd taken the liberty of ordering me a ham-and-cheese omelet, OJ, and coffee. So far, the coffee was all I'd had, and I'd only taken a few sips. Despite Jinx nagging me about not eating, he hadn't done much more than move pieces of fruit around on his plate.

"I'm sorry, Audra."

"I know."

Night Jinx had succeeded. The explosion had destroyed the entire building, along with the Incursion Engine it had housed. For several moments afterward, the sky continued to be filled with Maelstrom energy, but then it slowly faded, and the night returned to normal, stars and all. I'd had wanted to search the rubble for Russell, Bloodshedder, and Sanderson, but we heard sirens approaching, and we departed. Mostly because I didn't want Jinx to get in a fight with the cops and firefighters. I'd had enough violence to last me for a while.

We'd found Connie and the Deathmobile waiting for us on the street. The hearse had used its headlight beams to age the ground it was trapped in until it collapsed into dust, but it had taken a while. Connie had waited on the street, just in case we made it out alive. She didn't know what had happened to Cancer Jack and Lizzie Longlegs, but I figured they'd turn up sooner or later. Incubi like them always do.

"You did what you had to do," I told Jinx. I wasn't sure if I was trying to convince him or myself. "You saved the world. Two worlds, actually."

"Perhaps." He speared a pineapple chunk with his fork and lifted it up to examine it. "But we're supposed to be the good guys. A good guy would've found a way to save our friends, too." He looked at the pineapple chunk a moment longer, then dropped it and the fork to his plate with an expression of disgust.

I heard the door to the diner open and close, but I barely noticed. I was too focused on Jinx.

"They would've understood," I said.

He looked at me, and I saw a mixture of doubt and hopefulness in his gaze.

"Do you really think so?" he asked.

"I do."

"And you'd be right."

These last words were spoken by someone who'd

approached our table, and as we looked up, neither of us could believe what we saw: Sanderson, alive, collarless, restored to full health, and dressed in an undamaged and spotless blue suit, complete with his ever-swirling Maelstrom tie.

"Uh… not to state the obvious," I said, "but you blew up."

He smiled. "I got better."

There were only two seats at our table, so he pulled up a third and joined us. A server started our way, but Sanderson waved her off.

"Sorry it took me so long to get here. Reconstitution isn't an easy feat, even for me. Especially not when a good portion of my power was siphoned off to fuel the Lords' Incursion Engine."

I was so happy to see him that I couldn't help myself. I leaned over and gave him a hug. He hesitated. Then to my surprise, he hugged me back. Only a little, but it was enough.

"I'm going to be very busy for the foreseeable future, working to control the media fallout from the 'weather phenomenon' that took place last night, as well as redoubling our efforts to track down the Lords' agents. It's obvious they remain far more of a threat than I believed." He sighed. "And, unfortunately, I have to arrange a memorial service for Damon and Eklips."

None of us spoke for several moments before Sanderson continued.

"And I'll need to review the Rookery's security procedures and strengthen them so something like this can never happen again. If Neil had decided to do something to the Unwakened, the results could've been catastrophic for Nod."

"You couldn't have known Neil was a traitor," Jinx said.

"I could have and should have," Sanderson said. "But

forget that for now. The reason I came here was to thank you and tell you that you both did an excellent job – even if you weren't officially on the case." He smiled to show that this wasn't a rebuke. "I want you both to take a couple days off and get some rest." He gave me a pointed look. "I mean it, Audra."

"Message received," I said.

He nodded and then stood. "I need to get back to Nod. I'll see you in a couple days."

He turned and started to walk away.

"Sir?" I called.

He stopped and turned back to look at me.

"Yes?"

"It's daytime. You can't get to Nod now."

He smiled. "Maybe *you* can't."

He began to turn away again, but then he stopped.

"One more thing. Make sure to leave here in…" He cocked his head to the side and a faraway look came into his eyes, as if he were doing some kind of internal calculation. "Precisely five minutes. That's an order."

Jinx and I exchanged puzzled glances, but when we turned to look at Sanderson again, he was gone.

Like the good little officers we were, we waited five minutes before getting up and going to the register to pay for our uneaten food. More people had filtered into the diner by now, and more than a few eyed our less-than-pristine clothes with disdain. I was too weary to care, and Jinx and I left.

As we walked down the sidewalk, enjoying the cool morning breeze, I thought of how solid the concrete felt beneath my feet, and I was glad the world was as it was. Humans have the best of both worlds, don't we? Reality during the day, and an ever-changing playground at night when we dream. At least, for those of us who still can dream.

"I'm glad Sanderson's OK," I said, "but seeing him got me thinking…"

"If he could survive the explosion, perhaps the Fata Morgana did, too," Jinx said.

"Yep."

"A problem for another day."

"Yep."

We continued walking in silence for a time, and then I asked, "Is that exhibit still at the Art Institute? The one you went to yesterday?"

"You mean the Titian exhibit? Yes, it is."

"Good. I think I'd like to go with you. That is, if you don't mind seeing it again."

Jinx looked at me in surprise. "I'd love to, but didn't you promise Sanderson you'd rest?"

"I'll meditate for a few hours first, OK?" I caught a whiff of myself. "*After* I take a shower."

He smiled. "OK."

I tried to smile back, but I couldn't do it. As glad as I was that Sanderson was alive, I wished Russell was, too. It wasn't as if I'd been in love with him or anything like that. Hell, we'd only known each other for a couple days. As adults, anyway. But he'd been a good guy, someone who'd been willing to risk his life to do what was right. And I had to admit there'd been a spark between us. Who knows what might have developed if he'd–

Ahead of us, a man walking a dog on a leash turned the corner and headed in our direction. The dog was a dachshund, and the man was Russell, dressed in civvies. I understood then why Sanderson had told us to leave the diner when he had. If we'd left any sooner or any later, we would've missed Russell.

There were a number of pedestrians on the sidewalk – most of whom were giving us plenty of space because of our disheveled appearance – and Russell didn't see us at first. Bloodshedder detected us right away, though, and she barked to alert Russell. When he saw us, he looked almost panicked, but then he let out a long breath and relaxed.

We continued walking toward each other until the four of us were standing face to face. Well, in Bloodshedder's case, face to ankle.

"This is awkward," Russell said.

At first I was elated to see him, but that emotion was quickly replaced by anger.

"What, you mean the whole 'I survived an explosion that leveled a building and wasn't planning on telling Audra and Jinx' thing?"

"That would be it. The people I work for thought it would be advantageous if everyone thought I was dead for a while."

"And those people would be…?"

He looked at me for a moment, and I could tell he was debating what, if anything, to say.

"I can't tell you their name, but I can tell you this much: you've heard their whispers."

At first I didn't know what he meant, but then it hit me. The voices that I heard whenever I passed through a Door. The voices that whispered to me, that had urged me to hurry, hurry when we were headed to Perchance to Dream.

Shaken, I said, "They're the ones who rescued you."

Bloodshedder let out a sharp back.

"And you, too," Jinx said.

"Yes," Russell said. "They pulled both of us out in the nanosecond before the blast occurred. But don't ask me anything more. I shouldn't have told you as much as I did."

I wanted to stay pissed at him. After all, he'd intended to let me go on thinking he was dead. But despite everything, I was just too damn happy to see him. I leaned forward and gave him a peck on the cheek.

"I'm glad you're OK."

He smiled. "Likewise."

Bloodshedder yipped, and I bent down and gave her a scratch behind the ear. "You, too," I said, and was rewarded with a tail wag. I straightened and looked at Russell again.

"So what are you doing out on the street?" I asked. "Especially since you're supposed to be pretending to be dead and all."

He looked suddenly embarrassed. "Bloodshedder's really hungry. There's this Mexican place a few blocks over that serves this really spicy *huevos rancheros* that she likes."

Bloodshedder barked in agreement and licked her chops.

Russell leaned close, as if to impart a secret. "She's a really picky eater, and she gets incredibly grumpy when she's hungry."

"I can imagine."

She scowled but then wagged her tail again.

"Jinx and I will keep your secret as long as you want us to," I said.

Jinx nodded. "Of course."

"I, uh, suppose this means we won't be seeing much of you for a while," I said, trying not to sound as disappointed as I felt.

"Oh, I don't know. I might be able to sneak in a visit now and then. And who knows? Maybe another potentially apocalyptic disaster will occur and we'll find ourselves working together again."

I smiled. "It's a date."

Russell gave me a last smile, and Bloodshedder gave a last tail wag, and then the two of them continued on their way, and Jinx and I did the same.

After a few moments, Jinx said, "He's a good man."

I grinned. "Are you saying he's good enough for your mommy?"

"No. I'm saying he's good enough for my friend."

I wanted to give the big galoot a hug, but instead I punched him on the shoulder. But not that hard.

He smiled.

"Do me a favor?" I asked.

"Sure."

"Tell me who the hell Titian is."

Jinx shook his head. "Titian was an Italian Renaissance painter born in 1485..."

ACKNOWLEDGMENTS

Thanks to Lee Harris for helping me dream this book into existence, to Cherry Weiner for shepherding my flights of fancy, and to my wife Christine, for keeping the nightmares at bay.

ABOUT THE AUTHOR

Tim Waggoner is a novelist and college professor. His original novels include the Nekropolis series, *Cross County, Darkness Wakes, Pandora Drive, and Like Death*. His tie-in novels include the Lady Ruin series and the Blade of the Flame trilogy, both for Wizards of the Coast. He's also written fiction based on *Stargate: SG-1, Doctor Who, A Nightmare on Elm Street*, the videogame *Defender, Xena the Warrior Princess*, and others. He's published over one hundred short stories, some of which are collected in *Broken Shadows* and *All Too Surreal*. His articles on writing have appeared in *Writer's Digest, Writers' Journal* and other publications.

He teaches composition and creative writing at Sinclair Community College in Dayton, Ohio and is a faculty mentor in Seton Hill University's Master of Arts in Writing Popular Fiction program in Greensburg, Pennsylvania.

NEED ANOTHER FIX OF MR JINX?

GOOD NEWS

THERE'S A SEQUEL

READ ON TO GET A SNEAK PEEK AT DREAM STALKERS, BOOK II OF THE SHADOW WATCH SERIES

AVAILABLE FROM ANGRY ROBOT BOOKS

ONE

I'm not a big beachgoer. I look all right in a bikini, although I'm not going to get on the cover of *Sports Illustrated*'s swimsuit edition anytime soon, and not without some serious help from Photoshop. But in Chicago, "the beach" too often means sweaty tourists, gritty sand, and the nipple-poppingly cold water of Lake Michigan. My idea of a *real* beach is an out-of-the-way island in the Bahamas, but since Shadow Watch agents rarely get vacations, I suppose I'll have to keep dreaming. Get it? *Dreaming?*

Jinx and I sat next to each other, huddled in the large woolen blanket that smelled as if it had been used to wipe King Kong's ass. Our clothes didn't smell much better. Instead of our usual gray suits – standard issue for Shadow Watch officers – we wore thick winter coats, jeans, boots, gloves, and pullover caps. In Jinx's case, the boots were about ten sizes larger than normal to accommodate his gigantic clown feet. It was early December, and the wind coming in off the lake had a nasty bite to it that indicated the city was going to be in for an especially hard winter.

Normally, Jinx's body heat would've kept me warm. Incubi – at least in their Night Aspects – are suffused with Maelstrom energy, and as a result they gave off a significant amount of heat. But tonight, Jinx was wearing a negator collar, which prevented his body from absorbing more than a minimal amount of M-energy. At the moment, he was no stronger or more durable than a human. Unfortunately, he wasn't any saner.

He kept his voice to a whisper as he spoke. "If I cut my wrists right now, do you think I'll bleed to death, or do you think I'll still heal, only more slowly than usual?"

"Don't you dare," I whispered back, knowing full well he might give it a try. "I had a hard enough time cleaning up the mess the last time you slit your wrists. The living room carpet still has stains on it."

"I know. Sometimes they talk to me. They like to tell jokes, but they're not very funny. I laugh anyway, though. I don't want to hurt their feelings."

Jinx might've been joking himself, or he might've been telling the truth. After all, it was *his* blood he was talking about.

The night sky was cloudless and clear, and the stars were so bright, they almost didn't look real. It was sad, but, even though I knew I was looking at the real thing, I couldn't help thinking that the illusory starfield in Nod – called the Canopy – was more beautiful. Sometimes I don't know which world I belong to more, which only makes me feel like I don't really belong to either. I searched for constellations, but it had been a long time since my high school science classes, and I didn't recognize any. At one point, I thought I'd found the Little Dipper, but there were only six stars instead of seven. No North Star on the end of the handle.

I lowered my gaze and realized Jinx was looking at me. His normal skin tone is clown-white, with bright red lips and blue crescents around his eyes. But his white skin reflects light like nobody's business, and at night he sometimes looks as if he's glowing with a low-level phosphorescence – especially when there's a moon out, as there was tonight. It's a great effect for a lunatic nightmare clown, but not so useful when it comes to going unnoticed during a night-time stakeout. So before heading to Montrose Beach, I slathered flesh-colored makeup all over his face. His disguise wouldn't withstand close scrutiny, especially not in full light, but at least his skin wasn't gleaming blue-white.

"Nervous?" he asked.

He didn't have to ask, though. He was an Incubus, a nightmare given life, and I was his Ideator, the person who'd dreamed him up. We shared a bond that was deeper than that of siblings, or even parent and child. And, even if we hadn't been linked, I'm sure he could read my emotions on my face with ease.

"Yeah," I said. I didn't elaborate. I hoped Jinx would leave it at that, but I knew he wouldn't. If Jinx saw a button labeled DO NOT PUSH, he would immediately push it, keep pushing it until his finger bled, and then destroy the button with a vicious swing of his sledgehammer.

"What's the worst that could happen?" he asked.

"Melody and Trauma Doll will screw up somehow and get killed."

Jinx giggled softly. "I know. I just wanted to hear you say it."

I punched him on the shoulder as hard as I could, and I was gratified to hear him take in a hissing breath through gritted teeth. With the negator collar on, Jinx experienced pain like a human.

I could get used to this, I thought.

The collar was necessary because Incubi can sense each other's presence, especially when in close proximity to one another. Jinx's collar was easily removable – unlike the kind we use on Incubi we take into custody – so it wouldn't prevent him from going into action when the time came. But until then, I intended to enjoy the side benefits.

We had a bottle wrapped in a small brown sack, and we passed it back and forth occasionally, taking turns sipping from it. It was a Jim Beam bottle with water substituted for whisky. Not only were Jinx and I on duty, there was no way in hell I would let him drink alcohol. He was hard enough to control as it was. And the First Dreamer help me if he gets hold of caffeine. When that happens, he's like a combination of Freddy Krueger and the Tasmanian Devil.

Except for the two of us, the beach was deserted – or at least it appeared that way. We'd picked up word on the street that, if you wanted to score some shuteye, Montrose Beach was the place. Jinx and I had been here since ten o'clock, and although I didn't check the time on my wisper – the light from the device would be a dead giveaway that I was a Shadow Watch officer – I estimated it was well past midnight now. A police officer, one of the regular kind, came by to roust us off the beach at one point, but I showed him my ID with its stylized dreamcatcher symbol. He looked at it for a moment without speaking, then told us to have a nice night and left. The Shadow Watch has operatives in every major city on Earth – and some not-so-major – but I knew most of the operatives in Chicago, and that cop wasn't one. Thanks to the Somnocologists who designed it, the dreamcatcher symbol projects an almost hypnotic calming energy that tends to make people more... agreeable. But other than that one encounter, the night had been the very definition of uneventful.

Thanks to the wind, the waves were high tonight, and they broke against the beach with loud, rhythmic *shooshing* sounds. The effect was as hypnotic in its own way as my ID, and if I'd been capable of sleeping, I'm sure I would've dozed off right then. But the sound didn't help me concentrate. It invited me to relax, release my stress, and let my mind wander, none of which I could afford to do. I bit the inside of my cheek hard enough to draw blood, and the pain sharpened my senses once more, but I knew it wouldn't last. I would've killed for a hit of rev, but I was doing my best to stay drug-free these days, and I didn't have any on me.

Where the hell are Melody and Trauma Doll? They should've been here by–

Jinx interrupted my thoughts with a none-too-gentle elbow to my ribs. He nodded to the north, and I turned to see a pair of figures walking along the shore in our direction. Melody was a tall, thin Asian woman with prominent cheekbones, killer eyes, and a smile that could get her gigs modeling for toothpaste ads. Tonight she wore civvies – a black coat and jeans, and her dark hair was tucked under a black-and-white striped beanie cap. Trauma Doll hadn't done anything to disguise herself – which was the point. We wanted any Incubi in the area to recognize her for what she was.

Trauma Doll was Melody's Incubus, and her name suited her perfectly. Her porcelain skin was as white and smooth as polished bone, and, as she moved, small fissures appeared wherever her limbs bent, making soft cracking sounds. The damage healed almost instantly, only to reoccur the next moment she moved. Her only clothing consisted of loops of black barbed wire that encircled her arms, legs, chest, and torso. The wire didn't cover her completely, but, since she possessed no genitals or nipples, the parts that showed weren't especially sexy – unless you had a fetish for life-sized China dolls, that is. She wore her bright orange hair in pigtails tied with blood-stained ribbons. Her sky-blue eyes were anime-large, and they appeared to have been painted on, until she blinked. It was an extremely disconcerting sight, and one I hadn't gotten used to yet. The small nub above her mouth was only a suggestion of a nose, and her too-red lips formed a Betty Boop moue. All in all, Trauma Doll made an imposing, frightening figure, and I wondered what had inspired Melody to ever dream up such a sinister thing.

Then again, I imagine a lot of people wonder the same thing about me and Jinx.

Speaking of Jinx, he sighed as he watched Melody and Trauma Doll approach. "Don't you just love the sound her skin makes as it cracks? It's almost musical."

Of all the problems I've had having a nightmare clown for a partner, I never thought I'd have to deal with Jinx falling for a woman who was made out of porcelain.

"Next thing you'll tell me is how beautiful her skin looks in the moonlight," I said. "All shiny, cold, and hard..."

He scowled at me, but then quickly refocused his gaze on Trauma Doll.

"You know you can't go out with her," I said. "She's a trainee. *Our* trainee."

After the Lords of Misrule had nearly caused the dimensions of Earth and Nod to fuse into a single chaotic mess, the Nightclad Council had decided the Shadow Watch needed more officers – in both dimensions – to make sure something like that could never happen again. Director Sanderson had started a major recruitment drive, and almost all current officers had been assigned a pair of rookies to mentor. Melody Gail and Trauma Doll were ours.

Jinx grinned at me. "You know how I feel about rules."

"The faster they're broken, the better," I said. "But I don't want you doing anything that might interfere with her training."

"Why? Afraid something *bad* will happen?"

"Yes. And you damn well know why."

"Nathaniel," Jinx said, and then surprised me by letting the matter drop. We both fell silent and turned our attention back to Melody and Trauma Doll.

So far, there had been no sign that anyone besides the four

of us was on the beach tonight, but when it comes to Incubi, appearances don't mean squat. This fact was driven home to me once again as a patch of sand near our trainees rippled. An instant later a humanoid form rose forth from the sand not more than half a dozen yards from Melody and Trauma Doll. They stopped and turned to face the newcomer. I couldn't make out his features – or if *he* really was a he – so I turned to Jinx.

He reached up and tapped the negator collar around his neck. "Don't look at me. Right now, my eyesight isn't any better than yours."

Shit! I'd forgotten about that damned collar.

The spot where Jinx and I sat was several hundred feet farther back from the water than Melody and Trauma Doll, and even with the half-moon in the sky, I couldn't make out any details about the sand being's form. He/she/it was an Incubus, of course. A human couldn't have risen from the sand like that. But otherwise, I knew nothing. I *hate* not knowing stuff, especially when I'm working and *double* especially when my not knowing something might get someone else killed.

I started to rise to my feet, but Jinx put a hand on my shoulder and gently but firmly forced me to sit back down.

"I thought you'd be all for rushing mindlessly to attack," I said.

"Usually I am, but I'm working on being less predictable."

"But not less annoying."

He grinned at me, but he kept his hand on my shoulder. With the negator collar on, he was no stronger than an average human male, and I thought I could take him. But probably not before he could spring the catch on the collar and remove it. After that, it would be an entirely different story.

I knew Jinx was right to stop me. While I wasn't comfortable letting Melody and Trauma Doll make contact with the shuteye dealer, there was no way Jinx and I could've done it.

After our part in stopping the Fata Morgana and the Lords of Misrule, we were too well known throughout the Incubus and Ideator communities in both dimensions. If the two of us had been walking along the beach, the sand-figure would most likely have remained hidden as we passed. We needed to bust the shuteye operation, and, right now, Melody and Trauma Doll – two unknowns – were our best bet.

Relax, I told myself. *Let them do their job. It's what they've been trained for.*

Then again, they weren't fully-fledged officers yet, were they?

Shuteye is one of the most dangerous drugs ever produced in Nod. Once an Ideator brings an Incubus to life, they no longer have any need to sleep. We're linked to our Incubi, and, since they don't sleep, we don't either. We do need to rest several hours each day to continue functioning at peak capacity, however, so we read, watch TV, meditate, whatever, just as long as we're not working. I *hate* resting without sleeping. It's boring as hell, and it's a waste of time. But I'd learned the hard way that if I don't rest, my job performance suffers – which in turn means others suffer, the ones I've sworn to protect. So I do my best to refrain from working three or four hours a day. It's not as much as Somnocologists recommend, but it's about all I can stomach.

I don't miss sleeping all that much. To tell you the truth, I don't even remember what it was like. My life before I became an Ideator and a Shadow Watch officer sometimes seems like little more than – pardon the expression – a dream. But some Ideators would do just about anything to experience sleep again, and some Incubi – who've never slept – are curious about what it's like. Normal sleep drugs, the kind you can get in any pharmacy on Earth, won't work on Ideator or Incubus physiology. And that's why shuteye was created. The drug allows the user to experience a chemical simulation of sleep.

Some users begin to exhibit psychotic behavior and become a danger to themselves and others, and some poor bastards go crazy after taking only a single capsule. I know. I've seen it.

Melody and Trauma Doll walked back to the figure who stood motionless as he/she/it awaited them. Melody began talking to the figure, but she kept her volume low. I wished I'd made her wear a wire so I could listen in on her conversation with the dealer, but you can never tell what kind of special senses a particular Incubus might possess. And, if the dealer so much as suspected Melody was an officer, it wouldn't go well for her.

At first, everything seemed to go okay. Melody talked, the sand creature responded. Melody talked some more. The sand creature then reached inside its chest and pulled out a plastic bag containing several small capsules. I couldn't tell how many were in the bag from where I sat, but I guess there were a half dozen, max. The sand creature held the bag out to Melody, while at the same time holding his other hand out palm up, ready to receive payment. And that was the moment Trauma Doll decided to go into action. She shrugged her right shoulder, and the coils of barbed wire wrapped around that arm rippled, loosened, and shot toward the sandy being like a gigantic S&M Slinky, and with a not dissimilar *spronging* sound. The coils lengthened as they encircled the dealer, covering him/her/it from head to toe in an improvised cage.

"That's my girl!" Jinx shouted.

He took his hand from my shoulder, popped the catch on his negator collar, threw it to the side, leaped to his overlarge feet, and began running toward Melody and Trauma Doll, determined not to miss out on whatever action might be left.

As it turned out, Jinx didn't have to worry. Instead of being constrained by Trauma Doll's coils, the sand creature simply stepped out of them, the barbed wire passing through its substance without doing any apparent damage.

"Rookies," I muttered.

I threw the blanket off, got to my feet, and started running after Jinx. I'd kept my trancer tucked against the small of my back, and I drew it as I ran and flicked the activation switch. Melody drew her own trancer the moment the sand creature escaped Trauma Doll's coils, and she fired before the Incubus could attack either of them. A beam of multicolored Maelstrom energy shot from the weapon's muzzle and struck the sand creature in the chest. But either the beam passed through the Incubus' sandy body or else the creature had created a hole in itself for the beam to go through. Either way, the M-energy did the Incubus no damage and continued lancing through the air – straight toward Jinx.

I wanted to shout a warning to him, but there wasn't time. Yet just as Jinx was about to get a face full of M-energy, he veered to the side, and the beam missed him, continuing on for a few dozen more feet, weakening as it went, before finally hitting the beach's upward slope. Sand exploded with a loud chuffing sound. Jinx turned his head to give me a quick grin and a thumbs-up, and then faced forward once more and increased his speed.

I hadn't managed to shout a warning, but Jinx had responded as if I had. I remembered Sanderson telling Jinx and me – during one of our numerous dressing-down sessions in his office – that as Ideator and Incubus, we should have a bond so strong it would be almost telepathic. Since that time, Jinx and I had worked out some, if not all, of our differences, and these days we did function better as a team, better than we ever had before, in fact. So maybe I *had* projected my thoughts to Jinx, at least on some basic level. Or maybe it was nothing more than a coincidence. Right then it didn't matter. I had work to do.

I may be an Ideator, but that doesn't mean I have any special powers beyond having once dreamed an Incubus into existence. Unless you count having life-long insomnia as "special". I ran after Jinx, but I was nowhere near as fast as he was, and I knew he would reach Melody, Trauma Doll, and the sand creature before I would. I briefly considered taking a shot at the shuteye dealer with my trancer. Maybe if Sandy didn't see the energy blast coming, he wouldn't be able to avoid it. But I suck at firing on the move, and I didn't want to hit Melody or Trauma Doll by accident. So I concentrated on running faster and hoped I'd get there in time to do some good.

Our trainees had been startled by the ease with which Sandy had shrugged off Melody's trancer blast, but they recovered quickly. Trauma Doll retracted her coils and they wrapped tightly around her porcelain arm once more. She then thrust her hands toward Sandy, unleashing both her right and left coils. But instead of encircling Sandy, the coils straightened and she scissored her arms back and forth, causing the barbed wire to slash through the creature's substance like a pair of metal whips. At the same time, Melody fired her trancer at Sandy, only this time, she'd flicked the selector switch to wide beam setting, and moved her trancer up and down, spraying Sandy from head to toe with M-energy.

I was impressed. Melody and Trauma Doll were working together in an attempt to disrupt the cohesion of Sandy's substance in order to weaken and perhaps even injure him. It was damned smart. Too bad it didn't work.

Sandy raised his own arms, as if in imitation of Trauma Doll, and he hit the two of them with twin blasts of sand to the face. Melody dropped her trancer, turned her back on Sandy, staggered forward several steps, and fell to her hands and knees. Her trancer's beam winked out as it hit the sand, and it lay there for a split second before it sank into the sand and disappeared. Whatever kind of Incubus Sandy was, he was even more powerful than I'd thought. How much of the beach did the damned thing control? Could the very ground Jinx and I ran on be used against us as a weapon whenever Sandy felt like it? Talk about precarious footing.

The sand-blast had a far more dramatic effect on Trauma Doll. The impact caused the left side of her head to shatter in an explosion of white porcelain shards. She didn't go down, but her arms dropped to her sides and her barbed wire whips fell limp. I'd suspected that Trauma Doll was hollow, but this was the first time I'd had any confirmation. Incubi are tough and they can heal a lot of damage while in their Night Aspects, but they aren't invulnerable. If their heads are cut off or destroyed, they die. Trauma Doll had only lost half of her head, but I feared she still might be dead – or whatever the equivalent is for a giant animated toy.

I felt like I'd taken a blow to the sternum. My breath caught in my chest, and a cold pit yawned wide where my stomach had been. The thing I had feared the most had happened. Melody and Trauma Doll, rookies under my supervision, had gone down. And neither looked like she'd be getting up anytime soon. Shock gave way to anger – mostly at myself, but it provided the motive force to spur me on to greater speed.

As I continued running toward Melody and Trauma Doll, Jinx let out a bellow of rage, reached inside his jacket, and withdrew a sledgehammer. Part of his clown abilities was being able to store an insane amount of bizarre weaponry on his person, regardless of the size. The sledge – which he called Cuthbert Junior – was his favorite, and without pausing in his run, he lifted the hammer back over his shoulder, then hurled it toward Sandy like it was a steroid-infused tomahawk. Cuthbert Junior was a blur as it spun through the air. As if sensing the sledge's approach, Sandy started to turn to face the oncoming weapon, but, before the creature could do anything, Cuthbert Junior slammed into him with a loud *chuff!* Sand sprayed everywhere, and the sledge continued traveling a dozen more feet before it *thunked* to the ground, only a few inches from the water's edge. Its head sank into the wet sand, its wooden handle pointing skyward. I thought Jinx would go to retrieve Cuthbert Junior, pulling it out of the sand with a moist sucking sound as he shouted something like, *I am rightwise born King of England!*

But instead he ran to the spot where Sandy had been standing, unzipped his pants, pulled out a chalk-white portion of his anatomy I would've preferred not to see – *ever* – and unleashed a stream of urine. The sand sizzled and smoked as Jinx's piss struck it.

As I drew close, I called out, "I think you ought to give some serious thought to seeing a urologist!" Then I ran past him, giving him and his prodigious river of urine a wide berth. I saw the baggie of shuteye capsules lying on the sand. The sand creature must've dropped it when Trauma Doll first attacked. Or maybe it had gotten snagged on her barbed wire as he escaped her trap and was pulled from his hand. Whichever the case, there it was, and, despite my urgent need to check on Melody, I bent down, snatched up the baggie, and stuffed it in my pants pocket. We'd need it for evidence.

I hurried to Melody, who was still on her hands and knees, and crouched next to her.

"Are you all right?" I asked, knowing it was a stupid question but unable to think of anything else to say.

That's when I noticed that the sand directly beneath her face was wet. At first I thought the sand-blast had irritated her eyes and she'd been crying. But then I realized that what I was looking at wasn't the result of shed tears, but rather shed blood.

"I managed to avert my face in time to avoid the full impact." Her voice was strained, and she spoke through pain-gritted teeth. "But a half-blast did enough damage. I can't see out of my left eye." She paused. "I'm not sure I *have* a left eye any more."

My stomach did a flip at her words. I crouched lower to get a better look at the damage and immediately wished I hadn't. The left side of her face was little more than a mass of blood and ravaged meat. I had no idea if Jinx had destroyed Sandy or if even now the Incubus was working on reconstituting his body, and I didn't care. All that mattered was getting Melody to a hospital.

For an instant, Melody's face seemed to... shimmer is the best way I can describe it. Kind of like the way heat rising off hot asphalt can make the air seem to distort and ripple. It happened so quickly that I wasn't sure if I'd really seen it, and then it was gone, and Melody looked normal again. Well, as normal as anyone *can* look with half of their face reduced to bloody, shredded meat. I told myself that what I'd seen was only a trick of the moonlight, most likely intensified by stress, and I thought no more of it.

Jinx finished his vengeance-piss, shook the dew off the lily, zipped up, and then turned around. At that exact moment a breeze blew in off the lake, and Trauma Doll's half-headless body wobbled, then fell over backwards.

Jinx walked over to Trauma Doll and gazed down at her. Her body remained still, but the scattered shards of what had once been the left side of her head were already beginning to move of their own accord, sliding across the sand to rejoin the rest of her. They traveled slowly, with jerky, erratic motions, as if they were almost too weak to move. Jinx helped them along by moving them closer to Trauma Doll's ragged-edged face and neck with gentle sweeps of his giant feet. The pieces began to adhere to the main body and to one another with soft clinking noises, and I began to hope that Trauma Doll was going to recover. Unfortunately, Ideators don't heal any more swiftly than ordinary humans, and Melody's bleeding wasn't going to stop on its own.

I tucked my trancer into the back of my pants – no way was

I going to put it on the sand after what had happened to Melody's weapon. Then I pulled off my jacket, wadded it into a ball, and pressed it to Melody's wound. I helped her shift to a sitting position, and then she took hold of the jacket and held it in place, freeing my hands.

"Thanks," she said, her voice shaky but calm enough, considering the circumstances.

While I'd tended to Melody, Jinx had continued scooping pieces of Trauma Doll's head closer to her body. The porcelain shards were coming together to form larger sections of her face, and a number had rejoined her body to the point where her chin and lower jaw were mostly restored.

As if reading my thoughts, Melody said, "She'll be okay. She may look fragile, but she's one tough bitch." Despite the intense pain she must've been in, Melody's voice held unmistakable pride. I knew how she felt. Kind of.

There was a time when I'd have been holding any number of drugs that I could've given Melody to ease her pain, but all I had was the bag of shuteye capsules.

"How bad does it hurt?" I asked. "Bad enough to risk a shuteye?"

"No!" She almost shouted the word and then, as if embarrassed, she smiled and added, "You don't want me to have to report you for corrupting a rookie, do you?"

I smiled. "Guess not." I glanced over at Jinx. "How's Trauma Doll doing?"

"She'll need another ten minutes or so to finish pulling herself together," he said. Normally, he might've giggled at the bad pun, but he wasn't in a laughing mood just then.

One of Trauma Doll's ears was restored, although none of her facial features had reattached to her body yet. Still, her hand raised and gave me a thumbs-up.

I didn't think it was a good idea for Melody to wait much longer to get medical attention, so I lifted my wisper to my face and spoke into it. The device doesn't look like much, just a simple silver bracelet, but it can do anything a smart phone can, and more.

"Call Connie," I said.

Whenever Jinx and I need a ride, we call Connie Desposito. Her Deathmobile might be one of the most unsafe vehicles I've ever ridden in, but it's faster than ten kinds of lightning, and right now speed was what Melody needed most. But before the wisper could connect with Connie's cell, the sand beneath us began to shudder, and I had a bad feeling that our granular drug dealer wasn't quite finished with us. A large mass exploded out of the sand near Jinx's feet. It slammed into him with a sound like two colliding semis, and the impact sent Jinx soaring into the air. He arced up and out over the lake, then fell toward the water. He landed so far from the beach that I couldn't see where he hit, but I heard the splash. I looked back at the object that had struck him and saw it was a giant fist formed from sand. The fist raised a middle finger toward the lake, and then it shifted, reformed, and became a human figure, only this time it had facial features.

"*Nobody* pisses on me!"

The voice had a whispering quality, like sand sliding over sand, but it was unquestionably male. He turned toward me then, and his expression – already angry – became downright murderous. I still crouched next to Melody, but, as the sand Incubus started toward me, I stood, drew my trancer, and leveled it at him.

"Do I really need to identify myself as a Shadow Watch officer?"

His sandy mouth twisted into a smirk. "Your clumsy sting operation told me that. Did you seriously think I was going to be fooled by those two?" He nodded to Trauma Doll and Melody. "I could practically smell how green they are."

He stopped when he was within five feet of me. I kept my

trancer aimed at him, but he seemed unconcerned. Trancer fire hadn't been any kind of threat to him so far. I glanced at his feet, or rather where his feet should've been. His legs terminated at his ankles, as if his feet were buried in the sand. He was connected to the beach, *was* the beach. And that's when I guessed his name.

"Montrose," I said.

He smiled. "What else?"

"So what's your Day Aspect?" I asked, genuinely curious. "Do you become human or are you *really* the beach?"

All Incubi have Day Aspects, but those aspects aren't always human – or even made of organic material, for that matter.

"Let's just say that in the summertime I get pretty damned tired of people plunking their fat asses down on me."

"So your life sucked so much that you figured becoming a drug dealer would be a step up?"

He shrugged, the motion causing bits of himself to slide off and fall to the ground.

"It's more interesting than lying around and doing nothing all night," he said.

"So why not go live in Nod?"

Since there's no day in Nod, Incubi never assume their Day Aspects. In Nod, Montrose would be free to walk around as a pile of ambulatory sand all he wanted.

"That's boring, too." His voice turned wistful. "Besides, I'd miss the lake."

There wasn't any point in trying to understand Montrose. Incubi don't think like humans do, and we're not always the most rational creatures ourselves. Besides, I didn't have time to keep playing get-to-know-you with him. Melody needed medical attention.

"I shouldn't do this, but you seem like a nice enough guy, and you only tried to sell my colleague a few capsules. How about we go our separate ways and call it a night?"

I kept my tone relaxed, but I didn't lower my weapon.

Montrose didn't take any time to consider his reply.

"Where's the fun in that?"

And that's when I realized how much trouble we were really in. Montrose had swallowed Melody's trancer. He could do the same to us any time he wanted. Hell, he could probably slide his sandy substance into our mouths, down our throats, and into our lungs, asphyxiating Melody and me, and there wouldn't be a damn thing we could do about it. There could be only one reason why Montrose hadn't killed us all by now. The only reason we were still alive was because he wasn't done playing with us yet.

Fabulous.

I wanted to keep his attention off Melody and Trauma Doll, so I fired a quick blast of M-energy at him, and then I started running north along the beach. I knew my trancer blast wouldn't do much more than slow him down a little, but I'd take however much of a head start I could get. I put all the energy I had into my run, hoping to put as much distance as possible between myself, Melody, and Trauma Doll. I had no idea how big Montrose really was, but Chicago has twenty-eight miles of public beaches, and there was no way he could be *that* big. I hoped.

I have no idea how far I'd gotten before a wall of sand sprang up before me, but I was moving too fast to avoid it. I managed to angle my body so I hit the wall with my right shoulder. I expected the wall to be as solid as rock, but, while it provided some resistance, I plowed through it without much trouble. I was, however, off balance now, and I lost my footing and fell. A pit yawned open beneath me, and, as I tumbled into it, I almost screamed. But before I could do more than fall a few feet, sand rushed up to meet me, and my breath was driven from my lungs as it collided with me. The sand continued moving, taking me with it, and I realized I was being borne skyward by a pillar of sand. Montrose's laughter seemed to come from everywhere and nowhere all at once, and I had the impression that each individual grain of sand was laughing, their tiny voices merging into one eerie, omnipresent sound.

I felt my stomach drop as the pillar – no, the *tower* – rose swiftly into the air. I tried to grab hold of the sand beneath me, to dig my fingers in and steady myself. But the sand that comprised the flat surface of the tower was packed tight, and I couldn't get any purchase on it. I'd lost my trancer somewhere along the line – probably when I'd first fallen into the pit. If I'd had it, I might've been able to blast a handhold with a tight-beam setting. But then again, Montrose would likely just fill the area back in. The tower stopped rising so abruptly that momentum actually carried me several inches higher. Panic gripped me as I felt empty space between me and the top of the tower, and my limbs flailed as my body desperately attempted to find something solid to grab hold of. My momentum gave out, I seemed to hang motionless in the air for an instant, and then I began to fall. I hit the top of the tower belly-first, and I released a most unladylike "Blarg!" It was a good thing I hadn't eaten recently, or more than sound might've come out of me.

I lay there for several seconds, shaking with fear, but I forced myself to calm down. It took every ounce of willpower I had, but I managed to move into a crouching position, and from there I stood. My legs were shaky, but they held me up. From this height, Melody and Trauma Doll looked like actual dolls, and I estimated I was a hundred feet off the ground, maybe more. On my left was the dark expanse of Lake Michigan, and on my right was the city. The buildings were lit up so brightly, they almost seemed to glow, and, even in this moment, when there was no guarantee I'd live through the next few moments, the sight took my breath away. What can I say? I'm a Chi-Town girl born and bred.

Montrose's laughter had faded into the background somewhat, but it hadn't stopped. Now it became louder once more, and I understood why when the tower began to sway. It began gently enough, moving back and forth an inch or two at the most. But with each passing second the tower's range of motion expanded. To make matters worse, instead of following a regular pattern, the tower moved in unpredictable ways: slow circles, fast figure eights... It would jerk to a halt and then start moving again just as abruptly. I spread my feet apart and stretched my arms out, almost as if I were surfing. In a way, I guess I was. Even with the extra attraction afforded by the corrugated soles of my boots, my feet would slide several inches in one direction, and then when the tower changed course, they'd slide in another. The trick was to maintain my balance and not panic. I reminded myself that Montrose wanted to play with me, and that, as long as I amused him, he'd keep me alive. More importantly, the longer I stayed alive, the longer his attention would be off Melody and Trauma Doll.

Since I'd given Melody my coat, all I had to protect my upper body from the cold December air – not to mention the ass-biting wind blowing in off the lake – was a long-sleeved white shirt that was part of my official Shadow Watch uniform. I could feel the cold starting to seep into my bones, slowing me down and making me clumsy.

Evidently I was doing too good a job of not falling, for the sand on top of the tower became softer, looser, and Montrose's laughter rose in volume. I started sliding more then, and even my boots couldn't find me steady footing. Then it happened: my right foot slid out from under me at the same instant the tower jerked in a new direction. My left ankle twisted, and I fell. My left knee hit the tower's surface, followed by my left elbow. The sand had become hard again, and it felt like hitting solid stone. I was too terrified for the pain to register as anything more than a distant annoyance. I flopped onto my back and began sliding headfirst toward the tower's edge. The circular top wasn't especially wide, only ten feet across or so, and I knew I had only a couple seconds to prevent what would most likely be a fatal hundred-foot fall to the beach below.

I curled my fingers into claws and pressed them against the tower's hard surface. My nails tore with piercing pain, but I pressed my fingers down harder. I came to a stop with my head hanging over the tower's edge, and I made the mistake of turning to look down. A wave of vertigo hit me, and I closed my eyes and scooted back to the center of the tower's surface. I got to my feet, fingers throbbing, heart pounding, breath coming in ragged gasps, stomach roiling with industrial-strength nausea. But at least I wasn't dead. Not yet, anyway.

I realized then that the tower had stopped moving, and I could no longer hear Montrose's laughter. A small patch of sand near my feet shifted, bulged upward, and formed into a humanoid face.

"This is the most fun I've had in ages!" Montrose said.

My first impulse was to raise my foot and stomp down as hard as I could on the sonofabitch's face. I almost did it, too, but then I caught movement out of the corner of my eye, and I looked toward the lake. Jinx ran across the water, his already large boots swollen even larger to become miniature pontoons. His boots made loud slapping sounds as he came, and he moved surprisingly fast and gracefully.

So... Jinx can walk on water. I'll never hear the end of that.

Now that Jinx was coming, I knew I only needed to stall Montrose for a few more minutes. I knelt down next to his face, and he frowned in surprise. His face slid back a couple inches, but it didn't disappear into the tower.

"Is that all this is to you?" I asked. "A game?"

As I spoke, I reached toward the front pocket of my jeans, moving slowly and holding Montrose's gaze to keep his attention fixed on my face.

"Of course," he said, his tone indicating that this should be obvious to anyone with even a modicum of intelligence.

I inserted my bleeding fingers into my pocket, fighting to keep the pain I felt from registering on my face.

"It's not a game to me. And it's not to my friends. You hurt them, really badly."

Montrose giggled. "I know."

I slipped the plastic bag containing the shuteye capsules from my pocket. As I palmed the bag, I heard Jinx's splashing footfalls becoming louder. He was getting close to shore.

"So I guess it only matters if something is fun for you, huh?"

I dug my sore, bloody fingertips into the plastic, working to tear a hole in it. My blood made the plastic slippery, complicating the job, but I was determined – not to mention more than a little desperate – and I succeeded. I felt a single capsule fall into my palm. I wasn't sure one would be enough, but I knew I wouldn't be able to get any more before Montrose realized what I was up to.

His expression became puzzled then.

"Well, sure. Isn't that how it is for everyone?"

Shuteye comes in gel-coated liquid doses, and I pressed what remained of my thumbnail into the semisoft gel coating until I felt it break. I leaned closer to Montrose's face and was relieved when he didn't slide away from me.

"It's not that way for me," I said. "But I have to admit that I'm going to enjoy this."

I lunged forward and jammed my hand into Montrose's mouth.

Despite what I'd said to him, I really didn't want to do this. I'd seen the horrific results of what shuteye could do when someone had a bad reaction to it. But right then shuteye was the only weapon I had at my disposal.

Montrose tried to close his mouth, but I'd caught him off-guard. I shoved my arm down his throat almost all the way up to my shoulder and released the capsule. And then, while he was still too surprised to harden his substance and bite my arm off, I withdrew it and scooted back a couple feet. I had no idea if he had a true digestive system, but I hoped it wouldn't matter.

Montrose's features contorted into a distorted mask of hate. His face rose from the tower's surface, a humanoid body forming beneath it until he stood before me in all his gritty glory. His hands shot toward me, arms lengthening so he didn't have to step so much as an inch forward to reach me. I expected to feel sandpaper-rough fingers wrap around my neck and begin to squeeze. Instead, they fastened over my nose and mouth, and an instant later I felt sand begin to slide up my nasal passages and down my throat. I immediately started gagging – or at least I tried to. The sand was too thick, and there was too much of it. Panic took hold of me, and, if it hadn't been for my training, I might well have thrown myself off the tower in an attempt to get away from Montrose. Death by, as we call it in the trade, "sudden deceleration trauma" would've been preferable to choking slowly on living sand. But I forced myself to remain standing where I was, and, while there was nothing I could do to fight back the panic, I did my best to endure it.

Just a few more seconds, I told myself. *Just... a... few... more...*

Montrose's face had become a mask of savage glee as he drank in my suffering. But now his features went slack, and, considering what he was made of, I mean *slack.* Lines of sand began running down his face, and his facial features softened as they eroded. The process started slowly, but it picked up speed, and soon his entire body – arms included – collapsed into a lopsided pile on top of the tower. I began hacking and coughing and exhaling air through my nose to clear away the residue that Montrose had left behind. I didn't spend too much time congratulating myself on my brilliant ploy, however. Montrose's body was much larger than the humanoid extrusion that had tried to kill me – and I was standing on it, one hundred feet above the ground. The sand tower remained steady for several seconds after the collapse of Montrose's avatar, but then it began to shake, and I could feel the surface beneath my feet begin to soften. The tower was about to fall apart under me, which meant that I had only one option if I wanted to survive. I ran to the edge and jumped out into space.

As I fell, I relaxed my body and waited. I heard a distant *sproinging* sound, and, an instant later, Jinx – propelled by his powerful shoe springs – came flying toward me. He caught me easily, and, as we plummeted toward the ground, his springs extended once again to soften our landing. We bounced a couple times, and then something strange happened. Stranger than usual, I mean. For an instant – *just* an instant – a wave of dizziness came over me and my vision blurred. When it cleared, I was looking at myself, and I... *she* was staring back at me, wide-eyed with shock. We were descending toward the ground, and I realized that I was holding me. I mean *her*. I glanced at my hands and saw they were chalk-white. I was... Jinx?

The dizziness hit again, accompanied once more by blurry vision. But, just as it passed, I felt a jarring impact. When my vision cleared this time, I found myself looking at Jinx. We were lying side by side on the sand.

"Sorry," he said, his voice devoid of any hint of clownly lunacy. "Guess I didn't stick the landing."

He stood and held out a hand. I took it and he helped me to my feet. I ached all over, but I'd survive. Jinx noticed my wounded hands.

"I thought you didn't go in for manicures," he said, sounding much more like his usual demented self.

I displayed one of my injured fingers to him to show what I thought of his joke. Neither of us said anything about what had happened as we were landing. Maybe we were both hoping it hadn't really happened. Maybe we kept quiet about it because we knew it had.

Jinx and I turned toward the lake and saw a huge mound of sand where Montrose's tower had been.

"I could make an erectile dysfunction joke right now," Jinx said.

"I'd rather you didn't."

Before I could say or do anything else, a loud, low mournful tone came from the direction of the street. Jinx and I turned in its direction to see a midnight-black hearse with eerie green glowing headlights come roaring over the sand toward us. Evidently, my wisper call to Connie's cell had gone through, and she'd heard enough of what was going on to figure out where we were. I couldn't have been more relieved.

I waved to Connie and pointed to Melody and Trauma Doll – the latter of whom had sat up and was putting the remaining shards of her head back into place by hand. Melody, however, was no longer sitting and holding my bunched-up jacket to her face. She lay on her side, very, very still.

I ran toward her and Jinx followed. The Deathmobile came along behind us, and I prayed to the First Dreamer that the fact that a hearse had come to rescue Melody wouldn't turn out to be a bitter irony.

We are Angry Robot

angryrobotbooks.com

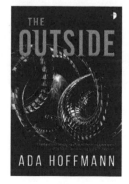